THE LAST HITMAN

Also available by Robin Yocum

The Sacrifice of Lester Yates

A Perfect Shot

A Welcome Murder

A Brilliant Death

The Essay

Favorite Sons

THE LAST HITMAN

A NOVEL

ROBIN YOCUM

NEW YORK

Published in the United States by Crooked Lane Books, an imprint of The Quick Brown Fox & Company LLC.

Crooked Lane Books and its logo are trademarks of The Quick Brown Fox & Company LLC.

Library of Congress Catalog-in-Publication data available upon request.

ISBN (hardcover): 979-8-89242-373-1
ISBN (paperback): 979-8-89242-374-8
ISBN (ebook): 979-8-89242-375-5

Cover design by Ashton Smith

Printed in the United States.

www.crookedlanebooks.com

Crooked Lane Books
34 West 27th St., 10th Floor
New York, NY 10001

First Edition: December 2025

The authorized representative in the EU for product safety and compliance is eucomply OÜPärnu mnt 139b-14, 11317 Tallinn, Estonia, hello@eucompliancepartner.com, +33757690241

10 9 8 7 6 5 4 3 2 1

For Rick Yocum
August 31, 1945—August 24, 2023

PROLOGUE

Once, I swore an oath.

It was an oath of silence. I pledged that I would go to my grave without ever revealing the atrocities I had witnessed or the lives I had ended on behalf of the Fortunato family. That oath was sacred. On the day that I swore to it, I couldn't have imagined a time when I would break my vow.

Now, I'm writing a book.

Yeah, that makes me a rat, which in my line of work was considered the lowest form of human life, just below FBI agents and newspaper reporters. I'm not sure what Alphonse Fortunato or Big Tommy would do if they knew I had broken my vow, but I think it's safe to assume that it wouldn't end well for me.

I didn't wake up one day and suddenly decide to go straight. I got into the mob by happenstance, and I got out the same way. Would I have flipped if Big Tommy was still around and I was a valuable member of the family? Not on your life. But things change. Big Tommy and his father are both gone. Little Tommy is in charge, and he has little use for his old Uncle Ange. A man—a real man—can only take so much disrespect.

That's what this book is about—my forced transformation from a respected member of the Fortunato crime family to a relic of a day long past. Rat or not, this is a story that needs to be told, and I'm the only one who can tell it.

The question is: What's my motivation? Am I writing out of anger? A little. Revenge? That's certainly a big part of it. Greed? Hey, if I can put a few beans in my pocket by telling my story, that wouldn't be so terrible. But maybe it does involve some soul-searching and cleansing. I will be the first to admit that I have a strained relationship with my conscience. No one wants to look back on their life and realize that the world would have been a better place without them.

People of privilege can't understand that there are others who have little or no control of their own destinies. For those of us, the world dictates the terms and conditions. When you're in this kind of a firefight, your first instinct isn't bravado, it's survival. Simply, what do I have to do to get to the next day? That was my life growing up. When you're young, poor, and living on buttered noodles and insults, and you see a path out of poverty, you don't ask a lot of questions. You simply put one foot in front of the other and follow the path. That's exactly what I did. I saw no need to analyze the ramifications or the world around me, because my life was better than it had ever been. I had food, money, and respect, and if I had to leave some bodies lying in the ditch along the way, so be it.

Looking back, would I have taken a different route? Probably. But, as they say, that is water over the dam. I can't change who I am, what I was, or what I did. All I can do is tell this story as straightforwardly as possible. I'm going to give it to you with all the warts, the blood, the tears, the disloyalty, the death. Am I sincerely trying to rectify the past by changing my ways at this late stage? Perhaps. Or maybe I'm just kidding myself and seeking some factitious redemption from the reader by baring my sins.

I guess you'll be the judge.

Angelo Cipriani

CHAPTER 1

May 2019

A GIRL SCOUT AND a couple of nuns.

Those were the only people who had knocked on my door in the previous three years. I saw the Girl Scout every spring. She was a cute kid, a little redhead with a gap between her front teeth, and she knew that I was a soft touch for those peanut butter cookies they sell. A cocaine addiction couldn't have a tighter grip.

The nuns showed up one morning as I was coming out of the kitchen with my first cup of coffee. I was barefoot, unshaven, wrapped in a terrycloth robe, my hair looking like it had been combed with a blender, when I heard the rap at the door. It wasn't a polite, nun-like tap, but a sharp, answer-the-damn-door kind of knock. I jumped like a spooked cat, slopping hot coffee over my hand and wrist. Yeah, I tended to get a little jittery when someone pounded on my door, but for good reason. First of all, I wasn't expecting company at seven-fifteen in the morning. Of greater concern, however, was the fact that there was no shortage of people out there who would like to see me dead. That nugget of reality tended to put me a little on edge.

I set the coffee cup on the end table and pulled the sawed-off shotgun from under the couch cushion. I prefer a handgun for my work, preferably a 9-millimeter with a suppressor, but for home protection, you can't beat a double-barrel 12-gauge and a couple of deer slugs. Not only would the slug go through my solid oak door, but it would exit out the spine of anyone in the hall who was hoping to do me harm.

Slowly, I slunk along the wall toward the door, the double-barrel held waist-high.

There was a second knock.

I heard a female voice and leaned across the door for a look out the peep hole. There were two spindly nuns in the hall, both squeezing cardboard boxes to their chests. I hid the shotgun behind my hip and opened the door as far as the security chain would allow.

The smaller nun, who had several wild, disconcerting white whiskers spiraling off her chin, smiled and said, "Mr. Cipriani?"

"Yeah."

"May we speak to you for a moment?"

I looked them over from the top of their habits to their little black shoes. They seemed legit. Never in all my years with the mob had I known the cops or a rival family to come looking for me disguised as nuns. The cops might try such a ploy, but no self-respecting mobster would pull a stunt like that. "Just a minute," I said. I shut the door, propped the shotgun against the wall and out of sight, disengaged the chain, and opened the door.

"Mr. Cipriani, we're from Catholic Social Services," said the taller nun, who had gray teeth and an overbite that would have hidden a golf ball. "We were told that you might be experiencing some financial difficulties, so we brought you some things that we thought might be helpful."

The smaller nun handed me a box that contained bread, peanut butter, and cans of soup and beans and Spam. The taller nun handed me a box of toiletries. It was very nice. It was humiliating beyond belief, but nice. I tucked a box under each arm.

"May we come in?" the shorter one asked.

"It's really not a good time, Sister," I said.

She peered into my apartment. "I see. Perhaps another time, then?"

"Yeah, perhaps. I'm curious. Who told you I might need some help?"

"Oh, I don't really know. We get a lot of calls from people who are, you know, concerned about their friends and neighbors."

The tall one said, "If you're looking for a way to help make ends meet, Mr. Schumacher at the M&K Market on South Fourth Street is looking for a part-time stock boy. Maybe you could apply for a job there."

A stock boy. That's what my life had come to. In that instant, the taller nun had taken our meeting from embarrassing to insulting. My jaw started to tighten, and I felt a wave of heat rising out of my robe and enveloping my ears. I didn't want to punch a nun, so I cut our meeting short. I thanked them for their charity and backed away from the door.

"We will pray for your soul," said the shorter one.

"I appreciate the thought, Sister, but I think you should save your breath. Even Jesus has a line in the sand where forgiveness is concerned. I crossed the Rubicon years ago."

"It's never too late to ask for forgiveness," the taller one said.

I shut the door with my foot.

It's a terrible thing to have outlived your usefulness, even if your primary contribution to the company involved putting conical lead into the brains of those who greatly displeased your boss. While I will readily admit that is not a profession that most people would choose, it gave me a purpose in life. I felt valued.

I'm out of money and self-respect. I'm sixty-nine years old, a time when most people my age are propping up their feet and relaxing at the beach. That works in theory, but not when you've spent your entire working career as a henchman for the Fortunato crime family. The Mafia generally doesn't offer a generous pension program. And let's be realistic. Most guys in my line of work don't die of old age. I didn't worry about my golden years because I didn't think I would make it this far. My old partner Carlo didn't, that's for sure.

I had become a nobody. Carlo and I worked together for more than three decades. Every cop and FBI agent in the tri-state knew who we were and what we did, but they could never put a finger on us. That's how good we were. Half the time, I don't think the cops even tried to solve the cases. If they were honest, they'd tell you they were secretly grateful, because we were not exactly taking out taxpayers or Sunday school teachers.

Little Tommy thought I'd lost my fastball, so he put me on the shelf. That means that while I was technically still a member of the Fortunato family, he had stripped me of most of my earning potential. I believed I could still be an asset. I was not an old sixty-nine, if that makes any sense. My résumé was somewhat narrow, but I wasn't ready to be retired. Unfortunately, most *Fortune 500* companies were not looking for someone with my skill set.

I spent most of my hours in virtual isolation, trapped in a Slack Street apartment. Out of this tedium, I watched too much television, and I would catch myself getting sucked into game shows and shouting out answers ahead of the contestants. It was pitiful. In my profession, I always figured that if you lived by the sword, you perished by the sword. In other words, eventually someone would put a bullet behind *my* ear. Instead, it looked like I was going to die of boredom. I'd given more than fifty years to the family, and I'll admit that at times it was a dysfunctional love affair, but other than sweeping floors and emptying the spit cans at the Steubenville Athletic Club, it's the only job I'd ever had.

But time marches on.

Now the rest of the old guard is gone—Alphonse, his brother Matteo, Big Tommy, Carlo, Jimmy Beans, Dommie the Clip, Muzzie Lollini, Mickey V, Sammy Avocado, and Constantine "Connie Bones" Bonelli, who died after eating some bad headcheese. Imagine that. You dance your way through decades of working in organized crime, you survive the Gemelli slaughter, and bacteria from headcheese is what gets you. It doesn't seem fair.

I read in the *Steubenville Herald-Star* that Connie's brother, Riccardo "Ricky Bones" Bonelli, had died. That only left me and

Joseph "Joey Nickels" Nicolosi. Nickels was still alive, but barely. They'd amputated his left leg just below the knee a few months back, and he was in a nursing home in Weirton. There were times when Nickels didn't know his own name, and I figured he'd be better off dead. Either way, Nickels and I were the last men standing. That's probably a bad turn of a phrase, with them cutting off Nickels's leg, but you know what I mean.

I was the only one left to deal with Little Tommy and his cast of yes-men and hangers-on, and they all looked at me like I was a dinosaur. I would still get the occasional phone call when Little Tommy had a job that he didn't want to entrust to guys who smelled like dope and combed their hair with their fingers. But those calls had become less and less frequent.

The disrespect made my hands ball up into fists. It was hard for me to believe that I was the same guy he had called "Uncle Ange" most of his life. I would be lying if I said I wasn't bitter.

A few months back, not long before her dementia took hold, I drove out to the compound to take Big Tommy's widow, Rosebella, a dozen raisin cookies from Downtown Bakery. They were her favorite, and Big Tommy had them delivered to the house every week. Rosebella had always been kind to me, especially when I first started working for the family and was the punching bag for all the capos. I felt an obligation to look after her, despite my tenuous relationship with her son.

The music—or what passes for music these days—coming from the compound was so loud I could hear it when I turned onto Rosemont Street. By the time I pulled into the drive, my windows were vibrating. I scooped up the box of cookies and headed for the back door. When I turned the corner at the side of the house, I saw Little Tommy and the rest of the hoodlum gang around the pool. A stereo with speakers the size of Volkswagens was pounding out some kind of rap shit. There were a couple of black guys, one of them sitting in Big Tommy's favorite Adirondack chair, passing a pipe back and forth. Two white girls and a black girl were in the pool splashing around and not wearing any tops. The smell of reefer was so heavy in the air that the birds were probably high. Liquor bottles and beer cans were strewn everywhere. It looked like some kind of fraternity party at the Fortunato compound. It was disgusting.

When Little Tommy saw me standing by the pool, he looked like I had caught him masturbating. He hopped out of the water and started walking toward me, his hair wet in his eyes, which were bloodshot, the pupils wide and fixed. He was coked out of his head. "What's this?" I asked, shouting to be heard.

"A couple of our suppliers were in town from Detroit, so I'm showing them a good time."

"You're mixing business and pleasure. That's a bad idea."

"Lighten up, Angelo. I've got this covered."

One of the white girls swam to the edge of the pool and said, "Take your clothes off and come on in, Grandpa."

Waves of heat were climbing up the back of my neck. "Where's your mother?"

"In the house."

"*Here*! Your mother is *here* while this is going on?"

My jaw tightened, and I had to take a couple breaths to calm down. I went into the house and found Rosebella in the living room, reading a book and wearing a pair of ear protectors that her late husband wore when he went to the pistol range. She smiled and peeled them off when she saw me. "It's so loud," she said. "That music makes the whole house shake."

I held up the white box wrapped in string. "I brought you your favorite cookies," I said.

"Oh, that's so sweet, Angelo. How did you know that chocolate chip was my favorite?"

I swallowed. "I didn't. I thought raisin cookies were your favorite."

The corner of her mouth hitched. "They are, dear."

She got me.

"Rosebella, do you want to get out of here, get away from the noise, and maybe go get some lunch?"

"I would love to, but I don't think it would be proper for me to be seen out in public with another man."

"It's just lunch, Rosebella. We'll go across the river, maybe up to Robinson Township. It'll be fine."

"I just don't know what Tommaso would say about that."

"Tommaso would be the first person to say get the hell away from this racket."

She nodded and said, "I think you're right. I will need to get cleaned up."

"You do that. I need to talk to your son for a minute, and I'll wait for you by the car."

I walked out back. The flare of anger that had reddened my ears and neck had moved down into my gut. It was a blast furnace of heat. I made eye contact with Little Tommy and nodded toward the garage. "Can I have a minute?" I asked.

"Sure," he said. He pulled a T-shirt over his paunchy belly and walked behind me into the garage. As soon as Little Tommy had latched the door, I grabbed him by the front of his shirt and slammed him against the side of his dead father's Cadillac. "What the hell is wrong with you?" I said between clenched teeth. "Don't you have any respect for your mother? You bring this trash into the house that your grandfather and father took such pride in? Every time I come over here, I have to run through a gantlet of bums and pot smoke just to get through the back door. You were raised better than this, Tommy. You ought to be ashamed of yourself."

His facial expression never changed. He didn't look angry or insulted, and he didn't try to fight back. He just stared at me with those blank eyes, the lids at half-staff, and said, "You need to be careful, Angelo. It's not 1967 anymore, so if you don't get your hands off me this instant, I'll have one of my associates from Detroit cut out your heart and dump you in Lake Michigan." I gave him a push and let go of the shirt. "I don't understand why we continually have this conversation. I'm in charge now. You don't have to like it, but that's the reality. And I'll run things the way I want to run them. And if I want to have a party at my house with drugs and strippers, that's what I'm going to do, and it's none of your fucking business. Never again. Don't you ever come around here telling me how to run my life or this business. I'm going to let this one slide because you've been like family my entire life, and I'm going to assume it was just some kind of brain fart, but don't ever do it again."

"I'm taking your mother to lunch."

"Good. Get her out of the house. She needs some fresh air."

I opened the door to leave, then closed it again.

"Something on your mind?" he asked.

"Just for future reference, Lake Michigan is clear on the other side of the state. If they cut out my heart and dump me in a lake, tell them that Lake St. Clair is much closer to Detroit. They'll save a lot of money on gas."

CHAPTER

2

1967

I GREW UP ON Bessemer Street in the Spaghetto, a sliver of a gritty neighborhood pressed hard against the shores of the Ohio River and darkened by the looming shadows of the Wheeling-Pittsburgh Steel plant. We were the poor dagos. The good Italians lived above the flood zone in Little Italy. They had nice houses on brick-lined streets with restaurants, butcher shops, markets, and the Catholic Church where the good Italians made confession—Our Lady of Fatima. The famous Dean Martin—then Dino Crocetti—grew up in Little Italy.

The Spaghetto had pea gravel and tar streets, and the facades of houses that had been scoured to the shade of driftwood by the acidic fly ash of the steel mill. The homes were wedged together, and even as a boy I could touch both our house and the Di Vittorios' next door. We had one little store, the dusty Mercato Sarefino with its expired milk and yellow fly strips that hung from the ceiling like party streamers.

My parents were Dario and Polina Cipriani. My father was a first-generation Italian who came to America looking for a better life. He never found it. He worked himself into an early grave on the docks of the Big Valley Brick Company, shoveling clay out of river barges for eight hours a day. My mother was from the Ukraine. She was a cripple, born with a withered left leg that caused her to drag the foot and wear holes in the sides of her shoes. She helped make ends meet by taking in laundry and mending. I was Italian-Ukrainian, which is why I have a penchant for veal parmesan and a head the size of a cement block.

Even by the standards of the Spaghetto, we were poor. But my parents were obedient Catholics, and my mother popped out thick-headed babies with stunning regularity. I was number ten of eleven kids, which is why we ate potato cakes or pasta noodles with butter four nights a week and got most of our clothes at the Salvation Army thrift store. During the morning restroom break the first day of the fifth grade, Steve Casey pointed to my shirt and said, "That's my old shirt. We gave it to the Salvation Army."

I said, "No, it's not. We bought it new at The Hub department store."

"You're a liar. The pocket's been sewed where I tore it." He started laughing. "Cipriani wears my hand-me-downs."

I drilled Steve square in the nose, knocking him backwards into a urinal. Blood was coming from both nostrils, coating his teeth red, while the seat of his pants sopped up piss. I got satisfaction and a three-day suspension before lunch. It wasn't my first fight. We scrapped on the streets of the Spaghetto all the time. Sometimes just out of boredom. But I learned something the day I bloodied Steve Casey. Violence can be a solution. No one at school ever screwed with me after that.

I wasn't much of a student. My younger sister, Gabriella, helped me as much as she could. She was a mathematics savant. She would try to explain a math problem, and I would look at her with slack-jawed confusion. I didn't get it, and she couldn't understand why. She'd put the pads of her hands to her temples and ask, "Are you retarded?"

I shrugged. "I don't think so."

But maybe I was.

I lasted in school until the spring of my junior year. They had a career day, and I wanted to listen to a fireman talk. Instead, our guidance counselor, Austin Adams, picked me and a couple of other guys out of the class and took us to the cafeteria, where a guy from Wheeling-Pittsburgh Steel was talking about being a laborer. Adams said, "I think being a fireman is out of your reach, Cipriani. Go to the steel mill. The most complicated task you'll ever have is figuring out which end of the broom to hold."

Maybe I was retarded, but I knew an insult when I heard one. I dropped my books on the floor and headed for the front door, and I never went back. In my mind, it was all Austin Adams's fault, and in case you're wondering, I wasn't going to forget that.

It was a good lesson, I guess. It taught me that every time you think you know how the world works, the world kicks you square in the oranges. I went home and sat on the porch for a long time before my mother looked out the screen door and asked, "What are you doing home?"

"I quit school," I said.

She shrugged her shoulders and said, "In that case, you better go find a job."

CHAPTER

3

May 2019

ON THE MANTEL of the bricked-up fireplace in my apartment was a clock that Big Tommy gave me one year for Christmas. While it was one of my most prized possessions, it also was the source of my madness, as the rhythmic click of its pendulum echoed off the walls. The sound was faint, but unrelenting, a second-by-second reminder of the prison in which I was captive. The clock was my perpetual enemy except for the few minutes before it struck noon each day.

When the sweep hand circled the globe and closed in on the twelve, I would begin my walk down the hill to the Starlighter Diner to take my lunch. It was one of the few highlights of my day. An hour before noon, I would shower, shave, and slap on enough cologne to hopefully mask the smell of the dog piss that saturated the carpet in the common hall and got on my shoes. Every widow in the apartment building had a dog, and none of the damn things could control their bladders. The place smelled like a pisser at a roadside rest.

I waited until the last minute to put on a white dress shirt as I wanted to arrive at the diner clean and pressed. You know, looking sharp. In the old days, I'd send my shirts out to the cleaners and have them laundered and ironed with extra starch. Not so much anymore. I was doing my own laundry in the coin machines in the basement of the apartment building and ironing my shirts in front of the television. It was just one more thing.

On my limited budget, I probably should have made a sandwich with the peanut butter or Spam the nuns gave me. But I liked getting out of the apartment and taking in a little sunshine. And, in all honesty, I had a thing for the waitress who worked the counter at the Starlighter—Carolyn Melvin. She didn't know I was sweet on her, and I didn't have the guts to tell her. It's funny, in a way, that a guy who made his living in one of the most brutal ways imaginable couldn't summon up the courage to ask out a waitress at the diner.

I figured my time for finding a good woman was in my rearview mirror. I hadn't been in a serious relationship since I'd lost my wife. What had that been? More than thirty-five years. It hardly seemed possible that so much time had passed. After Jolie's death, the wife of every capo in the Fortunato organization tried to set me up with a woman or a puppy. They were relentless. Their hearts were in the right place, but I wasn't interested, and I finally told them the only things I wanted brought into my house were mail and groceries. If it had a face, I didn't want it crossing my threshold. Quite simply, I didn't think I would ever love another woman after Jolie. But maybe I was wrong, because I sure wanted to give it a run with Carolyn.

I walked through the lobby of the apartment building and into a bright, clear day. Twenty years ago, bright, clear days in the Ohio Valley were rare. The sun was often blocked from view by the belching smoke from the steel mills—Wheeling-Pittsburgh Steel in Steubenville and Weirton Steel across the Ohio River in West Virginia. From the top of the hill where my apartment building sat, I could see the smoke stacks at Wheeling-Pitt that towered over my home as a youth. They were cold, silenced when the mill was shuttered. It was sometimes hard to believe this was the same city in which I'd grown up. The collapse of the steel industry had devastated Steubenville. It was hard to wrap your brain around the change. We made the steel that powered the Industrial Revolution and won two world wars. Steel was everything to Steubenville. And then it wasn't. You could now breathe the air and drink the water in the Ohio Valley, but nobody had work. It was a shame.

After Wheeling-Pitt shuttered, there were people in town who would look at that empty, hulking steel plant and say, "Someday, big steel is coming back." They didn't want to face the reality that the heyday of the industry that built their city was over. Steel was never coming back, but you couldn't convince them. I used to scoff and secretly laugh at them for their naïveté. But now, who was the one being naïve? Wasn't I guilty of refusing to face reality, believing that my usefulness to the Fortunato family would be resurrected like the days when Big Tommy was in charge? Of course I was. We're all capable of playing the fool.

I walked down the hill, over cracked sidewalks and past an asphalt playground where the basketball hoops had been torn off the metal backboards and a few pitiful swings swayed in the breeze. The paint store was still open, but the auto parts shop and the jewelry store where I bought Jolie her engagement ring were closed, the windows broken out of the front, shards of glass littering the concrete. The glass crunched under my piss-laden soles. The Starlighter Diner was on the corner just beyond the jewelry store. Somehow, it had survived the depression that had claimed so many of the city's businesses.

The Starlighter's owner was Kostos Mangos. The restaurant had been in his family for generations. He was a Greek and a good guy. I liked to tell him, "The Greeks may have invented the theater and culture and art, but they needed the Italians to perfect them."

He would tell me to go screw myself, and we'd laugh. He didn't know what I did for a living. He thought I was just an old dago from up the hill who came down to complain about the food and flirt with his waitress. He had no idea that he was one of the few people on the planet who could get away with talking to me like that, even in jest.

I took a seat on the far side of the horseshoe counter so I could keep my eye on the front door. Yes, I was a little paranoid, but that's what helped keep me alive. I carried a .22-caliber revolver in my pants pocket—a Saturday night special. It wasn't the 9-millimeter that could end any argument, but it would do the job in a pinch. Back in the day, when Big Tommy was alive, I wasn't nearly as cautious. That's because I knew he had my back. I'm not saying guys from other families didn't try to take me out when Big Tommy was alive, but they knew the risk. With Little Tommy in charge, I was flying solo.

Carolyn saw me; she smiled and said, "There's my darlin'." It was her common greeting for me. It was simply a term of endearment, something a young girl might say to her grandfather, but it still made my heart flutter a bit.

Carolyn was somewhere in her early fifties and still a fine-looking woman, with the darkest eyes I'd ever seen on a human being, a thick head of brown hair that she swirled on the top of her head, a full bosom that her waitressing dress strained to contain, and a little thick in the hips, just the way I like them.

She set an iced tea in front of me and said, "Whatta ya havin', sweetie?" She didn't bother to bring me a menu; I knew it better than she did.

It was Tuesday. The blue plate special was meatloaf. I wasn't a huge fan. I said, "How about the fish sandwich?"

Carolyn leaned down, put her face a foot from mine, smiled, and said, "I'm shocked."

"I'm a creature of habit, dear."

I ordered the fish sandwich at least three times a week.

Carolyn turned on a heel and headed for the open window separating the dining hall from the kitchen. I watched as she clipped the ticket to a stainless steel wheel and gave it half a turn, saying, "Order up."

I was looking over the sports page from that morning's *Wheeling Intelligencer* when he sat down beside me. I didn't know who he was, but I knew *what* he was. It didn't take me two seconds to figure that out. There were eighteen empty seats at the counter, but he sat right next to me. Everything about this guy was cheap, including his aftershave and a yellow necktie that looked like it was made from a kid's plastic raincoat. He had a haircut that belonged on a ten-year-old, slicked into place with Brylcreem. I'm sure my olfactory glands were damaged by decades of breathing in fly ash from the steel mills, but I could still smell a cop a mile away.

Carolyn came over to the man and he said, "A black coffee and a grilled cheese on whole wheat, please."

He looked down and played on his cell phone for a minute before tucking it into the inside pocket of his suit coat. I could no longer concentrate on the box scores. I was waiting for it, and only a few minutes passed before he said, "How's it going these days, Angelo?"

Let me say this: I knew it wasn't a big secret among law enforcement what Carlo and I did for the Fortunatos. I'm sure we were on the radar of every police department up and down the Ohio Valley. With that said, it was still a little unsettling to have a total stranger, who I knew had a badge and an ankle holster, sit down next to me and call me by my first name.

"Do I know you?" I asked.

After a moment, he slid a business card to the edge of my newspaper and said, "We'd like to talk to you."

I glanced down at the card. His name was Ross, Special Agent Lawrence G. Ross of the Pittsburgh field office of the Federal Bureau of Investigation. I put my fingertips on the card, pushed it back under his coffee saucer and said, "Christ Almighty, are you trying to get me killed?"

He kept drinking his coffee. I'll give him this, he was a pretty cool customer. Carolyn stopped over and topped off my iced tea. When she was out of earshot, he said, "Talk to us, and we'll make it worth your while, Angelo." He held the coffee cup in front of his lips, then whispered, "Things haven't been the same around the ranch since Big Tommy died, have they?"

"People die. Things change."

"That's true. But it still couldn't feel good when Little Tommy put you out to pasture."

That comment gave me chills. It was as though he'd been living inside my head and knew what I was thinking. Carolyn set my fish sandwich on the counter.

"I stay busy," I said.

"Yeah, you get a lot of work done coming down here to the diner a couple times a day and hanging out in your apartment, waiting for Little Tommy to call you."

"Have you got a tail on me?"

"Don't flatter yourself. We just know your habits. We only put tails on guys we think can outrun us, and that isn't you anymore. Let's be realistic, you're no longer an A player with the Fortunatos. In fact, you're not even a B or C player."

"Go screw yourself."

He grinned into his coffee cup. Carolyn slid his grilled cheese across the counter. He took a couple of bites, keeping his eyes straight ahead. "We hear Little Tommy's been moving a lot of cocaine and heroin. That's certainly not like the old days, is it? You remember the old days, don't you, Angelo? I mean, Big Tommy and Alphonse were corrupt as hell, but they still had standards. They weren't trying to poison the community with drugs. I wonder what Big Tommy would think about his kid turning the family business into a giant pharmacy."

"I don't know what you're talking about. The Fortunatos make their money in pizza parlors, car washes, and coin laundries."

He snorted. "You're a loyal soldier to the end, huh, Angelo? Let me tell you something. I don't know how long it's going to take, but I promise you this: Little Tommy Fortunato is going down. I flat guarantee it, and when he does, he's going down hard. When that happens, there'll be a lot of shrapnel flying. If you don't want to get hit and go down with him, you need to talk to me."

After a couple of minutes, he dropped a five-dollar bill on the counter and pushed his business card back under my newspaper. "You wouldn't look good in orange, Angelo. It's not your color. Give me a call. It won't you cost anything to talk."

"Only my life," I said.

He left. Carolyn came back over and cleaned up his place. "Who was your friend?" she asked.

"I don't know. Some guy trying to sell me life insurance."

"I thought so. I can smell those insurance guys a mile away."

It made me smile. But just about everything she did and said made me smile.

On my way back up the hill, I crumpled Ross's card and dropped it through a storm grate in front of the playground.

CHAPTER 4

April–October 1967

THE MORNING AFTER I'd dropped out of high school, I was at the kitchen table eating a bowl of cold cereal when Gabriella came downstairs. "I heard you quit school," she said.

"Yeah, I did," I said.

"Why?"

"Because old man Adams disrespected me."

"Oh, what a perfectly rational reason for dropping out of school. You are so retarded."

I walked downtown to the sweeper store where my brother, Michael, worked in the repair shop. When I started to explain what kind of job I was looking for, Michael put a hand up in the air and said, "Please, shut up. You're a seventeen-year-old dropout. That doesn't exactly make you management material."

Michael picked up extra cash working as a bartender for wedding receptions at the Steubenville Athletic Club, and he was able to get me a job as the club's night watchman. I think my most valuable qualification was that I had a pulse. The night watchman was really the night janitor. I swept and mopped floors and picked up wet towels from the locker room and laundered them. I also had to clean out the ashtrays and the spittoons in the lounge. If you want a humbling experience, get a job washing other men's towels and emptying their spit out of brass canisters. Any delusions of grandeur that you might've had about the working world will disappear pretty quickly.

The club's lounge was often where high-stakes poker and pinochle games played late into the night. The games interfered with my schedule, as any noise on my part was met with expletives from the card players—typically those who were losing—and I was accused of disturbing their concentration. Thus, I tiptoed around, trying to sweep and mop and be invisible. I had been working at the athletic club a few months when a pinochle game was extending past one AM. As I was sweeping behind the bar, one of the players said, "Hey, you, bring me a Rolling Rock."

"Hey, you" or "Boy" were the common refrains from those who perceived me as being of a lower social status. They weren't wrong. I knew my place in the world and obeyed their orders without complaint. I snapped the cap off a Rolling Rock and walked to the table, the bottle in one hand, my broom in the other. The man who had ordered the beer had his back to me. When he turned to take it, we were both surprised. It was my former guidance counselor, Austin Adams. He took the beer, pointed at me with the top of the longneck and said, "I guess I underestimated you, Cipriani."

I didn't understand the comment. "Sir?"

"The broom. You finally figured out which end to hold. Congratulations."

The men at the table laughed. Adams shook his head and went back to his game. I wanted to club him with the broom handle, but like I said, I knew my place. I went back to sweeping behind the bar.

I worked an eight-hour shift at the club. If I hustled, I could finish my work in four hours. While the towels were in the dryer, I could either work out in the gym or shoot pool. The club had a beautiful eight-foot mahogany pool table, and I would sometimes practice for as long as three hours a night. I liked pool, and I got to be good at it. I'd never really been good at anything, except hanging around the Spaghetto and looking for trouble. I became so good, in fact, that I entered a tournament at Bixby's Pool Hall across the street from the Paramount Theatre and beat some of the best players in the Ohio Valley. I got twenty-five bucks and a little trophy. I started dreaming about becoming a professional pool player.

In early October of 1967, I was at Bixby's on a Saturday evening, shooting stick by myself. There was another tournament coming up, and I wanted to practice on the home felt. I hadn't been there very long when a black sedan pulled up outside and three men in dark suits and fedoras got out and walked into Bixby's.

The first man through the door looked like a bear in a suit. He had more hair on his knuckles than I had on my entire body. The short walk from the car had winded him, and I could see tiny beads of sweat on his lip. He eyed me up like a prizefighter entering the ring. The second man through the door was Alphonse "Iceman Al" Fortunato, the head of the most powerful crime family in the Ohio Valley. They called him "Iceman Al" because if you got sideways with him, he wouldn't hesitate to put your corpse on ice. He controlled the illegal gambling, prostitution, and loan-sharking on both sides of the river between East Liverpool, Ohio, and Wheeling, West Virginia. He had casinos above Schulman's Music Store in Steubenville, in a windowless, cement block building near the Dallas Pike Truck Stop outside of Wheeling, and another in the back of what appeared to be an abandoned warehouse next to Weirton Steel. He ran the whorehouses on Water Street in Steubenville and on Wheeling Island, and had sports gambling and daily number sheets in every bar, American Legion, and VFW hall in the valley. He also paid off every sheriff and chief of police along the river, just so no one would get too suspicious when they saw two hundred cars parked outside of a supposedly abandoned warehouse in Weirton, West Virginia, on a Saturday night.

Everybody in the Ohio Valley knew of Alphonse Fortunato. He always claimed to be a legitimate businessman, and he did own a couple of motels, pizza parlors, coin laundries, and car washes, all of which he had obtained from the previous owners for payment of gambling and loan-sharking debts. While legitimate, they were maintained strictly as vehicles through which he laundered the hundreds of thousands of dollars he made every year from prostitution and gambling. If he was trying to project an image of legitimacy, he was doing a poor job of it. Everyone knew who he was and what he did. He wasn't exactly Clark Kent, is what I'm saying.

He was wearing a three-piece gray suit with navy pinstripes that probably cost more than our house. A gold chain was connected to a button on the vest and disappeared into a small pocket where I could see the outline of a watch. He was big all over. His thick belly looked like it belonged on a Russian weightlifter, and he had broad shoulders, powerful hands and wrists, and thumbs that could snap the cap off a bottle of beer. When he took off his hat, it revealed two streaks of gray racing back from his temples through hair that was slicked down with pomade.

Without saying a word, I racked my cue stick and started toward the door, avoiding eye contact with any of the three men. Like I said, I knew my place in the world, and it wasn't in the same room with Alphonse Fortunato. But before I could get to the end of the table, Iceman Al said, "No need to run off, kid. Let's shoot a game." It wasn't a request. He said, "Rack 'em." I nodded but couldn't speak. The head of the Fortunato crime family had just asked me—ordered, actually—to shoot pool with him. For me, it was like a brush with greatness, something I'd tell my grandchildren about. I racked the balls good and tight and stood back to let him break.

The house game was eight ball, call your shots, no slop. I was so nervous, I was shaking. Iceman Al peeled off his suit coat and handed it to the third guy, then loosened his tie. He was imposing in his vest and gold chain. He had a cigarette hanging out of his mouth when he broke; balls scattered over the green felt, but nothing dropped. The two ball was resting in front of a corner pocket. I clipped it in and proceeded to run the table, cleanly dropping ball after ball. I banked in the six and left myself with an easy one-rail to put the eight ball in a side pocket and win the game.

Then I realized I had left myself with an easy one-rail to put the eight ball in a side pocket and win the game . . . against the most powerful mob boss in the Ohio Valley. My mouth went dry, and my stomach knotted up. I lined up my shot and intentionally scuffed the cue ball. I said, "Aww," like I was upset with myself.

Iceman Al was standing at the far end of the table, two thick hands wrapped around the top of his cue stick. After I missed my shot, he stood there for a long moment, glaring at me, before slowly walking to the table. He put one of his massive hands on the cue ball and set it back where I had taken the shot. Without taking his hand off the white ball, he said, "First of all, kid, don't ever sell yourself short in this life. If you do, you'll never get anywhere because people will step all over you. Second thing, if you ever take pity on me again, I'll cut off your balls and put them in that rack for the next game. Are we clear?"

I wanted to say, "Yes, sir," but couldn't work up enough spit to answer, so I nodded my head quickly.

He moved his hand, and I took my shot. The cue ball went off the rail, clipped the eight and it dropped into the pocket. "See, that wasn't so difficult, was it?" he said.

Iceman Al grabbed the rack, dropped it on the table, and said, "Rematch." We played six games. I won four. I would've beaten him five times, but I scratched on the eight ball in the fourth game. When I did, I looked up at him, my eyes wide, and said, "I didn't do that on purpose."

"I know," he said. "No one's that stupid."

After I sank the eight ball to win the sixth game, Iceman Al put his cue stick back in the rack on the wall. "Good games, kid. What's your name?"

"Angelo, sir. Angelo Cipriani."

"Italian?"

"Yes, sir. Mostly."

"Uh-huh. So, Angelo Cipriani, what do you do?"

"For money?"

"Yeah, for money."

"I sweep floors and clean spit out of cans down at the athletic club."

"So, you're a janitor?"

"Yes, sir."

"Sounds awful."

"It is."

"How would you like a real job?"

"W-w-working for you?"

"Yeah."

"Yes, sir. I'd like that a lot."

"Good. Do you know where I live?"

"No, sir."

"It's a white house at the end of Rosemont Street. You can't miss it. Be there at seven o'clock tomorrow morning."

"Yes, sir."

"Do you have a car?"

"No, sir."

"How are you going to get there?"

"I'll figure it out."

He nodded, just a bit, and I thought he smiled, but it was no more perceptible than his nod. I think he liked that answer. He pulled out a money clip and peeled off a five-dollar bill and handed it to me. "When you get there, I want you to have a hot coffee for me from the diner at the corner of Sunset and Bryden."

He started for the door. "How do you take your coffee?" I asked.

This time, the nod and the grin were clear. "Very good, kid. Two creams."

If it was my first test, I passed.

Just before he walked out the door, he turned back and said, "Polish your shoes before you get there, and look sharp."

I didn't have a lot of nice clothes, but I did have a good white shirt and black slacks that Mom had bought me for Easter Sunday Mass. On the way home, I stopped at S.S. Kresge for a tin of black shoe polish. I buffed my shoes to a high gleam and laid out my clothes for the morning. I set two alarms, but was up and wide awake at four AM. I walked to Fourth and Market and caught the first bus up the hill at six. I figured when I got to the diner, I'd find out how to get to the Fortunato compound. When I asked the waitress for directions, her brows arched like a couple of caterpillars, and she pointed down the street with the eraser end of her pencil. "Go down Bryden to Rosemont. It's a white mansion at the end of the street. You won't miss it, I promise."

It was the biggest house I'd ever seen in my life. It looked like the White House, two-and-a-half stories of white-painted brick. The property was surrounded by a black iron fence with a fleur-de-lis at the top of each post. Red brick pillars stood sentry at the top of the driveway. A matching brick drive snaked around to the rear of the house. It was intimidating, and I had never felt more inadequate in my life, standing in front of this massive house and a seven-foot fence holding a paper cup of coffee. I didn't want it to get cold, so I walked up to the front porch and reached for the doorbell, but pulled my finger back at the last second. I didn't know if I was allowed to use the front door. In fact, I couldn't imagine that I was, so I ran around to the back.

I rang the back doorbell and a few moments later the bear in the suit with the hairy knuckles opened the door. He smelled heavily of cologne and hair tonic. "What the fuck are you doing using the back door?" he asked. "White people use the front door."

"Mr. Fortunato said—"

"I was there last night, remember? I know why you're here." I just stood there. He held out his hands, palms up, and shrugged. "The air conditioning's running, junior. We're not trying to cool the whole damn neighborhood."

I stepped inside, then followed him to an office in the back corner of the house. It was lined in cherry panels and smelled of leather and lemon oil and stale cigar smoke. Without comment, I walked over to his desk and placed the coffee on Iceman Al's blotter. I set a stack of four bills next to the coffee and put the ninety cents in change on top of the paper. I was quick to give him his change because I thought it might be another test.

Iceman Al looked at the stack of coins, then flicked the silver with a finger, spreading it across George Washington's face. He then ran his hand over the bills, splaying them across the blotter. "You didn't leave her a tip?" he asked.

"No, sir," I said. "You didn't tell me to, and it wasn't my money to give away."

Again, he nodded, and there may have been a hint of a grin. It was another right answer.

The bear sat down on a couch, and the long cushion turned up at the ends. I would later learn that he was Dommie "The Clip" Policaro, who oversaw the family's loan-sharking business and was something of Mr. Fortunato's chief of staff. If it wasn't a major issue that required Mr. Fortunato's direct approval, all requests went through Dommie.

The second guy from the pool hall was in a chair by the window, smoking a cigarette and reading the morning *Intelligencer*. His name was Joseph Nicolosi—Joey Nickels—who oversaw the Fortunatos' finances and the operation of the three casinos. Think of him as the chief financial officer. If an account was off by fifteen cents, Nickels knew it. When canvas bags full of quarters came in from the casinos, Nickels would count them by grabbing handfuls and determining the dollar value by the weight. It was impressive to watch.

Over time, I would learn just how much this crime family operated like a business. Granted, it was all illegal as hell but a smooth business nevertheless.

Iceman Al peeled the plastic lid off the coffee cup and said, "You never asked me what the job was, kid."

"It doesn't matter what the job is," I said.

"Are you sure you're up for this? It ain't no job for snowflakes. What I do, you know, can sometimes be construed as a rough business."

"I grew up in the Spaghetto. I can do rough."

"Good. Very good. Now, here's what you need to remember: Don't be thinking you're gonna come in here and be some kind of gangster. The last two guys I hired for this job didn't understand that, which is why they ain't here anymore. This job is whatever I decide it's going to be every day, and it's going to be a lot of scut work. This job is all the crap that I don't have the time to do, or don't want to do. There might be days when I tell you to go sit in the corner and twiddle your thumbs for eight hours, but when I need you, the only answer I wanna hear is yes. Got it?"

I nodded.

"Nodding ain't an answer."

"Yes, sir."

"Do you have a driver's license?"

"Yes, sir."

"Good. Now, we got a few rules around here that are not to be violated under any circumstances. Rule number one, and it's very simple: Nothing, and I mean nothing, that you hear within the confines of this house is ever to be repeated. Do you pray to our Lord and savior Jesus Christ?"

"Sometimes."

"When you do, you don't even tell Jesus what's going on here. It's none of his business. If I think he needs to know something, I'll be the one to tell him."

I wanted to grin, but knew better.

"Rule number two: You do what I tell you, when I tell you, exactly as I tell you. Rule number three: This one is very important, so I want you to listen closely. I have a couple granddaughters who come around here, sometimes to swim in the pool. They're about your age. If I catch you sniffing around either of them, I'll cut off your balls and staple them to your chin. Do you understand?"

He had a castration theme going. In all honesty, it was very effective. "Yes, sir."

"Then we understand each other. I don't ever want to have this conversation again." He reached into his pocket, pulled out a set of car keys and tossed them to me. "I want the Caddy washed, inside and out, and waxed."

When he turned his gaze back to the papers on his desk and wrapped his hand around the cup of coffee, I turned and walked out. Of course, I was tempted to ask where I would find the hose and soap and sponges, but I thought it might be another test. I could figure it out on my own. I'd save the questions for the important stuff.

It didn't take long for word to spread around the Spaghetto that I was working for Alphonse "Iceman Al" Fortunato. It made me a celebrity of sorts in the neighborhood, and the kids thought I was like Al Capone. One Friday afternoon, as I was walking back to the bus stop after work, Mr. Fortunato's Cadillac slowed down on Rosemont and the back window rolled down. Mr. and Mrs. Fortunato were on their way to their table at the Federal Terrace. He nodded toward the front seat and said, "Get in, kid. We'll give you a lift home." I got into the front seat with Jimmy Beans. "You live in the bottoms, right?"

"The bottoms" is what people who didn't want to be insulting called the Spaghetto. "Yes, sir," I said.

The Fortunatos talked amongst themselves. That was fine. I was enjoying the ride. It was a warm afternoon in the late spring of 1968, and Bessemer Street was full of kids playing a game of Wiffle ball. Parents and grandparents sat on the tiny front porches. The mill roared nearby. As the Cadillac approached, the ballplayers moved to the curb. There wasn't a single set of eyeballs in the Spaghetto that wasn't on that Caddy, and everyone knew who was inside.

When I stepped out, I leaned my head back into the car and said, "Thanks, Mr. Fortunato."

"See you Monday, kid," he said.

I walked toward the house, a little bit of a hitch in my lip. Working for Alphonse "Iceman Al" Fortunato may have made me somebody on the streets of the Spaghetto, but the admiration I enjoyed in the neighborhood for being a gangster was countered by the reality of the garbage details I got at work, where I was simply Angelo the lackey. I washed cars, cleaned ashtrays, ran to the diner to pick up lunch, ran to the corner store for cigarettes, and drove downtown to the Herald Square Cigar Store for boxes of Cuban cigars that you weren't supposed to be able to get in this country but could actually get quite easily if you were an influential crime boss.

Dommie the Clip sent me to the market one day for a pack of Pall Malls. When I got back, he looked at the cigarettes and said, "What the fuck is this?"

"Your cigarettes," I said.

"These aren't my cigarettes. I said Marlboros, numb nuts. Marlboros. Who the fuck smokes Pall Malls?"

He said Pall Malls. To this day, I'd stake my life on it. He was just bustin' my balls in front of all the other capos. I took the package out of his hand, said, "Sorry," and sprinted back to the store. I never wanted them to see me rattled.

I did well at my job. You know why? Because I worked hard, kept my eyes and ears open and my mouth shut. I did everything I was told. It didn't matter how many shit sandwiches his capos fed me, I ate every one without complaint. However, no one's orders took precedence over Mr. Fortunato's. If one of the capos was drowning in the pool and Mr. Fortunato told me to wash the Caddy, the capo would have to tread water or drown, because that car was getting spit-shined first. He was my first priority. I always gave him his change, and I answered him with "Yes, sir" and "No, sir," but mostly "Yes, sir," because that's all a crime lord really wants to hear. Oh, and when his granddaughters came around, I found something to do in the garage or the basement. Well, mostly. If I thought I could sneak a peek or two without getting caught, I did.

I did not set out to become a mobster. I thought I wanted to be a fireman. I thought wrong. One day I'm hanging around Bixby's shooting pool, and the next morning I'm working for the man who controlled the entire Ohio Valley and hanging around a cadre of capos who wore tailored suits, more gold jewelry than an Egyptian queen, and the most finely buffed shoes I had ever seen.

I knew what they did, and I knew how they got their money. My mother didn't approve. She said I would burn in hell. Maybe she was right. But it's hard to rationalize morality when you're hungry and someone shows you a way of life that doesn't include steel-toed work boots and the fire of the mills. I was motivated by money and respect.

And working for Alphonse "Iceman Al" Fortunato was giving me both.

CHAPTER

5

May 2019

I DROVE UP TO the funeral home in Wellsville for the visiting hours for Ricky Bones. It was pretty sad. A nephew stood by the casket and a few vases of flowers, and only a handful of people milled about the room. Riccardo Bonelli, his real name, had been divorced for years and was estranged from his two daughters. A couple years earlier, I ran into one of the girls at the Fort Steuben Mall. When I asked how her dad was doing, she said, "I don't know. I never see him. He's too busy trying to drink himself to death to be bothered with his family. I don't hate him, but if a semitruck were to go left of center and kill him, I wouldn't be upset."

That was a shame, but not surprising. Ricky was a hard guy to work with, so it was a safe bet that he was a hard guy to live with, maybe even harder to love. He was self-destructive and moody, one of those guys who thought the world had it out for him. Nickels Nicolosi said it best: "Ricky Bones has a good engine, but his hands are never on the steering wheel." If Ricky ever enjoyed a moment of introspection and admitted that he brought a lot of misery on himself, I never saw it.

Back in the day, Ricky was a powerful guy. I'd heard he was a pretty good athlete at Wellsville High School, a football player and wrestler. When he took off his shirt, he looked like a statue of a Greek god. But he looked puny in his casket, thin and shrunken by the ravages of alcohol, and it seemed like the lining of the casket was swallowing him up.

I spoke briefly to the nephew and offered my condolences. He asked how I knew his uncle, and I said, "We were business associates."

"Oh, I see," he said, forcing a smile.

Let me interpret that for you: *So, you're one of the Fortunato family bums he wasted his life with.* I got the feeling that the quicker the casket that was swallowing up his uncle was swallowed up by the earth, the happier the nephew would be.

I felt bad about not visiting Ricky when he was in the hospital. We'd worked together for years, but to tell you the truth, I was never a big fan. He was forever poking at me, trying to find fault with anything I did. I told him once, "Ricky, if I found a unicorn that shit gold coins, you'd have a problem with it." He never forgave me for showing him up with that Jewish florist. But like I said, Ricky was his own worst enemy. If he had just taken care of business, it wouldn't have been an issue. Again, never his fault.

It was a short, sad visit. I was glad that I went but was just as glad to walk back out into the sunshine. I didn't bother to sign the registry. The cops, they tend to keep an eye on things like that. Then they haul you into court and call you a "known associate." They're bastards.

From the funeral home, I drove to Weirton to see my buddy Nickels at Pinecrest Rehabilitation Center. This was a gross misnomer. It was a nursing home. They called it a rehabilitation center to give you the illusion that it was a place where people went to recover from surgery or an injury and would eventually go back to a normal life. Nothing could have been further from the truth. It was a warehouse where the owners didn't want you to get better because they wanted to keep the beds full and the Medicaid dollars rolling in. They're bastards, too. It was more of a cheap motel than a rehabilitation center. The doctor at the hospital told Nickels he'd only be at Pinecrest a couple of weeks, just until he learned to walk on his artificial leg. He'd been there months, and I'd yet to see him walk. I feared the only way Nickels would leave would be in a body bag.

Doctors had amputated his left leg just below the knee. Nickels had gotten a rough spot on his foot from a pair of ill-fitting shoes. Or maybe he stepped on a nail. Who knew with Nickels; he was a wizard with numbers and finances, but weak on the details when it came to the rest of his life. After the infection set in, Nickels used his acute understanding of medical science to self-diagnose the problem, which he determined to be of little concern. He ignored it until his leg turned black halfway up his shin and a couple of toes rotted off in his sock. He was lucky to be alive. Although, when I walked the halls of Pinecrest, I wasn't sure how lucky he really was.

Nickels loved my visits. He was a talker. If you called Nickels to tell him that his house was on fire, it would be a forty-five minute conversation. His stories would drag on and I'd finally tell him, "Nickels, for the love of God, land the plane." He'd laugh and keep on talking. The problem these days was that I never knew who was going to be in the room—the lucid and quick-tongued Nickels, or the one who couldn't tell you what day it was. A month earlier, I walked in and he was working a crossword puzzle. He looked up and asked, "What's a nine-letter word for constant, begins with a P?"

"Try perpetual."

"That fits. Thanks." Then, from clear out of left field, he asks, "Have you seen the cats?"

"Cats? What cats?"

"The cats that live here."

"It's a nursing home, Nickels. There ain't no cats here."

"Yeah, there are—a black one and little orange one. They come sleep with me at night."

"What? There ain't no cats sleeping with you."

"If it ain't a cat, then it might be a coon. If it's a coon, I'm going to kill that bastard with my ink pen."

"If a raccoon crawls into your bed, call a nurse, because you're not going to kill anything with that plastic ink pen. Mother of Christ, what kind of drugs are they giving you?"

A week later, we were having a perfectly wonderful visit when after thirty minutes he got all agitated and said, "How many fuckin' ducks have you killed?"

"Ducks? What ducks? What the hell are you talking about?"

"You heard me. How many have you killed?"

"None."

"I killed sixty-eight. My Ford F-150 will go a hundred and eighty miles an hour. I've got two silencers on my AR-15. I changed the damn furnace filter twice last week. Last night, I saw commandos parachuting into the trees out back. What do you got to say about that?"

There was nothing to say. He didn't even own a Ford F-150. I cut that visit short. I couldn't take any more.

When I walked into his room after visiting the funeral home, he gave me a weak wave and said, "Angelo, my man."

"How're you doing, Nickels?" I asked.

"It's just another crazy day in paradise. Can't you tell?"

As usual, he had the thermostat set on the Depths-of-Hell. The poor guy hadn't been warm since he entered Pinecrest. As I was pulling off my sport coat, I said, "Can I turn down the heat a little bit?"

"No. I'm freezin'."

"Nickels, it's hotter than hell in July in here."

"Yeah, well, I'm getting ready for my eternity."

He laughed. We covered several inane topics—the weather, the lousy food at the nursing home, women from the old days—when he asked, "Is the Super Bowl this Sunday?"

"The Super Bowl? They played that months ago; it's May. It's baseball season."

"*May!*" He winced. "I can't keep track of time in this shithole."

A nurse came in with a paper cup containing his pills. He washed them down with the last of his coffee. It wasn't five minutes before he had trouble focusing on our conversation and began drifting in and out. When the nurse came back, I asked, "How come he's not more aware? There was nothing wrong with his brain when he got here."

"We have to keep him slightly sedated," she said.

I pointed to Nickels and said, "*This* is what you call *slightly* sedated?"

"If we don't, he tries to leave."

"Who can blame him?"

She turned up her nose and left.

Nickels squirmed around on his bed and said, "My leg hurts like blue hell."

"Your good one?"

"What do you mean my good one? They're both good ones."

"Nickels, you only have one leg. They amputated the left one, remember? That's why you're in here."

He looked down, raised the stump a couple inches off the mattress so the sheet puffed up. "Fuckin' ay," he said. "When did that happen?"

"Are you kidding me? Months ago."

"I hate this place, Angelo. This ain't no way to live."

He drifted back to sleep. I read the *Intelligencer* until he woke up fifteen minutes later.

"What have you been up to, Ange?" he asked.

"I just got back from the funeral home. I told you the other day that Ricky Bones died, remember?"

He didn't.

"Ricky? Aw, that's too bad. How did he die?"

"I'm guessing he died of being Ricky Bones for the past eighty years. The guy drank a fifth of gin every day for the last three decades. I'm guessing that his liver finally waved the white flag."

He laughed. "How many of the old guard are left?"

"You're looking at them, partner. You and me."

"I hope it's just you soon. I lie here all day and shit and piss in that metal pan and try to remember my name. This ain't no way to live, Angelo. Did I mention that?"

"Yeah, you did."

He closed his eyes and asked, "Who did you say died?"

"Ricky Bones."

"Oh, yeah. Ricky. That's too bad. How did he die?"

He drifted back to sleep before I could tell him that I still didn't know.

CHAPTER

6

July 1971

Mr. Fortunato's granddaughters were regular visitors to the compound, especially in the summer when they were home from college—Bridget at Notre Dame and Yvonne at Xavier. They would lounge around the pool in their two-piece bathing suits, their olive skin slathered in baby oil, their hair long, straight, and the color of wet coal. Despite Mr. Fortunato's threats, I violated his admonition at every opportunity. I couldn't help myself. They were two of the most stunningly beautiful women I had ever seen in my life.

That first year I worked for Mr. Fortunato, I got invited to his Christmas party. This was a big deal for me. I had never seen so much food or gold jewelry in one place. The girls were there, and I was sneaking peeks at them when Mr. Fortunato busted me. We made eye contact, and he casually reached down and cupped his testicles. Message received, loud and clear. I didn't look their way the rest of the night. Later in the evening, couples began pairing off for a game of charades. I was walking up to Mr. Fortunato to thank him for the invitation to the party and head home when Yvonne said, "I want Angelo for my partner."

I was looking straight at her grandfather when the words came out of her mouth, and I started stuttering, "Oh, no, no thanks, no, I can't. I, I can't."

"Oh, come on, Angelo," she said. "It'll be fun."

"No, it won't. Not at all. No, really, I can't."

"What, my granddaughter's not good enough for you, Angelo?" Mr. Fortunato asked, furrows of concern stretching across his forehead. The room went silent, and I was facing a no-win situation. Did I leave the party and insult my boss and his granddaughter, or did I go home later with my testicles in a brown paper sack?

"No . . . she's great, no, I mean, yes, of course she is, good enough, I mean. I just . . ."

Mr. Fortunato started laughing, and the entire room followed suit. "This kid, huh?" He wrapped his arm around my shoulder and squeezed. "Go have fun, Angelo. It's Christmas." He kissed me on the top of the head, squeezed tighter, then leaned down and whispered, "Touch her, and you're a dead man." Then he smiled and pushed me toward her outstretched hand.

I think it might have been a setup, but I never asked.

* * *

The girls were in the pool on a hot Saturday afternoon in July. I had been in the garage washing the Cadillac and peeking glimpses of them through the windows. They were sitting on the edge of the pool, their legs in the water, ample cleavage oiled up and on full display, their dark eyes hidden by oversized sunglasses.

After finishing the car, I combed my hair, tucked in my T-shirt, and headed for the house. I was almost to the back door when Bridget said, "Angelo, why don't you come swimming with us?"

"You know I can't do that," I said

"Why?"

"Because Mr. Fortunato would not like that on several levels."

"What's that mean?"

"It means, one, he doesn't pay me to swim, and, two, if he caught me in the pool with his granddaughters, I am liable to lose a couple of body parts of which I am very fond."

They giggled. Yvonne said, "Nonno will let you swim if we ask him."

"Please don't do that."

"Why? What are you afraid of?"

"Mostly, your grandfather."

"He's a big softy."

"We must not be talking about the same Alphonse Fortunato."

As I reached for the back door, Bridget said in a sweet tone, "Angelo."

I couldn't not turn around. When I did, she rolled the tip of her tongue over her upper lip and winked. I could hear them both laughing as I slammed the door behind me.

I only got sideways with Mr. Fortunato a couple of times. These were missteps of my own devising. Missteps might not be a strong enough word. Stupidity is a better one. The first was a slightly forgivable sin, but certainly the most embarrassing story I will tell.

I fell in love with one of his hookers.

Mr. Fortunato had three brothels on Water Street. I was twenty when I walked into the one known as the blue house and met Dusty. She was beautiful, with long auburn hair, gray eyes, and perky breasts. She walked up to me and said, "How 'bout it, handsome, wanna dance?"

Oh, did I ever. Right there, I fell in love with Dusty. On the fourth straight night I went to see her, I took her flowers. Yeah, let me repeat that just so you can gauge what a dumbass I was at that age. I took flowers to a hooker. I became the first guy in history to walk into a brothel with a bouquet. I was young, naïve, and hard, which may have contributed to my clouded thinking.

I'm going to gloss over some of the ugly details, but I went back one night and when I saw her coming down the stairs with a steelworker, I made a scene and told her that I didn't want her seeing other guys. Yes, I told a prostitute not to see other guys.

The next morning, Mr. Fortunato called me into his office and said, "Have you completely lost your marbles? Those girls are my employees. They're not a dating service for stiff-dicked dagos." He threw a pencil at me. My face was surface-of-the-sun hot. "Get the fuck out of here, and don't pull a stunt like that again. Find yourself a nice girl and get married, but I don't want to hear that you're looking for her in one of my whorehouses."

The second time I got called on his carpet was for a much more serious infraction. I was at the Federal Terrace with Connie Bones and Nickels. I looked up to those guys and tried to emulate them. They were both classy dressers, and Nickels set me up with Morris Supovitz at the Phil-Mor Men's Store. Morris measured me for custom suits, suggested the material I needed, picked out my shirts and ties, and showed me how to tie a Windsor knot. The day I walked out of there in that custom suit, I thought I was Clark Gable. No kidding, I didn't know how good a nice suit could make you feel.

The three of us were eating in Mr. Fortunato's private room. I was wearing one of my new suits—worsted wool, light gray with blue pinstripes—and feeling like I looked successful. As we were leaving, I saw my old nemesis, guidance counselor Austin Adams, and his wife sitting in a booth. I said, "Hold up a minute. I need to talk to someone."

I walked up to the table and in a stupid, fake Brooklyn Mafioso voice, I said, "Hey, Mr. Adams, how ya doin'?" He looked blankly at me. In the years since he had mocked me in the lounge at the athletic club, I'd grown thick and muscled, and my face had become more chiseled. "You don't remember me?"

"I'm sorry, but no. I've had a lot of students over the years," he said.

"Yeah, but how many of them did you tell they couldn't figure out which end of a broom to hold?"

He blinked twice. "I'm sorry, but I'm drawing a blank."

"Let me help you out—Angelo Cipriani."

"Yes, Angelo. I remember you."

"Let me ask you a question. Do you think a guy who didn't know how to use a broom could buy a suit like this? It costs more than you make in a month." I pushed up the sleeves of my jacket to reveal a watch and cufflinks. "How about jewelry like this? Do you think a dumbass who couldn't use a broom could buy gold cufflinks?" Mrs. Adams started to squirm.

"What do you want?" he asked.

"I just want you to answer my questions."

"You seem to be very successful, Mr. Cipriani. I'm happy for you."

He said it in the same condescending tone that he had used that day back when I was a junior in high school. I wanted to punch his face. Instead, I picked up the bottle of cabernet from the table and poured it over his head. He made no effort to get up or to stop me. After setting the bottle back on the table, I peeled a twenty dollar bill out of my money clip and threw it on his plate. "Buy yourself another bottle of wine, douchebag."

I had waited years for that, and I walked out of the Federal Terrace feeling like a big man.

The next day was payday at Wheeling-Pitt, and I went down to the mill to collect on loans and a couple of payment plans we had set up with some gamblers. When I got back to the compound, I walked into Mr. Fortunato's office with a cloth bag stuffed with cash. It was just the kind of thing that usually made him happy. I set the bag on his desk, and he said, "I need to talk to you for a minute." He stepped out from behind the desk and slapped me full on the side of the face with a righteous right hand. And I'm not talking about a love tap. He hit me so hard that flecks of spittle flew out of my mouth, and the side of my face felt like someone had pressed a hot iron to it.

I would rather get punched than slapped. Getting slapped denotes that you are a lesser man. It's insulting. I put a hand to the burning skin and said, "What was that for?"

"Shut up," he said, slapping me again, this time with the left hand.

I just took it. What else was there to do? This was the mob. There wasn't a human resources department where I could complain because my boss was being mean to me.

"What the fuck is wrong with you?" he asked.

"What did I do?"

"I let you use my private room at the Federal Terrace, you eat on my dime, and you repay me by making a scene in the middle of the restaurant because you got your feelings hurt back in high school?" He slapped me a third time. The left side of my face was numb. "If you want to keep working for me, you better grow the fuck up. Do you think the people who were there last night think it was Angelo Cipriani showing his ass? No. I'll tell you what they think. They think it was one of Alphonse Fortunato's men showing his ass." He started poking me in the chest with an index finger. It felt like a piece of steel. "I pay a lot of people good money so that we don't have trouble in this town, and I'm not letting some snot-nosed punk ruin that for me. You understand me good. You pull another stunt like that and you'll be back emptying spit cans at the athletic club. Now get the fuck out of my sight."

One thing about Mr. Fortunato, once you screwed up and he either verbally berated you or slapped the holy shit out of you, it was over. He never brought it up again, and I never gave him any reason to.

After I ducked inside and escaped from his granddaughters, I could hear Mr. Fortunato holding a meeting with his capos in his office. I was thirty feet from the closed door and could hear him going scorched earth on the boys. He was in one of his moods. You don't want to ever piss off a Viking or a crime lord. At one time or another, we all took a turn in his doghouse. On this day, however, he was upset with everyone but the saints and the Holy Mother.

Mr. Fortunato was rarely in what I would categorize as a jovial mood, and gregarious was not an adjective ever used to describe him. I guess when you get up in the morning wondering if today's the day the FBI or the IRS is showing up at your doorstep, or if a rival family is going to put a bullet behind your ear—or in your forehead or your heart—it tends to make you a little less sociable.

When I walked into the room, all heads turned. Every capo looked like he wanted to make a dash for the open door. I lowered my head, gently pulled the door closed behind me, and went to my seat in the corner of the room. Mr. Fortunato was cursing, shoving papers off his desk, throwing pencils, more cursing, pointing fingers, yelling, more cursing. I figured it was only a few minutes before he took a swipe at me. I should have taken my chances with the granddaughters. He was complaining about one gambler's account, in particular, that was ten thousand dollars in arrears, and he wanted it cleaned up yesterday.

Here's what you need to understand about the mob, or at least guys like Mr. Fortunato. They don't go around killing everyone who's late on their gambling payments or someone who pisses them off. If that was the case, there would have been blood running down Market Street like it was the Ohio River, because Mr. Fortunato was always pissed at someone. Every once in a while, they might decide to make an example of a repeat offender, but not very often. Mostly, they just wanted their money, and if you were habitually late, they may not kill you, but they could make you very uncomfortable, if you know what I mean. Oh, and by the way, just because you're late on your debt and you haven't heard from anyone in a couple weeks, you should never make the mistake of thinking they've forgotten about you. The mob never forgets. Ever. They are the greediest sons of bitches I've ever seen in my life. If you were in arrears for twenty dollars or twenty large, believe me, they knew it.

The generalized ranting went on for another five minutes before Mr. Fortunato threw a stapler at Ricky Bones and yelled, "How can you let this happen?"

"I'm working on it, boss" Ricky said. "He's a good customer."

"Let me explain to you what a good customer looks like, Ricky. He pays his fuckin' gambling bill. How can he be a good customer if he owes us ten grand?"

"I'll talk to him."

"Not talk. Collect, goddammit. I want every dime, and I want it before I take my next piss."

"It's just that, he's my brother-in-law and I . . ."

There wasn't a guy in that room whose ass didn't pucker up when those words came out of Ricky Bones's mouth. I could always tell when Mr. Fortunato was ready to go nuclear. He would start running his tongue around the inside of his mouth in circles and shaking his head. Between clenched teeth, and in a surprisingly calm voice, Mr. Fortunato said, "The Jew florist, Stein, he's your brother-in-law?"

"Yeah, he's married to my wife's sister," Ricky Bones said.

"How come I didn't know that?"

"I didn't think it was important."

I cannot even begin to tell you what a bad answer that was. I thought Mr. Fortunato was going to have an aneurysm. "So, let me get this straight. You're telling me that you've been letting one of your relatives skate on my dime?"

"I just, I thought . . ."

Mr. Fortunato began screaming, having entered an entirely new level of rage. "See, that's the fuckin' problem right there, Ricky. I don't pay you to think. It's a travesty that stupidity isn't painful."

"Boss, please. My sister-in-law has been pleading with my wife for me to cut him a break. She's up my ass about it."

"And you expect me to take the hit? Unacceptable. If you can't do the job, I'll find someone who can."

"I'll do it," I said.

The words were out of my mouth before I had time to think of the ramifications of failure.

Everyone turned to look at me. I said, "I'll handle it. I'll get your money."

It was the first time I had ever spoken out at a meeting. When I said I needed to make my bones, I didn't mean it in the traditional sense of the Mafia. A lot of people think you need to kill a rival member to make your bones. Not necessarily. Within the house of Fortunato, you needed to show not only your usefulness and absolute loyalty to the organization, but your ability to make money. I'd been waiting for this opportunity. Up to that point, my usefulness had been limited to every crummy job that no one else wanted to do. This was the chance to show Mr. Fortunato that I could help put money in his pocket.

Alphonse stared at me for a moment, his nostrils flaring, and I wasn't sure if I would get the green light or get kicked out of the meeting. Finally, he nodded a couple of times and said, "Do you know who we're talking about?"

"Benny Stein at Sunset Florist, down by the bowling alley."

"He owes me ten thousand dollars, and you tell him I better see some money soon. Be persuasive, but he can't pay me back if he can't work. Don't break a bunch of bones—maybe a finger or two. If he's uncomfortable, that's okay." He pointed a finger at me and again rolled his tongue around the inside of his mouth before continuing. "Understand this, kid. You shot off your mouth that you could collect. This is your account now, and I'm holding you responsible."

I said, "Yes, sir," and headed out the back door to my car.

When I walked through the portico to the driveway, Bridget said, "Where are you going in such a hurry?"

"To make my bones," I said, never breaking stride. Suddenly, something was more important to me than the two beauties at poolside.

It was a little less than a ten-minute drive from the compound to the flower shop. I grabbed the screen door of the shop and threw it back so that it slammed against the outside of the building. The instant I came through the door, Stein knew why I was there. He had never laid eyes on me, but when you owe ten grand to the mob, you know there's going to come a day when someone in a bad mood is going to show up. There was a customer at the counter; he held up an index finger to the woman, gesturing that he had an urgent matter to take care of, and started walking toward a door to the back room. He motioned to me with his head to follow, as though I needed an invitation. When the door was closed behind us, I started toward him, my face pinched into a frown and one index finger extended toward his nose. He backed up, threw both hands in the air, and said, "Wait, wait, wait. No rough stuff. I've got the money." He bent down to a cabinet below a table of geraniums, reached far inside, and pulled out a brown paper lunch sack. "Here it is," he said, handing me the bag.

I opened it; it was full of neatly wrapped twenty-dollar bills.

"This is all of it?"

"All of it."

"Ten thousand."

"Every dollar."

In all candor, it was a little disappointing that it had been this easy. "You better not be lying to me."

"It's all there, I swear. Tell Mr. Fortunato I'm sorry, but my wife's been sick and . . ."

I knew that a lie was about to come out of his mouth, so I shoved my hand in my pants pocket and slipped my fingers into the holes of my brass knuckles. I hit him as hard as I could, right at the bottom of his nose. The cartilage snapping sounded like someone had cracked a walnut, and the skin split down to his upper lip. He flew backward, hitting the table. Three potted geraniums fell to the floor, their clay pots exploding on impact, potting soil spreading over the concrete. Blood was streaming from both nostrils over his lips and teeth.

"What the hell," he said, covering his face with both hands. "I paid you the . . ."

I grabbed his shirt under the collar and said, "Shut up, flower boy. You were late, very late, and I don't care how sick your wife is. From now on, you pay your debts on time. Don't stop betting with Mr. Fortunato, but don't ever make me come back down here again, because your brother-in-law is no longer in charge of the account. I am. I'm not gonna ask if you understand. I'm just gonna assume you do, because if I have to come back here to collect again, things are going to be a lot rougher on you."

I'll admit this: Stein was a skinny little florist, so it didn't take a lot of nerve to walk in there and rough him up. With that said, it's also easy to be a badass when you have the backing of Alphonse Fortunato.

Just a few minutes earlier, I had been wondering how I was going to make my bones with Mr. Fortunato, and then it was handed to me on a platter. I couldn't believe my good fortune. Ten seconds after I walked out the door of the florist, I had a plan in my head. I raced back to the compound, arriving less than half an hour after I'd left. Everyone was still in the flogging session. The conversation stopped when the door opened. I walked into the office carrying the folded paper bag; it looked like I was bringing the boss an oversized sandwich. I set it on his desk, then returned to my chair in the corner, never saying a word or making eye contact with anyone, like it was just another day at the office.

Mr. Fortunato looked at the sack, then at me, and then at the sack again. He peeled back the paper and looked inside. "It's all here?"

I looked like I was surprised that he asked me the question. I said, "Yes, sir. It's all there."

He reached into the bag and pulled out the stacks of bills. "How'd you get it so fast?"

I shrugged. "You told me to be persuasive."

"Does he understand that it better never happen again?"

"If he doesn't understand, he's either retarded, or he wasn't paying attention."

Mr. Fortunato took a deep breath and nodded, the anger seeming to release from his body. Then it returned like a meteorite breaking through the atmosphere. He hammered his fist into the stack of cash. Several of the paper straps broke, and twenties went into the air and helicoptered to the floor. "Goddammit," he yelled, looking around the room at his capos. "I wait weeks for you jagoffs to get me my money, and that snot-nosed kid does it in twenty minutes? What the fuck am I paying you clowns for?"

Out of the corner of my eye, I could see Ricky Bones glaring at me. I had pushed him out of the way and shown him up in front of the boss and the capos. He wouldn't forget this, and that was fine with me. As I've said several times, my job was to make Mr. Fortunato happy. Or, at least try. It obviously wasn't working at that moment. I'd just dropped ten thousand dollars on his desk, and he wasn't acting the least bit happy. He continued yelling, throwing things, and questioning the legitimacy of their births. During this tirade, Big Tommy, who was sitting on the couch across the room, gave me a sideways glance and a grin. I averted my eyes, fearing

I might smile, which could have been a fatal mistake in Mr. Fortunato's current state of displeasure.

Big Tommy was Alphonse's only son. I liked Tommy and he always treated me like a human being, which meant he didn't go out of his way to bust my balls every minute of the day. He was three years my senior and began working in the organization after earning a business degree from the University of Pittsburgh. He was probably the best educated mob underboss in the country. There was a lot of talk about Big Tommy going straight and establishing an umbrella corporation to manage the car washes, pizza parlors, and other legitimate businesses. But I never saw any movement in that direction. Frankly, there was too much money in gambling and prostitution to waste time on legitimate enterprises. He had a bachelor's degree framed on the wall, but at his heart, Big Tommy was still the son of a gangster.

Alphonse yelled for another twenty minutes. He didn't stop because he was no longer pissed off; he just ran out of steam. It's hard to maintain that level of anger.

After the meeting, I went back to the garage to clean up a few things before I went home. The granddaughters had left and the capos were scrambling to their cars, anxious to get out of range. Twenty minutes later, Mr. and Mrs. Fortunato got into the Cadillac with Jimmy Beans at the wheel and headed for the Federal Terrace. When the Caddy cleared Rosemont Street, Big Tommy walked into the garage. "That was a nice move today, Angelo," he said. "I don't know how you pulled that off, but you did yourself a solid in my old man's eyes."

"Thanks, Tommy."

"No kidding. He'll remember that."

"I hope so."

"There's no doubt about it. He runs a performance-based operation, and you proved yourself to be an A player. I guarantee you're going to get the call up to the big leagues. Ricky Bones screwed the pooch. Once you get sideways with my old man, it's a long road to get back in his good graces. Poor Ricky, he's going to be hauling bags to Flushing for a long time."

* * *

This might be a good time to explain the meaning of "hauling bags to Flushing" and how the whole sports book and daily number worked. The family took bets on sports and the daily numbers—three- and four-digit numbers that were drawn every night at the compound.

In order to make these operations work, the family needed dozens of couriers to deliver the spot sheets, collect the bets, and deliver the payoffs. This was referred to as "hauling bags." It was considered a task for low-level associates. Think of it like a paper route for wannabe goombahs. Flushing, Ohio, is a little town in western Belmont County, but the VFW and the Oriole Bar both made book on sports and the daily numbers for Mr. Fortunato. Thus, whoever was hauling bags to Flushing had a miserable job of driving out to the sticks over country roads twice a day, making deliveries and pickups.

The term was somewhat metaphorical in nature, as anyone who fell out of favor with Mr. Fortunato for any reason was said to be "hauling bags to Flushing."

Sports gambling, by far, was the largest revenue generator for the family. It was a massive operation. You could get spot sheets in nearly every bar and private club in the Ohio Valley. A spot sheet was a half-sheet of typing paper on which were printed the odds for the games that week. Football brought in the most gamblers and money, so I'll use that as an example.

On Monday morning, couriers would deliver that week's spot sheets to the locations that were taking the bets. The sheets contained the matchups and odds for the professional, college, and a few select local high school games being played that week. You could not bet on individual games. You had to play a minimum of a three-game parlay. That means you had to bet and win three games to collect at three-to-one. You could bet on more than three games, and the potential payoff increased with each additional bet. The payoffs looked good, but it was a sucker's bet. It wasn't impossible to pick three winners, but the odds were extremely high. That's why sports betting was so lucrative; it was virtually all profit. That's also why Mr. Fortunato was living in a sprawling compound, and a lot of the gamblers shuffled home to house trailers.

There was usually one person at each location in charge of accepting the bets. He wasn't a bookie in the truest sense of the word, but that's how we referred to him. The vig, or juice, on sports betting was 10 percent. That was the bookie's payoff for accepting the bet. The bookie was never out any cash, no matter the outcome of the bets. Mr. Fortunato took the risk of paying out the winners, but he also kept the profits.

So, you might ask, if winning a parlay is so difficult, why wouldn't a bookie just run his own business and keep the profits? The short answer is because he didn't want to become dead, which is what might happen if Mr. Fortunato found out someone was trying to cut into his turf. If he suspected that a bookie might be going through the spot sheets and looking for the sure losers to pull out and keep the bets, he would send in an associate to put down a couple hundo on an eighteen-game parlay. If that spot sheet didn't show up, the bookie was going to get a very unpleasant visit from one of Mr. Fortunato's associates. If it happened a second time, they probably wouldn't show up for work the next day . . . or maybe ever again. It happened very seldom, as anyone with a nickel's worth of common sense knew the consequences of cheating Iceman Al.

(Note: This was the reason Mr. Fortunato had Sammy Avocado in the fold. Sammy was expected to play the role of a complete psychopath, and by that, I mean that Sammy was a complete psychopath. He had a huge jaw and a misshapen head; the dimple in the middle of his chin was somewhere east of his left eye, which was always rattling around in the socket. He was built like a gun safe, had hands the size of boxing gloves with a mountain range of knuckles that were crisscrossed with white scars. All Sammy lacked was a couple of bolts in the side of his neck and the transformation would have been complete. There were few people in this world that I genuinely feared, but Sammy was at the top of the list. He had the brains of a bowl of stewed tomatoes, but Mr. Fortunato didn't keep him around for his intellect. When there was a collection problem with an account, Sammy would go out with an associate to square it up. Sammy's job was to stand nearby and scare the hell out of the problem child. He looked like he could go medieval on you and enjoy it, both of which were true. It was very effective. Mr. Fortunato never—*never!*—sent Sammy out on his own. The boy was weapons-grade stupid, so you could tell Sammy to go to Mr. Smith's bar and collect a thousand dollars, and he might interpret it as go to Mr. Smith's home and butcher his wife and children in the front yard. He was kept on a very short leash.)

On Friday afternoons, the couriers would return to the bars and American Legion posts to pick up the bets. Each sheet would have the name of the gambler and the cash stapled to the sheet. The bookie would hand them to the courier in a zippered canvas bag, the zipper held in place with a padlock that could only be opened by the counters at the compound. When the last pro game was over on Sunday, the counters would go through the bets, tossing the cash from the losing bets into a laundry basket on the floor, and stapling any winnings back to the spot sheet. On Monday morning, the process would start over again with the couriers returning to their routes, delivering the same canvas bags to their locations with that week's spot sheets and payoffs for the winners.

If you went to the grocery store and got a dollar bill back in change with staple holes in the middle, you knew it had previously been wagered with Alphonse Fortunato.

CHAPTER 7

July 1971

TWO DAYS AFTER I collected the ten thousand dollars from the florist, I stopped by Mr. Fortunato's office late in the afternoon to see if he needed anything before I went home for the day. His feet were crossed at the ankles and resting on the corner of his desk, and his hands were folded over his ample belly. The local news played on the black-and-white television in the corner of the room.

He said, "Hey, kid, come here. I want you to see something." I walked to the side of his desk. He pointed and said, "Watch this."

A news reporter from WSTV was standing in front of Schulman's Music Store downtown. He was holding one finger to an ear and looking very grave. A fleet of police cars, their red lights flashing, surrounded the building. Uniformed officers were exiting a back door, hauling out roulette wheels, craps tables, slot machines, and cardboard boxes containing decks of cards and dice.

The reporter said:

Steubenville Chief of Police Walter Snodgrass said this raid above Schulman's Music Store was the result of an investigation by a joint anti-gambling task force.

Mr. Fortunato slapped my arm. "A joint task force . . . that's a good one," he said.

Snodgrass said today's raid ended a six-month investigation into illegal gambling in the city. We have Chief Snodgrass with us. Chief, can you give us any more details about this operation?

The chief stepped into the camera, pulled a cigarette from his mouth, and used it to point at the third floor of the building.

We had a tip that an illegal casino was operating on the top floor of that building. We were able to infiltrate the operation with undercover officers. That led to today's raid. We are not going to tolerate this type of illegal activity in our community. Gambling ruins families and causes financial hardships. They say it's a victimless crime, but there are no victimless crimes. This is a step toward ending vice in Steubenville. It was the first bust, but it won't be the last.

"Chief Snodgrass, he's pretty good in front of the camera, don't you think?" Mr. Fortunato asked.

"I guess," I said.

I felt like I'd entered an episode of *The Twilight Zone.* They were hauling all the gaming equipment out of Mr. Fortunato's casino, and yet he seemed to be in a particularly jovial mood, when he should have been throwing staplers and overturning his desk.

As the last of the gaming equipment was loaded into a panel truck, the reporter asked Chief Snodgrass who was responsible for running the casino and if any arrests were imminent.

We're still working on that. It's obviously a complicated system, and we suspect this operation has out-of-state ties to organized crime.

Out-of-state ties? I thought. Are you kidding? He's right in your backyard.

I can tell you this . . . Chief Snodgrass turned to face the camera. *You can run, but you can't hide. You're not bringing your vice to our community. We're going to find out who's responsible, and we're warming up a jail cell for you.*

Mr. Fortunato got up from his chair and turned the television off. "You've got to give Chief Snodgrass credit," he said. "He's working to keep our community safe." He started chuckling. "Stick around, kid. I'll need you a little bit later."

The cook had made rigatoni and meatballs for dinner. Mr. Fortunato ate at his desk. I ate with the cook and the maid in the galley kitchen in the basement. I didn't know how long he wanted me to hang around, and I didn't ask. I'd wait all night until he told me otherwise. After dinner, I went to the living room and turned on the television. It was a few minutes before ten when he walked in and said, "Come on, kid. Let's go for a ride." We got into the Cadillac and he said, "Head downtown." I drove down Sunset Boulevard; he sat in the passenger seat, blowing cigar smoke into the night air.

We didn't converse; he just pointed with his cigar and said, "Here," when he wanted me to turn. I took an easy right onto Market Street and another right onto South Fifth Street. I was watching the orange end of his cigar more than the road. I drove past the pigeonhole parking garage and into the parking lot at the side of Schulman's Music Store. At the back of the lot there was an open space. A metal sign on a steel post read: Reserved for A. Fortunato. I slid the Caddy home.

I followed Mr. Fortunato to the back of the building, where we got into a freight elevator lined with moving blankets. Halfway up, I could hear what sounded like a party. The elevator door opened on the third floor onto a small foyer where an associate I knew only as Bobo was sitting on a stool next to a solid steel door. His eyes widened at the sight of Alphonse Fortunato, and he hopped off the stool. He said, "Mr. Fortunato. I didn't know you were coming down tonight." The old man didn't give Bobo a second look; he just pointed at the door. Bobo hit a buzzer and opened it, and we stepped inside.

It was a little difficult wrapping my brain around what I saw and heard. There were no fewer than a hundred people pulling the arms on slot machines, rolling dice at the craps table, plopping down chips at the roulette wheel, and playing poker and blackjack. A three-piece jazz band was playing in the corner. People were laughing and cheering. Two guys and a woman were working behind an ornate bar that spanned one entire side of the room; everyone in the place had a drink in their hand.

Nickels was in the back of the room, talking to a woman in a red dress and pearls. The instant he saw Mr. Fortunato, he touched the woman on the shoulder and headed toward the boss. Mr. Fortunato said, "Good crowd."

"Great crowd," Nickels said.

"Especially considering all that negative publicity we got earlier."

They both started laughing.

I still hadn't pieced it all together.

As we got back on Sunset Boulevard for the ride back to the compound, Mr. Fortunato looked over at me and said, "You figured it out yet, kid?"

"No, sir. I don't think so."

"It's not as complicated as you might think. The chief, he's got his own constituents to think about. Steubenville is a pretty wide-open town, but we've still got a lot of Bible-thumpers who don't like gambling and whoring. So, every two or three years, they need to make a big gambling or prostitution raid, you know, so the church crowd thinks they're getting their money's worth. We save our worn-out and broken equipment in the back room. When it's time for the show, we let the cops call the television stations and the newspaper and they raid one of the casinos." He started laughing. "It's all a big show. All they're doing is hauling out our trash, but it makes for good television, and it makes all the holy rollers happy because they think the gambling is getting shut down. In another week, they'll haul that junk into a field and set it on fire for the TV cameras."

"But the chief said they're going after the owners."

"Kid, please. Do you know how much I pay the chief every year to keep the casinos and brothels open? The answer is plenty. The attorney general will read about this and he'll send out some crime-fighter certificates, pat some people on the back, they'll all get their picture in the paper and everyone's happy. They don't need to arrest anyone because in two weeks everyone will have forgotten about it and moved on to something else." He looked at me, his brows arching. "You didn't know the chief was in my pocket?"

"Of course, but I guess I just didn't know it was this . . ."

"Blatant?"

"Theatrical. I think theatrical is the word I was looking for. That was all theater this afternoon."

Alphonse Fortunato sat back in his seat and smiled. "People say what I do is an ugly business, but at least it ain't politics." He fired up another cigar. "I've got a meeting in the morning, and I want you to go along. I'm going to show you how things really work in Steubenville, Ohio."

* * *

At a few minutes before nine the next morning, I walked to the Cadillac with Mr. Fortunato and Ricky Bones. As we reached the car, I opened the back door for Mr. Fortunato and was reaching for the handle on the front door when he said, "You sit back here with me, Angelo."

Angelo?

He rarely called me anything but "kid." The only time I recalled him calling me Angelo was at the Christmas party when he thought I was insulting his granddaughter. And I had never ridden anywhere with him that I wasn't in the front seat. I slid into the back seat, and Ricky Bones pointed the car toward downtown.

Now, I've got to tell you, this was the biggest day of my life up to that point. I was sitting there, trying hard not to smile, thinking that this was the day I was getting the call to the big leagues, just like Big Tommy predicted. I sat erect and looked out the window and acted like this was the kind of thing that happened every day. You know, me and the head of the largest crime syndicate in the Ohio Valley having our driver take us to a meeting. We took Washington Street across Route 7 and turned right on Water Street, where Mr. Fortunato's whorehouses were open for the boys coming off the night shift at the mill. A pair of mill workers were climbing the steps of one of the houses, their hard hats and tin lunch pails in their hands.

We drove down to the warehouse district, where cobblestone wharfs still reached out into the brown Ohio River; warehouses of brick were divided by streets of brick in a near-perfect grid. The southern terminus of Water Street was the old Fort Steuben Brewery. Mr. Fortunato owned the warehouse and used it as a redistribution center for hijacked semitrucks—also a lucrative business, particularly if you could heist one carrying alcohol or cigarettes.

(Note: Jimmy Beans hijacked a refrigerator truck full of frozen beef halves and parked it in the warehouse over the July 4 holiday. Unbeknownst to Jimmy, the power to the refrigeration unit in the truck went out and the thawed beef sat in the stifling heat for a week. When Jimmy's customers came to pick up their beef, the rancid smell ran them out of the warehouse. Jimmy got the refrigeration unit working and the beef refroze. We all had to go down in the middle of the night and drag a trailer full of frozen beef to the Ohio River. The lead article in the newspaper two days later was the mystery of how twenty halves of rotten beef clogged the main water intake line at Wheeling-Pittsburgh Steel.)

Ricky Bones drove through a gravel and weed parking lot and nosed the Cadillac to the freight door of the warehouse. It wasn't a minute before it began to rise. Muzzie Lollini was already inside, pulling on the heavy chain that raised the steel door.

Bones stopped just inside the door and rolled down the passenger-side window. Muzzie leaned down and said, "They're already here."

Mr. Fortunato nodded, and Ricky drove to the far end of the warehouse. The freight door came down behind us. Tucked into a dark corner was a black sedan with a government license plate. Two men stood in the deep shadows of the warehouse. Before we exited the car, Mr. Fortunato said, "Ricky, go have a smoke with Muzzie."

For a moment, I locked eyes with Ricky Bones in the rearview mirror. I couldn't tell if the look in his eyes was anger, disappointment, or simply resignation. I tried to keep mine neutral, but we both knew what was happening. We were trading places in the organization, and he hated it to the depths of his tiny, black heart.

Mr. Fortunato exited his car with a brown paper bag twisted around a bottle. As we walked toward the two men, the only instruction he offered was, "Listen and learn."

The man who stepped forward to greet Mr. Fortunato was Armand Mickelson, who was a deputy chief in charge of the detective bureau at the Steubenville Police Department. He and Mr. Fortunato clasped hands. "Good to see you, Armand," Mr. Fortunato said.

"You too, Alphonse."

Mickelson turned sideways and said, "This is one of my detectives—Gabe Carson."

Mr. Fortunato gave the slightest of nods, a sign of disinterest in the underling. Then, he looked again, squinting for a long moment. "Do I know you?" he asked.

"Sort of," Carson said. "I used to play American Legion baseball with your son Tom."

"Oh, yeah. I thought I recognized you. You were the shortstop."

"Good memory."

He grinned. "You shoulda stuck with baseball, kid." He nodded toward Mickelson. "You'd be associating with a better class of people." He extended a hand toward me. "This is my associate, Angelo Cipriani."

Mickelson looked at me and said, "I know Mr. Cipriani well. I see he's moved up in the world since the days when I caught him boosting comic books from the A&P."

"Well, we all get our start somewhere, huh?" Mr. Fortunato said.

If Mickelson smiled, I didn't see it. He said, "Two women were raped in their homes in the Greenwood Addition. There were two more break-ins in the area, same MO."

"I read about it in the paper. Any leads?" Mr. Fortunato asked.

"One. We heard he works for you, a guy by the name of Paulson."

"Never heard of him." Mr. Fortunato looked at me.

"Richie Paulson," I said. "He used to be a courier. Complete psycho. Dommie fired him, probably two years ago."

"You want that I should handle it?" Mr. Fortunato asked.

"No," Mickelson said. "He knows we're looking for him and he's gone underground. Just help us find him. One of the women he raped is the mother of a cop. We'd like to take Mr. Paulson for an elevator ride that stops between floors."

Mr. Fortunato nodded. "Understood. I'll see what I can do."

"Someone is dealing greenies out of one of the whorehouses. It's either Mickey V or one of the girls. We can't have that."

"I doubt it's Micky V; he's smarter than that. Either way, I'll handle it."

Mickelson nodded. "Good. So, what have you got?"

It was Mr. Fortunato's turn. "One of your third-shift bluebirds has been harassing my girls on Water Street, wanting freebies. I'm making enough payments to the guys with the gold badges that my girls shouldn't be getting on their knees for every Dick Tracy in the department."

"Who is it?"

"Batterson."

"It won't happen again."

"We've had some problems with a Polack mill rat named Yablonski. He roughed up one of my girls. Drunk. He's a nephew of the mayor. If that wasn't the case, he'd already be in a body cast. This happens again, I don't care who he's related to, he's going to get a visit that he really won't like."

"I know the kid. He's a punk. I'll make a call to the mayor and make sure he's aware of the situation. But if he acts out again . . ." Mickelson shrugged. "I guess street court will be in session."

(Translation: Mr. Fortunato had been given the green light to square things with Yablonski.)

"Is that it?" Mickelson asked.

"One more thing. I've got this connection down south. He scored me some excellent bourbon." Mr. Fortunato extended the hand holding the brown-wrapped bottle toward Mickelson. "Here, I brought you a bottle. Try it. It's premium stuff. I was able to secure quite a bit of the product, and I'd like to get it into the bars around town, but I don't want any hassle."

(Translation: Mr. Fortunato had hijacked a semi full of bourbon and needed a way to unload it. He wanted Mickelson to get the inspector from the Ohio Department of Liquor Control to look the other way.)

"That's a decision that will have to be made further up the food chain. I'll let you know."

Mr. Fortunato nodded. "Fair enough. When?"

"Soon, I hope, but I've got one more thing."

This was the reason for the meeting. Mickelson was holding his big request until the end. He pulled a mug shot photo from his jacket pocket and handed it to Mr. Fortunato. "I'd bet my last dime that this guy has been sexually abusing his stepdaughter. I don't know what kind of sick shit is going on in that house, but it's going on."

"Why can't you take care of it?"

"The mother's an alcoholic and slathered in crazy sauce. She's also terrified of the old man. She won't let us near the kid. An aunt, the sister of the little girl's blood father, said she's witnessed the old man with his pants down, standing over top of his naked stepdaughter, masturbating."

"Jesus H. Christ, how much proof do you guys need?"

"It's not us; it's the prosecutor. He says it's not enough to get a conviction. It's his word against hers, so he won't bring charges without something more substantial, and we can't get near the kid. We go to the house, and the mom won't come to the door. We know she's in there, but the blinds are drawn down tight. She has to know what's going on but is probably trying to protect the security of the old man's paycheck."

"Doesn't the kid go to school?"

"No. She's only three."

The muscles in Mr. Fortunato's jaw tightened. "So, in the meantime, this little girl keeps taking the heat for this creep?"

"Our hands are tied, Alphonse."

"How do you know the aunt doesn't have an axe to grind against the old man?"

"She might, but this isn't his first rodeo. He has a previous charge of sexual abuse of a minor a few years back. He beat the rap because the mother of the little girl didn't want to put her through further trauma. You want the particulars?"

"Not especially."

"Good. Because repeating them makes me want to find a brick wall to punch."

Mr. Fortunato slowly shook his head and looked at the photo, then turned it over and read the name Mickelson had printed on the back. "Woodrow Golightly."

"He works at Harmony Nut and Washer, has a side hustle selling dildoes out of the trunk of his car, and spends most of his evenings at Wellman's Bar on Lincoln Avenue."

"Do you want him to understand the error of his ways, or . . ."

"In all candor, Alphonse, I doubt Mr. Golightly is the kind of man who will listen to reason."

We live our lives in that vast gray area between black and white, good and evil. Mr. Fortunato may have been a mob boss, but he loved his family and had a soft spot for kids. And there are crimes that humanity and the mob mutually can't tolerate, and child abuse is at the top. Mickelson knew this. He also knew the mob's sense of justice was pretty simple.

Mr. Fortunato slowly nodded his head and said, "Enjoy the bourbon."

That morning, I learned a lot more than I ever did sitting in the corner at the meetings with the capos. It wasn't just about the payoffs. The cops and the Fortunato family were uneasy allies. I had long wondered how Mr. Fortunato operated with impunity, but that was no longer a mystery.

A week after the meeting in the warehouse, the wife of Woodrow Golightly filed a missing person report with the Steubenville Police Department.

A few days later, Chief Snodgrass gave Mr. Fortunato the nod to unload his bourbon.

Woodrow Golightly was never seen again.

CHAPTER

8

May 2019

IT WAS LATE morning on the last Friday in May, and I was slouched on the couch, watching a game show. I fantasized about being a contestant on the show and having the host say, "Tell us a little about yourself, Angelo."

Well, I'm from Steubenville, Ohio, where I'm a semiretired contract killer for the Fortunato crime family. I enjoy eating at the local diner and lusting over a waitress I have no chance of ever dating and trying to keep from being murdered by enforcers of rival families. And I'd like to say hello to my Aunt Florentina.

I was slaying it from my couch; the game looks like easy money. I thought about trying to get on, but that would have been more embarrassing than being a stock boy down at the M&K Market. As they were lining up contestants for the big deal of the day, my cell phone began humming in my pocket. I pulled it out and read the words on the screen: Blocked Caller. I figured it was someone wanting to sell me something I didn't need and couldn't afford. I pushed the red button, sending the call to voicemail.

Before I could put the phone back in my pocket, it was again vibrating, again from the Blocked Caller, and again I sent it to voicemail. Another call came in. And then another, and another. Someone was punching the redial button with stunning rapidity.

On the sixth call, I finally answered. "This better be important."

"Or what?" the caller asked.

"Or, maybe I track you down and kick your sorry ass."

"Relax, Angelo. You're going to get yourself all riled up, then you'll have to ask Doctor Baughman to have your blood pressure medicine increased."

He had my attention.

"Who the hell is this?"

"You know who it is."

A lady from Topeka who was dressed like a bunny and holding a giant rubber carrot missed badly on the big deal. She was trying to act like she was just happy to be on the show with her fake carrot and floppy ears, and not disappointed to have missed out on an all-expenses paid trip to Spain and Portugal. What a loser.

I said, "Agent Ross, I assume."

"You assume correctly."

"How'd you get this number?"

He snorted into the phone. "I'm with the FBI, Angelo. I got your phone number the same place I found your medical records. There's a lot of information in cyberspace if you know where to look."

"Whatta you want?"

"Let's not go through the whole drill again, okay? You know what I want. I want you to tell me what you know about Little Tommy Fortunato and his drug operation."

"First of all, I don't know anything about any drug operation, and I'm obviously not interested in talking, because I didn't call you back, did I?

"How could you? My number was on the business card that you threw down the storm sewer."

I had to admit, this cop, he was pretty good.

He said, "I don't get it, Angelo. Why are you trying to protect Little Tommy after he's turned his back on you?"

"I don't know what you're talking about."

"Really, you're telling me you're still a valued member of the family? The new CEO brought in his own management team. You're the guy left over from the old regime, walking around the office with a cup of coffee, bitching because, 'That's not the way we did things in the old days.' That's why you're sitting in your apartment watching game shows."

"How do you know what I'm watching? Are you sure you're not spying on me?"

"No. You just need to get your hearing checked. You've got that TV turned up so loud I can hear it clear from Pittsburgh."

I pushed the clicker and turned it off. "If I talk to you, I'm signing my own death warrant. You know that, right?"

"It'll just be me and you talking, that's all. No one else will know."

"Right. No one else in your office will know that you're talking to a member of the Fortunato family. Sure, I believe that. Give me some credit, Ross."

"I can make you a very good offer, Angelo, and I can give you a better life than the one you're living. All I want to do is talk. You don't have to agree to anything. Just meet with me for thirty minutes."

"Okay. Just talk, thirty minutes."

"Great. Come by the office and . . ."

"No, no, no. There's no way in hell I'm walking into an FBI office. No way."

"Where, then?"

"North of town a couple of miles there's the abandoned Big Valley Brick Company. It's overgrown, but the sign is still on the side of the main building. I'll meet you on the back side by the old loading docks."

"I can be there in a little over an hour."

It was ten-forty. "I can't make it until later. Three o'clock."

"Oh, that's right, you need time to go see your girlfriend at the diner."

"You're not ingratiating yourself to me with the cute remarks, Ross."

"I'll see you at three. Maybe we can get a nice little place in the sun for you and your sweetie."

CHAPTER

9

May 2019

A WEEK BEFORE MY sixtieth birthday, Big Tommy said, "Let's get out of here for the day, what do you say? We'll take a ride and clear our heads."

It was unusual for Big Tommy to take a day off work. But when the boss says let's take a ride, you take a ride. He drove. This wasn't unusual. Alphonse, he never drove, and in all candor, I don't think he could have squeezed behind the wheel. But Big Tommy, he loved to drive. We cruised up through East Liverpool and continued north on Route 7 to East Palestine. We talked about baseball and Little Tommy and walleye fishing on Lake Erie. Not one time did he bring up business. It was the most relaxed I'd seen him in years. We caught Route 14 west, crossed over Beaver Lake and into the community of Columbiana. When we hit the city limits, Big Tommy pulled a piece of paper from his shirt pocket and looked at an address he had scribbled in pencil.

"What's up?" I asked.

"There's a car lot up here that I wanted to check out."

A few minutes later, he pulled into Warren's All-American Rides. It was a classic car lover's dream—GTOs, Camaros,

Thunderbirds, Impalas, Firebirds. We walked through the lot and traveled back in time for a few minutes. I loved it. It was fun watching Big Tommy away from the compound and acting like a kid around those cars. We walked into the small showroom where sat a completely restored 1980 Oldsmobile Cutlass 442, black with red leather interior with a 350 V8 engine. It was a beautiful set of wheels and my dream car back in the day.

Big Tommy slid into the passenger seat and waved for me to get in on the driver's side. I climbed in and grabbed hold of the wheel. "Sweet ride, don't you think?" Big Tommy asked.

"Oh, man. Back in the day, this was *the* car as far as I was concerned," I said.

"I'm glad you like it, because you're going to drive it out of here."

I wasn't sure I heard him right. "What do you mean?"

"It's yours. Happy sixtieth birthday, my friend."

"No way."

"It's all yours. I knew this was your favorite ride, so I had a friend of mine who's a car guy track this one down. It's been totally restored, top to bottom. New paint job, upholstery, refurbed engine and tranny. It's probably in better shape now than when it came off the assembly line." He smiled and ran his hand over the leather seat. "You know, for my money, my family has never had a more loyal soldier than Angelo Cipriani. Every time my father needed you, every time I've needed you, you've been there, and you've never turned down an assignment . . ." He let that hang for a moment. We both knew what he meant.

I started to tear up. I hated that. "If it wasn't for you and your father, I'd still be emptying spit at the Steubenville Athletic Club," I said.

"The athletic club closed down years ago."

"See, if it wasn't for you, I'd be unemployed."

We both laughed. Big Tommy said, "How about we just keep this between us, okay? No reason the other capos need to know."

That was Big Tommy. What a guy.

I was proud of that car, but I was prouder of what he had said to me.

The subsequent years had been hard on the old girl. She was rusting under the wheel wells and along the bottom of the doors. The upholstery was coming apart at the seams, and yellow foam spewed between the faded red leather. The engine sounded like a washing machine full of nickels. I parked her beneath a spreading maple behind my apartment. The shade kept her cool, but the birds added further insult.

I fired her up, drove over to Route 7 and turned north. It was a five-minute drive to the old Big Valley Brick Company and my meeting with Agent Ross.

The entrance was still accessible, though the asphalt drive had crumbled, leaving the narrow passage soft and muddy. Waves of foxtails leaned in from both sides. It was thirty minutes before my meeting with Agent Ross when I pulled onto the grounds of the place where my father worked himself to death. The brickyard, as it was known locally, went out of business in the mid-1970s. As I was told, the Environmental Protection Agency was up the owner's ass about the pollution from the furnaces, and he decided to shut it down rather than retool. It sent four hundred workers to the unemployment line. Thank you, federal government. Over the years, nature had reclaimed most of the property. The cement block building that held the kilns still stood, but vines, weeds, and honey locust trees had assaulted it from every angle.

This overgrowth made for a good cover and an ideal place for a meeting that you wanted to keep private. Also, I was familiar with the grounds because, well, there may or may not be the body of an Irish shylock from Cleveland named Rory Masterson buried in the soft dirt down by the riverbank. I mean, I can't say for sure one way or the other, but I will say that there are some people in this world who apparently don't understand good English when they're told not to encroach on the territory of Big Tommy Fortunato. And when these same people don't get the message after a couple of beatings . . . well, unfortunate things can happen.

I snaked through the old gravel parking lot, trying to dodge the low-hanging branches from the thorny honey locust trees. Thistles scraped the side of the Cutlass, not that they could do that much more damage. I backed the Cutlass under a canopy of trash trees and slipped my 9-millimeter under my untucked shirt. There were empty beer cans and used condoms strewn across the high grass under the trees. Apparently, I was not the only one who knew this place was hidden from the rest of the world.

A cobblestone wharf extended into the Ohio River where the barges used to dock. At the water's edge, tiny waves lapped in the shoals, and the smell of oil and mud was heavy in the air. I was pitching tiny pebbles into the water when Ross walked up and stood beside me, taking in the river and the decaying brickyards without greeting.

Neither of us made eye contact. Still looking out over the water, I said, "In the old days, when this factory was humming, they used to bring barge loads of clay to this wharf, and my father and a few of the other grunts who couldn't speak English would start shoveling. The company worked them like rented mules. They'd unload the whole damn barge by hand. It would take them days."

"Honest work," Ross said.

"Fool's work," I countered. "The old man, he'd come home so stoved up and tired that he could barely walk. In the winter, his skin would crack and his fingers would be covered in blood. He got so that he couldn't even go out in the yard and toss around the baseball. He died when he was fifty-seven years old, his body completely shot."

"Is that why you got in with the Fortunatos, so you didn't have to unload barges by hand?"

"What do you think, Sherlock?"

He picked up a flat stone and skipped it on the dark water. "We want to make you an offer, Angelo." I said nothing. "In exchange for your help in our investigation of Little Tommy Fortunato, we're prepared to give you complete immunity for any and all transgressions, and put you in the witness protection program."

"Are you miked up?" I asked. Ross said nothing. Of course he was. "Why would I want immunity? You're implying that I've done something wrong. I'm sure you checked me out before coming down here, so you know that I've never been arrested, not once."

"Not yet, anyway. They're making a lot of advances in DNA research these days. Sooner or later, someone is going to make a link to you and one of the corpses that you and Carlo caused to be dead. Maybe that bookie down in Little Washington or Woodrow Golightly. Who knows? All it takes is a little blood, maybe some saliva or a hair follicle. You didn't cap all those guys without leaving some kind of evidence behind. It may not have been evidence that could convict you in 1980, but it's 2019, Angelo. Technology is improving every day."

"I don't know what you're talking about. Besides, you'd have to have my DNA to compare it to something."

Ross smirked. "We've got your cell phone number and your medical records. Do you seriously think we don't have your DNA?"

That made my ass pucker.

"We don't want you," Ross said. "We want Little Tommy. He's a bad guy, Angelo. He's hauling drugs into the area in truckloads. We want him off the street, and you're the key."

"Why am I so important?"

"Because you know how the system works. Look, this might hurt your ego, but if you were still a vital part of the organization, we wouldn't bother with you. But we both know you're not. Little Tommy's pushing drugs onto the streets and you to the curb."

"Did you have to graduate from the FBI Academy to figure that one out? So, you get Little Tommy, but what do I get?"

"Along with revenge on the guy who moved you out of the organization?" I nodded. "You get a new identity and a nice little place far from Steubenville. I heard your lungs aren't so good—cigar smoke and growing up next to Wheeling-Pitt has probably turned them to leather. The dry air in New Mexico would be good for you, and you'll receive a generous stipend. You'll be able to buy yourself a new car." I took a breath and looked away. It was tempting. Ross sensed that I might be leaning his way. He said, "Those were pretty good days when Big Tommy was around. I'm sure you miss it."

"You don't know the half of it," I said.

"Probably not. But I'm willing to learn."

"If you want to talk, lose the wire."

There was no argument or feigned outrage. Ross unbuttoned a couple of buttons, fished around inside his shirt, and a few seconds later pulled out a small disc microphone and an accompanying wire. Without direction on my part, he threw it into the Ohio River.

"Okay, there you go," he said. "Now we're just talking."

"No bullshit," I said.

"None. Nothing you say goes beyond this meeting."

"Okay, so you've done your research. You know Little Tommy's got no use for me. But he started pushing me out the door years ago. What makes you think I know how the operation works these days?"

"You're a smart guy, Angelo."

"Don't patronize me, Ross."

"I'm not. I know, for example, that your mantra over the years has been to keep your eyes and ears open and your mouth shut. That's how you got so far up the ranks with Alphonse and Big Tommy. So I know you've been observing how Little Tommy works."

I could feel the skin across my forehead furrowing. "Who have you been talking to?" He pushed his hands in his pants pockets and stared at me. "I thought you agreed to no bullshit."

"Joseph Nicolosi," he said.

"Nickels? Jesus Christ, Ross, he doesn't even know where he is half the time. You need to leave him alone. He's a sick old man."

"What he told me would never stand up in court, but he's got no love in his heart for Little Tommy either. He said, 'You can't make good wine with bad grapes, and Little Tommy is bad grapes.' He also said you were the key. Here's the bottom line: The organization you grew up in is gone forever. In your heart, you've got to know that. Help us out, and I'll give you a chance to go somewhere and live a good life." He looked out over the water, as though distracted, and said, "As long as we're talking about the old days, whatever happened to your partner, Carlo Della Russo?"

He was trying to lull me into a false sense of security and let down my guard. "I haven't seen him in years. He got out of the game."

"Really? I thought once you were in the game, you were in forever."

"You've been watching too many movies, Ross."

"Where is he? You must know that much. You two were tight for a lot of years."

"So, I tell you where he is, and you run down there and try to flip him?"

"You're the one I'm interested in flipping, Angelo. No one else."

"This is probably hard for someone like you to understand, but this is all I've ever done. I grew up with nothin', and this life, it's all I know. I wasn't born a silver-spooner like you."

"Excuse me? You think I was born with a silver spoon in my mouth?"

I hit a nerve. Good. "I'll bet you didn't grow up eating buttered noodles four nights a week."

"Jesus Christ, you're a piece of work. Do you think you're the only person in the world to grow up poor? I used to pick apples for twelve hours a day to help my mom make ends meet. I delivered pizzas and stocked shelves to work my way through college. My old man divorced my mother and bailed on both of us. I hardly ever saw him. He wanted to be a cop, then he made every bad move a cop makes—married and divorced three or four times and had at least as many stints in rehab. He thought the world hated him because he wore a badge."

I laughed. "He didn't patrol the Steubenville Spaghetto, did he?"

"He most definitely didn't patrol the streets of Steubenville, Ohio, that's for sure." He threw another stone into the water. "My mom was an only child and both her parents were dead, so it was just the two of us. There was no other family. I was pretty close with one of my old man's brothers, my uncle, but you know how it goes. You end up getting divorced from the entire family. It was kind of a lonely time, but we made it."

"Are you trying to prove to me that FBI agents can be human?"

"Would it work?"

"Probably not."

"No, probably not." Ross pawed at the gravel with the toe of one shoe. "You're not the only one who took one or two in the mouth growing up, Angelo. You and me, we're not so different. Tough upbringing, we're both single and married to our jobs. The difference is, I'm still getting paid, and Little Tommy has you on welfare."

Now he was the one who hit the nerve. I'd had enough. I turned and started walking up the wharf.

"Did you ever hear of Christina Mosser?" he asked.

I turned to face him. "No."

"If you come to Pittsburgh, I'll take you over to Homewood Cemetery and introduce you."

He was punching below the belt. But what did I expect? The FBI didn't fight by the Marquis of Queensberry rules.

"She was a sweet kid, seventeen, beautiful, an honor student, and the star of the cross-country and track teams. She was everything you'd want in a daughter. Then, one night, one time, one pill, and she was dead. She thought she was taking a pill to help her study. It was counterfeit and loaded with fentanyl. Her mother found her in bed the next morning, something no parent should ever have to do. We found the classmate who gave her the pill and traced it back to the dealer. He was one of Little Tommy's boys."

"If you can trace it back to Little Tommy, bust him. What are you waiting for?"

"It's not that easy. The federal prosecutor won't touch it. There's not enough evidence to get a conviction."

"Sad story, but I don't see what it has to do with me."

"Show a little humanity, for God's sake. There'll be a lot of Christina Mossers if we don't nail Little Tommy. So, tell me, Angelo, are you interested in my offer or do I need to move on?"

"I'll think about it."

"Don't think too long. My bosses are very impatient. When we take down Little Tommy, it'll be like rats leaving a sinking ship.

Everyone at the compound will want to spill their guts in exchange for immunity. The first guy to the door gets the deal. In the meantime, we're still working on that DNA. There's no statute of limitations on murder."

"I said I'd think about it."

I'd taken a few more steps toward the Cutlass before he asked, "Didn't you take the omerta?"

I turned again and stared at him for a long moment. The omerta is the sworn oath you take when you become a made man in the Mafia. It is an oath of loyalty and silence. Breaking the omerta is equivalent to a death sentence. Admitting that I took the omerta would be admitting that I had sworn my allegiance to the Fortunato family. I said, "I don't know what that means."

Ross rolled his eyes and laughed. "Of course you don't. Okay, hypothetically speaking, let's say a guy takes the omerta and swears his loyalty to a mob family. In this hypothetical situation, wouldn't you think that door should swing both ways? If you swear loyalty to the family, isn't the family obligated to return that loyalty?" He let the words hang in the air for a moment, then grinned and said, "I'm asking for a friend." He walked up the grade and handed me another business card. "Try to keep this one out of the storm sewer."

I had to admit, I didn't totally dislike this guy.

CHAPTER

10

December 1974

WE HAD BEEN teetering on the edge of a border war with our brethren in Pittsburgh and Youngstown from the first day I stepped onto the Fortunato compound in 1967. In fact, no one around the compound could remember a time when there wasn't tension between the three families. No one wanted a war. The Mafia doesn't like killing people. Well, they like killing some people. But they don't want to make a public display of it and start causing a panic. Once you start shooting up downtown streets, and grandma or a kid catches a bullet, that's when the feds get involved and the heat really turns up. It's much tougher to bribe a fed than the locals. It's not impossible, of course, but it takes a lot more work.

The territorial borders between the Fortunatos in the Ohio Valley, the Gemelli family in Youngstown, and the Santoro family in Pittsburgh were loosely mapped out in the 1920s during Prohibition. That is when organized crime became firmly entrenched in the Ohio River Valley. Alphonse Fortunato's father, Aldo, began illegally importing liquor and beer from Canada and opening speakeasies all along the river between East Liverpool and Wheeling. Once the speakeasies were established, Aldo hired some girls to take care of his better customers. This little enterprise expanded into riverfront brothels in every town with more than a thousand population. He then established a daily number and sports gambling in the speakeasies. It was a very lucrative venture.

(Note: Aldo Fortunato was a revered player in organized crime, and a personal friend of Al Capone and Public Enemy Number 1, Charles Arthur "Pretty Boy" Floyd. In fact, Floyd and his wingman, Adam Richetti, spent the night of October 19, 1934, at one of Aldo's brothels in Steubenville. They were on the run following the Kansas City Massacre the previous year. Floyd needed a place to hide out for a while, so Aldo gave them the keys to a hunting lodge he had deep in the Allegheny National Forest of Pennsylvania, just south of the New York state line. The next morning, en route to the lodge, Floyd and Richetti got into a shootout with cops in Wellsville, Ohio. Richetti was captured and later went to the gas chamber, but Floyd escaped. He hid out in the hills for the next few days until he was shot and killed by FBI agents in an East Liverpool cornfield on October 22. When he died, he still had the keys to Aldo's hunting lodge in his pocket.)

Throughout Prohibition, the Santoros and Gemellis were content to take care of business in their own backyards. The Santoro family controlled Allegheny County and western Pennsylvania. The Gemelli family controlled the entire Mahoning Valley. There was plenty of business, and everyone was making a lot of money. Ergo, no bloodshed. However, after Prohibition ended in 1933, the families started looking for ways to make up the income generated from bootleg liquor, and both the Santoros and the Gemellis started eyeing Aldo's turf in the steel mill–rich Ohio Valley. Aldo had a smaller operation, and they figured he was an easy mark.

Big mistake.

Marcello Santoro arranged for a meeting with Aldo, during which he suggested that it would be in everyone's best interest if the Santoro family took over the bookmaking and prostitution business in the Ohio Valley. He told Aldo that he could continue with his operation, but 60 percent of the income would henceforth be sent to Pittsburgh.

"That doesn't seem like such a good business deal to me, since right now I'm my own boss, and I get one hundred percent of the profits," Aldo said.

"Be reasonable, Aldo," Marcello said. "You'll make it up on volume, and you'll have my protection."

"Your protection?"

"Absolutely."

"You'll give me a couple days to think about it, right?"

Decisions between mob families were rarely made at such a meeting. It was customary to return to the compound, consult the consigliere, and consider their options. Marcello Santoro nodded and said, "Of course, my friend."

Aldo had been preparing for one of the two rival families to try to muscle in on the Ohio Valley, and his response was exactly what you would expect from a mobster of his repute. Within the next seventy-two hours, eleven of Santoro's capos were gunned down on the streets of Pittsburgh. One of them was Marcello's middle son. The first five capos killed were shot to death in a poker room at the Sunnyvale Social Club in what became known as the Sunnyvale Massacre. At the conclusion of the bloodbath, Aldo sent Marcello a note by courier that read: *I've considered your proposal for my territory. I don't believe that will work for me. My best to Annabelle.*

The tensions and killings continued for years, but Aldo never lost an inch of territory. After Aldo died of a heart attack in 1947, Alphonse took over. One of the first things he did was to have Cleveland mob boss Lenny Esposito mediate an agreement between himself and the Gemellis in Youngstown, in which they agreed to stay north of East Liverpool and Columbiana County. For the most part, they abided by the agreement. Most of our problems came from the Santoro family, and if you think they had forgotten that Aldo had gone trophy-hunting on the streets of Pittsburgh more than four decades earlier, you'd be very wrong. I swear to Christ, Arabs and Jews get along better than the Santoros and Fortunatos.

On December 11, 1974, Alphonse Fortunato received an emissary from the Santoro family at the compound. The emissary said that Federico "Fat Freddie" Santoro, don of the Pittsburgh family, requested a meeting with Mr. Fortunato.

Mr. Fortunato never got out of his chair or extended any greeting to the emissary. "What's he want?" he asked.

"He wants a chance to talk to you in person," the emissary said.

"Yeah, I assumed if he wants a meeting, he wants to talk in person. *Specifically*, what does he want to talk about . . . in person?"

"Mr. Santoro feels there has been unneeded tension between the two families for too many years. He believes there is enough meat on the bone for both families if we establish permanent borders and work together against outside intrusion. Mr. Santoro would like to establish a binding and permanent alliance between the Santoros and the Fortunatos."

"Really? Binding and permanent, huh? Interesting. And why now?"

"As I said, Mr. Santoro says the hostilities have existed for too long, and they don't serve the interests of either family."

Mr. Fortunato sat at his desk for a long moment, tapping a pencil eraser against his blotter. After a while, he slowly nodded and said, "Okay, tell Fat Freddie I'll meet with him, but not in his backyard."

The meeting was arranged for the following week at Cavaretta's, an Italian restaurant in Burgettstown, Pennsylvania, the midway point between Steubenville and Pittsburgh. Carlo drove the Cadillac to the meeting. I sat up front with him; Mr. Fortunato and Big Tommy sat in the back. Mr. Fortunato had wanted his right-hand man, Dommie the Clip, in the meeting, but Big Tommy insisted on Carlo. "I don't think there's going to be any trouble, but if there is, we want Carlo close," Big Tommy said.

(Translation: Carlo could put bullets into the skulls of three of the Santoros before they had their guns out of their belts.)

A second car carried Muzzie Lollini, Dommie the Clip, Connie Bones, and the muscular Ricky Bones. They would not be in the meeting but would be in the restaurant in case there was a problem.

It was a show of force, making sure the Santoros saw that we had plenty of dry powder.

(Note: "Dry powder" was the term that Mr. Fortunato used to describe our personnel and firepower. If we had more dry powder than our rivals, we could outmuscle them.)

"I'm skeptical about this," Big Tommy said during the ride. "Why does Fat Freddie suddenly want an alliance? We've been at war since the Sunnyvale Massacre, then out of the clear blue he wants a truce. I'm not buying it."

"We haven't checked out the landscape yet," Mr. Fortunato said. "We listen and see what's in this for us. If it leads to less bloodshed and more money . . ." He shrugged his massive shoulders. "Let your universe expand, son. Don't eliminate opportunities before they are presented to you."

Big Tommy looked at his father and grinned. "You've become quite the philosopher."

"It's not philosophy; it's business."

We were fifteen minutes early for the meeting, but the Santoro family representatives were already in the private dining room at the rear of the restaurant—Fat Freddie, his son and heir apparent, Odi, the emissary and a fourth man who was not making eye contact and trying to cover a harelip with a thick moustache. If there were problems, he was the one I had to watch. How did I know this? It was the harelip. He had grown up as an outcast, the butt of teasing and jokes by other kids. Fat Freddie had given him an opportunity, much the way Mr. Fortunato had given me, and he would be fiercely loyal, as in give-up-his-life loyal. I made sure I sat right across the table from him.

Salads were already on the table. Soon after we sat down, two waitresses took our orders and our food was in front of us in minutes. This had all been orchestrated by the Santoros for expediency. After twenty minutes of pasta and pleasantries, the same two waitresses brought out plates of tiramisu and put pots of coffee at each end of the table. They then left the dining room and closed the doors behind them.

Fat Freddie was, indeed, morbidly obese and somewhere in his late sixties. He said very little during lunch; he ate less. I also noticed that he had used the edge of the table to steady himself when he stood after we entered the room. Given his weight and age, I didn't read much into this.

When the waitresses closed the doors, however, all eyes turned to him. He cleared his throat and said, "I apologize for my lost voice. I'm fighting a bad case of laryngitis." You could hardly hear his straining words, yet he had smoked three cigarettes through lunch, blowing smoke out of the side of his mouth and away from the table. "I appreciate you accepting my invitation to meet. I think Rocco [the emissary] expressed my desire to come to a working agreement with the Fortunatos. There's been too much blood shed over the years."

I watched the man with the harelip. He sipped his coffee and seemed relaxed. The emissary rested his forearms on the edge of the table, alternately staring down and at his boss. The son, Odi, was overweight and slovenly. His hair was unkempt, and I noticed a dark ring of dirt around the collar of his shirt and food stains on his necktie. While the meeting could potentially produce a new era of peace and profits for his family, Odi seemed bored with the proceedings. I interpreted this as him having no input in Fat Freddie's plan.

"I want to suggest an alliance between the Fortunatos and the Santoros," Fat Freddie continued. His voice was strained and had the high-pitched whine of a fishing reel on the run. "We are willing to give you a portion of western Pennsylvania that would include Midland and the areas of Monaca and Aliquippa west of the Ohio River. We'll keep the territory east of that line. We draw up these lines to exist in perpetuity, and together we'll strenuously protect those borders from intruders."

(Translation: The Gemellis.)

Rocco handed out a two-page document that showed the proposed borders and explained how the transition would take place. Fat Freddie watched without comment. I watched with interest when he moved his forearms from the table and rested his clasped hands on its edge.

After Rocco explained the plan, Mr. Fortunato nodded and looked at Fat Freddie. "Why now, Freddie? After all these years, why are you now seeking this alliance?"

"I told you. I want no more fights with the Fortunatos. It benefits no one. We have no interest in the Ohio Valley, and we don't need these outlying territories. They'll benefit you. We work together and create an alliance, everybody wins. No more spilt blood."

Mr. Fortunato nodded. "Of course, I'll want to talk this over with my consigliere."

"Understood," said Fat Freddie, who struggled to his feet and extended his right hand to Mr. Fortunato. "I look forward to hearing back from you." My eyes remained focused on his left hand and wrist. What, I wondered, was he hiding?

On the ride home, Mr. Fortunato said, "What do you think?"

Big Tommy said, "I don't know what his motivation is, but on the surface, it seems like a good deal."

"What do you think, Carlo?" Mr. Fortunato asked.

"I don't know, boss. I've been dealing with those bastards ever since I've been with you. They've been trying to worm their way into Weirton and Wheeling for years. Why are they suddenly open to firm borders and willing to give us the western Pennsylvania territory? I don't get it, and I smell a rat. Fat Freddie doesn't do anything for the common good. He hates all the Fortunatos, so why would he offer us this?"

There was silence in the car for a full minute before I said, "I know why."

I turned around to Mr. Fortunato, waiting for permission to continue. "Don't keep us in suspense," he said.

"He's playing you."

"Really?"

"Absolutely. Fat Freddie doesn't have laryngitis. He's sick. There's something seriously wrong. Unless I miss my guess, he's got a tumor in his throat the size of a plum. I think he's on his way out with throat cancer."

"If the son of a bitch has throat cancer, I can't think of a more deserving recipient," Carlo said.

"As we were walking out of the dining room, Freddie was still sitting at the table, and if I had to bet, I'd say there was a wheelchair hidden in the trunk of his car. That's why they were there so early. They didn't want us to see it. Also, I saw a little piece of tubing under one of his cuffs, the kind you see when they're giving someone an IV or medicine in their veins. He hardly ate and didn't talk until he had to. He's dying, I guarantee it, and he knows that kid of his is weak and won't be able to hold the territory. That's why he wants an alliance. He wants to seal the deal without letting anyone know he's on the way out. He's not too concerned about you, but he's afraid of Youngstown. If they know he's dying, they'll start moving into Pittsburgh like the jackals they are. That kid of his is too weak to fend them off. He wants to establish firm borders and a—what do you call it?—mutual defense pact, because he needs you in order to protect his legacy and the kid."

In my gut, I knew I was right. I instinctively knew the laryngitis thing was a ruse. I watched how Fat Freddie kept bringing his hand up around his throat when he was swallowing, trying to clear a pathway for the food and stifle the pain. Sure, I was a high school dropout, but I'd grown up on the streets of the Spaghetto. I knew how to fight and read weakness, and Fat Freddie was weak.

Mr. Fortunato sat back in his seat and nodded. "If that's the case, we can certainly squeeze him and work a better deal. What would you suggest, Angelo?"

"You've got an opportunity here to really stack some chips. I'd hit him square in the face. Tell him you know that he's dying and that his family will need your protection after he's gone. You'll give it to him, but that kind of a commitment is going to come with a price. You ask for all the territory you think we can cover and a percentage of the Pittsburgh profits. He'll take the deal, because without your muscle, Youngstown will steamroll his kid and they'll lose everything, and the legacy and name of Federico Santoro will be lost to everyone but his widow."

Mr. Fortunato looked out the side window, slowly nodding his head. He said, "That's smart, Angelo. Very smart."

Big Tommy gave me a wink.

* * *

The next day, we drove to Pittsburgh, where Mr. Fortunato and Big Tommy sat with Fat Freddie and Odi and talked alone in a gated courtyard. It was cold, and the pine trees in the yard had been decorated with strings of white lights and silver garland. A concrete Virgin Mary, a hand pressed to her bosom, looked down on us from a terrace, her hair and shoulders covered with ice. Dommie the Clip and I sat on a wooden bench a hundred feet away, hidden behind a row of arborvitaes. While I couldn't hear their conversation, I could clearly see the look of resignation in Fat Freddie's eyes, and that of bewilderment on the face of his hapless son. After thirty minutes, Mr. Fortunato stood, grasped his rival's hand, and headed toward us. It was a clean deal. In exchange for helping protect the Santoro turf, Fat Freddie agreed to pay a 5 percent "honorarium" of all income within Allegheny County, and turn over control of the western Pennsylvania counties of Beaver, Washington, and Greene to Mr. Fortunato. This would more than double the family's income. The only provision Fat Freddie demanded was that nothing change while he was alive. Mr. Fortunato agreed to the term.

After we were all in the car, Big Tommy said, "Merry Christmas to us."

When we returned to the compound, Big Tommy and Dommie headed home. As I was walking toward my car, Mr. Fortunato came out the front door and said, "Come here, Angelo. I want to talk to you."

He put his hand on my shoulder, and we walked back to his office. There were two bourbons already poured and sitting on either side of the desk. He closed the door behind us and extended a hand toward the chair that was in front of his desk. "Sit down, please."

I was hoping that this was my moment. Mr. Fortunato had seen my good works and my value to the family, and he was going to make me a made member of the Fortunato crime family.

"Angelo, your keen sense of observation led to this deal today." He picked up his bourbon and held it in the air over his desk. "Salud." We toasted and tossed down the bourbon and we both sat down. He pressed his fingertips together and squeezed his eyes closed for a moment before speaking. "This is a difficult conversation for me to have with you. But you deserve to know the truth, and you deserve to hear it from me." My elation popped like a kid's balloon, and my gut cinched up. I started to fight back tears, because in my heart, I already knew what was coming, and it wasn't good. He continued. "You've got a future with this organization. You've done good. Real good. And I love you like a son. But I want to be very clear, because I know it's on your mind. I can never make you a made man with this family. No matter how good your work is, no matter how big of an earner you are, I can't. I believe in the omerta, and to become a made man, you have to be a full-blooded Italian. That Ukrainian blood you've got, it's poison. I don't ever want you to leave, and I'll always take good care of you, but . . ."

"But I'll always be a second-class citizen."

"I'm sorry for that."

"Iceman Al" Fortunato was not one to pull punches.

CHAPTER

11

February 1975

FAT FREDDIE SANTORO died two months after the meeting in Burgettstown. Mr. Fortunato sent an enormous spray of roses and carnations to the funeral home, and his brother, Matteo, attended the service. Even though the Fortunatos and Santoros had hated each other for decades, Fat Freddie had ceded three lucrative counties to Mr. Fortunato's control, which was a gesture that he deemed worthy of a two-hundred-dollar flower arrangement.

The minute word reached the compound that Fat Freddie was no more, Mr. Fortunato called a meeting of his capos and trusted subordinates, which included those who were in line to become made men and anyone banished to the back of the bus because of their Ukrainian blood. It was the first time I had ever seen Mr. Fortunato not sitting behind his desk at a meeting. On one wall of the office, he had thumbtacked a large map to the cherry paneling. It outlined what was now the Fortunato family's new territory, which extended from eastern Ohio, across the West Virginia panhandle, into Beaver County, Pennsylvania. It was as if we had annexed Texas. He had set up a war room, preparing for the impending attack from Youngstown. All he needed was a little swagger stick and a pair of jackboots and he could have passed for General Patton—cursing and all. On the map he had pinpointed every bar, VFW, American Legion, and AmVets that had made book with the Santoros and were now our customers. "We're going to set up a northern perimeter and it is not to be penetrated," he said.

By a northern perimeter, Mr. Fortunato did not mean we were going to dig foxholes and set up machine-gun nests, although that wouldn't have been a bad plan in anticipation of an attack by the Gemellis. Here's how the system worked. Let's say there's an American Legion post that isn't taking bets. The Fortunato capo who is in charge of that territory goes into the post and speaks with the commander. He might speak forcefully, but usually that isn't necessary. In exchange for taking bets on behalf of the Fortunato family, the post will receive a 10 percent vig on the total dollars bet. In most cases, the commander sees that it's a victimless crime and he can bring in another five hundred dollars a month for the club, and more than that when the playoffs begin. He's a hero to his members because they can now make bets while they're drinking beer and telling war stories, and the additional revenue keeps the dues from increasing. Setting up a perimeter means you don't let the Gemellis or anyone else into that American Legion hall. You do this because the Gemellis would be looking for ways to make inroads in our territory. They'd send one of their capos into that American Legion, offer the commander an 11 percent vig, and promise to burn down his house and roast his family alive if he doesn't take the offer. At this point, the commander wants to resign his post and move to Brazil, but he accepts the offer, knowing that the next time the Fortunato courier comes in to collect the receipts, there's going to be an explosion. Typically, this is when mobsters start shooting each other in the street. Thus, it was highly important not to give them an inch of our territory.

The day after Fat Freddie's funeral mass, Mr. Fortunato received a letter by courier from Anthony Gemelli. It read: *I suggest that we meet immediately to discuss a business transaction that would be mutually beneficial to both our organizations. We are amenable to meeting at a site of your choosing.*

Mr. Fortunato read the missive and passed it around to his capos. He said simply, "And so it begins, boys." There was little doubt as to the subject of the "business transaction." Fat Freddie hadn't cooled in his grave before the Gemellis were on the move.

The Gemelli family was headed by two brothers known in our circle as the Gems—Anthony "Tony Gem" Gemelli and Franco "Frankie Gem" Gemelli. Technically, Tony was the head of the family, but there was very little separation of power between the brothers. They made up a two-headed beast that acted with impunity, knowing they had the backing of the powerful Cleveland mob. Of the Gems, Mr. Fortunato said, "They're ruthless and stupid, which is a very dangerous combination."

The meeting was held at Delmonico's Steakhouse, a restaurant that Mr. Fortunato had acquired in Empire, a tiny burg along the Ohio River north of Steubenville. "Acquired," as in the owner had gotten so far in debt with gambling losses that the deed was turned over to Mr. Fortunato in lieu of the owner having his fingernails removed with a pair of needle-nose pliers. The meeting was held at nine in the morning, when the restaurant was closed. Mr. Fortunato, his brother, Matteo, Dommie the Clip, and Connie Bones went on behalf of the family. Big Tommy and I were in a box truck driving back from the Upper Peninsula of Michigan with a shipment of stolen Canadian liquor that had been smuggled down the Keweenaw Waterway to Hancock. On a good day, this was a sixteen-hour haul. We left at four in the morning, taking turns driving, and parked the truck with the stolen hooch inside the old Fort Steuben Brewery warehouse. By the time we got back to the compound, it was nine PM.

The instant we turned onto Rosemont Street, Big Tommy moaned like a wounded animal. "Oh God, no," he said. Black sedans and police cruisers surrounded the compound. We both knew what had happened.

Connie Bones was in the intensive care unit at Ohio Valley Hospital.

He was the only one to survive the slaughter.

* * *

According to Connie Bones, the meeting was brief. Tony Gem led the contingent, along with his brother and two hulking henchmen whose sole purpose, it seemed, was to try to intimidate Mr. Fortunato, which was a laughable waste of time. A lowland gorilla could not intimidate Alphonse Fortunato.

After a few pleasantries, Tony Gem said, "The passing of Freddie Santoro provides us with a unique opportunity, wouldn't you agree?"

"I'm not sure. What do you mean?" Mr. Fortunato asked, playing along.

"The kid, Odi, is the new boss. He's sloppy and weak, and he's got no stomach for a fight, and I know he don't have the balls. He won't be able to hold his turf. If we move in now, it will be easy to divide the territory. We thought you'd want a piece of the action."

"Tony, how about we cut the bullshit and put the cards on the table? You know that Fat Freddie ceded Beaver, Washington, and Greene counties to me. So what's with the charade?"

"Yeah, we heard that. I've discussed it with my brother. We're willing to let you keep Greene in exchange for Allegheny, Beaver, and Washington."

Mr. Fortunato's eyes widened. "You want to run that by me again?"

"Look, Beaver and Washington should have been ours. We were planning on taking it when the old man died. Naturally, we want Pittsburgh and all of Allegheny. We'll let you have Greene. It's a good deal. You should take it."

Waves of red heat erupted from within Mr. Fortunato's collar. "You're being very disrespectful, Tony, and I don't appreciate it. The Santoros once tried to make my father a similar deal back in the day.

It didn't end well for them. It was in all the papers; you should take the time to read about it."

"You need to listen to reason, Al. You don't want a war over this. We don't either, but I've explained our position, and it's not going to change. This is in stone."

"In stone?" Mr. Fortunato sat back in his chair, his arms crossed, waves of anger rolling across his jaw, his teeth grinding. "In that case, let me explain my position. Fuck you, Tony. I negotiated with Fat Freddie for that territory before he died. It was a business transaction. The borders remain where they are, and that means we keep our counties and Allegheny stays with the Santoros."

Tony Gem chuckled. "A business transaction, huh? Really? And what did Fat Freddie get in return?"

"You're looking at it."

"Wait a minute. Let me make sure I got this straight. They're paying *you* to keep *us* out of Allegheny County?" The entire Gemelli contingent started laughing out loud. "You know, Al, that whole David and Goliath thing only works in the Bible. I've got three times more men than you and backing from Cleveland. I guarantee you won't like it if you cross us."

The gloves were off. Mr. Fortunato said, "Don't push me, Tony. You're the one who won't like the results."

"You're bluffing."

"You can't bluff stupid."

The insult stung Tony Gem like a left hook. His jaw stiffened. "Is that your answer?"

"Did I stutter?"

"If that's the way you want it, then I guess we got nothin' else to discuss."

Mr. Fortunato pointed toward the door and said, "You know the way out."

After the Gemellis left, Connie Bones locked the door and watched the foursome walk across the gravel parking lot, where their sedan was backed up to a chain-link fence. Tony Gem took off his suit coat and wiped his forehead with a handkerchief before getting into the back seat. Connie watched until the car left the lot and turned north on Route 7 toward Youngstown. "They're clear," he said.

That's when things went south. Matteo, Connie Bones and Dommie the Clip all looked at the boss. He said, "Gentlemen, we're at war."

They were the last words he ever spoke.

Mr. Fortunato was the last one out of the restaurant. He turned and locked the door, and as they were walking out from under the green canvas awning, a second sedan sped around the corner of the building, the passenger-side windows down, the barrels of three Thompson submachine guns extending from the opening. Connie Bones said they didn't have a chance. The submachine guns opened fire and all four Fortunato family members were splattered with lead, red blooms expanding over white shirts, brain matter splattering the awning, glass shattering, the wooden façade splintering. The car stopped in the gravel lot and dust rolled up from under its tires. Two of the men exited the passenger side doors and fired another burst into our guys. Matteo had fallen backward onto Connie Bones, who was finally able to pull his pistol from his shoulder holster and return fire. He thought he hit one of Gemelli's men but couldn't say for sure. They jumped back in the car, and he remembered hearing the gravel sling off the wheel wells as they sped away. He struggled to stay conscious, his eyes losing focus. The last thing he remembered was seeing an old woman in a pink housecoat standing in her yard in the trailer park beyond the parking lot, both of her hands cupped over her mouth.

And then everything went dark.

* * *

I was devastated. That's the only word that fits the situation. This wasn't just death. This was the slaughter of a man I revered more than anyone in the world and two of my compatriots, all three riddled with bullets and butchered so badly that they couldn't be shown in their caskets. I tried to stay busy helping with any detail that needed attended to, because it kept my mind off the reality of the moment, and kept me from trying to offer stupid consolation to the inconsolable.

I'm not sure what to say about Alphonse Fortunato. I don't want to be trite and say he was like a father to me. To say such a thing would be disrespectful to Big Tommy. Maybe he treated me the way a father should treat a son, but my only frame of reference was my own father, a man who labored under the yoke of another and allowed the world to beat him down. That certainly was not Alphonse Fortunato.

Here's what I know to be true: Without Alphonse Fortunato, I was destined for a life of slopping spit at the athletic club and hanging out at the pool hall. He was a paradox—charitable yet vengeful, thoughtful but violent, smart and yet capricious. He told me to demand respect. He also told me that people shouldn't have to earn my respect. On numerous occasions he said, "You give respect to everyone until they prove they are unworthy of it. The first time someone disrespects you, you're the victim. If you continue to take it, you're a volunteer." He taught me about honor and love and loyalty.

Granted, becoming a mob enforcer is not a career path most people would choose, but my options were limited. Mr. Fortunato took me under his wing. In doing so, I learned some things that most fathers probably don't tell their sons. He liked to say, "The first punch counts, too. If you know a fight is coming, take it to him." He also said, "There are very few arguments that a half a brick to the side of the head won't settle." I learned about business. Not the kind they teach at Wharton or Kellogg, but how the real world works—how to grease the skids with the cops and politicians, and how to dispose of those individuals who are trying to take bread out of your mouth. Yeah, that's a nice way of saying that you're going to make someone disappear, but that's the way my world worked.

I was frustrated with the fact that I would never be able to pay him back for all he had done for me. And now I could not even tell him thanks. He didn't wake up every day thinking about my welfare, but I woke up every day thinking about his. While I would never be able to pay him back, here's another fact I knew to be true: I wanted to exact revenge on his behalf.

CHAPTER

12

June 2019

AFTER MY MEETING at the brick factory with Agent Ross, I felt like my life was on the cusp of upheaval. I could deal with upheaval in the moment. It's the anticipation that always set me on edge. My stomach has all the stability of a Jenga tower. When my nerves shift into high gear, my gut goes DEFCON 1—fire, ice, cramps, you name it. The other capos would say, "Just relax." Oh, good idea, why didn't I think of that? Like I had any say in the matter.

That was one thing I always admired about Carlo. His pulse never raced in the run-up to a hit. He always acted like we were heading out for a cup of coffee. Me? My heart would pound anticipating what could go wrong. When I expressed my concerns to Carlo, he'd say, "Relax. It'll be fine. We ain't splittin' atoms here."

You can tell someone not to worry, but that doesn't solve their problem. My brief association with Ross had my stomach feeling like I'd chewed up a Pepsi bottle for breakfast. The potential for something to go badly wrong was great. I didn't believe for a minute that Ross wasn't telling everyone in his office—bragging, actually—that he'd gotten a potential flip in the Fortunato organization. That kind of information is dangerous on the street, and I knew those numbskulls at the FBI ran their mouths. Pretty soon, word would get back to the compound and Little Tommy.

That would be very bad.

It was raining the next day when I headed to the diner. I put on my galoshes and grabbed an umbrella for the trip down the hill. When I arrived, there were only a few people at the counter. I propped my umbrella in a corner by the door and took my usual seat, and Carolyn greeted me with her usual refrain, "There's my darlin'."

I ordered a cheeseburger and the tater tots. I like tots. It wasn't what my cardiologist would have preferred, but you'll have that. Carolyn was all smiles and spending a lot of time chatting it up with me and largely ignoring the other customers. She refilled my iced tea and asked, "Any plans for the weekend?"

"Nothing particular," I said. "I'll play it by ear. What about you?"

"My niece is getting married on Saturday."

"Nice."

"She's always been my favorite, and she's got herself a nice guy. I'm happy for her. The wedding and the reception are at some fancy arboretum near Canton. I'm going to ride up with my sister and her husband. I'm going by myself, I guess. I always feel like a third wheel when I go alone, but what are you going to do, huh?"

I said, "Yeah, what are you going to do? But that's nice of them to take you."

She nodded, and I saw little dimples appearing on her chin and her lips pinched tight. "I better check on your cheeseburger." When she came back, she slid the plate in my general direction, poured tea into a full glass, slopping it on the counter, then said, "Enjoy your lunch," in a tone that indicated she would be fine if I choked to death on my cheeseburger. She took two steps toward the kitchen, then spun on a heel and walked back toward me. With her fists digging into her hips, she said, "What's your story, Angelo Cipriani?"

"My story?"

"Yeah, what's your story?" She crossed her arms and leaned back against the stainless steel cabinet that ran down the middle of the horseshoe counter. "I'm curious. What is it?"

I set my cheeseburger back on the plate. "I'm not sure what you're talking about," I said. In all candor, guys in my line of work don't like questions like that.

"It's not a difficult question, Angelo. What's your story? Are you married? Were you ever married? Do you have a girlfriend? Do you have kids? What do you do for a living? Are you retired? Do you have a hobby? Where are you from? You've been coming in here nearly every day for two years. You eat, joke around with Kostos, flirt with me a little bit, and then go home. The next day is the same as the one before. Tell me something about yourself. *Anything*."

This was not a friendly conversation. This was an inquisition, and I had yet to figure out the source of her anger.

"Okay. I'm semiretired."

"Really? Oh, that's fascinating. Thanks for sharing that intimate detail about your personal life."

"I, I, I do some contract work for the Harrison Cement Company."

She looked at me for a minute, her eyes narrowing. "The Harrison Cement Company. Isn't that one of the companies the Fortunatos own?"

It was a jab to the throat. I felt like I was trying to swallow a tennis ball. "Yeah, they own it, but I don't really know much about them."

"What do you do for them?"

"This and that."

"This and that. What's that mean?"

"Consulting."

"Consulting? For a cement company?"

"Uh-huh."

"Sounds fascinating."

"It pays the bills."

"Are you married?"

"No."

"Ever been?"

"A long time ago. She died."

"I'm sorry for that. How long ago did she die?"

"Nineteen eighty-three."

"Nineteen eighty-three. That was more than thirty-five years ago."

"Uh-huh."

"And you never remarried?"

"No."

"Why?"

"I don't know. I guess I just never found anyone that I thought could put up with me."

"That's not true. That's the kind of thing guys say when they don't want to give you an honest answer."

No, it was the kind of answer you give when you're stuttering around because you're afraid to tell the truth. Carolyn was the first one I'd met in years that I wanted to have a relationship with, but I'd had been afraid to ask. Given her temperament at that moment, I didn't want to make such an admission while she had a glass pitcher of iced tea within arm's length.

The assault continued.

"Do you have any kids?"

"No."

"No girlfriend or significant other?"

"No."

"Are you interested in a relationship?"

"That would be nice."

"How old are you?"

"Sixty-nine."

She stopped to take a breath. I'm thinking, I should call Ross and tell him to hire her as an interrogator.

She nodded and pulled her order pad from the pocket in her apron and started writing out my tab. Then the exasperation returned. She put her hands on the Formica countertop, her pen in one hand and the pad in the other, and leaned in toward my face. "If you're sixty-nine years old, Angelo, just out of curiosity, how many more chances do you think you're going to get to have that relationship?" My mouth dropped open, but again I didn't know how to answer. "It's not a hypothetical question. How many? How many more chances in this lifetime do you think you're going to get to find someone who cares about you?"

"I don't know," I said. "Not many, I suppose."

"Bingo. Not many is the correct answer."

She slammed my tab on the counter and walked away. As God is my witness, I never saw that coming. I pulled out my wallet to pay the tab, but when I turned over the grease-stained ticket, the only thing written on it was her name and phone number.

CHAPTER

13

February 1975

IT WAS A couple of minutes before midnight when I pulled onto Rosemont Street, returning from dropping off Mr. Fortunato's ninety-three-year-old mother—Miss Maxine—at her home outside of Bloomingdale. She was a tough cookie, and she'd held up at the funeral for her two sons better than the rest of us. I left Jimmy Beans there to stand guard at her home. Everyone was understandably on edge. Ricky Bones was at the hospital watching over his brother, who looked like he was going to pull through. Muzzie Lollini was patrolling the front of the Fortunato compound with an Uzi. I cut the headlights, turned on the inside dome light, and drifted slowly up to the gate. On a good day, Muzzie was a little jittery, and I didn't want him spraying down the Caddy because he mistook me for a Gemelli.

I pulled the car into the garage, then walked around the back of the house, intending to put the keys to what was now Big Tommy's Cadillac in what was now his office on what was now his desk. When I entered the screened-in veranda, I saw the orange glow of Big Tommy's cigar. He was slouched in the corner of the wicker couch, his feet crossed at the ankles and resting on the matching coffee table. A bottle of bourbon and a half-filled glass sat next to his shoes.

"I was just bringing you the keys to the Caddy," I said, handing them to him. "Sorry to disturb you, Tom."

Big Tommy uncrossed his feet and sat up. "Not at all," he said. "Sit down, Angelo. I could use the company." He pulled a cigar from his shirt pocket and handed it to me. "Go get yourself a glass out of the kitchen."

I returned, and he poured me a drink and refreshed his. I bit off the end of my cigar and struck a wooden match, its flare illuminating the room and the wan face of my new boss. For several minutes, we sat in the darkened room, the glow of the cigars casting a faint light. Big Tommy blew a stream of smoke into the screened window and said, "It was a hell of a thing, wasn't it?"

"That's putting it mildly," I said. "I'm still trying to get my head around it."

"I went over to the hospital early this morning to see Connie Bones. He's in pretty rough shape, but he was able to talk for a few minutes. He said the meeting went south in a hurry. Tony Gem announced what territory they were taking, and apparently the old man told him to go fuck himself. Tony and Frankie Gem and a couple of their mouth-breathers left the meeting and drove off in their sedan. Dad, Uncle Matt, and the boys assumed the coast was clear. They walked out of the restaurant, and a second car came around the corner and unloaded. Connie said it was over before it started. He was in the infantry in Vietnam, and he said it was worse than any firefight he saw over there. Before they all walked outside, Connie said he watched Tony Gem stand by the car, pull out a handkerchief and wipe his face. He didn't think anything about it at the time, but now he's guessing that was the signal to the guys in the second car that the meeting hadn't gone their way and to take Dad out."

"So, now what?"

"I'm thinking on it. *What* I'm going to do is a foregone conclusion. It's the *how* that's still a question mark for me. I don't want to start dumping tea in the harbor without a plan."

This was the difference between Big Tommy and his father. Tommy was more calculating and thoughtful. If this had been reversed and Tommy had been killed, Alphonse would already have driven a tank and two armored personnel carriers through the front of Tony Gem's manse, and there would be bodies stacked to the ceiling.

"You know, when I was in business school at Pitt, they never offered a class on what to do after a rival sprays down your family with machine guns," he said, drawing on his cigar.

"No, I don't suppose that's part of the curriculum at any business school," I said.

"I talked to the sheriff. I told him we didn't know who my dad was meeting with, then I told him that I'd appreciate it if he didn't get too aggressive in the investigation."

I knew what that meant. Big Tommy had already convicted the Gemellis and appointed himself judge, jury, and executioner. All that remained was to determine the time and place.

"I want to be the one to do it," I said.

Behind the glow of his cigar, I could see his face tighten. "I don't know, Angelo. I'll talk to Carlo and see what he thinks."

"I don't care what Carlo thinks. I want to do it."

"Look, no one doubts your loyalty to this family, or your courage, but for a job like this . . . Carlo has a few more notches on his gun handle, if you know what I mean. And I think I owe it to him. He was supposed to be there. He got sick and couldn't go. Connie Bones went in his place, and now Connie's in the ICU, all shot to hell. Carlo feels terrible and thinks if he had been there, things could have been different. Of course, he couldn't have changed a damn thing, and he'd probably be dead, too."

"I understand that. Carlo's a lion. Doesn't matter. I want to be the one who sends those cowardly bastards to the gates of hell."

"Have you ever killed anyone?"

"You know the answer to that. No, but I can't think of a better time to start. Your dad, he did a lot for me. I can never pay him back for all he did, but I can avenge his murder. In fact, it would give me great pleasure to do so."

"Taking out the Gemellis means you're entering a whole new level of commitment."

"I understand that. Tom, look at this from a practical standpoint. The Gemellis know who Carlo is. He's not going to sneak up on anyone, and they'll be looking for him. They don't know me. I'm telling you, I'm your guy."

"It's a hell of a thing to take another man's life, even if they're trash like the Gems."

"I feel confident that I'll still be able to sleep at night."

"Once you cross that line, you can't uncross it."

"I'm well aware of that, too."

He sat in silence for a minute, then lifted his bourbon and tossed it down. "All right. You're in. However, I want you to work with Carlo and go on a practice run."

"You mean a hit?"

"We try not to use that term out loud, but yes. Carlo can teach you a lot, and I need to know that you're familiar with the process."

I pulled the cigar from my mouth and smiled. "You mean, you want to make sure I've got the stones to pull the trigger."

"That's exactly what I mean."

CHAPTER

14

July 1975

THE DAY BIG Tommy said I would be working with Carlo Dello Russo, I was awestruck. As far as I was concerned, I was working with a legend.

Even by the standards of the Spaghetto, the Dello Russos were a tough bunch. They lived around the corner from us on Carnegie Avenue and were a family of one girl and eight boys, all of whom were sweaty roughnecks, including the sister. Mostly, they drank, fought, and got arrested. The exception was the next to the oldest boy, Gilberto, who was something of a black sheep in the Dello Russo family. He graduated high school, enlisted in the army and later became a police officer in McKees Rocks, near Pittsburgh. This made him a pariah with his brothers.

Carlo was the shining star of the Spaghetto. He was eight years my senior and a boxer. A good one, too. He won the Ohio Valley Golden Gloves Tournament three years straight. There were always articles about him in the newspaper, and Mr. Dante at the Mercato Sarefino would clip them out and tape them to the store's front window. One article had a picture of Carlo standing bare-chested with his arms crossed, the Wheeling-Pittsburgh Steel plant belching smoke in the background. The caption under the photo read "Steubenville's Iron Mauler." He had ripped abs, a wide chest, and a jaw that came to a point and gave him the look of a Spartan warrior.

Carlo had a heavy bag hanging from the limb of an oak tree and a speed bag hanging off the back of their house, and when he was practicing you could hear the steady rhythm of his punches echoing a block in every direction. All the boys in the Spaghetto would run down the alley to watch him pound the bag. He would be shirtless, sweat rolling down his back and into the waistband of his shorts, his fists banging the bag with such rapidity that it sounded like machine-gun fire, and you could hear the windows in their house rattling. In a place that didn't have many heroes, Carlo was a guy you could look up to. Every kid in the Spaghetto wanted to be like Carlo "The Iron Mauler" Dello Russo.

One of the Dello Russo brothers, I was never sure which one, had a young son of maybe four or five who idolized Carlo. The little guy would go out in the yard and shadowbox alongside him. Every once in a while, Carlo would put the gloves on his nephew and let him punch the heavy bag. For all his toughness, Carlo had a real soft spot for the kid. It was nice to see, because Carlo Dello Russo didn't have a soft spot for many people.

He was strong and tough, and eventually he started fighting professionally. Early on, he recorded knockout after knockout, but he was mostly fighting bums. At one time, Carlo was the thirteenth ranked light heavyweight in the world. Three years after he went pro, Carlo won a match in Atlantic City, but took a slew of hard punches to the side of his head. He collapsed in the locker room after the fight and woke up in a hospital three days later, having lost his peripheral vision on the right side. He tried to fight twice more, but he couldn't see the left hooks coming, and he became more of a target than a boxer. Seeing he was never going to be world champion and fearful that he was going to end up dead or blind, he gave up the sport.

When Carlo and I began working together, he was immediately like a brother. Unfortunately, he was like an older brother who didn't want his aggravating little brother hanging around and asking questions. He was always rolling his eyes, shaking his head in disgust, and offering condescending remarks. This is your life when you're an apprentice hitman. Six weeks after my late-night meeting with Big Tommy, Carlo walked down to the safe room where I was counting the daily number take with Nickels. He said, "I just talked to Big Tommy. Tomorrow's the day."

"Okay, good, good," I said. "Like, are we going to meet for breakfast or something?"

Carlo rolled his eyes and said, "Yeah, let's meet for breakfast, kid. Let's go down to Elby's Big Boy, sit in the middle of the restaurant, and discuss the intricacies of how we're going to put a bullet in someone's brain."

(Note: Big Tommy called me Angelo or Ange, I was "kid" to everyone else in the organization. Later, I would be known as Angelo "The Kid" Cipriani. My apologies to Ted Williams.)

Nickels snorted.

Carlo turned and headed out of the safe room. As he left, he said, "I'll see you here tomorrow, my dear pupil."

Nickels was still laughing.

The next day was like the first day of school and the teacher doesn't show up. I'm keeping busy around the compound, and Carlo is nowhere to be found. I finally asked Big Tommy if he knew where Carlo was, and he shrugged and said, "Not my day to watch him."

A simple "yes" or "no" would do, but no one in the mob can give you a straight answer.

Carlo showed up midafternoon carrying the black canvas bag that he referred to as his "tool kit." It contained an assortment of handguns, ammo, suppressors, a sawed-off shotgun, duct tape, a roll of plastic, a bottle of bleach, rubber gloves, leather gloves, ball caps, four or five pairs of sunglasses, a flashlight, a roll of toilet paper, and a length of piano wire, which he used when he wanted "to get up close and personal" with his mark. Big Tommy had left for a meeting, so class started in his office.

"Here's what you've got to remember," Carlo started. "Where these jobs are concerned, Big Tommy is just like the old man. He doesn't like to see any theatrics."

"I don't know what that means," I said.

"Use your head, kid. It means when he sends us out to do a job, all he wants to see in the paper the next day is a small headline that says a man was found shot to death or a man was reported missing. What he doesn't want is a front-page story about a car explosion that tears up a city block and kills some young mother and her baby. No theatrics. Get in, get the job done, and get out. You don't get no style points in this business. In the movies, the hitman's always talking to his mark, explaining why he's got to kill him, blah, blah, blah. First of all, the mark *always* knows why you're going to kill him. But none of that matters. When Big Tommy gives you a name, your only responsibility is to make sure that guy becomes a corpse. Period. Big Tommy will never ask if he begged for mercy. He doesn't give a shit. All he wants is to make sure the guy's dead and that there's nothing connecting him to the hit. Remember that, and don't let your personal feelings get in the way. One of these days, and trust me it's going to happen, he's going to give you a name and it's going to be someone you know. Maybe it's a childhood friend or a business associate, but you got to take personal feelings out of the equation. Big Tommy's the boss now. Your job is to take care of business and do as he says, just like he was the old man. Do the job, and he'll reward you handsomely. Screw it up, and . . . well, don't screw it up. And I probably don't have to tell you this, but I will anyway: you never mention what we do to a living soul. Are we clear?"

"Absolutely."

"Good. Now, when you're on a job, you have to exploit your opponent's weakness. What does he do that makes him vulnerable and distracts him from his situational awareness? In many cases, the weakness is gross stupidity. Obviously, this plays to our advantage. I haven't taken out a lot of rocket scientists, if you know what I mean. A lot of times, guys get drunk and put themselves in a position that makes my job a lot easier. Take Paulie Gasparino, for example.

Paulie had been skimming from Alphonse. He was a low-level guy and someone Alphonse could make an example of, you know, put a little blood on the floor so the other grunts take notice. He tells me to take care of it. The next Saturday night, Paulie was at the Merriment on Wheeling Island. Paulie liked the young girls and the place was always loaded with 'em. I walked in and pretended like I was surprised to see him. Paulie was already half in the bag, so I bought him a couple more drinks, doubles, and by midnight he was blind drunk. We were getting ready to leave and I tell him, 'You've been drinking a lot. How about you let me drive you home?' He insists that he's okay, so I tell him that I'll walk him to his car. He gets in, and I tell him to buckle his seat belt. He grabs the clip and turns his head to look for the plug. Pop, pop. I give him two in the back of the head and shut the car door. I love it when they make my job easy." He chuckled to himself and then sat silent for several moments, as though deep in concentration. "I guess that's all I've got. Did you bring a piece?"

I pulled a .32-caliber semiautomatic from the back of my waist.

"Let's get you something with a little ass," he said, reaching into his bag and pulling out a Beretta. "In close quarters, I always use a semiautomatic with a suppressor. I like a 9-millimeter because it's a no-doubter. I've never seen it happen, but I've been told that people have been shot in the head with .22s and .25s, and the bullets ricocheted off their skulls."

"I imagine they end up with a hell of a headache."

"That's funny, but I don't want to come back and tell Big Tommy that someone he wanted dead is running around with a headache and the knowledge that he's a marked man." He reached into the bag and pulled out a revolver. "Now, if you're out in the woods or someplace where no one is going to hear the shots, my weapon of choice is a .38 revolver with hollow points. You don't have to worry about your gun jamming, and you don't have to pick up your brass. It's very clean." He returned the revolver to the bag and handed me the Beretta. "Tonight, it's going to be close quarters, so you'll use that one."

I looked at the pistol in my hand and then at Carlo. "Tonight? Me? I'm going to do this?"

"Yeah. Who did you think was going to do it?"

"I don't know. I thought you were teaching me."

"I just did."

"I mean, I guess I thought I would just watch the first one."

"You guessed wrong, kid. You talked like a big man around the boss. You said you were ready for this."

"I am. I just figured we'd go somewhere like the Mingo Sportsman's Club and shoot some first. You know, practice."

"Jesus H. Christ, kid, we're not shooting clay pigeons." A smirk slowly crept over Carlo's lips. "Oh, I think I know what the problem is here. You've never shot a gun before, have you?"

"Of course, I've shot a gun before. I practice with my .32 all the time."

Nope. Not once. Not ever. I'd had the .32 semiautomatic for several years, but I'd never fired it a single time. Mostly I just liked carrying it around because it made me feel like one of the guys. Okay, it made me feel like a total badass, but I'm not sure I'd even had the safety off more than a couple of times. This is a little embarrassing to admit, but at that stage of my career, I was afraid of guns. I was always terrified that I'd do something stupid like shoot my balls off.

"Look, I could teach a monkey to do this," Carlo said. "You walk up to your mark, you put the muzzle about three inches from his head and exchange his brain matter for lead." He looked down and pointed to the muzzle. "That's this end of the gun, in case you're wondering." He started laughing. "Don't overthink this, kid. It doesn't take a Marine sniper to pull this off. It takes more balls than skill. Do you know what a guy's ear looks like?"

"Yeah. I've seen ears before."

"Beautiful. Find his ear, put the muzzle behind it and pull the trigger. Trust me, the bullet will do all the heavy lifting for you."

We drove Carlo's Lincoln Continental down to the old Fort Steuben Brewery warehouse. Just past the loading dock, Carlo took a ramp to the lower level and parked next to a storage area. He slid a wooden door to the side, walked into the shadows, and drove out in a 1968 Ford Galaxie, four-door sedan. We loaded his tool kit into the trunk and pulled out of the warehouse. He said, "Before you ask, I'll tell you. If you're driving someplace where you don't want to be seen, you don't do it in a white Lincoln Continental. It screams for attention. You want to drive a car that nobody pays attention to because it looks like a thousand other cars on the street. What color is this car?"

"Kind of a yellowish brown, maybe tan or beige. I don't know."

"Exactly. If someone sees us and the cops ask 'em to describe the car, that's what they're going to say."

I thought that was good information.

"So, this guy we're going after. What's his story?"

As we were driving over the Market Street Bridge, he looked at me and asked, "Are you fuckin' retarded?"

"I don't know. Ask my sister."

"What?"

"No, I'm not retarded. Why are you asking me that?"

"Were you listening to anything I said back at the compound? It doesn't matter what his story is. He's displeased Big Tommy to the point where the head of the Fortunato family believes he shouldn't be wasting valuable oxygen. Got it?"

"Yeah, I got it."

"Good. Then don't ask me no more stupid questions." He rolled down the window and fired up a little cigar with a plastic tip. After drawing hard on the cigar, he blew smoke out the window and said, "There are no exact rules to this business, but we have a code."

"A code. Like a code of ethics?"

"Sure, if that's what you want to call it. I'm not sure the word ethics is the correct word when you're talking about putting a bullet in someone's cranium, but if that makes you feel better, fine. Number one, don't shoot nobody in the face. Sometimes this can't be avoided, but you do your best out of respect for the family. They can't have an open casket if you blow his face all to hell, so you go for the back of the head or the heart. Besides, if you slip one into the back of his head, there's no fighting and none of the crying and begging for mercy. God, I hate that. Some guys in our business, the more devout ones, let's say, they'll only kill their marks from the front—shoot 'em in the heart. They believe you need to give the condemned time to ask Jesus for forgiveness. That's a crock. The last thing those guys are thinking about is getting right with God. When you're standing in front of a mark pointing a 9-millimeter at him, he ain't thinking about Jesus. He's thinking, 'How can I get that gun and make him eat it?' Trust me, take the easy way out, shoot 'em in the back of the head. Two, don't go fishing through the mark's wallet or stripping off his jewelry. It's bad form. And three, never clip anyone in front of the wife and kids. That's a hard and fast rule for me. They don't need to see that."

We cut through Weirton and across the West Virginia panhandle into Pittsburgh. I wanted to know where we were going, but was smart enough not to ask. We crossed the Monongahela River at Elizabeth and followed Route 51 south. "There's a road atlas under your seat," Carlo said. "Find us a way back across the river into Donora."

"Donora? Stan Musial is from Donora," I said.

"Who's that?"

"Stan 'The Man' Musial. The baseball player."

"Baseball and useless information. I got no use for either of them. Just get me across the river."

Once we crossed the bridge into Donora, we followed Route 837 as it snaked along next to the Monongahela to an area known as Victory Hill. Carlo pulled off the road and into the parking lot of the Victory Hill Church of Christ. He shut off the engine, checked his watch, and said, "Okay, since you didn't ask no more stupid questions, I'll tell you. Big Tommy has a cousin, Melanie or Melissa, something like that, who's married to a guy with a bad temper and the IQ of bait. He likes to beat the shit out of her, and he's been sticking it to her fourteen-year-old daughter from another marriage. This guy has no redeeming social value."

"Are we going to kill him or rough him up?"

"You ask a lot of questions that you should already know the answer to. Did I put a gun in your hand earlier today because we're going to rough him up? He's screwing his fourteen-year-old stepdaughter and beating the hell out of Big Tommy's cousin. Do you think a prick like that deserves to live? Think about it really hard, and make sure you give me the right answer, because it's very important."

"I'd say no."

"And you'd be right. I hope you weren't guessing."

"I wasn't."

"Good. Maybe you're not retarded, after all."

Carlo put his seat back and dozed off. I was astonished. I figured he would have maps and synchronized plans of how this would go down, and we'd be working out the details until the last minute. I was sweating like I was in a sauna and my stomach was in knots, and Carlo was gently snoring.

Thirty minutes later, a green Ford Country Squire station wagon with fake wood paneling pulled into the lot. I tapped him on the knee and said, "Carlo." The station wagon pulled up next to us so that the driver's-side windows were only a foot apart. The driver was an attractive woman, a brunette, her face caked with makeup, which I assumed was covering up bruises. A teenage girl with long, straight hair sat in the passenger seat. Her face was pale and unadorned, and her eyes had the scared, distant look of someone who had already given up on life.

Carlo reached into his jacket pocket, pulled out a thick, white envelope, passed it out the open window to the woman, and said, "Enjoy your vacation."

She handed Carlo a half sheet of notebook paper. Pressed between her thumb and the paper was a house key.

Carlo looked at the paper, nodded, and said, "We're good." Without uttering a word, the woman drove off. When the dust in the parking lot had settled, Carlo checked his watch. "It's too early," he said. "Here's the deal. She and the kid are going to take a little trip to Disney World. The husband likes to get hammered at a bar called the Lame Duck. When he gets back tonight, we're gonna have a little welcome home party for him."

Carlo went back to the trunk and returned with a brown paper bag, two ball caps and two pairs of sunglasses. He handed me one of each and said, "Put these on." I read the directions that were on the notebook paper while he drove. We did a drive-by of the neighborhood. It was middle-class, a cluster of split-level homes built into the hillside so that the garages were directly under the house and part of the basement. The house was in the middle of the neighborhood. "Not ideal," Carlo said. "But we'll be all right." There were cars parked on the street, kids playing in backyards, and a mother pushing a baby in a stroller. "Don't ever make eye contact with anyone, sunglasses or no. If you make eye contact, it causes them to remember."

We drove five or six miles out of town, crossed back over the river, and pulled into the parking lot of a shopping center with a multiscreen movie theater. The lot was crowded, and we slipped into a spot in a back row. He opened the brown paper bag and handed me a peanut butter sandwich, an apple, and a warm can of Dr Pepper. "When you're out on a job, don't ever go in a restaurant," he said. "Eat before you leave, or bring something with you. Gas up the car before you leave. If you have to stop at a gas station or a store, always pay cash. No credit cards. Have as little interaction with people as possible, and get back home as soon as you can. No stopping or celebrating until the job is over."

"Celebrating" seemed like an odd word choice, but such is this business.

After dark, we cruised through the parking lot of the Lame Duck. He pointed at a red Chrysler and said, "Our boy didn't disappoint us." It was past eleven o'clock when we parked down the street from the mark's house. Carlo said the most dangerous part of the mission was about to begin. There was no place to park our car except on the street. We had to get to the back of the house and inside without a nosy neighbor seeing us and calling the cops. He said, "Always take the bulbs out of your interior dome light and the trunk. Keep it as dark as possible. I'm going to get in the trunk and get my bag. When you get out, push the door closed, but don't lock it. You don't want it locked if you've got to get away in a hurry. I'm putting the key under the floor mat. That way, if things go south and we've got to make a run for it, we're not fumbling around trying to get the door unlocked."

"Got it."

"Walk along the shrubs between the houses and get to the back door. I'm right behind you."

Carlo used the key the woman had given us to unlock the door. The tiny light on the kitchen stove was the only one burning. Wearing rubber gloves, Carlo pulled the door shut behind us, and we went straight to the basement. A streetlight near the front of the house cast a faint glow through the garage door window. After our eyes adjusted, there was ample light to see. There was a baseball bat propped in the corner. He brought it over to where I was standing and said, "We'll need this. Maybe it's a Stan Musial autographed model."

He was laughing at his own joke as he walked up the stairs and came back with a couple of Iron Citys and a bottle opener. We sat in the dark, sipping beer and waiting to kill some guy I'd never met. My intestines were doing the merengue. Carlo, he sat there drinking his beer like he didn't have a care in the world. And I think that was because he didn't.

I don't want to say that Carlo didn't have a conscience, but there was a strong possibility that he didn't have a conscience. I wanted to kill the Gemellis because of what they had done to Mr. Fortunato, Matteo, Dommie the Clip, and Connie Bones. I felt justified in my feelings of hatred and my desire for revenge.

For Carlo, it didn't matter who Mr. Fortunato or Big Tommy had marked for death, or why. To him, it was just another day at the office. He fetched us two more beers. "Might as well drink them," he said. "He's not going to need them after tonight." After popping the caps off the bottles, he reached into his tool kit, pulled out the

9-millimeter, and attached the suppressor. He took it off safety, jacked a round into the chamber, and handed it to me. "It's live."

I must admit, I liked the feel of it in my hand.

Carlo said, "Guys like this, they're big men when they're slapping around women, but they're cowards at heart. A few years back, before you came on board, these two guys broke into an apartment and raped the woman who lived there. Bad enough, but what the dipshits didn't know was that it was Alphonse Fortunato's aunt, who was in her late seventies. Some neighbor was letting the dog out, hears the old lady crying, and calls the cops. They catch the two guys in the house. They've got them dead to rights. They're locked up in jail, and Alphonse goes down and tells the prosecutor that the family doesn't want to press charges. He says he doesn't want the old lady to have to endure a trial after all she's been through, so they can go ahead and let the two guys go. You see what's happening here, right?"

"I've heard bits and pieces of the story."

"The cops were laughing their asses off when they pushed them out the back door of the jail. There were five of us waiting to pick them up—Dommie, Muzzie, the Bones brothers, and me. They see what's happening and try to get back in the jail . . ." Carlo had to take a break in the story because he was laughing so hard. "They know their lives are over. We threw them into the car, took them out to the compound and tied them to a couple of chairs in the safe room. We beat the dogshit out of them for a long time, then I pulled the nine out of my waist. They started begging and crying, like they think they don't deserve to die. Fuckin' pussies. Like I said, nothing pisses me off more than guys who can't take it like men. I can tell you this, kid, none of us in this business live to old age. One of these days, someone is coming for me, and I swear to Christ, when that happens, I'll take it like a man. I'll never give them the satisfaction of seeing me beg for my life. Anyway, I shot them each in the knee cap just to give them something to cry about. Eventually, Alphonse comes downstairs; he's dressed up because he and the missus were heading to the Federal Terrace for dinner. I hand him my nine and boom, boom, that quick, he puts one in each of their foreheads. The only words he spoke the whole time were, 'Get that scum outta my house.' Then he went to dinner and had crab legs."

He took another sip of his beer, then reached out and tapped me on the side of the knee. A car was pulling into the driveway, its headlights shining through the garage door window and illuminating the back wall. Carlo pointed toward a dark corner that was in shadow. He whispered, "Wait over there." He stepped back between two steel cabinets, the baseball bat tight in his hands, the left gripping the barrel, the right wrapped around the thin handle. The car stopped short of the garage. A few moments later, I heard the handle twist, and the steel slide that had locked it in place fell out of its moorings. The springs squeaked as he lifted it open. A few seconds later, the car door shut and the Chrysler pulled nose-first into the garage.

My eyes darted between Carlo and the mark. Carlo never moved, not an inch. He reminded me of a big cat ready to pounce on its prey. The mark turned off the engine. The headlights continued to glow for another few seconds before he turned them off and exited the car. He pulled down the garage door, slid the steel slide back into place, and started across the basement toward the stairs.

Carlos stepped out from between the cabinets and rammed the business end of the bat into the mark's sternum. I heard bone and cartilage snap and the air rush from his lungs. In the next instant, Carlo whipped his right foot across the mark's legs, just above the ankles, dropping him to the ground. He landed on the side of his face; it sounded like a melon splattering on concrete. He moaned and pulled for air. Carlo rammed a knee into his spine, grabbed a handful of hair, and jerked the mark's head back. From the time Carlo stepped out of the shadows to when he had the man by the hair hadn't been five seconds. It was the work of a pro.

I stepped out of the corner. Carlo leaned down close to the mark's ear and said, "You like to smack your wife around and screw little girls? I hope it was worth it, because it's never going to happen again."

The man was trying to speak, still straining to catch his breath. Carlo slammed his head to the floor, then stood back. After a few seconds, he looked at me, his brows arching, and said, "What are you waiting for, a formal invitation?"

I was scared to death, but I didn't hesitate. I extended my arm and started firing 9-millimenter rounds into the back of his skull; blood splattered everywhere. His body was twitching around on the floor like he'd bitten into an electric cord. After six or seven shots, Carlo reached out and grabbed my wrist. "You can stop anytime you like, kid. I think he got the message."

It's a little difficult to explain how I felt. I'm not a psychopath and not the kind of guy who fantasized about taking another man's life. But I had, and to tell you the truth, I was kind of proud of myself. It had been a test to see if I had the nerve to pull the trigger, and I'd passed. More times than necessary, I'll admit, but I'd still passed. I justified it by telling myself that I had saved that little girl future torment and her mother plastic surgery, and that I had ridded the earth of one of God's mistakes. That was all true, but I had still killed a man that I had known for all of twelve seconds.

Such is life and death as part of the Fortunato family.

Carlo said, "Jesus, kid, what a mess."

The basement looked like a splatter art project. Carlo pulled the roll of plastic out of his tool kit and we spread it on the floor next to the corpse. He grabbed his feet and I grabbed the material around the shoulder of his shirt. As we lifted, the man I believed to have been a corpse moaned, and I dropped him. Carlo looked at me and shook his head. "It's just air coming out of his lungs," he said. "Trust me, he's negotiating with Jesus by now. I hope he has a good lawyer."

We set him on the edge of the plastic and started rolling him toward the middle. Once he had four layers of plastic over him, we began binding him up in duct tape. When he was secure and very mummy-like, we wrestled him into the trunk of the Chrysler. "Why are we taking the body?" I asked.

"Because the boss said to."

That was all the answer I needed.

I got a pair of rubber gloves, the bleach, and a rag from the tool kit and started looking for blood to clean up. There was plenty. Carlo used his flashlight to look for splatters. We threw the gloves and the empty beer bottles into Carlo's tool kit. The basement and garage were as we found it.

"You're going to drive the Chrysler," Carlo said. "Drive two miles over the speed limit and stay ahead of me. I'll guard your tail. If you need gas, stop at the first exit on the interstate. Otherwise, you don't stop for any reason. None. Take one of the empty beer bottles with you in case you've got to piss. When you get back to Steubenville, drive straight to the Hilltop Funeral Home on Stony Hollow. If we get separated, just wait for me there."

I knew the Fortunatos had for years enjoyed a special relationship with the owners of the Hilltop Funeral Home. Bodies went into the crematorium, no questions asked, and Carlo made the payment for services with a wad of green money. Once we cleared the funeral home, we drove back to the warehouse, leaving both cars and driving out in Carlo's Lincoln. The next day, the Chrysler was driven to a local scrapyard, which Mr. Fortunato owned, crushed into a brick and put on the next truck heading to Weirton Steel. It would be melted down in a blast furnace before anyone knew the mark was even missing.

To the best of my knowledge, he never again beat Big Tommy's cousin.

CHAPTER

15

July 2019

THERE ARE SOME people who work very hard at being disrespectful. There are others for whom it comes naturally. Little Tommy falls into that latter category. I'd just finished my second cup of coffee when the phone rang. He said, "I need to talk to you. Come out to the house." Then he hung up. When he does that, I can't not visualize my hands wrapped around his scrawny neck. I assumed that he had another schmutz for me to train as my replacement, which would be a disaster, but at least he would pay me for my time.

I was at the compound within the hour. Little Tommy was in the office, shoeless and wearing a wrinkled T-shirt and blue jeans. He looked like he just rolled out of bed. The place smelled like reefer. A cell phone was pressed to his ear. "I'll call you back in a minute," he said before pushing the phone into the front pocket of his jeans.

"What's up, boss?" I asked, showing him a degree of respect that I didn't believe he deserved.

"I got a call last night from Silvio Lombardi," he said.

"In Rochester?"

"How many Silvio Lombardis do you know?"

Sweet mother of Christ, I wanted to smack this kid. "I guess that's the only one."

"He needs help with a situation. He asked for you specifically."

"Silvio Lombardi knows who I am?"

"Apparently, since he asked for you."

"What's the job?"

"I didn't get into the weeds with him, 'cause I don't give a shit, but he's dealing with some kind of issue and he wants a little outside influence."

"How much?"

"It pays ten large."

In the old days, ten thousand dollars was carrying-around money. On this day, it was serious cash. "Silvio's got a big organization. He doesn't have anyone to take care of his problems?"

"It's ten G's, Angelo. Are you interested, or no?"

"Yeah, I'm interested. What's your cut?"

He handed me a scrap of paper off his desk with a phone number scrawled in green ink. "It's yours. Just take care of it, and keep him happy." Little Tommy was already punching buttons on his cell phone. "I got a lot going on this morning." He turned his back to me, a tacit signal that I was excused.

I put the paper in my pocket and headed out of the office. As I walked toward the back door, I saw Rosebella standing in the living room, a dirty nightgown falling off of one shoulder, staring at the wall. I kept walking.

I should have been excited about the payday, but I couldn't shake the belief that everything wasn't copacetic. Little Tommy gave new meaning to the word greedy. When a Mafia don sends one of his capos to do a job for another family, he always takes a percentage of the fee. It's the benefit of owning the franchise. Maybe the kid felt sorry for his old Uncle Ange and was throwing me a bone, but something in my gut told me that wasn't true.

After lunch, I went back to the apartment and called the number. One of Silvio Lombardi's capos answered with a curt "Yeah."

"This is Angelo Cipriani."

There was a moment of silence before a man with a voice like a grinding transmission picked up the phone. "Mr. Cipriani" was all he said.

"Mr. Lombardi, sir, how may I be of assistance to you?"

"I'm looking for a man of your skill set, but for obvious reasons I'd prefer not to talk on the phone."

"I understand that completely."

"Can you be here tomorrow?"

"I can be there this evening, if you like."

"That won't be necessary. I'll expect you tomorrow."

He gave me the address and the phone went dead.

Why would Silvio Lombardi be looking for outside help? I couldn't get that question out of my head. He controlled Rochester and was one of the most powerful crime lords in the eastern United States. It didn't make sense. While the old guard in a lot of cities had forsaken the drug trade, Silvio had embraced it. The money was rolling in and he was ruthless in his approach. If overdose victims were stacked a hundred feet high in front of his mansion, he couldn't have cared less. I suspected that much of the product that Little Tommy was dealing was being wholesaled to him by Silvio. That was none of my business, but I feared there might be a tight relationship between the two of them and maybe I was the one with the bull's-eye on his forehead. Did he know I'd been talking to the FBI?

After hanging up with Silvio, I got in the car and drove over to Weirton to see Nickels. When he was lucid, he had good instincts for this kind of stuff. He was in his bed, watching a soap opera on television.

"You watching daytime dramas now?"

"Yeah, the news is too depressing, and they've got all those smokin' hot news babes who don't even know I'm alive, which is even more depressing." He pointed the remote at the screen and turned down the volume. "You usually visit in the morning. What's up?"

A nurse walked into the room with a tiny paper cup of pills. She handed it to Nickels, who dutifully tipped the cup to his mouth and washed them down with a bottle of water. I closed the door to the room after she had left.

"I've got a little bit of a situation I want to run by you," I said.

"Lay it on me, my man."

"I got a call from Little Tommy this morning. I drove out to the compound and he hands me a sheet of paper with a phone number for Silvio Lombardi."

"Rochester?"

I nodded. "Yeah. I called him just before I came over here. I'm supposed to meet him tomorrow about a job."

"Does he want you to paint a house?"

"I'm guessing, but I won't know until I meet with him. My question is: Why would Silvio Lombardi want someone from Steubenville, Ohio, to do his heavy lifting?"

"It's not unheard of. Families share resources all the time. What's your concern?"

"My concern is that I am not the painter, but the wall. I think Silvio supplies Little Tommy with a lot of drugs. Maybe the kid is calling in a marker to get rid of me."

"I don't want to be insulting here, Angelo, but are you really that important? Are you so much of a threat to Little Tommy that he'd want to get rid of you?"

"Maybe he thinks I know too much."

"Maybe you're being paranoid."

"Maybe he knows the FBI is trying to flip me."

"Maybe you're being more paranoid than usual."

"You're the one who told me that paranoid helps keep you alive in this business."

Nickels yawned and stared back at the television. "Is the juice worth the squeeze?"

"Ten grand."

"Nice payday."

"So, you're telling me that if it was you, you'd go to Rochester and hear him out?"

"Rochester? What the hell's in Rochester?"

"What do you mean what's in Rochester? I just told you—Silvio Lombardi."

"I'll tell you who was a real son of a bitch—Hirohito."

"Hirohito?"

"The emperor of Japan."

"I know who Hirohito is. What's he got to do with Silvo Lombardi?"

"And Hitler, everyone thinks he was such a bad guy."

"Hitler was a bad guy."

"He was a saint compared to Stalin, I'll tell you that much."

"Nickels, I don't think we should be conferring sainthood on Adolph Hitler, regardless of who we're comparing him to. Who cares, anyway? They're all dead."

He laughed. "You believe that? Don't be a chump."

That quickly, the train had completely left the tracks. His drugged-out eyes looked back at the television. He turned up the volume and was pulled back into the story. I never did get my answer, and at six o'clock the next morning, I left for Rochester.

* * *

Silvio Lombardi lived in a three-story brick mansion that was four times the size of the Fortunato home and located in the tony suburb of Brighton. The home was built in the eighteen hundreds when Brighton was considered the brick manufacturing capital of northern New York, or so the welcome sign claimed as I pulled into town.

After leaving the nursing home the previous day, I drove to the old Fort Steuben Brewery warehouse and swapped out my Oldsmobile Cutlass for the nondescript Ford Galaxie that we kept for such occasions. It was the same car that Carlo and I had used the night we drove to Donora and he introduced me to my new profession.

It didn't get used much, and I had to jump the dead battery with the Cutlass.

I parked the Galaxie on the street in front of the Lombardi mansion and stuffed the key into the seat. If I was going to be a mark, I didn't want to make it easy for them to drive my car to some scrapyard. As I walked up to the house, I had my 9-millimeter tucked into a shoulder holster, a .380 in my ankle holster, and my snub-nose .22 in my belt.

A guy roughly the size of Paul Bunyan answered the door. He pushed it open and filled the void. "You Cipriani?" he asked.

"I am," I said.

"Are you carrying?"

"Of course, I'm carrying."

"I need your weapon."

"Not happening, big man."

His face screwed into a quizzical vortex, like a kid looking at long division for the first time. My bet is, Mr. Bunyan wasn't used to having people disobey his orders. He said, "Wait here." He closed the door, and I heard the dead bolt slide into place. Several minutes passed before he returned and said, "This way." We walked to the back of the mansion, our footfalls echoing off the wide hallway. The place was massive, bright, and immaculate. Who says crime doesn't pay? He opened the wooden door to the office of Silvio Lombardi and motioned me in with the sideways movement of his head.

In the room were Silvio and his son, Vito. Silvio was in his mid-seventies with silver hair and a Roman chin. He was trim and tanned and looked more like a country club tennis instructor than a mob boss. Vito was shorter and thicker than his father, handsome, but with a hairline that was in full retreat. We shook hands, and Vito gestured toward a couch and a couple of chairs in the corner of the room. "Please, sit down," Silvio said. "I appreciate you coming here on short notice. Your reputation precedes you, Mr. Cipriani."

"Thank you, Mr. Lombardi," I said, sitting on the couch at an angle so I could survey the entire room. "I consider it an honor that you asked for my assistance."

Vito turned to Mr. Bunyan and said, "We're good here."

The big man gave me a quick glare, then left the room.

You never let down your guard. What appears to be the friendliest of environs can turn south in a hurry, but I was probably needlessly worrying at this point. The don or the underboss rarely did the dirty work themselves, unless it was a personal grudge and they wanted the satisfaction of taking a life, like Mr. Fortunato and the rapists. From a practical standpoint, he wouldn't want bloodstains on his good couch.

"What can I do for you gentlemen?" I asked.

The two Lombardis looked at each other; Silvio nodded. "My father is facing a bit of a dilemma," Vito said. "My sister, Jeannine, is married to a man who has no regard for our family, our ways, or my sister."

"What's that mean, exactly?"

"It means he beats the blue Jesus out of her every night. It's a problem that needs to be remedied."

"You don't have the resources to take care of this?" I asked.

"Of course. However, my father would like to keep his distance from this one. My sister, for reasons that I can't explain, thinks this creep walks on water and smacks her around because he loves her. I've offered to handle it, but she doesn't want any outside interference in their marriage. Once he's out of the picture, we'll deal with her mental health issues. My father wants him gone, and he wants to be able to raise his right hand to God and tell my sister that neither he nor one of his capos had anything to do with it."

"I see."

"That's why I'm doing the talking, and not my father."

Silvio nodded.

Word games are a very big thing in the mob.

(Note: Here's something I've never understood. If you can't control your temper and are inclined to beat your wife, for the love of the Madonna, don't marry a Mafia princess. It's not going to end well for you. No, I don't believe it's okay to smack your wife under any circumstance. I'm just making a point about the inherent dangers of punching the daughter of a crime boss who is most likely dealing with his own anger management issues.)

Vito handed me a photo of his brother-in-law. "His name is Philip Murphy."

"Murphy? So he's not . . ."

"No. He's Irish, stupid, and not involved in our business. He just likes to take the money we give to my sister." He handed me an index card. On it were two of the bars he frequented, with addresses.

I memorized the information and handed it back to Vito. "Burn that paper."

Vito said, "When?"

"I don't think it will be necessary to make an extra trip to Rochester."

"So, today?"

"If I can find him. Where's he work?"

"He's got an automobile repair garage. He's a mechanic. Don't try anything there. It's on a busy street and there are too many people around. Try the Blue Harbor Grill first. He's banging the barmaid and likes to hang out there after work. Plus, he'll have a couple pints in the tank by then."

"What's he drive?"

"A white company van, mostly."

"Okay." There was a moment of silence. "About my fee."

"What about it?"

"I take it up front."

"Don't take this personal, Mr. Cipriani, but I don't pay the gardener until the flower beds are edged and the sidewalk swept," Vito said. "When the job is finished, you'll get your fee."

This is not the way I worked. "With all due respect, Mr. Lombardi, when the job is over, I want to put as many miles between myself and Mr. Murphy as quickly as possible. Returning here could muddy the waters for both of us."

"When the job is complete, you come see me."

I was on their turf, and there was no room for debate. I left and continued to worry that this was a massive setup. I picked up a burger and diet cola at a fast-food drive-through, gassed up the car, pissed, then drove around until I saw a van with Murphy Auto Repair stenciled on the side parked outside of the Blue Harbor. It all seemed too perfect; he was right where they said he would be. I settled back into my seat, watching from a couple hundred feet down the street.

Murphy was in the bar another two hours before I saw him come out and fumble with the keys getting into the car. I assumed he was drunk and could be easily goaded into doing something stupid. I drove up as he was pulling out, cut him off and laid on the horn. As I passed, I flipped him off. That's all it took. He started following me up close, and twice bumped the Galaxie. In the rearview mirror, I could see him flipping me off; he was flashing his lights for me to pull over. We were in an old industrial area that reminded me of the warehouse district in Steubenville, and I felt like I was on familiar ground. My 9-mil was in my lap. My plan was to turn down an alley between two abandoned brick buildings and stop. I'd wait for him to open the door and try to drag me out of the car. I'd put two in his chest and go get my money.

But when I turned into the alley, he didn't follow. Pussy, I thought. I didn't want to back out into the street, fearing he might have turned around and would be waiting for me. He could ram the side of my car before I saw him coming. I decided to drive on through the alley and make another run at him tomorrow. I dropped the Galaxie into gear and started creeping forward, keeping my eyes on the rearview mirror, waiting for the ambush.

It came, but not from the rear. What a rookie mistake. My attention was so focused on the mirror and the maw leading into the alley, that I didn't look forward until the first bullet hit my windshield. I heard it go past my right ear as a spiderweb of cracks spread over the glass. I laid down, and a second bullet went through the glass right above the steering wheel. It would have been a kill shot if I had not ducked. My pistol had fallen to the floor. I grabbed it and peeked over the dash. Through a sliver of unbroken glass, I could see Murphy coming toward the car, a revolver in his hand of his extended arm. This guy was no mechanic; he was a pro.

I opened the passenger-side door and fired two blind shots in his direction. He swore, then fired a bullet that buried itself into the warehouse wall to my right. Chips of brick flew into the open door. I reached outside, rested the side of my hand on the fender and took another shot. The gunfire sounded like cannonade in the narrow alley. I took a fourth shot. It may have hit him. He was running back toward his van with a hand cupped over the side of his face.

Maybe he wasn't a pro. A pro would have kept coming after me. Maybe he was just an Irish mechanic with a bad temper and a .38-caliber snub nose. I closed the door and kicked what was left of the windshield onto the hood. The car was still running. I slammed it into reverse and floored it, backing out of the alley as busted glass slid off the hood and into the gravel.

I was shaking as I pointed the Galaxie west and headed toward the interstate. It shimmied between forty-five and fifty-five, and shards of busted glass were dancing all over the dashboard. It was the first time in my life that I had botched a hit. Silvio Lombardi had been smart not to pay me in advance. I didn't know if I had been set up, or if it was just a bad day at the office. I almost hoped it was a setup. At least that way I wouldn't have been bested by a drunken Irish mechanic. Either way, I was going home without my payday, and it looked like Little Tommy was right. I *had* lost my fastball.

Fortunately, I had filled up the gas tank, just like Carlo had taught me. I was driving down the freeway with no windshield, picking glass out of my clothes and hair and knocking down the clingers that hung from the molding around the windshield opening like icicles. It was getting dark, so the lack of a windshield didn't attract the attention of the cops, but the rushing air kept drying out my eyes. I got the car back to the warehouse and drove the Cutlass home. At that point, it qualified as a bad day, but I was ten minutes away from it getting worse. I was about three steps inside my apartment when a kidney stone broke loose, or whatever happens when you get a kidney stone. The pain was so jarring that it dropped me to my knees, and I thought for a moment that maybe one of Murphy's bullets had hit me in the gut. I know that doesn't make sense, but the pain was short-circuiting the rational thought process. It was awful. The damn stone was riding a bucking bronco and giving it the spurs. I curled up on the bathroom floor, spiked a fever, threw up twice, pissed blood, passed out from the pain, and sad as this is, shit myself. By the time I passed the stone late the next morning, my bathroom looked like the site of an exorcism. As things turned out, getting shot at was the better part of my day.

* * *

After the stone passed, I skipped going to the diner and took the longest shower of my life. Afterward, I wrapped myself in my bathrobe and stretched out on the couch and slept for the rest of the day. The next morning, I went over to see Nickels.

"Where in hell have you been?" he asked. "I ain't seen you forever."

"What are you talking about? I was here the other day, right before I left for Rochester."

"What the hell were you doing in Rochester?"

"We talked about this. I told you I had a job with Silvio Lombardi."

"You didn't tell me that."

I took a breath. I had to keep reminding myself that this wasn't the old Nickels. He couldn't help this. "Nickels, I asked if you thought I might be getting set up as a target, which may have happened, and you started talking about Hirohito and Hitler and Stalin."

"You know, Angelo, I'm starting to think that you're the one who needs to see a doctor. Where are you getting this stuff, and what do I care about those assholes? They're all dead, you know?"

CHAPTER 16

May 1976

THE BRAZENNESS OF the attack by the Gemelli family made it evident that they didn't fear the Fortunatos. They had the backing of the Cleveland mob and didn't believe we had enough dry powder or the balls to launch a major counterattack or defend our perimeter. The Gemellis were like a mouthy little kid from the Spaghetto who thought he could taunt and bully with impunity because his big brother was standing behind him. This was a miscalculation of major proportions on their part. We would retaliate but on our terms.

We would wait until they let down their guard.

After Carlo and I disposed of the predator in Donora, Big Tommy asked Carlo how the mission had gone. Carlo responded, "The kid might end up causing a worldwide lead shortage. He was still pumping bullets into the guy's skull fifteen minutes after he was in hell. He's green, but he didn't hesitate when it was time to take out the trash."

With Big Tommy's blessing, I began preparing for my battle with the Gemellis. First of all, I needed a new identity. Muzzie Lollini was able to use his contacts with the Chicago mob to get me a driver's license and a Social Security card. Muzzie had business cards made up to go with it. My new name was Pete Cola. I was from Indianapolis, where I worked as a field rep for Consolidated Bearings, a ball bearing distributor. I was divorced, no kids. I had a car registered in Pete's name with Indiana license plates that was kept in the basement of the Fort Steuben Brewery warehouse. For weeks, none of the capos called me anything but Pete. For the time being, Angelo Cipriani was dead. I had to get used to my new identity so that it became second nature.

(Note: I later learned that there had been a real Pete Cola. I don't know what happened to Pete, but I think we can assume things didn't end well.)

Frankie Gem had a known weakness for women, particularly those who were not Mrs. Frankie Gemelli. We planned to use this weakness to our advantage. Guys who are always sporting boners tend to not think very clearly. Their situational awareness decreases as their erection increases. It's science.

"We'll need a decoy," I told Big Tommy.

"Got anyone in mind?" he asked.

"We need someone we can trust to keep their mouth shut."

"Obviously," he said. I looked at him without speaking. He nodded and said, "Okay. Maybe. I'll talk to her."

"Her" was Roxanne Louise Marquette, Big Tommy's girlfriend. She had come to town from Fort Wayne to work in one of the Fortunato brothels. She was a smoke show with wine-red hair, eyes the color of a Carolina sky, and a two-hundred-dollar-a-day cocaine addiction. Tommy fell in love and wanted to save her, so he pulled Roxanne out of the brothel and sent her to a rehab clinic somewhere in Kentucky. When she returned, he gave her an allowance and put her up in a penthouse suite at the Fort Steuben Hotel. Over the years, I had been out with Big Tommy on many occasions. Around Steubenville, he was always with his wife, Rosebella. When we went out of town, to Pittsburgh, Columbus, or Las Vegas, he would take Roxanne.

Big Tommy never flaunted his relationship with Roxanne. In fact, for years, he thought he was putting one over on Rosebella. Then came the evening when they went to the Federal Terrace for dinner, and Roxanne was at a table with a couple of friends. Rosebella never broke stride or missed a beat. She said, "Oh, look, Tom, your girlfriend's here, too." Of course, as every male in the world would do, Big Tommy vehemently denied even knowing Roxanne. Rosebella just smiled, and that was the last word she ever said about it.

(Note: Yes, I see the hypocrisy of Mr. Fortunato dressing me down for falling in love with a hooker, while his son kept a former prostitute in a penthouse suite at the Fort Steuben Hotel. However, those are the privileges of being a crime lord.)

The Gemellis controlled the Teamsters union in Youngstown and owned both the landfill and the only refuse company permitted to operate in Mahoning and Trumbull counties—Eastern Ohio Refuse and Hauling. It had a nice, non-mob sounding name for a corrupt money-laundering organization. Frankie served on the board of directors of the American Garbage Packers Association, and we knew he would be attending its annual convention in Jacksonville, Florida. What better time to strike than when he was a thousand miles from home and pounding alcohol like a good conventioneer?

I wanted to use Roxanne to trap Frankie Gem. Once a cock hound like Frankie got a look at her, he would no longer be in control of his faculties. I knew how guys like Frankie operated. When they picked up a girl, they would never take her back to their room. They always went back to the girl's room. That's because once they've nutted, they can get up and leave. If the girl is in his room, there was always the chance she wouldn't leave after sex.

(Note: Yes, I know that's crude, but we're talking about Frankie Gem, not Prince Charming.)

Muzzie got Roxanne a fake identity – Dixie Lee Jackson of Austin, Texas – and we headed for Orlando. We drove to Columbia, South Carolina, and spent the night. We left just before eight the next morning and arrived in Jacksonville about noon. On the way down, I kept asking Roxanne to review the plan with me. When I suggested we review it a fourth time, she looked at me and said,

"Angelo, do you know how many times I've seduced men back to my room and put them in a defenseless position?" Before I could respond, she said, "Wait. Don't answer that. I might consider your answer insulting. Let's just assume that I'm perfectly capable of luring Frankie Gemelli back to the room. And for the record, I've never had a man turn me down. So just relax and do your part. I've got my end covered."

Dixie Lee Jackson had booked a hotel room at the Palms Hotel, which was attached to the convention center. We stopped at a diner a couple of miles from the hotel for lunch. We drank coffee out of cups that had handles shaped like mermaids with their little pink breasts exposed. I don't know why I remember that. Maybe because it was the kind of thing I never saw growing up in a Catholic household in the Spaghetto.

While I waited at the diner, Roxanne was going to go check into the hotel under her alias. When I handed her the key to the car, I said, "When you park the car, back it into the slot in the garage. Don't lock the doors, and put the key under the mat on the driver's side."

"Okay. Why?"

"You don't want the car locked in case one of us needs to leave in a hurry. Let's say we get into a situation with Frankie and things go south—maybe I get shot and you've got to make a run for it. If the key is in my pocket, you're screwed. This way, you get to the car, it's unlocked, reach under the mat and you're off and running."

Carlo would be proud, I thought.

She said, "Why didn't you just get an extra key made?"

This girl, she was a handful.

She got the phone number from the pay phone on the wall near our booth, then left to check in. I had another coffee and massaged the mermaid's ceramic breasts while I waited. It rang thirty minutes later. She said, "Room 2107." I put on my sunglasses, hailed a cab, and went to the hotel.

There was nothing to do but wait until evening when the garbage packers would hit the hotel bar. She had seen several photos of

Frankie Gem and knew her target. She wanted room service for dinner, but I nixed it. The only other person I wanted in the room was Frankie Gemelli. "We'll eat later," I said. I didn't know how she could possibly eat. My stomach felt like the core of a volcano, and I was popping antacids by the handful.

When she came out of the bathroom at 6:45, she literally took my breath away. She turned around once and said, "Do you think this will work?"

"If he's breathing, it'll work."

"Ahh, Angelo, that's the nicest thing anyone's said to me in a long time."

There was not a red-blooded man on the face of the earth who wouldn't have melted in her presence. She was wearing maroon pumps, black seamed stockings, and a maroon dress that was tight over her hips and rear, and had one of those—what do you call them, plunging necklines? She was showing plenty of the right kind of skin. Stunning is the only word that described her, and I had to keep reminding myself that she was Big Tommy's girlfriend.

She looked in the mirror, rolled her lips together to even out the lipstick, then started toward the door. As she walked by me, she reached out and let her fingernails scrape down my jawline to my chin. It tingled my loins.

Big Tommy's girlfriend. Big Tommy's girlfriend. Big Tommy's girlfriend.

As she grabbed the door handle, she turned and said, "Battle stations, love. It's almost showtime."

For the dozenth time that afternoon, I snugged the silencer on my 9-millimeter, clicked off the safety, and checked to make sure a round was chambered. I took a quick piss, then moved into the closet. It was tight, but I was able to squeeze myself into the front corner. It had two slatted doors, and I could see the carpet in the room through the lower openings. When I heard her key enter the lock, it would be my last breath before I moved.

Dixie Lee walked into the hotel bar and spotted Frankie Gem with a group of six or seven other guys. Three were on barstools; the others clustered around. They were loud and laughing. She assumed he was at least five scotch and waters to the good. The bartender came over, and Dixie Lee ordered a rum and Coke. As she stirred it with a plastic swizzle stick, she could feel Frankie's eyes burning in on her. She finally looked over and made eye contact with him. She offered the faintest of smiles before returning her attention back to the drink.

It wasn't a minute later that she saw him leave his friends and head her way. She pretended not to notice until he slid onto the barstool next to her. She would tell me the conversation went something like this:

Frankie said, "How is it that a spectacularly gorgeous woman like you comes in here alone?"

She sipped her drink through the little plastic straw, then said in a breathy voice, "Well, if you come in with someone, you might not have the opportunity to meet someone better-looking and more interesting." She raised an eyebrow.

"Well, you're in luck, because I'm a very interesting guy."

"Is that a fact?"

"It is a fact. So, maybe we could go back to your room and you could find out how truly interesting I am."

She reached up and gently ran her fingers down his necktie. "I would love to go back up to my room with you, handsome. The only problem is, I paid a lot of money to get here from Texas, and now I'm finding myself a little short on cash. Do you think we could work out an arrangement?"

"I'm sure we could. How much of an arrangement are we talking about?"

"Five hundred dollars."

His face took on a pained look. "I can't do five hundred, but I'd go two hundred."

(Note: In defense of that scumball Frankie Gemelli, he was probably used to Youngstown, Ohio, prices.)

Roxanne said, "Oh, no. I'm sorry. I mistook you for a real player. The two-hundred-dollar girls are down the street at the corner. Good luck with them."

She pulled her clutch purse off the bar and turned on her stool to leave when he said, "Wait, wait, wait." He nodded and smiled. "Okay, a woman who knows when she's dealing from a position of power. I like that. So, what exactly do I get for five hundred dollars?"

She put her right hand on the back of his neck, digging her lacquered nails into the skin, and breathing enough hot air into his ear to launch a balloon, said, "Anything you want, for as long as you want it."

"Let's go."

She unsnapped the clasp on her purse and said, "In advance, handsome."

As furtively as possible, he pulled his wallet from his suit coat pocket, counted out ten fifty-dollar bills, and slipped them into her purse. She smiled, took hold of his elbow and walked across the lobby to the elevator.

I took the deep breath when the key hit the lock. I saw her shoes pass by, then his. Through a small crack I had left between the closet doors, I watched Frankie Gemelli start to take off his suit coat. She grabbed his lapels and said, "Uh-uh, handsome. That's my job." She ran her lips over the side of his face and moaned while she undid his necktie and top button, then gently started pulling off the jacket until it was halfway down his back, pinning his arms against his side. She then dropped to her knees and began panting and wrestling with his belt and zipper. He had zero situational awareness. She had stolen it. When his pants and underwear were around his ankles, I pushed open the closet door closest to me. I could see myself in the reflection in the mirror on the other side of the room. Fortunately, Frankie had his head back and his eyes closed, enjoying a moment that wouldn't last long.

I grabbed the collar of his suit coat with my left hand and jammed the pistol into the back of his head with the right.

Roxanne rolled away. Frankie said, "You fuckin' whore. You set me up for a hustle?"

"Shut up," I said.

Frankie Gem looked into the mirror, squinting to get a good look at me. "You have no idea in the world who you're screwin' with," he said.

"You're wrong, Frankie. I know exactly who I'm screwin' with, and just so you know, this is no hustle; it's payback from Big Tommy Fortunato."

I know that Carlo said we didn't get style points. Just shoot them and be done with it. But I wanted Frankie Gemelli to live just long enough to know his death came straight from Steubenville, Ohio. For just an instant, I took my eyes off the mark to see his reflection in the mirror. I couldn't tell if the look on his face was fear or resignation, or simply disbelief. It didn't matter. I fired a single round from my silenced 9-millimeter into the base of his skull. Frankie pitched forward onto the bed, his half-naked body twitching as his central nervous system shorted out and sent a shower of electrical charges through every nerve.

"Oh, my God," Roxanne said. "Shoot him again. He's not dead."

"He's dead. He just doesn't know it yet. Get out of that dress and into something that won't draw the attention of every guy in the hotel, and let's get the hell out of here."

She went to the bathroom to change. I wrapped my handkerchief around the silencer, unscrewed it, and put it in Roxanne's suitcase. I put the 9-millimeter in my waistband, then walked around the foot of the bed for a last look at Frankie Gem. There was a silver chain and a St. Christopher medal around his neck. St. Christopher supposedly offers travelers protection from sudden death. I wrapped the medal in my hand, let the chain slide between my fingers, then gave it a quick pull. I was putting it in my pants pocket when Roxanne came out of the bathroom in a plain black skirt, a white blouse, flats, and her hair wrapped on the top of her head. "Did you go through his wallet?" she asked.

"No."

"Why not?"

"Carlo says it's bad form."

Her beautiful face screwed up like it was the most insane thing she had ever heard. "Well, it's a good thing that Carlo's not here, isn't it?" she said. "Give me your handkerchief."

She wrapped her hand around the cloth and reached into his jacket pocket and pulled out the wallet. Using the tip of a fingernail, she splayed the leather and plucked out twelve hundred dollars in fifties and twenties. "Cheap son of a bitch. He had all this money and he tried to work me down to two hundred dollars," she said, dropping the wallet on the floor. Roxanne counted out six hundred dollars and handed it to me. "Don't tell Carlo."

"Trust me, I won't. When he was in the bar, did you see a bodyguard?"

"I don't know. There were five, maybe six guys around him."

"You can't take a chance being seen in the lobby. Take the stairs."

"We're twenty-one floors up."

"Sorry for your luck. Go out the side of the hotel and walk to the gas station next door. I'll be there in ten minutes."

We turned off the lights and walked out of the room together. I put the "Do Not Disturb" hanger on the doorknob. That might give us an extra day before the maids found him. Roxanne disappeared in the staircase before the elevator stopped on our floor. There were two guys in the elevator, talking about garbage. I stepped in and kept my head down. I didn't lift it up until I had cleared the lobby and was heading toward the parking garage. I threw the suitcase in the back seat and met Roxanne in the gas station lot.

As I pulled away, she said, "I'm famished. And don't be taking me to some cheap dive. I've earned a good meal."

We headed north and found a seafood restaurant near the airport. We had a bottle of cabernet and calamari for an appetizer. Roxanne ordered the New England clambake and I had fried shrimp. I'd never had shrimp in my life until the first Christmas party that Mr. Fortunato hosted. I was afraid to eat them at first. After that night, I rarely passed on them.

We were back on the road before eleven PM. I was running on fried shrimp and adrenaline. I think I could have made it all the way to Ohio, but Roxanne said no dice. It had been a long day, her performance had been flawless, she had to watch Frankie Gem get his brains splattered with his pants down around his ankles, and by God, she wanted a room with a comfortable bed. Fine, I said. We drove a couple hours north and found a hotel near Savannah. We were up early the next morning and headed back. I dropped Roxanne off at the Fort Steuben Hotel and went straight to the compound. It was almost eight o'clock. Big Tommy was circling the pool with a screen, fishing leaves from the water. The tree frogs and crickets were singing in unison. As I approached him, he said, "Well?"

I held out a fisted hand until he put his beneath it, then I opened mine, dropping Frankie Gemelli's St. Christopher medal into his palm. "Here's a little keepsake for you," I said. "St. Christopher must have been on vacation, because it turned out to be a bad night for Frankie."

Big Tommy bounced the medal in his hand, a thin smile pursing his lips. "Carlo doesn't approve of taking trophies, you know."

"Yeah, I know. I probably did a couple of things that Carlo wouldn't approve of, but Frankie Gem is just as dead."

We went to his office. He normally never asked for the particulars of an operation, but in this case, he wanted a blow-by-blow account. "So he died knowing it was payback for killing my father?" he asked.

"Without question."

"Good . . . that's good . . . very good. He can think about that while he roasts in hell."

Before I left, Big Tommy handed me an envelope containing the biggest wad of cash I have ever seen in my life. "This is a lot, Tom," I said.

"You earned it." He leaned back in his chair. "And Roxanne did good, huh?"

"She's a champ." I held up the envelope. "You want that I should cut her in on this?"

"No, I'll take care of her."

"That's good." I got up to go. "One Gemelli down, one to go."

"That's right. This might look like a random murder to the cops, but I'll guarantee that Tony Gem will know who was behind it. Let's see how good he sleeps after this."

* * *

Here's something I didn't tell Big Tommy. There was a reason why I wanted Roxanne as my partner. Yeah, she was easy on the eyes, and I knew she was up to the job, but there was another reason. I was afraid if I took one of the other girls from the brothel, that after she'd held up her end of the deal, Big Tommy might consider her a liability and tell me that I was the only witness he wanted leaving the hotel room. I loved Big Tommy, but he was a crime boss. I knew he trusted Roxanne, and he definitely wouldn't punch her ticket. That's why she was my choice.

For the record, I've never whacked a woman. Carlo did. A couple of years before I came on the scene, Dommie the Clip dated this hairdresser from Mingo Junction for more than a year. About the time she thought he was going to propose, he broke up with her. Apparently, Dommie had been loose-lipped between the sheets, and after the breakup she threatened to go to the FBI with everything he had told her.

Big mistake.

I asked Carlo about it once, and all he'd say was, "She should have walked away and shut her mouth."

CHAPTER

17

July 2019

I'D JUST GOTTEN back to the apartment from visiting Nichols when the call came in. I was expecting it. "Angelo here," I said.

"How'd you manage to fuck up Rochester this badly?" Little Tommy asked.

"I set a trap, but things went south."

"That's your explanation? Things went south. I get you a job for ten large with one of the most powerful bosses in the east and you tell me things went south?"

"You know how these things go. It's complicated."

"It's not complicated. In fact, it's very simple. All you had to do was put a bullet in his ear instead of shooting it off."

"I think it might have been a setup. That guy acted like a pro."

"A pro? He's a fuckin' mechanic with an eighth-grade education; that's who schooled you. Now Silvio's pissed. I vouched for you, and he thought he hired a pro, and yet that one-eared bastard is still walking around today."

"Tell Silvio I'll take care of it."

"Oh, no. No, no, no. You don't go anywhere near Rochester. The guy reported the shooting to the cops. He said he was ambushed and that he believed his father-in-law was behind it. The cops have been to Silvio's place, asking questions. I'm probably going to have to drive to Rochester and kiss his ring or his ass or whatever he wants kissed to square this. I want to tell you something, if this comes back on me, it's going to be a bad day for you, old man."

* * *

Later that afternoon, I drove up to Robinson Township near Pittsburgh to buy new clothes for my first date with Carolyn. It was one of those huge men's stores, and a young kid with gauges in his ears—what the hell's with that, anyway?—an eyebrow piercing, and a crappy attitude acted like it was a major undertaking to direct me to the sport coats. It was nothing like the old days, when Morris Supovitz fussed all over me at the Phil-Mor. I don't know why I continue to make those comparisons. *Nothing* is like the old days.

A woman about my age with a cloth tape around her neck saw me struggling and came over to help. We tried on a few sport coats before I settled on one that was navy with orange window panes. I looked pretty snappy in it, if I do say so myself. I bought a new white shirt, a pair of khakis, and a pair of fake alligator skin loafers and a matching belt. I also bought some cologne. The good stuff, not the colored water you get at the drugstore.

All this I could ill afford, but I needed to look sharp. I knew I was punching above my weight class with Carolyn, so the pressure was on. If she didn't like me, or I screwed up our first date, she'd probably change her phone number, and I'd have to find a new place to eat. I called her the same evening that she gave me her number and stuttered and stammered through the entire call. I was always free and breezy at the diner, because I never thought I had a chance with her. But now that things were real, my collar was tightening up.

I got a haircut Saturday morning, then drove down to the Dodge dealership in Martins Ferry, where one of my nephews was the head of the repair center. I told him, "I need to rent a car, and a nice one."

He smirked and said, "Why? You got a big date or something?"

"Just get me a car, wiseass."

"We've got loaners for our customers, but I'm all out. How long do you need it?"

"Just for tonight."

"Let me see if I can set you up for an overnight test drive. We'd need it back by noon tomorrow."

"This is why you're my favorite nephew."

I'd made dinner reservations for seven o'clock at Ernie's Esquire, a classy place on the hill in Bethlehem, just outside of Wheeling. I picked her up at six. When she opened the door, I felt like I was eighteen years old again. She was gorgeous and smelled like springtime. I didn't mention this to her, of course, but most of the time she smelled like french fry grease. The hazards of the job. Her hair was up, and there were little ringlets hanging just outside her eyes. She was wearing a lime green dress with a slit on the side, white pearls, and cream heels. I didn't realize how little that waitressing uniform did for her figure. I'm here to tell you, Roxanne Marquette had nothing on this gal.

For years I had been grinding my teeth and agonizing over Little Tommy Fortunato and my place in the universe. At that moment, none of that mattered. I wanted my place to be right beside her for as long as I was taking in oxygen. I said, "Sweet Madonna, you're a vision."

"And you're sweet for saying so," she said.

When we walked out the door, she saw the black 2019 Dodge Challenger sitting in the driveway. "Where did you get the car?" she asked.

"How do you know it's not mine?"

"Because I've seen you in that boat you usually drive. Actually, I usually hear you coming down the street before I see you." She laughed at her own little joke.

"I'm test-driving it for tonight. If I like it, I might buy it. We'll see."

I opened the door and looked away, fearing she would see the scope of that massive lie spread across my face.

At Ernie's, we had a window booth overlooking the valley below. We split a shrimp cocktail and a bottle of pinot noir. After we ordered our entrees, I said, "Tell me about yourself."

"What do you want to know?" she asked.

"Everything."

"It'll be a short story. There's not much to tell."

"That's not true. Everyone has a story."

"Well, let's just say there's nothing interesting to tell."

I smiled and said, "I'll be the judge of that."

She had grown up Carolyn Marie Gregorski on the south side of Steubenville. Her father had been killed in an accident at the Wheeling-Pittsburgh Steel plant in Mingo Junction when she was only a few weeks old. Like my father, he had been a first-generation immigrant. She had been married three times. "I got pregnant at the end of my junior year in high school," she said. "We got married, and that was my second mistake. I was barely seventeen and he was only a year older. I thought we were going to have a family and be happy forever. He thought he was going to be a rock 'n' roll star. Eventually, I realized he was more interested in the band than me, so we got a dissolution. The next guy was a plumber with three kids under the age of five. He didn't want a wife; he wanted a babysitter. I think the nicest thing I can say about him is that he was jealous and stupid."

"Why did you marry him?" I asked.

"Because I was young, single, working at the Green Mill Restaurant, and raising my son on my own. He had a good job, and at the time that made him look like a life raft in the middle of the ocean."

It was ten years before she married Edgar Sweetwater. He was a high school math teacher at Wintersville High School and perfect. "He was everything the first two husbands weren't—educated, attentive, loving, and generous."

"Sounds like it was what you were looking for."

"It was, until the night he confided in me that he had been having an affair with one of his students."

"Not good."

"Not good at all. Wintersville is a small town, so of course everyone knew but me. The school let him resign, and it was all covered up."

"Didn't her parents come after him?"

"You mean *his* parents?"

"Oh."

"No, they didn't. I'm sure they simply wanted it to all go away, as did I."

She finished her pinot noir, and I refilled her glass. "When it comes to men, I choose very poorly."

My eyebrows arched. "Not exactly a ringing endorsement for me."

She slid her left hand across the table and rested it on mine. "Let me correct that," she said. "I've chosen poorly in the past, but certainly not tonight."

"Much better."

I was tingling from toes to treetops.

We had a wonderful evening. We ate steaks, laughed, told stories, and shared a chocolate lava cake for dessert. As we walked back to the car, she took hold of my left arm and pulled in close. Her breast pressed against my arm. That simple act of affection caused a reaction that reminded me of how long it had been since I'd been with a woman.

On the drive home, Carolyn asked, "Do you have relatives in the area?"

"Some. There were eleven of us kids. Seven of us are still alive. I've got nieces and nephews strewn all over the tristate. I think there's thirty-four or thirty-five of them. My parents died a long time ago. How about you?"

"Not much. I have a younger brother who lives out around Carrollton, but we haven't spoken in years. His choice, not mine. My son retired from the Navy. He and his wife live in San Diego with my two grandsons and granddaughter. I get to see them once or twice a year. I was raised by my Aunt Paula. She's my only relative in the area. God bless her, she's in her eighties and still going strong. She still lives in the house I grew up in."

"What happened to your mother?"

"She was around, but she had a lot of psychological problems and addiction issues. She remarried after my father died, but he abandoned us. I don't know if her psychological problems ran him off or if his running off exacerbated her mental health issues. I guess it doesn't matter, either way. My aunt said it was a good thing that he left. I guess he wasn't a very good man. My brother and I were fortunate that we had my Aunt Paula."

"I've always thought there should be a special corner of hell reserved for guys who abandon their families." (Note: Yes, I realize that it is both hypocritical and absurd for a guy who made his living as a mob hitman to pass judgment on other people for lesser crimes, but I have opinions, too.) "Where did he go? Did you ever find out?"

She shook her head. "No. I was pretty young when he left. I hardly remember him. According to my aunt, he told my mother that he was going down to Wellman's Bar for a beer. He walked out our front door, and that's the last time we ever saw him."

"Wellman's Bar?"

"Uh-huh."

Icy pinpricks rolled up my spine and expanded out into my shoulders and scalp, and without considering my actions, I said, "Your stepfather was Woodrow Golightly?" The words were out of my mouth before I had a chance to engage my brain.

Her head whipped toward me like she'd been slapped, a perplexed look consuming her face. "Yes," she said. "Woodrow Golightly. How did you know that?"

It was dark in the car, and I hoped she couldn't see my nervous swallow. "I remember reading about it in the newspaper."

"You remember reading about a guy going missing fifty years ago?"

My throat was tightening. What I really remembered was a meeting at the abandoned Fort Steuben Brewery warehouse between Alphonse Fortunato and Deputy Chief Armand Mickelson, in which the police were unable to get charges filed against a pervert who was molesting a three-year-old girl. I did the math. That little girl had grown up to be the beautiful woman sitting by my side. He didn't abandon his family. Carlo clubbed him with a crowbar behind Wellman's Bar. His body taken to a dog food manufacturer in East Liverpool where it was thrown into a front-end loader and dropped into a processor that reduced Mr. Golightly to a pulp the consistency of wood glue. I know this for a fact, because I went to East Liverpool with Carlo and waited until the mass was pushed into a slurry and on its way to a pressure cooker.

I thought, perhaps, that a first date might not be the time to divulge what I knew about her stepfather.

"I've always been fascinated with missing persons," I said. "Jimmy Hoffa, Amelia Earhart, the Lindbergh kid. It's a thing with me."

She looked at me, and her left eye crinkled. "I don't think you're being honest with me, Angelo. But I don't have any other plausible explanation for why you would remember my stepfather's name."

"Maybe we should just leave it there."

And we did.

When we got to her house, she said, "Angelo, this was one of the best nights I've had in a long, long time. Thank you so much. I'd invite you in, but I've always heard that girls who sleep with guys on the first date don't get asked back out for a second. So . . ." She got up on her toes and kissed me on the cheek. "I'll just say good night here."

As I was driving home, I turned on the oldies station on the radio. Katrina and the Waves were singing *Walking on Sunshine.*

I said, "Me too, baby, me too."

C H A P T E R

18

May 1976–June 1977

Four days after I returned from Jacksonville, the Steubenville *Herald-Star* ran an Associated Press story that was buried in the first section alongside a lingerie ad. The two-column headline read:

Youngstown Businessman Found Shot to Death in Florida

> Francisco Gemelli, a businessman and owner of the Eastern Ohio Refuse and Hauling Company in Youngstown, Ohio, was found shot to death in a Jacksonville, Fla., hotel room, where he was attending a convention.
>
> A later paragraph read:
>
> Police are searching for an Austin, Texas, woman identified as Dixie Lee Jackson for questioning in connection with the murder.

We had information that Tony Gemelli, terrified for his life, left Youngstown right after his brother's funeral and was hiding out in

Reno or Las Vegas. When Big Tommy heard this, he said, "That's fine. Eventually, every rat sticks his nose out of the sewer."

With Frankie dead and Tony in hiding, Big Tommy said it was time to fix bayonets and launch an assault on our perimeters in East Liverpool and Beaver County, Pennsylvania. The Youngstown mob had been acting with impunity, and their couriers and bag men had no concern for their own safety. Another big mistake. We took out nine of their men in a two-day blitz. We also took the gambling proceeds they were carrying. Connie and Ricky Bones, Nickels, and Jimmy Beans set up territories to monitor, with low-level associates in the bars as stakeouts. In the next week, three more Gemelli associates were killed. We didn't lose a single man.

The bloodbath was national news. The FBI was investigating. After the twelfth member of the Gemelli organization was killed, Big Tommy got a phone call from John Scardino, who had taken over the Cleveland mob after a car bomb blew Lenny Esposito through the windshield of his Lincoln Continental. Scardino requested a meeting in Akron to discuss "the Youngstown situation." Big Tommy agreed, and the two men met for lunch at the Tangier Restaurant.

Scardino said, "Your actions are bringing a lot of unnecessary attention to the Youngstown operation."

"When you slaughter my father, uncle, and a long-time associate, that's what you get in return—a pile of bodies and unnecessary attention," Big Tommy said.

"What's happening is not good for anybody, and it's bad for business."

"I couldn't agree more, John. So you tell that trained chimp of yours, Tony Gemelli, to stay out of Beaver and Allegheny counties, and don't go near East Liverpool, and maybe we won't have any more problems."

"Maybe?"

"I'm not making any promises. And let's remember something: My grandfather and Lenny Esposito established those boundaries years ago. Tony Gemelli takes his marching orders from you. He wouldn't dare cross them without your knowledge or your blessing, so let's not pretend that your hands are clean."

Scardino wiped his mouth on a napkin and swallowed, a line of red heat climbing up his neck. "I think you need to remember who you're talking to, Tom. Give me trouble, and I'll back Tony's play with more men and more guns than you can imagine. I'll make sure the Gemellis control everything from Youngstown to Portsmouth."

"You heard my terms. Keep the Gemellis out of my territory, and we won't have any problems."

I wasn't at the meeting, but Muzzie Lollini gave me the account I just relayed. I swear to God, Big Tommy Fortunato had balls the size of cantaloupes.

With the Gemellis in retreat, our operation was back in full business mode. The take from the three additional Pennsylvania counties was bringing in more money than anticipated. It more than doubled our Ohio Valley take. While the Gemellis had been defeated in the land battle, the war wasn't over for Big Tommy. Tony Gem still had to pay for the death of his father.

We knew that Tony had come out of hiding and was back in Youngstown running his operation. He had no doubt talked to Scardino, who had ordered him to limit his operation within the old borders. This doubtlessly infuriated Tony, who believed the Cleveland mob should have backed his play. It was good that he was angry with Scardino. It gave him less time to be concerned about us.

A year after I dusted Frankie Gem, I made my first reconnaissance mission into Youngstown. I had seen photos of Tony Gem, but I wanted to put eyes on him before we put a plan into place. I now had a moustache and hair feathered back over my ears and hanging over the collar of my shirt. I was still Pete Cola, the ball bearing rep from Indianapolis.

On a Thursday evening, I went to the Vine Cliff, an Italian restaurant in the Smokey Hollow section of Youngstown. The restaurant had reportedly been struggling, and the Gemellis offered to purchase a stake in the operation to help revive it. Once they had their foot in the door, they eventually muscled the original owner out of the picture and took over.

(Note: If that sounds familiar, it should. This sort of thing happened more often than you would think. Mr. Fortunato got a couple of restaurants, three car washes, a pizza parlor, a hotel in Weirton, and the Dairy Dream in Georges Run the same way. I loved Alphonse and Big Tommy, but I can't even begin to express what a bad move it is to go into business with the mob. It doesn't matter what kind of deal they make you up front; eventually they push you out the door.)

We had information that Tony Gem was spending a lot of time at the Vine Cliff. He liked the attention he got as the owner and supposedly was there nearly every night, glad-handing and playing the big shot.

I walked in wearing an old, shabby gray suit, a solid blue tie loosened at the collar, and brown shoes that I had intentionally scuffed up. I was trying to look like a corporate gear, a guy who spent too much time on the road and pounded enough gin and tonics to simultaneously kill all his brain cells and his liver. I sat at the end of the bar, which gave me a view of most of the restaurant. I ordered a gin and tonic and asked for a menu. When the bartender brought me a second gin and tonic, I asked what he recommended. He said the entire menu was good, but the chicken Parmesan and the lasagna were his favorites. I ordered the lasagna, which came with a salad and Italian bread. I had him bring me a merlot with my dinner.

Tony Gem walked into the restaurant at a little after seven, and every set of eyes in the place turned toward him. He was in his early forties and a magnificent physical specimen—slathered in muscle, his traps bulging between his shoulders and ears. His sculpted arms were massive, and he wore a golf shirt a size too small for added effect. He was handsome, with a wide jaw, a dimpled chin, and a beard so dark it looked purple. The guy was Samson in the flesh.

I concentrated on my salad, occasionally looking up to catch a glimpse of him as he worked the crowd. After twenty minutes of dancing around the room, he walked behind the bar, poured himself a bourbon, and looked over at me. "How you doin'?" he asked.

"It's a good night."

"How's the lasagna?"

"Going away, the best I've ever had."

"Yeah? Good to hear. The secret is to keep the layers very thin. It's my mother's recipe."

"Your mother's a goddess in the kitchen. This is phenomenal."

"She's passed, unfortunately."

"I'm sorry to hear that, but her legacy lives on in her food." I took my glass of merlot and offered it up as a salute. "To your mother." We tapped glasses. He seemed to appreciate the gesture.

He extended his hand and said, "I'm Tony. This is my restaurant."

"Nice to meet you, Tony. I'm Pete. This place is very nice. Homey. I like it."

"First time here?"

"Yeah. I'm in town on business. I was in a meeting today over at Youngstown Sheet and Tube. One of the guys recommended your place, said it was the best Italian in northeast Ohio. I gotta tell ya, I'm not disappointed."

"Good to hear. What's your business?"

"It's boring. I'm a rep for a ball bearing distributor."

"Do you buy your steel for your ball bearings from the Sheet and Tube?"

"No. We don't make ball bearings. We just distribute them."

He frowned. "Distribute ball bearings. That's a thing?"

"Oh, yeah. It's a big thing. You see . . ." I pulled a radial bearing out of my suit pocket; it was a prop that Muzzie had given me for just such an opportunity. "If a bearing goes out in the wheel of your car, whatta ya do? You just go down to the auto parts store and buy a new one. Right? No problem. But if you're General Motors, or Ford, or John Deere, and a bearing goes out on your assembly line, you've got to have a very specific bearing to get the line back up and running." I dropped the bearing back in my pocket. "When their assembly line goes down, they're hemorrhaging money like you can't imagine—easily over a million bucks an hour. So, what do you think they'd pay for the bearing that gets that line back up and running? The answer is, whatever we say. It's like extortion. I swear to Christ, it's like I'm in the Mafia or something."

I started laughing and he laughed, too, but not very much. I wanted him to think that I was so naïve that I had no idea in the world who I was talking to.

"Are you a salesman?"

I pulled out a business card and slid it across the bar to him. "Not sales. Marketing. I take the guys from the purchasing departments out golfing and to dinner, maybe pay for a lady, if that's what they want. I just make sure that when that ball bearing goes out, my company is the first one they call."

"So, when they need these bearings, you're the only one who has them?"

"We make an agreement with the manufacturers, so all sales go through us."

Tony Gem smiled. "That's a killer business model."

"No doubt. We've got all our customers by their short hairs. It's a beautiful thing." I wiped my lips with my napkin. "Can I ask you a question about your business?"

"Sure."

"I don't want to be insulting, but why the hell are you giving away this lasagna?"

His brow furrowed. "What do you mean?"

"I just paid seven ninety-nine for the best lasagna I've ever had, an Italian salad, and bread service. I guarantee you this, I could go down the street and find crappy lasagna for seven ninety-nine, and I'd probably pay extra for salad. People should be paying a premium for this. What was your mother's name?"

"Maria."

"Maria, whatever your last name is, original recipe lasagna. You charge twelve ninety-nine, and they pay extra for the salad."

"This is Youngstown, Ohio. People are only going to pay so much for . . ."

"Bullshit, Tony. I don't care if this is West Bumfuck, Egypt. People will pay for quality, and *this*, my friend . . ." I used my fork to point down at my lasagna. "Is quality."

Tony scratched at his chin, his brows bearing down on his nose as he considered this. "You really think it would go at that price?"

"I know I'm right. You work with me here, and I'll teach you how to squeeze balls."

I hit a nerve. He was insulted. His tone changed when he said, "You think I don't know how to squeeze balls?"

"Maybe you do, but not where this lasagna is concerned. You're leaving money on the table. If that was my mother's recipe, I'd call my brother-in-law in the frozen food business, and I'd have it in every grocery store in the country." I put a twenty and a five on the counter and extended my hand to Tony. "I've got to hit the road. It was nice meetin' ya, Tony."

"No, wait. I want to hear more about that frozen food thing. Can you stick around?"

I looked at my watch and pinched up my face a bit. "I've got a meeting in Pittsburgh in the morning."

"It's only an hour's drive. We close at nine. Stick around so we can talk. Whatta ya drinkin'?"

"Gin and tonic."

"Sit down. I'll set you up."

I slid back on my seat at the bar. This was supposed to be a reconnaissance mission, but the greedy bastard was leaning right into the pitch. When the last customer left at ten after nine, Tony told the other bartender that she could go home. A busboy was moving chairs and sweeping the floor. A waitress was filling salt and pepper shakers and ketchup bottles. I could hear clattering from the kitchen.

Tony pulled some liquor bottles from a cabinet beneath the bar and set them on a glass shelf that lined the wall. "I want to hear more about the frozen food thing," he said.

"I got a brother-in-law. He's a piece of shit; treats my sister like dirt. He's a chef, and he works for this frozen food manufacturer in their test kitchen. I didn't even know that was a thing until I got to know him. Anyway, he's always making product—that's what he calls it, product—and he brings stuff to the house for me to try out. You know, like an impromptu taste test. Some of the stuff he brings tastes like yesterday's garbage, but some of it still makes it to the freezer case at the grocery store. I'm telling you right now, Tony, he doesn't have anything that tastes as good as your lasagna. He could package that up in a deep aluminum tray—Mama Maria's Original Lasagna. You'd make fuckin' millions."

He nodded, considering this. "Millions?"

"No doubt about it. You negotiate for twenty percent of the retail price. I know that's doable because their markup is crazy. They'll have to put on another shift just to keep up with demand for your mother's lasagna."

"What's in this for you?"

"Two percent of your net."

The waitress was walking toward the door, finished for the night. Tony walked around the bar and let her out, locking the door behind her. "You can't be too careful around here, you know what I mean?" he said.

"I do. Youngstown has a reputation for being a rough city. Didn't they used to call it Little Chicago?"

"They still do." He turned to the busboy who was sweeping under the tables. "Andy, go help the boys in the back." I watched in the mirror as a boy of about sixteen propped his broom in the corner and pushed through the swinging doors into the kitchen. "I don't like to talk business where people can hear. Why only two percent?"

"One, if I don't get greedy, you don't call in a lawyer to start negotiating. Everybody wins. And two, with as much lasagna as you're going to sell, two percent puts me on easy street. I can tell my boss to go market his own fuckin' ball bearings."

We both laughed.

He bent down to get more bottles of booze. I arched my back, stretching. No one was watching from the kitchen. I slipped my hand into the back of my waist and wrapped my hands around the handle of my snub-nose .38. Tony was still rummaging through the inventory when I brought it around and hid it between my thighs.

"So, what are the next steps?" he asked.

A cook walked into the bar. "Can I have a beer, Tony?"

"Get it and go," he said, pointing at the cooler.

As he was fishing a beer from the cooler, I said, "I'll talk to my brother-in-law and see what he needs from you besides the recipe. He'll probably want you to come to Indianapolis and oversee the test kitchen phase, you know, to make sure they've got the recipe right."

"I could take one of my cooks over to make the first batch for them."

"See, now you're thinkin'."

"And after that?"

"I think he said it takes something like eight months from concept to store shelf."

The cook went back into the kitchen.

Tony opened up the cash register and started counting bills. "After that, no more ball bearings, huh?"

"It's no big deal. It's a ghost gig, anyway."

"A ghost gig? What's a ghost . . ."

Tony Gem looked up and found himself staring into the barrel of my .38. I pulled back the hammer, locking it into place.

"What's a ghost gig? It's what I pretend to do while I'm settling scores for Big Tommy Fortunato."

Tony's eyes widened but only for an instant.

The first bullet hit him square in the forehead. Bills and blood flew everywhere, and I could hear pots and pans falling as the kitchen crew scattered out the back door. Tony flew back against the glass shelves; shards of shattered bottles and shelving rained down on him. His body slumped to the ground. I leaned over the bar and pumped two more into the top of his skull.

I ran out of the Vine Cliff and down the street. A few people in the neighborhood had heard the roar of my .38 and were coming out on their porches. It was dark enough that they could never give a description of me. I cut across a yard to the side street where I'd parked the car. I'd left it unlocked with the key under the mat, exactly the way Carlo had taught me.

Unfortunately, they must teach the same thing in car thief school, because my ride had been boosted.

Now, in the movies, the hitman is always cool and collected, right? That's not reality, because I was in a raging panic. I could hear sirens in the distance and getting closer. This was not good. I took off running down alleys and between houses, trying to put as much distance between myself and the restaurant as possible. While this wasn't difficult, I had no idea where I was or how to get home. As I ran down one alley, I pulled out my handkerchief and began wiping my prints off the .38. I opened the lid on a trash can and stopped long enough to ditch the piece. I remember crossing some railroad tracks, my lungs burning. I ran through a little neighborhood of rundown houses and past a cement block bar with a bunch of black guys hanging around outside and a neon Carling Black Label sign in the window. It didn't look like friendly turf, so I ducked down another alley and ran between two darkened houses. Dogs were barking everywhere. I felt like a fox in one of those English hunts. I ran down a dead-end street where a guardrail with orange reflectors marked the end of the asphalt. I hopped the guardrail and traversed down a steep, wooded ravine covered with weeds slick with the night dew. I went down three times. When I climbed to the other side, I stopped to take a breath, hidden by the dark shadows of the trees, my pants slick with dew and mud. Across the street, I could see a neighborhood bar called the Olde Dubliner.

Irish. Great. I wasn't sure they'd be up for helping a dago down on his luck, but I was out of options. I went in, ordered a beer, and tried to make a collect call to Big Tommy's office at the compound. He didn't pick up. I had another beer and tried another call. And another, and another, and another. Still no answer. In my wallet back in Steubenville, I had the phone numbers of the capos. But that wallet belonged to Angelo Cipriani. I was still Pete Cola.

I nursed another beer. I probably called the office phone twenty times. I had to be looking desperate. It was almost eleven when the bartender said, "Slow night, pal. I'm closing up. You need to finish your beer."

Now what? I assumed that the busboy or the cook had given the police a description of me. I also assumed the Gems had the kind of pull with the police department in Youngstown that the Fortunatos did in Steubenville. In other words, if I was hauled in, I'd never make it to my preliminary hearing. I'd meet the same fate as the two guys who raped Alphonse's aunt.

I made one more failed attempt to reach someone at the compound. When I hung up and turned around, the bartender had a pistol on the bar a few inches from his hand. "I said, I'm closing up. You need me to call you a cab?"

Cab companies keep logs of all their trips, and the police have access to those records. Carlo taught me that. A cab ride from Youngstown to Steubenville or any point south would be a red flag. "I need a lift to East Liverpool."

"So call a cab."

"I can't call a cab."

He shrugged. "Not my problem."

I started to reach for my wallet. He grabbed the pistol. "Easy, partner. I'm just going for my wallet." I turned around so he could see my grass-stained ass. I reached back and lifted out the wallet. "I've got three hundred and sixty-two dollars here. It's yours for a ride to East Liverpool."

I had his attention. "Are you in trouble or something?"

"Do you think I'd offer you three hundred and sixty-two bucks for a forty-minute ride if I wasn't?"

He pointed to the bar. I set the bills on the counter. He scraped it off and put it in his pants pocket, then slid the pistol into his waist. "No funny stuff."

"I just need a ride out of Dodge."

We walked out back and climbed into his pickup truck. When we had pulled out of the neighborhood, I took a breath. "What did you do?" he asked.

"You don't seriously think I'm going to answer that, do you?"

After that, it was a mostly silent trip. When we cleared the Youngstown city limits, he turned on the radio. Of course, the murder of Tony Gem was the lead story was on the news.

Youngstown businessman and suspected mob kingpin Anthony "Tony Gem" Gemelli was found shot to death in his Smokey Hollow restaurant, the Vine Cliff, earlier tonight. Youngstown police have released few details in Gemelli's murder and say they have no suspects. His death comes just one year after the murder of his brother, Francisco Gemelli, who was found shot to death in a Jacksonville, Florida, hotel room. Stay tuned for updates as they become available.

When the broadcaster began giving sports scores, the bartender of the Olde Dubliner clicked off the radio and kept his eyes looking straight ahead. After a minute, he said, "I'd sure like to find out who killed Tony Gem."

I swallowed hard and looked at him. "Why's that?" I asked.

"So I could shake his hand for ridding the world of that guinea bastard. No offense intended."

"None taken."

He looked at me and grinned. I guided him to the Alhambra Tavern on Pennsylvania Avenue. They made book for us, and it was open twenty-four hours. I could hang out in a booth and call Big Tommy for a ride in the morning. Before I stepped out of his truck, I said, "Can I have ten bucks? I'm busted." He reached into his pocket and gave me back a twenty. As I climbed out, I said, "It would be best if you didn't—"

"Say nothing to no one?" He extended his hand across the seat and we shook. "Don't worry. I don't think I want a guy like you on my bad side."

He backed out of the parking space and was gone.

I made a collect call to the compound at seven, and Big Tommy picked up. He jumped in the Cadillac and drove up to get me. He was ecstatic. "I thought you were just going up on a scouting mission," he said.

"That was the plan. But things fell into place. There was no one else in the room but the two of us. I couldn't pass up the opportunity."

"What a night, huh? You didn't report the car stolen, did you?"

"What? No, I wouldn't—" He started laughing. "Quit busting my chops, Tom. I've had a rough night."

"How was the restaurant?"

"A pretty nice place, actually."

"What did you have to eat?"

"The lasagna."

"How was it?"

"I wouldn't feed it to a dog."

CHAPTER

19

July 2019

NURSING HOMES ARE proof that there is an upside to massive coronaries.

I went back over to Pinecrest to see Nickels. The place smelled like piss, and the nurses' aides, or whatever you call them, had pink and purple hair, piercings in their lips, and those gauge things in their ears. It was another reminder that perhaps I had lived too long. Nickels was in his room and propped up in his bed. His breakfast tray was still at his side, untouched except for the coffee. He smiled when he saw me at the door and said, "Hey, paisano."

I gave him a hug and set a crossword puzzle book on his nightstand. He liked those. "How're you doing today, Nickels?"

"How am I doing? How do you think I'm doing? They amputated my leg, I can't get to the whorehouse, and the food here is shit. Other than that, how was the play, Mrs. Lincoln?"

An attractive nurse with long dark hair and even darker eyes walked in to pick up the breakfast tray. She looked at Nickels and said, as though she was talking to a four-year-old, "You didn't eat anything, Mr. Nicolosi."

He looked at me and said, "This is my new girlfriend, Georgia. Prettiest nurse in the joint. If I had two good legs, I'd ask her to dance."

"Don't try to change the subject. Why didn't you eat your breakfast?"

"You know, Georgia, when I was in Vietnam during the war, I ate grilled rat and live coconut worms."

Her face pinched up and she said, "That's positively disgusting."

"And yet, not nearly as disgusting as that tray of slop they call a breakfast."

She shook her head and walked out with the untouched food. Nickels stared at her rear end until she disappeared out of the room. "The saddest part of my pathetic life is knowing that I'll never again have a shot at a woman like that."

"Time marches on, my friend."

"If that's the case, what's the use in living? How about you doing me a favor?"

"Name it."

"Have you got your 9-millimeter with you?"

"No. I got my .32."

"Close enough. I'll roll over and you put one right in the back of my head. Give me the Frankie Gemelli treatment and put me out of my misery."

"You know I can't do that."

He looked at me, smiled, and said, "Pussy."

We both laughed. It was a good morning. He was alert and happy.

I told him about my date with Carolyn. "She's a total sweetheart, Nickels. You'd love her." It was like every cogent conversation I'd had with Nickels. No matter how hard I tried to keep the conversation about women or sports or money, he dragged me back to talking about the family. Other than his time in Vietnam, I'm not sure Nickels had any frame of reference for a life beyond working for the Fortunatos.

"You getting any work from the kid?"

I shook my head. "He's pretty much put me on the shelf. He'll call when that bunch of amateurs he has working for him screw something up."

"Cleanup on aisle three?"

"Pretty much. So, as long as we're talking about Little Tommy, I got something else I need to ask you."

"Ask away. I got nothin' but time."

"I told you, the FBI's been knocking on my door. They're offering me a deal to flip on Little Tommy. I heard they talked to you, too."

"Yeah, a guy named . . . something. I can't remember."

"Ross."

He snapped his fingers. "That's him."

"What did he want from you?"

The nurse came back with two small paper cups containing pills. She stood by the bed until he had put them in his mouth and washed them down. "Open up," she said.

He dutifully did as he was told.

"Wiggle your tongue."

He did, then said, "Come by after your shift and let me put that to good use."

She rolled her eyes and left.

"The same crap they always want," Nickels said. "Information to take down the family. I told them I didn't know anything about the operation. Did I? Once upon a time, yeah, but that's ancient history. Little Tommy, he doesn't even know I'm alive. I'll tell you something, paisano, and I've never said this out loud in my life, but that kid's been a shit from the day he took his first breath. He's the most spoiled, entitled human being I've ever known in my life, and that was all Big Tommy's fault. He gave that kid everything he wanted; he never heard the word no. The kid wanted a go-kart, he got a go-kart. He wanted a new ball glove, he got a new ball glove. Bicycles, trampolines, BB guns. There was sporting goods equipment strewn all over the compound. As soon as the kid got tired of it, he'd drop it right there and walk away. I remember the day Big Tommy came home with that motorcycle. We were out front, and the kid was riding up and down the court. He was only fourteen or fifteen and still not allowed to ride it on the street legally. Of course the term legal never meant anything to the Fortunatos. Big Tom says to me, 'He loves it. Ain't that great?' What am I supposed to say? It wasn't my job to tell him that he had terrible parenting skills. He's was the boss, right? So I say, 'Yeah, Tom, that's great, just great.' But this morning, I'd finally had all I could take. I finally unloaded on Big Tommy. I told him that he wasn't doing that kid any favors by giving him everything he wanted and that he'd better get control of him."

I sat there for a long couple of seconds, digesting Nickels's words. I said, "Who did you tell that to?"

"Big Tommy."

"Big Tommy Fortunato?"

"How many Big Tommies do you know?"

"When did you see him?"

"I just told you. This morning. He and Alphonse stopped by."

I could feel the overwhelming sadness collect in my chest. It was like someone had flipped a switch. He had seemed so clear and alert up until this moment. I said, "Alphonse and Big Tommy were in this room to visit you this morning?"

"Yeah, Big Tommy was sitting in that same chair you're in right now. What's the big deal? They stop by all the time. We have some coffee and shoot the shit. The other day Alphonse brought me a prune Danish from Hornung's Bakery. It was delicious."

Hornung's Bakery had been closed at least twenty years.

"You're sure it was them?"

"What, am I blind? Yesterday, they brought along Dommie the Clip. We had a hoot. It was good to catch up on old times."

"Nickels, Alphonse and Dommie have been dead since 1975, and Tommy died six years ago."

He started laughing. "That's a good one. I'll tell them about that the next time they stop by. Who told you they were dead?"

It was not a fight I was going to win. I said, "I don't remember. Maybe I got some bad information."

"I guess."

I got up to leave. "What about the FBI, Nickels? What should I do about them?"

"If I had a shot, I'd cram it up that kid's ass sideways. He's no good."

"If Little Tommy finds out the FBI is trying to flip us, he'll come after you, too."

"At this point, he'd be doing me a favor. Look, if you're worried about the promises you made to Big Tommy, forget about it. I made a lot of promises to my dear mother and Jesus Christ. Those got broken, too. Life goes on, paisano."

I drove back across the river and parked the car on the street outside the diner. It was the first time I would see Carolyn since our date. When I walked in, she grinned at me but didn't greet me with the usual, "There's my darlin'."

That made me nervous. I sat down, and she brought me my iced tea. "Am I not your darlin' anymore?" I asked.

"Oh, you're my darlin', I just don't want any of the girls to know that because they might try to steal you away from me."

What a top-drawer babe.

I called her that night and asked her out again. She said, "Why don't you come over to my place tomorrow night, and I'll make us dinner."

"I'll bring the wine," I said.

"Don't be late."

CHAPTER

20

January 1981–June 1983

I MET MY DEAR Jolie under the most unusual of circumstances.

Her husband was a guy named Danny "Irish" McHugh. I called him Danny "Irish" McScrew, because he was forever trying to cheat the Fortunatos. Danny was a wiseass who always thought he was the smartest guy in the room. Plus, he had a chip on his shoulder the size of a coil of steel about being Irish and working for the Italians, and I'm sure he never called us Italians when we weren't around.

He had been working as an independent contractor for the Fortunatos for years. That may sound unusual for the mob, but it's a real thing. We allowed Danny to collect bets for us at Weirton Steel. The more bets he took, the more money he made, and as we liked to say in the business, taxibus freebus, because it was an all-cash operation. It was a good side hustle if you could keep your nose clean and resist the temptation to skim the take, which Danny couldn't do.

We had a guy taking bets for us at the Wheeling-Pittsburgh Steel plant in Yorkville—Walter Barrett. Every day at lunchtime, he'd set up in the break room at the hot mill and take bets for the sports parlays and daily number. Guys lined up around the building to place bets. It looked like the line at the soup kitchen in the projects. After his shift, Walter would walk to the parking lot with a tin lunch pail full of gambling sheets and cash. A courier would be there with an identical lunchpail with any payoffs from previous bets, and they'd make an exchange. So it went for years. I don't think Walter ever skimmed a dime. He turned over his receipts, took his vig, and went home. He had a cabin at Beech Flats, a boat at the marina in Rayland, and paid for his kids' college with his take. He was a very smart guy.

Danny McScrew, not so smart.

As I explained earlier, these were all parlay bets, minimum of three games, along with the daily number. It was virtually all profit. Middlemen like Danny were always trying to find ways to beat the system. This was a bad move because it was *our* system. Nickels was a mathematical wizard, probably even smarter than my sister. He knew when a middleman was shorting us.

Nickels told Big Tommy that Danny was skimming. After collecting the bets, Danny was looking at the spot sheets and picking out the ones he thought were sure losers and pocketing the money. Nickels knew this because he saw the drop-off in bets. Danny blamed it on the bad economy. "Bullshit," Nickels said. "Mill rats might not have enough money for bread and milk for their kids, but they can always find the extra cash for a bet."

Big Tommy told me to go have a talk with Danny. "Make sure he understands that we know what he's doing. It's unacceptable, and if the numbers don't improve, and I mean immediately, it's going to be a problem."

(Translation: In mob speak, "it's going to be a problem" means they're going to break both your legs across the shins with an axe handle.)

I wasn't to confront Danny at the mill because Big Tommy didn't want to bring undue attention to the fact that we were running a major gambling operation inside Weirton Steel. This was another difference between Alphonse and his son. Had the old man been calling the shots, I would have been waiting for Danny outside the gates with a baseball bat. The only direction Big Tommy gave me was, "Be subtle."

Danny liked to go out for dinner on Saturday nights at the Anchor Room in Wellsburg. This was no cheap evening, but money wasn't an issue if you were flush from skimming Big Tommy's profits. I was at the bar when he walked in with his wife. I didn't like to confront guys in front of their family, but sometimes it was unavoidable. I ordered another glass of wine and a shrimp cocktail. I'd wait for him to go to the restroom. It's difficult to defend yourself with one hand wrapped around your member.

Here's where guys like me get into trouble. His wife was beautiful, a full-figured woman with short, sandy hair, a flawless complexion, and perfect teeth. I couldn't stop staring at her. Guys like Connie Bones, he would lock in on Danny and wouldn't see another human being in the restaurant. Not me. All I could think was, how did a beautiful woman like that get hooked up with a mill rat like Danny McHugh?

They were in a booth with the open end facing the bar, so I had a clear view. I hadn't yet gotten my shrimp cocktail when I saw Danny reach across the table and smack her full in the face. It sounded like a tree branch snapping in the wind. He hit her so hard, her head slammed against the back of the booth. She was crying, and there was a scarlet stain on the side of her face from her ear to her chin.

It was then that I violated a major tenet of my job: Keep emotions out of it. But there I was, sitting at the bar staring at this goddess when this piece of shit busts her face. It was more than I could take. I got up from my seat, walked over to the booth, and put my hands on the corners of the table. I leaned in close and said, "I need you to step outside for a minute, Danny. We need to have a talk."

"Who the fuck are you?" he said, loud enough to draw eyes from half the restaurant.

"Who I am doesn't matter. Who I represent does. And I represent Tommaso Fortunato."

He said, "Go fuck yourself, wop."

More eyes turned toward us. This was the kind of ugly confrontation I wanted to avoid. I've been called dago plenty of times, and I really never took offense to it. But there was something about the word wop that went up my spine. Wop stands for "without papers," a derogatory term for foreigners who came here illegally.

"Just for the record, Danny, my father came through Ellis Island. He had his papers." I slipped my hand into my pocket and my fingers into a set of brass knuckles. Danny started to say something about my ancestry, but I didn't want to hear anything else he had to say. I brought my hand out of my pocket and drove it into the top of his mouth. His front four teeth exploded. It sounded like hot glass crackling in the snow. I brought a second punch right down on top of his nose. I don't know if you've ever seen what happens when someone gets hit on the bridge of the nose with brass knuckles, but it ain't pretty. The cartilage snapped as easily as his teeth. The front of his face was a faucet for blood, saliva, and chips of enamel.

I grabbed a handful of hair with my left hand, jerked his face close to mine, and made no attempt to whisper. "Big Tommy knows you're skimming. If the receipts don't go back up next week, I'll be seeing you again, and this little visit will seem like a hot fudge sundae compared to what happens next." I looked at his wife and said, "What are you doing with a bum like this?" I swear she was fighting off a smile. I headed for the door and threw a twenty on the bar as I passed my shrimp cocktail.

When I told Big Tommy what happened, he said, "You call that subtle? I just wanted you to talk to him."

"I know, Tom, but some guys, they just aren't very good listeners."

This is when I violated another tenet of my job. I could not get the image of Danny McHugh's wife out of my head. Two weeks after the altercation—that's a good word, right?—at the Anchor Room, I drove over to Wellsburg and parked down the street from their house. I watched Danny come off the front porch and get in his car. He still had blue circles around his eyes and bandages across his nose. After he pulled out of the driveway, I waited five minutes, then knocked on her door with a dozen yellow roses. When she answered, she was still in her housecoat, her face puffy from sleep, but she didn't seem the least bit surprised to see me. She said, "If I'd known my knight without shining armor was coming, I'd have made myself a little more presentable."

I handed her the flowers and said, "I wanted to apologize for making a scene at the restaurant."

"Really? That's why you're here? I thought maybe you came to see if you could lure me away from Danny."

She was the boldest babe I'd ever been around.

"Actually, that's exactly why I'm here."

She pushed open the door and led me upstairs to the bedroom. She slipped off her housecoat and nightgown, and we were making love inside of five minutes from the time my knuckles hit the door. I was not going to let this woman out of my life. She filed for divorce, and when she told Danny that she was leaving him for me, he said he would contest it. She said, "If you contest it, you'll end up in a shallow grave." He wisely changed his mind.

Jolie's father was Herman Frankfurth, a Wellsburg cop who knew that I worked for the Fortunatos. He was not a fan. I tried to make him understand that I would take care of his daughter. "She's already the most important thing in my life," I said.

"I know all about the Fortunatos and the oath you swear to them," Herman said. "You swear allegiance to the crime family, first and always, ahead of God and your own family, so don't tell me she'll be the most important thing in your life, because I don't believe you. It never ends well for people who get involved with the Fortunatos. Never."

To a large degree, he had a point.

I married Jolie on Saturday, June 19, 1982. We held the wedding in Big Tommy's backyard, next to the swimming pool. Her parents didn't come, but mine did. It was the first time in their lives that they had been around such opulence and tuxedos. My mother still thought I was going to hell. As my elderly father surveyed the surroundings, I think he believed the lifestyle he was seeing would be worth eternal damnation.

Jolie moved into my apartment in the Hollywood Addition. We were a little cramped, but it was a nice place with a park and a baseball field across the street. I was crazy about her. And I told her that I was not a made man with the Fortunatos and never would be, and that I could still get out of the life, if that's what she wanted.

That made Jolie laugh. "And do what, Angelo? Sell cars or insurance? Maybe work in the steel mill like my ex-husband?"

I shrugged. "I'll do whatever it takes to make you happy."

"I knew who you were and what you were when I married you."

That's a good woman.

Two weeks before our first anniversary, Jolie told me she was pregnant. A child. My child. I was going to be a father. It was the most exhilarating moment of my life. For the first time since I'd met Alphonse Fortunato at Bixby's Pool Hall, I seriously considered leaving the family. I wanted to talk this over with Carlo. We had been a team for years. I trusted his counsel and that he would keep our conversations private.

It had taken Carlo and me a while to bond. After my two successful hits on the Gemellis, I think there was a little jealousy on Carlo's part. He had always been the Fortunatos' main man. Suddenly, there was an interloper at the compound. But over time we became fast friends and partners. We had a routine. Thirty minutes after we'd completed a job for Big Tommy, Carlo and I would be at Undo's eating bucatini with a nice clam sauce, a bottle of chianti between us. And for dessert, maybe a cannoli. Carlo loved cannoli. We would laugh and talk, never about business, but about women, cars, or politics. Other than boxing, Carlo didn't care for sports. "Men box. Boys play baseball," he liked to say.

About the time of my anniversary, the Gemellis were again making intrusions into Beaver County, Pennsylvania. Those guys, they never learned. Frankie Gem's son, Donato "Donny Gem" Gemelli, was now head of the family and seeking revenge for the execution of his father, uncle, and the dozen lieutenants we had taken out during their last incursion into Pennsylvania.

Big Tommy said, "Frankie Gem was a dumbass, and the fruit didn't fall far from the tree." He sent word to Donny Gem that any intrusion into Fortunato territory would be met with the appropriate response. This meant, unless you want to end up at the cemetery next to your father, stay the hell of Beaver County. Donny, however, misinterpreted this to mean please trample all over our turf.

Carlo and I drove up to Monaca to the River Lounge, where one of the Gemelli capos had been pressuring the owner to make book with them. I always had a soft spot for the bar owners in this situation. First, they had armed mobsters from Steubenville come into their place and tell them to make book with them. Then, armed mobsters from Youngstown show up and say either you make book with us, or things will be bad for you. All this guy wants to do is pour draft beers and go home at night and turn on the ball game without bullet holes in his chest.

Big Tommy told us that the chief of police in Monaca was a choirboy. In mob speak, that means he was an honest cop and not on the take. For the record, we hated honest cops. Tommy gave us specific instructions to rough up the Gemelli capo but not to kill him, because he didn't want any trouble in Monaca. Easy enough.

I was at the bar with a gin and tonic when the Gemelli capo came in. He was a rough character named Orly Lanaro. There was no pretense of being cordial. He slammed the bar owner against a wall and said some very unkind words about Mr. Tommaso Fortunato. This must have been a regular occurrence in Monaca, because no one paid much attention to the bartender's head being bashed against the gargoyle carving on the back of the bar. I threw a five on the counter and walked outside, giving a simple nod to Carlo, who was sitting on a bench at the bus stop, pretending to read a newspaper.

My job was to get the capo between a couple of cars. Carlo was going to come up from behind and hit him in the back of the head with his brass knuckles. Once he was on the asphalt, we'd put the boots to him for a couple of minutes, then leave. Mission accomplished. When Lanaro came out and got into his car, I pulled my car in front of his, pointed down and said, "Your tire is flat."

He frowned, like I was a total jagoff, but he opened the door to get out and check the tire. Carlo, slick as you please, came up from behind. But instead of waiting for Lanaro to get out of the car, he shoved his pistol into the open door and calmly put two rounds in the side of his head. I was in an immediate panic. It was the middle of the afternoon in a crowded parking lot, and Big Tommy had said to rough the guy up, not blow his brains all over the dashboard. In fact, he specifically said not to kill him. You never, and I mean *never*, clip a guy from a rival family without a direct order from the boss.

Carlo shut the door to Lanaro's car, tucked his 9-millimeter into his jacket, and jumped into the Galaxie. "Let's get the hell out of here," he said.

It was an order I didn't need to hear. I was busting it across the parking lot and heading toward the freeway. "What the hell, Carlo? Why'd you do that?"

"Do what?"

"*Do what*? Big Tommy said not to kill him."

"I had to. He drew on me. It was me or him."

"Carlo, he didn't even know you were there. You shot him in the side of the head."

His jaw tightened. "He drew on me. You saw it, too. If Big Tommy asks, that's the story. Understand?"

In all our years together, I had never seen Carlo panic. Not once. What the hell had gone south? I didn't know. Maybe it was something personal. What I did know was that he was my partner, and I had his back. "Okay. Sure. He drew on you. I saw it."

Carlo winked. "That's my guy."

After we had crossed the state line and my nerves calmed, I said, "Carlo, I need to talk to you about something in confidence."

"I'm listening."

"My first anniversary is Friday, and Jolie is pregnant."

"What? That's great news. Congratulations, kid."

"Thanks. So, I'm thinking it might be a good time for a career change."

The smile melted off his face. "You're thinking of leaving the organization?"

"Yeah, I am. Carlo, I don't want my kid to someday ask me what I do for a living, and I have to tell him the truth, that I'm a hitman for the mob. I've got a beautiful wife, and I don't want her subjected to this."

"Big Tommy's not going to be happy. When you're in, you're in for life."

"That's exactly the point. I'm not in. I'm not a made man; I'll never be a made man. Mr. Fortunato told me that. I'm basically a second-class citizen."

"What do you want me to tell you, kid?"

"I want you to tell me what you think."

"Whether you're a made man or not, you know the operation. You'd be a prime target for the FBI to flip. That won't sit well with the big man. Not even a little bit. On a personal note, I'd hate to see you go. I'd always considered myself something of a loner, but not anymore. I'd hate to lose my partner."

I blew out my breath. I was already wishing I hadn't mentioned it to Carlo. It wasn't the response I'd been hoping for. We pulled into the parking lot at Undo's. I think Carlo could tell I was rattled. He said, "These things have a way of working themselves out. Just give it some time and think about it. You'll do the right thing."

We went into the restaurant and took a corner booth. He said, "So, what did you get the little lady for the anniversary?"

"A diamond tennis bracelet, quarter carats all the way around."

"Wow. First class."

(Note: Yes, it was screaming hot. A friend of a friend of Jimmy Beans had a line on some merchandise from a jewelry store heist in Toledo. I got it for pennies on the dollar. But it still counts. I'd still get points for being a thoughtful husband.)

"Yeah, she's going to like it. And Big Tommy gave me his room at the Federal Terrace. I'm having them fix us something special—chateaubriand for two."

"Fancy. She'll be putty in your hands."

"She already is."

We laughed, and Carlo poured the chianti.

CHAPTER

21

Sunday, June 19, 1983

We had a beautiful night at the Federal Terrace. The chateaubriand was amazing. We had no sooner sat down when Ricky Bones walked in with a chilled bottle of Dom Perignon. "Compliments of the boss," he said. "Happy anniversary, lovebirds. Enjoy your evening." He leaned down and whispered in my ear, "In this life, you never know how many more you're going to get, huh, pal?"

They weren't exactly the kind of well wishes you'd expect on your anniversary, but that was Ricky Bones. He could be a horse's ass, even when he wasn't putting forth much effort.

I gave Jolie the diamond tennis bracelet, and she started crying. She said it was the most beautiful gift anyone had ever given her. My life had never been so full. I told her that I was considering getting out of the life. Maybe we could move to the Carolinas and start fresh.

She said, "I want you to be Angelo Cipriani. That's the guy I married. How you decide to make a living is your business."

For dessert, we had a bite of our wedding cake, which she had kept frozen. I guess that's a tradition or something. It was terrible, so we split a bread pudding with cappuccinos. When I walked out of the restaurant with Jolie on my arm, I felt like the luckiest man alive.

I gave my parking ticket to the valet, who hustled out the back of the restaurant to the alley where the cars were parked. We stood in the foyer and waited. Jolie had both hands wrapped around my elbow, the sparkling tennis bracelet on her right wrist. We walked out the door as the car pulled into the yellow-striped spot reserved for Federal Terrace parking. The valet hustled around and opened the door for Jolie, then ran back around to get my door. I handed him a five-dollar bill and slid behind the wheel.

I should've been more alert.

I did exactly what I waited for the Gemellis to do. I let down my guard. It wasn't until I grabbed the gearshift to put the car in drive that I saw a sedan stopped crossways on Fourth Street, just north of the Market Street intersection, blocking traffic from the south. A quick glance in the side rearview mirror revealed a second car across Fourth Street at Washington. It was a barricade to prevent any cars from getting down the street.

After that, everything seemed to happen in slow motion. I reached behind me to grab the .38 snub-nose out of my waist. That's when I saw the guy running across the street toward us, a pistol in his right hand—maybe a 9-millimeter, but I ain't for sure. He fired just as I grabbed the .38. The bullet exploded the driver's-side window. It went past me; I heard Jolie scream.

I think it was the first bullet that killed her. I hope so.

He fired again. The bullet went through my arm and into my back. I slumped down and fired two shots—maybe three—that probably went through the driver's-side door. Glass broke on Jolie's side of the car. A second gunman was firing from the sidewalk. A bullet that I think came from the second gunman hit my hand and the pistol and flew under the brake pedal. I tried to reach under the seat where I'd hidden my 32-caliber revolver. I think I got my hand on the pistol, but I'm not sure. My spine was on fire. More bullets hit my body. There was less pain with each impact. The first gunman seemed just outside my door. I was hit in the head—a graze; hot blood poured down the side of my face.

I started to black out. I could see the darkness rushing in from the sides of my vision; there was blood in my eyes and the roar of a jet engine in my ears. I reached for Jolie; I felt her head slump against my back. There were more shots and breaking glass. A shot went through the windshield, and shards of glass rained down on me. People were screaming. It seemed that I heard footsteps running away and tires squealing. Everything was blurry. I was sure this was the end of my life. I fought the darkness. I heard sirens echoing off the downtown buildings. I said, "Jolie, please, Jolie. Oh God, Jolie."

And everything faded to black.

What I know now and what I'm telling you came from Big Tommy and Carlo. The cars that had blocked Fourth Street had been stolen from Mahoning County. That implicated the Gemellis. The two gunmen ran through an alley to a car that was waiting for them on Commercial Street. They were probably in a Youngstown bar celebrating before I got to the emergency room.

I was rushed to Ohio Valley Hospital, where the priest gave me last rites as they were pushing me into surgery. As must be obvious to you at this point, I survived. They stopped the bleeding, gave me a transfusion, maybe two, and life-flighted me to Allegheny Hospital in Pittsburgh. I lost a lot of blood. They kept wheeling me into surgery to pluck lead from my body and repair bones and tissue and organs. There's still a chunk of bullet near my spine that the doctors said was too dangerous to remove.

I re-entered the world of the semi-aware on a Thursday morning. That was the day they began weaning me off the drugs that had kept me in an induced coma for nearly three weeks. I'm not sure of the exact number of times they operated to repair my bullet-riddled body, but it was north of a half dozen. The process of re-entry was not like flipping a switch. Rather, it was slow and stuttered. The first few days were swirls of bright lights and disjointed dreams and hallucinations and nausea, interspersed by flashes of reality with faces fading in and out and voices beckoning me to emerge from the fog. Try as I might, my tires wouldn't hold the road. It was like some kind of evil amusement park ride. My head felt like a cannonball. My eyelids refused to open more than a sliver. The piece of the 9-millimeter bullet that had lodged in my spine and, miraculously, had not left me paralyzed, burned like the head of a torch. I had no concept of time, just blurred snapshots of the world around me.

There was a nurse with an angelic voice who gently, but repeatedly, slapped at my chin, saying, "Wake up, Angelo, you've been asleep long enough." The first time she fed me saltines and lime Jell-O, I promptly returned them to her in a violent and brackish upheaval that flooded her cleavage and left a Rorschach stain the color of swamp water on the front of her white dress. I remember her taking the Lord's name in vain.

My only clear memory of those first few days was forcing open my eyes and looking into the bristled puss of Jimmy Beans, who had been standing guard over me. He grinned and said, "Welcome back, sunshine."

Each breath felt like there were shards of hot glass in my lungs. Past cracked lips and a dry throat, I uttered, "I'm alive?"

"Yep. You ain't any prettier, but you're alive."

"How?"

"Wasn't your time. Almost, though. You didn't buy the farm, but you were looking at property for a couple weeks."

For a long time—I'm not sure if it was hours or days—I couldn't remember why I thought I should be dead. Something traumatic had occurred, but what? Finally, a video replayed in my brain. It had the stutter and stop of an ancient black-and-white film reel, grainy and stark, and I saw the car blocking Fourth Street at Market and the first gunman coming in from my left as I sat in the car. I had been ambushed.

That was the first and only instant that I felt joy to be alive. It was lightning-strike brief, as in the next instant I remembered that Jolie had been in the car with me. No one had to tell me she and our unborn child were dead. I instinctively knew that. That realization was a ball bat to the gut. Everyone else had had time to grieve, but the wound was fresh to me. I'd been shot seven times, but none were as painful as losing my beloved Jolie. The guilt was suffocating. I would never believe that it wasn't my fault. I put her in that position. Even Big Tommy would try to tell me that I was a victim. That might have been true, but she was collateral damage for my actions.

It was another week before I began to feel like a human being. The room had quit swirling, and I could finally keep down food. I was choking my way through a breakfast of undercooked bacon and oatmeal the consistency of lard when Father Patella came to visit. He may not have been the last person I wanted to see that morning, but he was a sparkling top five contender, standing just a rung below the Gemelli capos who shot me up. I never liked Father Patella. He was the priest at Big Tommy's church, the Church of the Holy Cross, and I assumed that Big Tommy had sent him up to see me. Father Patella was a humorless, sanctimonious little man with a thin face, a few wisps of black hair combed straight back, and a beaked nose the size of a lemon. He looked like a toucan. I assumed that joining the priesthood and abstaining from sex was probably not a big sacrifice for him. He always wore a long, black frock and his cleric's collar so that no one could possibly mistake him for anything but a man of the cloth.

He walked into my room and without preamble asked, "Angelo, do you want to give confession?"

"Confession? What the hell for? I've been in a coma after getting shot seven times. It's a miracle that I'm still alive."

"You didn't answer my question."

"You must not have been listening too good, Father." I lifted up the front of my hospital gown to display the cross-stitch of scars left by bullets and scalpels. "Here you go. Take a look at this road map. One of those sons of bitches put a bullet within a millimeter or a centimeter, one of the meters, of my heart." I dropped the gown and picked a paper napkin off my breakfast tray and pinched it between my thumb and middle finger. I held it up and said, "If that bullet was that much closer, you and me are not having this conversation. So, I think God's already on my side."

"God doesn't take sides."

"No? Well, in that case, he needs to re-examine his operational policies, maybe call in a consultant or something and update the manual, because he should be taking sides."

"I'm not here to be concerned about your attackers. On Judgment Day, God will sort out the evil from the chosen. I'm here for you, Angelo, and you need to confess *your* sins."

"How many of them?"

"All of them, of course."

"All of them?"

"Every last one."

"How old are you, padre?"

He frowned, and I assumed that he thought it an odd question. "Thirty-eight."

"In that case, you don't have enough years left in your life to listen to all my sins." I thought it was a good line, but he failed to see the humor. "Here's another thing that you and Jesus need to understand. I've got a pretty good idea who was behind this, so when I get out of here and back on my feet, my list of my sins is going to grow exponentially, because I'm going to flay them alive."

"Vengeance is mine, sayeth the Lord."

"Not this time. I plan to take extreme vengeance before God gets the chance. He and Jesus can have whatever's left when I get done with 'em."

This was probably not what a man charged with saving my soul wanted to hear. But here's the rub with Father Patella: He cared more about the attendance at the Tuesday night bingo game than he did whether or not I burned in hell. He figured he had already punched his ticket to heaven, and if he could get a sinner of my caliber to the confessional, it was just going to get him a better seat at the dinner table for all eternity.

* * *

Muzzie Lollini stopped by one day and dropped off one of the little cards they have printed at the funeral home for the deceased.

Daughter of Herman and Sylvia Frankfurth.

There was no mention of a husband.

I no longer felt like a tough guy. I felt small and stupid and cowardly. I felt like I didn't deserve to wake up from the coma, and that whatever power existed in the universe should have condemned my still-breathing body to the other side of the dirt.

I had been back among the conscious for three weeks when Big Tommy came by for another visit, this time alone. "The doctors said they're going to parole you in another week or so," Big Tommy said. "When you get out, I want you to go up to the hunting lodge to recuperate."

This was the same lodge in the wilds of the Allegheny National Forest where Pretty Boy Floyd was heading before he was killed by Melvin Purvis and the FBI. I was familiar with the lodge, as we used it as a meeting point when rotating prostitutes with the mob from Buffalo and Rochester. The lodge sat in a remote area, high in the hills overlooking the Allegheny River. It would be the perfect place to dispose of a body. "Are you taking me up there to finish the job, Tommy?" I asked.

He looked genuinely perplexed. "What's that supposed to mean?"

"Did you try to have me killed?"

His eyes widened and he looked like I had slapped him in the face. He walked over and shut the door to my room, and not gently. "Where in fuck did you get an idea like that?"

"Well, I . . ."

"Shut up your stupid face. I'm going to hope to Christ that you're under the influence of some kind of heavy pain medication, because otherwise we've got a big problem here. And just so we're clear, if I wanted to turn out your lights, we wouldn't be talking. I would have had Carlo put one behind your ear and you'd already be worm food instead of lying there like a piece of Swiss cheese, all shot up and with stupid shit coming out of your mouth."

"Did Carlo tell you I was thinking about getting out?"

"Yeah, that night, in fact. For whatever that's got to do with anything. I was in the backyard with Rosebella and Ricky Bones when Carlo stopped over and told me."

"Even after I told him in confidence?"

"You should know this by now, Angelo, but I'll repeat it since you seem to be having some kind of major brain malfunction at the moment. Carlo works for me, not you. There is no confidence when it comes to the business of this family." Big Tommy rubbed his hand over his chin and looked like he wanted to throw something. He took a deep breath and walked toward the only window in the room. "Jesus H. Christ, I cannot believe we're even having this conversation. And have you ever known me to take down someone's wife and dismiss it as collateral damage?"

"I'm sorry, Tom. But I couldn't make any other scenario work. I figured you were worried about me leaving, knowing what I know, and you decided the best way to keep me quiet was to have me clipped."

"That's ridiculous. I trust you like my brother. So, just so we're very clear, no, I did not try to have you killed."

"Who did?"

"As best we can tell, it was the Gemellis. Maybe it was retaliation for killing Frankie and Tony. That makes the most sense."

"How would they know that I pulled the trigger?"

"I don't know that yet."

"How did they know I'd be at the restaurant?"

"I don't know that, either."

"There's a lot you don't know."

"Give me time, goddammit."

For the first time since the shooting, my mind replayed a scene from that night. I saw Ricky Bones walking into the private dining room with a bottle of Dom Perignon. What had he said? Compliments of the boss and something about my anniversary . . . I squinted into space for a moment, then it came to me. *In this life, you never know how many more you're going to get, huh, pal?*

"Where'd you go?" Big Tommy asked.

I snapped out of my trance. "Huh?"

"Where'd you go? You drifted off."

"Ah, nowhere. These meds make me loopy. It's hard to focus sometimes."

"I see. So, if you're convinced that I'm not trying to kill you, I'll make arrangements for you to go to the lodge."

"I'm good with that, but the doctors are telling me I'll need weeks of rehabilitation."

"I know. I talked to them. It'll be taken care of."

"Okay. I appreciate it, Tommy, and I'm sorry for what I said."

"It's forgotten."

Big Tommy stood at the side of my bed and fidgeted for a moment, like he had something important to say but was struggling to find the words. Then he slowly reached into the inside pocket of his sport coat and pulled out a small manila envelope. He held it for a second, looked as though he might put it back in his pocket, then handed it to me. "It's Jolie's wedding ring and the bracelet you got her for your anniversary," he said. "They took them off of her at the hospital before they sent her body for the autopsy. I didn't know when it would be a good time to give them to you, so . . ."

It was another gut punch; I was fighting back tears and not doing a very good job of it. I handed the envelope back to Big Tommy and said, "How about you hold on to them for me until I get out of here? I've got no place to keep them."

He nodded and put them back in his pocket without comment. As he headed for the door he said, "I'll make the arrangements to get you to the lodge."

"I appreciate it, Tommy. By the way, I never had a chance to thank you for that bottle of Dom Perignon."

"What bottle of Dom Perignon?"

Every hair follicle on my head felt like it was on fire. "Never mind. I think it was a dream. These drugs, I tell you. I can't separate fact from fiction."

"Get some rest."

I forced a smile. I'd get some rest, and then I'd settle the score with my old nemesis, Ricky Bones.

CHAPTER

22

September–October 1983

THE HUNTING LODGE sat in the middle of more than two hundred acres of Pennsylvania forest and had been passed down through the Fortunato family since Aldo purchased it in 1908. It was a wooden, ranch-style building that sat on a bluff with the Allegheny River far in the distance. It was quiet, peaceful, and the ideal place to convalesce, but I couldn't look out over the expanse of green without thinking of how much I wished Jolie was by my side.

My only job was to rehabilitate my body. I lifted weights to regain full use of my arms and hiked the hills to build up my wind and stamina. It was the first time in my life that I hadn't lived in the gritty streets of Steubenville, Ohio. I was surprised how the hills, trees, and fresh air helped my mental outlook. Having grown up next to the steel mill, I didn't even know fresh air was a thing.

There were three Fortunato associates living in the lower level. They never came upstairs and did not interact with me. I watched them taking eight-hour shifts patrolling the grounds with sidearms and Uzis. I only saw three people on a regular basis. One was the cook, an Oriental woman named Saachee. She was a sweet little thing who brought me breakfast, lunch, and dinner, each time announcing, "Time to eat."

When she returned to pick up the plates, she would ask, "You like?" If I asked her a question or tried to engage her in conversation, she would say, "Yes, yes, uh-huh, uh-huh." I don't think she understood a word I was saying, but she was a great cook and a nice lady.

Two therapists worked with me on a rotation. One was a wispy little guy named Alvin, who was more cheerleader than therapist. He would have me lifting weights or riding a stationary bike, all the while clapping and saying, "Come on, Mr. Cipriani, you can do it. I know you can. You're the man, Mr. Cipriani. Push, push, push. You're doing so great." I wanted to slap him about four times a day.

The other was a brute of a woman named Gretchen, who put me through workouts as if she didn't like me. And maybe she didn't. She would stretch and twist me around until I yelled and clamped my teeth down on a towel. When I was so exhausted that I couldn't go any further, she would say, "That's fine, if you want to be a cripple for the rest of your life, then just keep dogging it. It makes no difference to me. I get paid either way."

I wanted to slap her, too, but in all candor, I was afraid she'd slap me back.

Once or twice a week, Big Tommy would send one of the boys up to check on me. During one visit, Muzzie Lollini said Big Tommy had offered to send one of the girls from the brothel up to keep me company for a weekend. I said no. I was far from being over the loss of Jolie, and I didn't want anyone else. The thought of crawling into bed with a whore would besmirch her memory.

When I thought of Jolie and how she died, a rage boiled inside of me. I wasn't without responsibility, but I hadn't emptied two handguns into a car with an innocent woman inside. I also hadn't forgotten that Ricky Bones owed me an explanation for the bottle of Dom Perignon that Big Tommy couldn't remember sending. I was sure that Ricky was somehow in bed with the Gemellis. When I figured out who set me up, I was going to get my revenge, the consequences be damned.

* * *

There was no board of directors or points system for advancement within the family. It was strictly up to the boss. The family was a dictatorship, not a democracy, and his word was law. Thus, there was always a lot of jockeying in the ranks to curry favor with the supreme leader.

It was a very competitive environment, and the capos were not always one big happy family. There were rivalries and frequently dissension in the ranks. There were times when Big Tommy was more babysitter than mob boss. Part of that was his own fault. Big Tommy tolerated a lot more nonsense than Alphonse, who had the management style of a caveman.

Shut up and do your job.

What are you, six? Grow the fuck up.

What's the matter, Nancy, are your ovaries hurting today?

You know, there are tap dancers out there that complain less than you.

I need a bulldog and get a fuckin' toy poodle. Mother of Christ, help me.

Either do your job or go down to the pie factory and work.

(Note: There was no pie factory. It was a figure of speech to indicate you were too soft for the mob and you'd be better off making pies. The capos considered it the ultimate insult.)

I hadn't had any particularly hard feelings toward Ricky Bones, but he'd had a hard-on for me since the day I collected on his account from Stein the florist. He resented the fact that I had endeared myself to Alphonse and set back his trajectory to become a made man by four years. Mind you, Ricky was the one who wasn't staying current on his books, but he blamed me. That was fine. I could live with that.

He liked making fun of my half-Ukrainian ancestry and called me Uke to see if he could get under my skin. He did, actually; I just didn't let him see it. There were a couple of times when I wanted to punch Ricky right in the mouth, but this was after he was a made man. You don't do that to a made man, especially if you're a half-Ukrainian associate. So I just took the little digs and jabs and let them roll off my shoulders.

Digs and jabs are one thing. But if he tipped off the Gemellis that I had been the triggerman for Frankie Gem and Tony Gem, then told them when they could find me coming out of the Federal Terrace, we had entered an entirely new level. I would choke the life out of him.

Ricky made a trip to the hunting lodge during the third week of my rehabilitation. He unloaded a trunk full of groceries into the kitchen, then walked out on the veranda where I was waiting for him. "Beautiful view," he said.

"Yeah, it is."

"You need anything before I head out of here?"

"Just a minute of your time, Ricky. I need to talk to you."

"Okay, but my time's valuable; let's have it."

Always with the attitude.

"The night Jolie got killed, you dropped off a bottle of champagne and said compliments of Big Tommy."

"Yeah, so?"

"I tried to thank Big Tommy for the gesture, and he didn't know anything about it."

"Jesus Christ, you asked him about it?"

"What's the big deal?"

"He doesn't like thanks for stuff like that. You're supposed to accept it and keep your mouth shut."

"Why didn't he know about it, Ricky?"

"If you've got something on your mind, Uke, spill it."

I began by jabbing a finger at Ricky. "Someone tipped off the Gemellis that I was the triggerman on Frankie and Tony. Someone also told them I was going to be at the Federal Terrace. Someone got my wife and baby killed and I . . ."

I never saw the punch coming, it was that fast. Ricky Bones hit me in the middle of the face. It was like a concussion blast. It knocked me over a table and into an Adirondack chair. My head hit an armrest, and I saw flashes of light. Blood was running out of my nose and into my mouth. I made a feeble attempt to get up, but Ricky was on me. He grabbed two fistfuls of the front of my shirt, shook me, and said through clenched teeth, "I'll give you a pass on this one, Uke, but I swear to Christ, if you ever make an insinuation like that again, I'll fuckin' kill you. And just so you know, I was in the backyard of the compound late that afternoon with Big Tommy and Rosebella when Carlo came by. He told us that you were thinking of leaving the organization. When Big Tommy asked where you were, Carlo reminded him that it was your anniversary and you were at the Federal Terrace. After Big Tommy and Carlo went inside, Rosebella pulled me aside and asked me to deliver the champagne on behalf of Big Tommy. She wanted you to think it came from him. Now, that's the end of this conversation, and we better never have another like it. I don't like explaining myself to anyone, let alone you."

He dropped me back to the floor and left. I was still trying to get my bearings when Saachee came out on the veranda with the lunch tray. She said, "Time to eat," set the tray on the table and left. It didn't seem to register that I was lying on the deck, my shirt stretched out of shape and blood all over my face. Either she was single-focused, or she simply didn't care.

It was the first beating I'd taken since my days in the Spaghetto. Maybe I deserved it. But I knew that Ricky's reaction was not unusual for a wiseguy. Just because he acted outraged didn't mean he wasn't guilty. If I accused him again, I would be much better prepared.

* * *

After seven weeks of rehab, I went home. The apartment looked the same as it did when Jolie and I left for the Federal Terrace. The anniversary card she had gotten me was still standing on the kitchen table. The dozen red roses I had sent her that morning were in a vase. The water had evaporated, and the petals had browned and littered the countertop. I drove across the river to Oak Grove

Cemetery in Hooverson Heights. The caretaker looked up her name on the log but couldn't find it. I said, "Look under her maiden name—Frankfurth."

"Oh, yeah. Here it is," he said.

He directed me to the grave, which was still crested and without a headstone. I sat cross-legged at the foot of her grave and cried for an hour. I apologized over and over—for not protecting her, for putting her in harm's way, but mostly for being who I was, a bum. Jolie married me in spite of that. She had deserved much better than this. She had deserved much better than me. When I had no more tears, I drove over to her parents' house. Her mother answered the door and smiled momentarily, until she recognized me. She turned away and said, "Herman, it's him."

Jolie's father, Herman Frankfurth the career cop who had rightly predicted that no good would come from our marriage, came to the door. He was in his stocking feet and a white T-shirt. "What do you want?" he asked.

"I wanted to talk to you and your wife."

He shook his head. "No chance. We don't want to hear anything you have to say."

"I'm so sorry for what happened. I didn't . . ."

"You didn't what? Didn't mean to get her killed? Maybe not, but she's just as dead, isn't she? I warned her about you and what she was getting herself into, and you know what she told me? She said, 'Angelo will protect me.' Well, you didn't protect, did you? You can go out and get yourself a new wife. I'm sure there's someone out there idiotic enough to get involved with trash like you. But we can't get our daughter back, can we?" His nostrils flared, and the heat came up out of his white shirt like a scalding rash. There wasn't another man in the world who I'd let talk to me like that, but I stood there and took the abuse because I deserved it. "Don't ever set foot on my property again. Today you're just an unwelcome visitor. Come back and you're a trespasser, and I'll kill you. I don't care who you work for."

CHAPTER

23

July 2019

I WAS HELPING CAROLYN clean up the dinner plates when she asked, "How did your first wife die?"

"What's that?" I asked. I'd heard her perfectly; I was stalling for time.

"I said, what happened to your first wife? How did she die?"

This was the heart of my problem with Carolyn. I'd been dancing around some of the questions she had asked me. Dancing is a bit of a misnomer. Actually, I'd been lying my ass off. How do you explain to someone as sweet as Carolyn that you've been a contract killer for the Fortunato crime family? It's not an easy conversation and most likely a deal-breaker.

My cell phone hummed in my pants pocket. The caller ID was blocked. It was the third time he'd tried to call me since I had arrived at Carolyn's house. I had sent the first two calls to voicemail. This one, however, was a lifeline. "I'm sorry, but I need to take this call," I said, walking out the back door into the yard. "Hello."

Without preamble, he said, "You were supposed to call me for a follow-up meeting."

It was Special Agent Ross. I wasn't about to tell him that he had just rescued me.

"No, I said I would *think* about calling you for a follow-up meeting."

"Fair enough. Have you thought about it?"

I had, but I was still struggling mightily with my oath. Somewhere in my naïve brain, I still harbored hope that I would return to prominence within the family. In my heart, I knew this was never going to happen. The organization I had grown up in was as dead as Alphonse and Big Tommy. I was a lingering vestige of a bygone era, and I wasn't sure that Little Tommy wasn't trying to have me killed.

"I'll come in, but that doesn't mean I'm committing to anything."

"I understand. When are you coming?"

"I'll let you know."

"Not this again, Angelo. I need a date."

"I'll call you."

"When?"

"Soon."

"Angelo!"

"Soon. I'll call soon."

The phone hummed in my hand. I pulled it away from my ear and looked at the caller ID. It said: Compound. "I need to take this other call."

"It's more important than trying to save your life?"

"It's not a high bar to clear, Ross. My life ain't worth much anymore."

I hit the button to accept the incoming call. "Hello."

"Angelo."

"Tommaso."

(Note: Not long after Big Tommy's death, Little Tommy insisted that he be called Tommaso. He said the name Little Tommy was insulting. Okay, fine, sure, whatever.)

I've got to admit, it creeped me out that Little Tommy suddenly called when I was on the phone with an FBI agent. I chalked it up to coincidence, but it still gave me chills.

"I need to talk to you," he said.

"I'm listening," I said.

"Not on the phone. Here."

"Okay. When?"

"When? Right now. In ten minutes."

That was Little Tommy—call out of the clear blue sky and expect me to drop everything and come running.

"I can't tonight."

"Why the fuck not?"

"Because I'm busy. If you gotta know, I've got a date tonight."

There was a moment of silence on the phone before he started laughing. "A date. Way to go, Angelo. Who's the lucky girl?"

"Just someone I know from the bank. It's nothing serious." I didn't want to tell him the truth. I always felt like he was storing away information to use against me. Was I being paranoid? Maybe. But that didn't mean that he wasn't out to get me.

"Tomorrow morning, then."

Carolyn was standing at the back screen door holding up two plates of strawberry shortcake. I held up an index finger and mouthed, "One minute."

"What time?" I asked.

"Ten."

"I'll be there."

I slipped the phone back in my pocket and went inside. Carolyn had dessert and coffee on the table. "Important call?" she asked.

"Just business," I said.

"Your consulting work?"

"Yeah."

Her hair was down on her shoulders, and she was wearing sandals and a sundress with green, yellow, and red tropical designs. She smelled like orange blossoms. I was in love.

We sat down to dessert, and she picked up right where she'd left off. "You never answered my question. How did your first wife die?"

"It was in a car accident."

"Oh my, that's terrible."

"It was a long time ago."

"Still, that's a terrible ordeal. Where did it happen?"

"Here in town. It's still hard to talk about."

"Sure. I understand."

"Let me ask you a question, Carolyn. Do you want to stay around here, you know, long term? Do you ever think of retiring and moving south?"

"I don't know. I guess if I had the proper motivation, I might consider moving. Why do you ask? Are you thinking of leaving?"

"Maybe. I don't know. The winters around here are starting to get to me."

"But what about your job? You're still doing some consulting for the cement company."

"Yeah, a little. In fact, that was one of the foremen on the phone just now. They want to talk to me tomorrow about a problem at the plant."

"What kind of problem?"

"I'm not sure. Some kind of supply-chain issue."

"I see." She set her fork on the edge of her plate and said, "Angelo, I know this is only our second date, but we've been doing something of a courting dance for a while. Isn't that fair to say?"

I smiled. "That's fair, yes."

"And I'm very attracted to you, and it seems to be mutual."

"Very mutual."

"So, would it be fair to say that we both are very much interested in seeing if this relationship can work?"

"Carolyn, there's nothing I want more."

"Good. I'm so glad to hear you say that, because I feel the same way. But if the relationship is going to work . . ." She pushed a silver serving tray that held the cream and sugar off to the side, reached under the maroon tablecloth, and pulled out an oversized sheet of copy paper and set it on the table facing me. It was the front page of the Steubenville *Herald-Star* from Monday, June 20, 1983. The headline read:

Reputed Mobster Clinging to Life;

Wife Killed in Downtown Shootout

Carolyn let me stare at it for a minute before pulling it back to her side of the table. She started reading:

> Angelo Cipriani, a reputed member of the Fortunato crime family, was shot and critically wounded yesterday in a downtown gun battle that claimed the life of his wife, Jolie. Mr. Cipriani, 33, and Mrs. Cipriani, 32, had left the Federal Terrace restaurant shortly after 8 p.m. when, according to witnesses, two gunmen approached their car and began shooting. Police said between sixteen and twenty rounds entered the vehicle.
>
> Mrs. Cipriani was dead on arrival at Ohio Valley Hospital. Mr. Cipriani is in critical condition after undergoing surgery for what a hospital spokesman said was multiple gunshot wounds.
>
> Steubenville Police Detective Hugh Fellows said the two assailants fled on foot. Police have no suspects in the shooting.
>
> A waitress at the Federal Terrace, who asked not to be identified, said the Ciprianis had been at the restaurant celebrating their first wedding anniversary.

She folded the sheet of paper and set it aside. "You know, Angelo, trying to hide something like this would be like the captain of the *Titanic* trying to hide the hole in the front of his ship. How did you think I wouldn't find out?"

"Sometimes you have to commit to the lie, just say it with confidence and see how long you can pull it off."

"Excuse me?"

"I didn't know how to tell you about my past, Carolyn. Well, that's not exactly true. I knew how to tell you, but I was afraid you'd run like your hair was on fire."

"So you lied?"

"Yeah, a hundred percent. That's what you do when you're in a wild panic. You lie to save your skin. Look, I'm sorry, but it just seemed like my best option until I found a better way to tell you."

"And when, exactly, was that going to be?"

"I don't know. You're the first woman since Jolie that I wanted. I was trying to do whatever I could to keep you." I blew out a stream of air. "How did you find that, anyway?"

"I was talking to my Aunt Paula, the woman who raised me, and I was telling her about what a wonderful time I'd had on our first date. She asked me your name, and I told her. She said, 'Angelo Cipriani, the mobster?' I laughed and said, 'There must be two Angelo Ciprianis. The one I went out with is a consultant in the cement industry.'" My face was so hot I thought the skin was going to peel back. "She said, 'Horsefeathers, he's a gunman for the Fortunatos. He's the one who got all shot up and his wife got killed back in the day. Stay away from him. He's bad news.' After that, it just took a visit to the library to look through the *Herald-Star* microfilm."

"I see. So, are you?"

"Am I what?"

"Are you going to stay away from me?"

"You mean, break up after two dates?"

"I guess. Your aunt thinks I'm bad news."

"Angelo . . ." She massaged her temples for a moment, squeezing her eyes tight before looking up. "Here's where I am. I've had a crush on you since the first day you walked into the Starlighter Diner. I thought you were the most handsome man I'd ever seen. And you were friendly and funny. I thought, there's the man of my dreams. Then for two years you wouldn't get off center. *Two years!* I asked the other waitresses what they knew about you, but nobody seemed to know anything. You were the mystery man. Finally, I had to beat you up at the counter and give you my number just so you'd ask me out. I would love for this relationship to work, but it can't be built on lies. What's in the past is in the past. If you want this to work . . ." She waved back and forth between us with four of her fingers. "I need to know who Angelo Cipriani is."

"We're going to need more coffee," I said. "And if you could add a little bourbon to mine, that would be better."

We sat at her dining room table for a long time. Hours. I can't tell you exactly how long, but dinner was at six and there was a full moon climbing over the West Virginia hills by the time I'd finished. She said, "That's quite a story. Is that everything?"

"I think so." I thought for a moment, then said, "Wait a minute. I guess there's something you ought to know about your stepfather." I told her everything I knew about Woodrow Golightly.

"He was clubbed over the head and made into dog food?"

"That's pretty much it, yeah."

"So he didn't abandon us."

"That's probably the nicest thing that can be said about him. He was a pervert. He got what was coming to him. Vigilante justice can still be just."

She slouched back in her chair and shook her hair off her face. "You've absolutely worn me out tonight, Angelo." She pushed back her chair. I started to pick up my coffee cup and plate. "Don't worry about that. I'll clean up tomorrow."

She took my hand, and we walked through the kitchen into the hallway toward the front door. We had only taken a few steps when she squeezed my hand and said, "Wrong door, cowboy," and led me back to her bedroom.

CHAPTER

24

Easter Sunday, April 22, 1984

On the afternoon of Holy Saturday, more than a year after Jolie had been killed, Big Tommy announced that he wanted all his immediate capos to attend Easter services at the Church of the Holy Cross. He made it sound like a request, but the word "please" was rarely part of his vernacular. It was an order. While I was not a made man, it also was to include me.

The last time I had stepped inside the Church of the Holy Cross was for the funeral mass for Alphonse and Matteo. Given my history, I almost thought it was sacrilegious of me to be there, but an order from the boss was an order from the boss. His only other directive was to "dress for Easter Sunday," which meant he wanted you there in a coat and tie. I thought maybe it was some kind of show of force, but who was he trying to impress? I mean, we'd be there to celebrate the resurrection. Talk about your ultimate show of force.

He wanted us at the compound by seven-thirty for breakfast. I arrived outside the gates at seven-twenty-five. There were plenty of cars in the cul-de-sac and in the drive, but I didn't see a single person. As I walked up the sidewalk, Jimmy Beans opened the front door. "Where is everybody?" I asked.

"Downstairs," he said.

"I thought we were having breakfast."

"Yeah, downstairs."

He shut the door and walked down the steps ahead of me. When we got to the door of the counting room, he grabbed the doorknob, turned, and said, "Straighten your tie." I did. He gave the door a pull and said, "After you."

I walked into the counting room and froze. Big Tommy was standing in the middle of the room behind a table draped in a black cloth; a candle burned at each end of the table. In a semicircle behind Big Tommy were his capos—Carlo, Mickey V, Joey Nickels, Sammy Avocado, Muzzie Lollini, Ricky Bones, Connie Bones. They were in dark suits, their hands clasped at the belt, all looking solemn.

My first thought was that it was to be a ritual killing. I didn't know what my offense was, but I knew this wasn't good. Jimmy Beans took the condemned by the elbow and walked me to the front of the table, then took his place in the semicircle.

"Years ago, my father brought you into his office to tell you that you would never be a made man in the Fortunato family," Big Tommy began. "This was completely understandable. You are not of pure Italian blood. My father adhered to this tradition, as did his father before him. You told my father, 'I'll always be a second-class citizen.' But not after today, Angelo Albert Cipriani. You've given your blood and your soul to this family, and in my eyes, that makes you as worthy of being a made man as anyone of pure Italian ancestry."

It was all I could do not to start bawling.

"And just so you know, because this is a move away from tradition, it was not my decision alone. Before you could join the ranks of these men behind me, it had to be a unanimous agreement among them."

I glanced over at my oft-times adversary, Ricky Bones. One eyebrow arched, and the thinnest of smiles pursed his lips. I nodded in his direction.

The ceremony was simple. I'm not going into the details because it was sacred to me. I spilled blood, took an oath, and pledged my undying loyalty to the family.

And that was that. I was a man of honor in the Fortunato family. I'm not sure I can adequately explain what this meant to me. Maybe it was like being made a partner in a big law firm or becoming the chief of surgery at a prestigious hospital or being promoted to general. I don't know. All I can tell you for sure is that a guy who was a high school dropout had become a capo in the crime family that ruled the Ohio Valley.

I went to the Church of the Holy Cross that morning, got on my knees and thanked Jesus for making me a made member of the Fortunato family. Organized crime is probably not the kind of thing Jesus gets involved in, but I still expressed my thanks . . . just in case. I have never been particularly a religious person, but I've always believed in a greater power and that there was something beyond this life. I will tell you that during the ceremony, I pledged my loyalty to the Fortunato family above my family and above my God. While I was thanking Jesus for the promotion, I did apologize for that transgression.

After church, we returned to the compound for a feast. It was the second best day of my life, right behind my wedding day. I wished Jolie could have been there. I hoped she was watching.

CHAPTER 25

August 19, 1989

ROSEBELLA HAD GIVEN birth to two girls, then miscarried the next three times she had gotten pregnant. Big Tommy had given up on having a son to carry on the family name. When she became pregnant for the sixth time, quite unplanned, no one expected her to carry the baby to term. The doctor ordered bed rest for the last five months of the pregnancy.

She fooled everybody. Tommaso Cristian Fortunato came into the world at seven pounds, one ounce, pink, wailing, and healthy. It was the happiest I had ever seen Big Tommy. Except for the day we pulled onto Rosemont Street and he instinctively knew his father had been murdered, it also was the only time I ever saw him shed tears. He was overjoyed. A son. The Fortunato name would live on beyond him.

We were again on the veranda that night with cigars and bourbon when he said, "I'm not going to let him take over the business. I want better for him. He's going legit."

"The business has been pretty good to you," I said.

"He can do better. He'll do something where he's not always worried that someone's going to put a bullet in his head."

He was baptized at our Lady of the Holy Cross on the first Sunday in October. Afterwards, Big Tommy and Rosebella hosted a party at the compound that would have made a presidential state dinner look like a wiener roast. There was enough food to feed a third-world country for a month. Lobsters were boiled in copper kettles, shrimp were piled on tubs of ice, and an ox was roasting over a spit. The champagne fountain looked like it belonged in a Paris park.

The families from Buffalo, Cleveland, Pittsburgh, and even Youngstown all sent emissaries with gifts and good wishes.

(Note: For the record, I didn't understand this, either. We were fighting the Gemellis in Youngstown all the time, but for some reason they sent two guys with gifts to help celebrate the birth of a son who, eventually, they'd want to kill. This organized crime, it can be a funny business.)

Rosebella and Big Tommy presented their son to the crowd under the shade of a sprawling oak. Big Tommy was crying again. Jimmy Beans nudged me in the ribs with an elbow and whispered, "I didn't think Big Tommy had tear ducts."

I was happy for Big Tommy. He got the son he had long prayed for. I didn't know, of course, that Tommaso's birth signaled the moment the clock began ticking down my time as a valued member of the family.

CHAPTER

26

July 2019

I WOKE UP AT Carolyn's the next morning to the question of "What do you want for breakfast?" It had been one of the best nights of my life, and no, I'm not giving you any more details than that. I loved this woman, and I was determined not to let her get away. I asked if I could come see her again that night, and she said, "I would expect nothing less." She got dressed for her gig at the Starlighter Diner, and I went home to clean up before my meeting with Little Tommy.

When I turned the Cutlass onto Rosemont, the morning sun was shining on the face of the manse that Alphonse's father, Aldo, had built during the heyday of Prohibition. The place was showing her age. It was in bad need of a paint job, and the gutters were bowing across the façade. Weeds and untrimmed grass were creeping up around the steel fence, and the driveway was cracked and pitted. Big Tommy had the house and fence painted every other summer, and in better days, Rosebella always had flowers growing out front, and the place looked like some botanical garden. Rosebella was in bad shape these days. She had never gotten over Big Tommy's death and was sliding deeper into the darkness of dementia. For all the money

Little Tommy was bringing in, you'd think he could spend a couple dollars to keep the place up and take care of his mother.

The front door was unlocked, and I went in and made my way back to the office in the corner of the house. The office smelled like reefer and body odor. I remembered a day when it smelled like strong men and old wood and cigar smoke. The place hadn't been cleaned since Big Tommy died. When I walked in that day, there were two stoners playing a video game on a screen that looked like it belonged in a drive-in movie theater. It was some combat video game where they were pretending to shoot up Russian commandos. Simulated machine-gun fire filled the room. Mother of Christ. Piss would run down their legs at the sight of a real Russian commando. "Where's Tommaso?" I asked.

"Search me, dude," said a guy who had one leg draped over the arm of the couch. His thumbs kept dancing over the controller, and he never took his eyes off the screen.

Dude.

I had to walk away.

I found Tommaso in the kitchen, dressed in cargo shorts, a T-shirt, and flip-flops. No one wore a suit anymore. He had one finger in an ear and a cell phone up to another. When he saw me, he moved the phone away from his ear and mouthed, "Give me a minute."

I backed into the hall, and as I was standing there, Rosebella came down the stairs. This woman, who had gone through life so perfectly coiffed, was in old bedroom slippers and stained pajamas. Her hair hung around her shoulders in black and gray tangles. Her lipstick looked as though it had been applied with a vibrator, the poor thing. It extended beyond her lips in every direction, giving her a clownish look. I said, "Good morning, Rosebella."

She smiled and said, "Oh, Muzzie, it's so good to see you."

Muzzie Lollini had died two years earlier. She was confused; I didn't correct her.

"Are you going to make yourself some tea, Rosebella?"

"Yes." She smiled for a moment before her face took on a perplexed look. "Have you seen my Tommaso?"

Her Tommaso, of course, had been dead six years.

"I haven't seen him lately, dear."

"I'm starting to worry. I can't imagine where he's gone."

"If I see him, I'll send him right over."

"Thank you." She toddled on to the kitchen.

Little Tommy came into the hall with a diet soda and waved for me to follow him. The king would see me now. We walked to the concrete pad between the garage and the swimming pool.

He looked agitated, and he repeatedly ran his hand down the lower part of his face, as though trying to squeegee off the perspiration. "I've got a problem, Angelo," he said, nodding for me to take the seat in an Adirondack chair.

"Tell me about it," I said, trying to hide my glee. When the boss had a problem, it usually meant an assignment for me, something that would put some cash in my pocket.

"The Mexican cartels have been hijacking my trucks out of Texas. Sometimes they steal our product. Sometimes they hold it hostage. They've got MS-13 gang members on their payroll. They're expert extortionists. I'm supposed to be the extortionist. I've got spooks in Detroit trying to steal product and sell it back to me, and the Chinese syndicate in Florida is paying twice the going rate for product. They're trying to buy everything they can so they can run me out of business. Once they do, they'll force the supplier to sell it to them for a third of what I'm paying. That's what I'm dealing with these days."

(Note: "Product" was Little Tommy's euphemistic term for cocaine, meth, fentanyl, and heroin, like he was selling disposable diapers or spark plugs.)

"What can I do to make your life a little more comfortable?" I asked.

"I need you to train my guys."

In other words, train my replacement. You'd think that after six years of this, I'd be prepared for the gut punch. But I wasn't.

"Tommaso, how many times have we been down this path in the past couple of years? You want me to train your guys to take my place, but they either don't have the stones or they don't have the smarts. And let me tell you something, the guys I clipped for your father were meaner and smarter than any of these bums you're dealing with now."

"Maybe so, but I can't send an old white guy into this mix. They'd make you in a minute, and you'd be dead. In the old days it was very calculated. They were precision hits, and you were executing guys who looked like you. You couldn't get near this bunch. I've got to recruit Asians, blacks, and Mexicans to keep pace. I love you like you were my own blood, but it's a different world now. I need younger and—what's the politically correct word these days?—more *diverse* guys in your role. But I need someone who can teach them techniques that will keep them alive. And it will keep you alive, and that's important to me."

I didn't believe that for two seconds. My life wasn't worth anything to Little Tommy. Once I taught his guys my business, I would be as expendable as any of his low-level drug runners. Maybe he was right. Maybe my day had truly passed. "You asked me to do this before, and we both know how it turned out. Your boys thought it was great to shoot people in a video game, but when it was go time, they froze. You know what your grandfather once told me? He said, 'This ain't a life for snowflakes.' And that's who you want me to train."

* * *

The first guy I tried to train was named Timmy Sweets. It was the lamest name for a mob hitman in history. I took him to an abandoned strip mine outside of Hopedale and let him practice with a 9-millimeter and a .38-caliber revolver. He could barely hit the side of the strip-mine wall, which is roughly the size of a football field. I told him not to worry because his work would be done at close range—three or four inches. The mark was a drug dealer named Isaac Jackson from Youngstown who had pistol-whipped a Fortunato courier into a coma and ripped off fifteen thousand dollars in cocaine. It wasn't the kind of situation where you worked out a repayment plan. I would distract Isaac, and Timmy would come up from behind and put one into the back of his skull. It was as simple a plan as I could concoct.

There's a trick fathers will use when taking their young sons fishing. They'll catch a fish, then hand the pole to the boy and say, "Here, try mine for a while." And, bang, they think they caught one. That's what it was like when I took Timmy Sweets out for the hit. I caught the mark getting out of his car near the housing projects on Youngstown's east side. I said, "Hey, Isaac, I need to talk to you for Tommaso Fortunato."

"I don't know nothin' about no ripped off drugs," Isaac said.

"Whoa! No one's accusing you of stealing anything."

"Good thing, motherfucker, because I don't take no disrespect from some old peckerwood."

"No need for that kind of talk. I just want to chat for a minute."

This was perfect. Isaac wanted to argue. He was distracted. No situational awareness. Timmy walked up behind him and promptly froze. Once Isaac realized what was going on, he took off running. I pulled my .38 snub-nose from my pants pocket and shot him in the back. It was a spine shot, and he dropped, most likely paralyzed from the waist down. It was like I'd just handed the fishing pole to Timmy. "Finish it," I said. Lights were coming on in the projects. Timmy walked over, his arm extended, the 9-millimeter shaking in his hand like he had Parkinson's disease. "Do it and let's go." Isaac was screaming. Timmy shot twice, hitting him in the shoulder and the armpit. Isaac was screaming louder, which, quite frankly, was totally justified. More lights came on. "In the head," I said. The next shot took off an ear and came out his eye. "Christ." I walked up and put two in the back of his head. It ended up being more of a mercy killing than an execution.

On the drive home, Timmy said just eleven words. "I don't think I'm cut out for this kind of thing."

"I think you should trust your instincts," I said.

The second trainee was Bruno De Luca, who supposedly came to work for Little Tommy from the mob in Camden, New Jersey. This led me to ask the obvious question. "If he worked for the mob in Camden, why does he need me to teach him how to clip someone?"

"Just make sure he's ready," Little Tommy said.

I took Bruno to the same abandoned strip mine. I've got to say, he was very good with the gun. He had the swagger of a New Jersey mobster who thought he was doing the pikers in Ohio a favor by coming to work for them. He could wear out your ears in about five minutes, always running his mouth, telling me about his multimillion-dollar drug deals, how much money he made, and the fancy cars he drove. His wealth was exceeded only by the number of beautiful women he had bedded. I finally asked him, "So why the hell did you come to Ohio if you had all this going for you in Jersey?" He just shrugged, which meant it was all bullshit.

Our target was a biker from Parkersburg, West Virginia, who went by the name of Apache. He had stolen a shipment of drugs, shot up the house of one of Little Tommy's best dealers, killing him and his girlfriend, and sent word up the river that he, and not the Fortunatos, would be controlling the drug trade south of Wheeling.

Apache's pronouncement was a death sentence; he was just too stupid to realize it.

His base of operation was a cement block fortress that was the headquarters for the River Warriors motorcycle gang. He spent a lot of time there and was rarely without fellow gang members at his side. However, he was known to frequent a bar in south Parkersburg near the Little Kanawha River called the Oarsman, where his girlfriend was a bartender. Again, a mark with a weakness for drink and the ladies.

I drove the Galaxie. Bruno sat in the passenger side with his 9-millimeter Winchester magnum in his lap, the silencer attached, incessantly talking about how he couldn't wait to put one in Apache's brain. His potential seemed a little more promising than Timmy Sweets. One of Little Tommy's local couriers went into the Oarsman to scout for us. He met us down the street from the bar and said, "He's in there. He's riding a black custom chopper parked by the back door. He's got long hair in a ponytail and a braided chin beard."

"What's he wearing?" Bruno asked.

"What, you want a fashion report? If a fat fuck with a braided chin beard gets on that bike, it's him, Einstein."

Bruno turned red. I couldn't suppress the laugh.

I moved the car around the block and parked it on the street where I could see the side door of the bar and the bike. All of a sudden, the chatter about making the hit stopped. His right leg was shaking, his heel pounding out a staccato rhythm on the floor mat. He said, "I don't think this is a good time. We need to call this off."

"What are you talking about? Tonight's the night."

"No. It's bad timing. He'll make me before I get to him."

"How would a biker from Parkersburg, West Virginia, recognize a wiseguy from Camden, New Jersey? Besides, who gives a rat's ass if he makes you? He's going to be dead."

"Yeah, yeah, it's a bad time. I feel it in my bones. Call it off. We need to call it off."

"I see. Mr. New Jersey tough guy can't make it happen. You're all hat and no cattle."

"What's that mean?"

"It means you're a pussy."

No sooner had the words come out of my mouth than Apache emerged from the side door. He was alone and unsteady on his feet. Drunk and sloppy. Perfect. "There's your mark. Are you in or not?"

"No, we need to abort."

I couldn't afford to abort. I needed the payday. I got out of the car and walked toward Apache just as he was hoisting his right leg over the bike and settling onto the seat. He didn't see me until I materialized in front of his bike. His eyes were at half-staff, and his face had the soft glow of drunkenness. "Are you Apache?"

He squinted, trying to focus on my face. "Who wants to know?"

"Close enough." I pulled my .38 from my pants pocket and fired three times into his chest. I snapped off the shots so fast that the third bullet struck home before he blew backwards off his motorcycle. It had been a rush decision, and I hadn't thought to grab Bruno's 9-millimeter with the silencer. The back of the bar was buried in a little basin, and the reports of the .38 sounded like someone had tossed TNT down a well. I sprinted back to the Galaxie and backed up the street without headlights until I came to an alley. I followed the alley in darkness for two blocks, then cut back to a paved road that took me to Interstate 77. When I was several miles up the interstate, I reached over and snatched the 9-millimeter out of his lap and threw it on the driver's-side floor. "Give me that before you hurt yourself, Nancy," I said.

"It wasn't the right time," he said. "We could have been busted because . . ."

"Shut your chickenshit mouth," I said.

The next day, he went back to Camden, or wherever it is that disgraced dagos go.

* * *

Little Tommy said, "You think I'm putting you on the shelf because you're part of the past generation, but I'm putting you on the shelf to keep you from getting killed."

"The last two guys I trained pissed down their legs. Both of the bad guys ended up corpses, and I'm still here talking to you."

"We can go round and round like this all you want, but I need someone to school my guys. Are you going to help me or not?"

I blew out a breath of frustration and exhaustion. "I promised your dad I'd look out for you. Of course, I'll help you. I'll do whatever you need."

"I want you to work with my new guy. His name is Gaetano. You'll like him. You're kindred souls. He grew up in the Spaghetto, just like you, and he's fearless."

"Fearless in this business means he's Sammy Avocado, and he's likely got a screw loose."

"He's my guy, Angelo. I want you to work with him."

"Do you know how much training Carlo gave me back in the day? 'Here's a gun. Shoot him.'"

Little Tommy was tired of hearing me talk. "When can you take him out?"

"Tomorrow."

"Good. Come by in the morning. I'll have him ready to go." He dug into his pocket and peeled off five hundred-dollar bills. "Here's a down payment." I had a couple of questions about this Gaetano, but the conversation was over.

CHAPTER

27

July 2019

I certainly did not approve of the way Little Tommy was running the family business, but I had to give him this: The kid wasn't stupid, he wasn't lazy, and he knew how to make money. A lot of money. Obscene amounts of money. And like gambling and prostitution, the drug game is an all-cash business. One income number I'd heard was twenty million dollars a year, and I don't think it was an exaggeration. He kept stuffing cash in the safe in the lower level of the house. It was stacked in every corner—wrapped twenty-, fifty-, and hundred-dollar bills. It was more than you could launder through the pizza joints and car washes in ten lifetimes.

Little Tommy set up a system of wholesalers, including Silvio's operation in Rochester, and had a steady stream of drugs coming up from Florida and Texas. Drugs were brought north in semis, panel trucks, cars, and vans. If it had at least four wheels, Little Tommy's team could figure a way to pack it with drugs. He had warehouses in Charleston, West Virginia; Erie, Pennsylvania; and Martins Ferry, Ohio. Behind false walls and in basements, the drugs were cut, packaged, and sent to the distribution warehouse in Weirton that once housed the Fortunato casino. From there, they went to dealers in western Pennsylvania, West Virginia, Ohio, and lower Michigan.

This was the target-rich information the FBI was anxious to get its hands on. So, you might ask, if I had been cut out of the organization, how did I know all this? I used a tried-and-true technique of the mob. I picked out the weakest link in the organization and exploited him. His name was Alphonse Fortunato II, the grandson of Matteo Fortunato. Alphonse II was a bit of a lost soul. His mother, hoping to distance her son from a career in organized crime, refused to allow him to be called Alphonse and instead called him Alfie. It was an unfortunate name that had followed him into adulthood. After he dropped out of college, Little Tommy reluctantly brought him into the organization at Rosebella's insistence. "He's your blood," she said. This meant nothing to Little Tommy, but he agreed and gave the kid little more responsibility than a janitor. He might as well have been emptying spittoons at the athletic club. The other mongrels in the organization referred to Alfie as "Tommaso's little bitch."

I was walking out of the compound one day when I ran into Alfie. He was so thin he looked malnourished, with sunken cheeks and eyes. He always carried that whipped-puppy look on his face, like he didn't have a friend in the world, and he probably didn't. I said, "Let's go grab something to eat, you and me." He actually looked over his shoulder to make sure there was no one else walking with us. I took him to Naples Spaghetti House in downtown Steubenville and bought him dinner. You'd have thought I had handed him a million bucks. I don't think anyone at the compound had ever shown this kid any degree of friendship. We got a booth and split a couple bottles of wine. I asked a lot of questions and let him tell me his story, then slowly worked the conversation to Little Tommy's drug operation. He was softened up by the alcohol. He knew intimately how it worked.

When we walked to the parking lot, I said, "I think it would be best if this conversation stayed between the two of us."

"Tommaso would slit my throat on the spot if he knew what I just told you."

"We don't want that, right?"

"No, sir."

"Of course not."

I kept the communication open with Alfie. On occasion, I'd buy him a spaghetti dinner and a bottle of wine. It was a cheap way of keeping myself connected to the inner workings of the new Fortunato crime family. This was long before Agent Ross invaded my lunch at the diner, but I always figured it would be useful information to have in my pocket.

* * *

After my meeting with Little Tommy, I went to the Starlighter Diner for lunch. I walked out to find a squat cop leaning against the passenger door of an unmarked Steubenville Police car. I must be a terrible creature of habit. The cops always know exactly where to find me. Detective Dennis Logston's arms were crossed over a gut that hung below his belt, stretching the material of his white dress shirt like a water balloon. Steubenville had some competent cops, but Logston wasn't one of them.

"Well, well, well, if it isn't one of Steubenville's finest," I said. "Oh, check that, I meant, if it isn't one of Steubenville's fattest."

His partner, a guy named McCarthy, was standing near the front of the car and choking back laughter.

"So, you're the one, huh, Logston?"

"The one what?" he asked.

"I heard the Downtown Bakery was being kept in business by a single cop. It must be you. Looks like you've got a jelly donut addiction."

I could see the red heat of embarrassment creeping up around his collar, and the muscles in his jaw rolling under his ears. "You're a funny man, Cipriani. Except I don't think you're going to be doing a whole lot of laughing when we get done with our conversation today."

"I'm not much of a conversationalist. You're welcome to talk at me, but I probably don't have much to say."

"How about we go down to the station and chat?"

"I got a better idea. How about you kiss my rosy red ass. I'm not going down to the station unless you've got a warrant for my arrest. Have you got a warrant?" Logston continued to stare, saying nothing. "That's what I figured. Have a good day, Detective."

I started walking up the hill; Logston fell in beside me. "I've gotten some very interesting, very detailed information about you and your buddy Carlo," he said.

"I don't know what you're talking about. I don't have a buddy, Carlo."

"Let me refresh your memory: Carlo Della Russo."

"Sorry, but it's not ringing a bell. I used to shoot pool with a guy at Bixby's whose name was Carlo, but I haven't seen him in years. He must've moved away or something."

"Yeah, I'll bet he disappeared because of the 'or something.'"

"Is there a point to this conversation?"

"My information tells me that you and Carlo killed Willie Valentine. Carlo strangled him in the car and you helped dump him in the ash ponds up behind Brilliant."

"Willie Valentine? Not ringing a bell." I looked over at Logston. We weren't yet halfway up the hill. He was already sucking hard for air. "You need to get in shape, Detective. You're going to have a heart attack, and what a tragic blow that would be for the police department."

I heard a chortle from McCarthy, who was following a few steps behind us. Logston's face was the color of an eggplant. I couldn't tell if it was the result of embarrassment, anger, or exertion, but I'm guessing it was a combination of all three.

"You're telling me that you and Carlo had nothing to do with Willie's murder?"

"Just out of curiosity, it sounds to me like you don't even have a body. If you don't have a body, how do you know anyone was murdered? Maybe this Willie fella is just on vacation or visiting relatives, or something. To tell you the truth, I'm a little offended by your line of questioning, intimating that I'd be involved with something as nefarious as murder."

"How about Woodrow Golightly?"

"You're going to have to help me out."

"He disappeared off the streets. The information I have is that it was the handiwork of your buddy Carlo and that caveman Sammy Avocado. However, it was you and Carlo who took the body to the dog food factory in East Liverpool where Mr. Golightly became kibbles."

"Where are you hearing these horrible stories? You better not be out there slandering my good name."

"Do you have a good name, Cipriani?"

"No need to get insulting, Detective. It's not my fault you're fat."

We were nearly to my apartment building. Sweat was beading on Logston's forehead and soaking the collar of his shirt. Waves rolled across his gut as he sucked for air. "I'm going to be working on these cases, Cipriani, and here's what you need to understand. When Iceman Al and Big Tommy were running the organization, they would regularly give the boys upstairs a thick envelope of cash. In exchange, the cops ran interference for the Fortunatos, and they were free to run the whorehouses and casinos. But Little Tommy, being the greedy prick that he is, isn't passing out envelopes, so there's no longer a moratorium on the Fortunato family. In fact, it's open season. I'm going to piece this all together and hang your ass."

"Logston, you couldn't piece together a kid's jigsaw puzzle." We got to the door of the apartment building. "I'd love to hear more of your fantasy tales, but I'm giving myself a pedicure this afternoon. The next time you visit Neverland, give my regards to Tinker Bell."

I was laughing when I disappeared into the apartment building. However, by the time I got to my apartment, I thought I was having a heart attack. It felt like someone was stabbing me in the chest with a giant icicle. Who in the hell was talking to the Steubenville cops? Logston was a dumbass of the first degree, but the information he had was right on the screws. I got into the contacts of my phone and found the phone number I had listed under the name Fred Pitts.

(Note: I recorded the number in my phone, then flushed Ross's business card down the toilet. Want to know the easiest way to become a dead mobster? Get caught with an FBI business card in your wallet.)

The FBI receptionist wanted to know my name. "Just tell him I'm calling from Steubenville," I said.

It was another couple of minutes before he picked up. "This is Ross."

"Someone up there talking to the Steubenville cops?"

There was a moment of silence. "I'm assuming this is my friend from the brick factory?"

"Yeah. Do you have a rat up there trying to sink my ass?"

"I don't know what you're talking about."

"What I'm talking about is, I just had a very disconcerting visit from a Steubenville detective who . . ." I paused. ". . . seemed to know some things."

"You're going to have to give me a little more information."

"He knew things he shouldn't have known."

"About you?"

"No, about Winston Churchill. Yes, about me. Why the hell do you think I'm calling?"

"I don't understand why you're blaming me."

"Because I think you're squeezing my balls by feeding the Steubenville cops information so they put pressure on me, and I'll agree to flip on Little Tommy."

"Good God, would you listen to yourself? I don't need the locals to do my heavy lifting, and here's a little inside baseball for you, Angelo. I don't involve the locals because I don't want them screwing up my operation. Did you ever think it might be Little Tommy feeding them information to get you out of the way? Instead of paying off the cops with cash, maybe Little Tommy's paying them off with information to get rid of you? Angelo, you're like the former high school jock who can never quit talking about things he did when he was seventeen. The old days aren't coming back. It's a whole new world. These guys aren't operating like the old mob. They operate like the Mexican cartels. There's no honor there. I'm opening a door for you to get out. If you want the opportunity, take it. And just so you know, if you get indicted on state charges, all deals are off, because I can't help you. So, what do you think? Are you ready to join forces with the good guys?"

"To tell you the truth, Ross, I don't know who the good guys are these days."

* * *

People have the misconception that cops are not allowed to lie. That's not true. If you lie to the cops, it's a crime. But they can lie to you all day long. Cops will lie to get the information they want. They will lie when the truth sounds better. So I didn't know if Ross was being square with me or blowing smoke, trying to put my nerves on edge so I'd jump to his side.

I was not ready to jump, but my nerves were definitely on edge.

CHAPTER

28

1991

I loved Carlo Dello Russo.

I spent more time with Carlo than any other human in my life, including my parents. I also learned more from him than anyone else. We were a hell of a team.

Carlo was a thirty-thousand-foot guy most of the time. He never paid any attention to the details unless we were on a job or at the horse track. Then no detail was too insignificant. On the job, he was the consummate pro. Sometimes he would just park one behind a guy's ear. If we confronted someone head-on, he would make them stand up and take it. He hated when guys begged for their lives. I never understood why this was important to him, but it was. He would say, "Do you want to die blubbering like a little girl, or go out like a man?" In all candor, his words never made a difference. Once a guy realizes that his time on earth is over, it's difficult to reason with him.

Some people might find it odd that I took pride in my work, but I always did. Carlo said we were professionals, and we should take pride in the craft. I can't tell you how many people Carlo and I took out. It was hard to keep track. After all, it's not the kind of thing you log in a journal. I sometimes feel like an old man trying to recall his many sexual conquests. The faces start to blur after a while. I was there, I remember the hit, but did I do the deed or did Carlo? Who knows, but I can tell you that our body count together was easily north of thirty. It's all I did my entire adult life. And I believe every son of a bitch we killed is rotting in hell. I may be headed there, too. I'll worry about eternity later.

It's funny—maybe funny isn't the right word; interesting is probably a better choice—how when I drove through the Ohio Valley, I would pass landmarks that sent me back in time to one of our hits. Every time I drove past the Logan Avenue exit to Mingo Junction, for example, I remembered the time we picked up a boost artist named Willie Valentine outside of the Herald Square Cigar Store and told him we'd give him a hundred bucks if he helped us out with some troublemakers at Big Tommy's whorehouse on Wheeling Island. Willie was always up for an opportunity to inflict a little pain, and if he got some cash in the process, all the better. We were just passing the Logan Avenue exit, and Willie was telling a joke about some guy giving away his wife's golf clubs or something like that. Willie mumbled a lot and I could only understand about every third word that came out of his mouth. He was about to the punchline when Carlo reached up with a piano wire, wrapped it around Willie's neck and started pulling hard, like he was trying to stop a runaway horse. Willie was a big guy, and he was trying to fight back, and I'm sitting over there like I'm a chauffeur, acting oblivious to the fact that a giant black guy was getting strangled to death next to me. There was spittle flying everywhere, and Willie was kicking and trying to get loose when his shoe hit one of my radio buttons and put on a country music station where Patsy Cline was singing "Walkin' After Midnight." I said, "Willie, my man, I didn't know you black guys liked country." I started laughing, then Carlo started laughing. He was still trying to choke Willie to death, but he couldn't stop laughing. As you might imagine, there wasn't anything about the entire situation that Willie thought was funny. His eyes were bugging out and his fingers were bleeding where he was trying to get the wire off his neck. I don't think he died until we were past the Georges Run exit. It wasn't one of Carlo's better efforts. I drove out New Alexandria Road behind Brilliant and we dumped Willie in one of the ponds where the power plant pumped its fly ash. It was highly acidic and Willie would be reduced to pulp in no time.

(Note: Two of Big Tommy's lower-level associates were walking down an alley in downtown Steubenville after collecting gambling receipts when a guy stepped out of the shadows and clubbed one of the couriers in the back of the head with a baseball bat. The second guy took a shot to the side of the face. The attacker tossed the bat and stole the receipts. The first guy never came out of the coma, and the last I knew he was staring into space at the same facility where Nickels was living. The other guy lost half his teeth and had to have about a dozen surgeries to reconstruct a face that looked like a squashed pumpkin. He didn't know Willie Valentine but said the assailant was a huge black guy who smelled like mildew. That narrowed down the possibilities to Willie Valentine. He was the only guy in Steubenville who was black, six-foot-five, smelled like mildew, and was dumb enough to rip off Big Tommy Fortunato.)

Carlo loved the ponies and was forever reading the racing forms. He considered himself an expert on horse racing, but I swear to God the guy had lost a fortune over the course of his lifetime betting on long shots that never failed to live up to their reputations. When he gambled, Carlo was usually wrong but never in doubt. Consequently, he never had any money. Carlo was the kind of guy who was always reaching into the couch cushions looking for change. If we went out to eat, the only thing that came out of his pockets was lint. He once had his car repossessed. That made Alphonse furious. He said, "This looks bad on me. You're one of my guys. Everybody knows you're one of my guys. Take care of your business."

There was a goombah from Washington, Pennsylvania, named Nelly Stefanelli, a small-time bookie who had been working in Washington County for years. After the Fortunatos took over Washington County from the Santoro family, Big Tommy allowed Stefanelli to continue to operate in exchange for 15 percent of the gross.

It was a very fair deal. Stefanelli was one of those guys who would agree to anything and thank you profusely for the opportunity, just so you would leave and he could figure a way to screw you.

It only took a few weeks before we were having to beat on him for his agreed-to 15 percent. He always had some lame excuse for not paying. This was a constant aggravation. We were making so much money in the area, and Washington was on the outskirts of our territory, that Big Tommy put up with a lot more from Stefanelli than he would have if he had been operating in downtown Steubenville. After a year, Big Tommy learned that Stefanelli had been making book in the south end of Wheeling out of a bar called the Ironmen's Huddle. Carlo and I paid him a visit, and he had a cast on his left hand for the next ten weeks. He was given specific instructions to keep current on his payments to Big Tommy, and under no circumstances was he to venture out of Washington County.

"Do you understand, Stefanelli?" I asked.

"Yes sir, yes sir," he said. "You'll never have another problem with me. I swear."

But some guys in this business, they just don't learn too good. The payments didn't come in, and after a few months he was weaseling his way back into Wheeling. Big Tommy called us into his office. We knew what was coming. He handed Carlo a piece of folded flash paper. Carlo looked at the name that was written on the paper, then handed it to me. I refolded it and passed it back to Big Tommy. He placed it in his ashtray, then touched it with the orange tip of his omnipresent cigarette. The paper and the name were gone in an instant.

(Note: Why did Big Tommy put his name on paper instead of just telling us to go kill Stefanelli? It had something to do with an old Mafia tradition where the head of the family refused to speak the name of the condemned. I was never exactly sure why. I heard that speaking the name was to give the condemned undue respect, but I also heard that speaking the name was bad mojo and it would put a curse on the head of the family. Who knows? In all honesty, there were a lot of mob traditions and superstitions that I didn't understand. Sometimes you just nod and keep moving down the road.)

Big Tommy said, "You know what to do."

We left for Washington late that afternoon. The plan was to catch Stefanelli at his apartment over a garage just outside of the business district, talk our way inside, and make it happen. We knocked on the door, but there was no sign of Stefanelli, and Carlo went crazy. I said, "He'll show up. We can wait for him. It's no big deal."

"It is a big deal," Carlo said. "I got a hot horse in the seventh race at the Meadows, and if this dumb fuck doesn't get back here so I can kill him, I'm gonna miss out on a sure thing."

"First of all, you've never had a sure thing in your life, and I can't believe you're worried about a horse race when we're on the job."

I took a credit card out of my wallet, wedged it between the door and the jamb, and pushed. It slid the latch bolt away, and the door popped open. Once inside, we made sure he wasn't hiding, then set up for the hit. I stood in his bedroom and looked out a window with a view of the alley and the stairs to his apartment. Carlo hid behind the refrigerator.

When Stefanelli's beater Chevy stopped in the alley, I moved into the hall and pointed toward the stairs. Carlo nodded. Thirty seconds later, Stefanelli walked in the door. Two seconds after that, he was dead on the floor. It was the quickest hit I'd ever seen in my life. One shot to the side of the head. Dead. Carlo said, "Let's get out of here. We can still make the race."

We drove over to the Meadows in time for the fifth race, which meant Carlo had two races to lose money on before he got an opportunity to lose serious cash on his "hot horse" in the seventh. He was ecstatic. He put two grand to win on Archangel, and the damn thing lost by eight lengths. I'm standing next to him in the stands, and remember, our operations are supposed to be covert. The number one rule is to not draw attention to ourselves, and Carlo is swearing and tearing up his betting ticket and throwing scraps of paper. That was another thing about Carlo: When he lost a bet, it was never because it was a stupid bet. The jockey threw the race, or the owners were in collusion, or everything was fixed.

"If that's the case, why do you keep betting on them?" I asked.

"Kiss my ass," he said.

He would be in a foul mood for days after a loss like that. I can't say that I blamed him, because I'd also be in a foul mood if I'd dropped two grand at a horse race. His bad moods were so legendary around the compound that Alphonse sometimes started off his meetings by asking, "Which Carlo is with us today? Happy Carlo, or the world-is-ending Carlo?" But as soon as he got some more cash and a line on another also-ran, he would be back to his old chipper self.

Carlo and I had a well-deserved reputation for efficiency. Not once in all the years we worked together were we ever questioned by the cops for one of our hits. And I know this sounds crazy—perhaps morbid is a better word—but we always had a good time. I mean, in the car on the way to a job, we'd be joking and kidding with each other, telling stories and jokes. Mind you, we were on our way to end someone's life, but after a while, it was just a job. I headed out to work in the same fashion that the old man went to the brick factory.

Carlo and I were driving to Pittsburgh on a job one night, and I mentioned that I had heard our mark was a pretty rough character.

Carlo said, "Nah, I've known him for years. He's all bluster. He's nothing but a big blowfish."

"A what?"

"A big blowfish."

"A blowhard?"

He frowned and said, "Whatever."

I loved that guy.

CHAPTER 29

August 2019

I HEARD THE BACKUP beeper of a truck in the narrow parking lot behind the apartment building. I was in the kitchen, still in my bathrobe and pouring a cup of coffee. I peeked out the window to see a flatbed tow truck being directed into the lot by Steubenville Police Detective Dennis Logston. There was no time to dress. I set my cup on the counter and headed for the door.

By the time I got outside the tow truck was backed up to my Cutlass. "What the hell's going on, Logston?" I yelled to be heard over the rumble of the diesel engine. "I don't have any outstanding tickets."

He smirked and reached into a pocket inside his sports coat and produced a folded document. "It's not about tickets, Cipriani. Your vehicle is being impounded by court order as part of a criminal investigation." He extended his arm and handed me the document. It was a search warrant for the Cutlass.

"What criminal investigation?" I scanned the document. "Oh, for the love of Christ. You've got to be kidding me. You're trying to link me to the murders of Willie Valentine and Woodrow Golightly?"

"What murders? You said you didn't know anything about Golightly and that Willie was probably on vacation. Do you know something that you're not telling me, Cipriani?"

"I know a lot of things I'm not telling you, numb nuts." I held up the paper and pointed to Logston's own narrative to obtain the search warrant. *The vehicle may be linked to the disappearance and possible murders of William Leonard "Willie" Valentine and Woodrow Thomas Golightly.* "Looks like you're pretty sure they're dead."

"Tell me what you know, and I'll leave the car here."

Here's where a lot of guys get themselves in trouble. One of Alphonse Fortunato's first directives to me was to keep my mouth shut. He said, "You don't admit to spitting on the sidewalk. If some cop sees you standing on the curb with slobber on your chin and a big goober on the concrete, you say you don't know nothin' about it."

"How long are you going to keep it?" I asked.

"Until we've searched every nook and cranny of it for evidence of the murders of Valentine and Golightly."

"Well, good luck to you, tubby," I said, turning to head back to my apartment.

"That's it," Logston said. "I'm taking your car in an attempt to link you to these murders, and you tell me good luck. What gives?"

"I'm in full support of our law enforcement agencies and the detectives. Even the fat ones. Best of luck with your investigation."

I walked away, not happy that I was losing my wheels for a couple of days, but smiling nevertheless, realizing that Willie Valentine and Woodrow Golightly were taken off the boards before my 1980 Cutlass came off the assembly line.

I swear, it's a miracle that any crimes ever get solved in that town.

CHAPTER

30

Thursday, September 20, 2007

I called Carlo at nine that morning. The first call went to his answering machine. I hung up and called him right back. Unless Big Tommy had called an early morning meeting of the capos, Carlo rarely got out of bed before eleven. The second call went to the answering machine; he answered my third. His voice was hoarse and groggy. "Yeah."

"Time to hit the deck, soldier," I said.

"What time is it?"

"About three hours after the rest of the working world got moving. Get up and get dressed. Big Tommy has a job for us."

"Okay. I'll jump in the shower and be at the compound in an hour."

"No need. I'll come by and pick you up."

"Doesn't the boss want to see us both?"

"It's not that kind of an assignment."

The phone line was silent for a long moment. "Is there new talent coming in?"

"Yes, there is."

"Outstanding. And you and me, we're making the run?"

"Yep."

"Where are they from?"

"Buffalo."

"Aww. I love those Buffalo gals."

"Get dressed. I'll be there in about a half hour."

Every few months, Big Tommy would send a couple of capos up to the hunting lodge in Pennsylvania to make an exchange of prostitutes. It wasn't good to keep the same girls in a whorehouse for a long time. The johns get tired of seeing the same talent, while other poor saps fall in love with their hookers. (Note: Yes, yes, I know.) Either way, it's not good for business. We would ship our hookers to Cleveland or Fort Wayne, the Cleveland girls would go to Buffalo, Erie, or Rochester, and the New York state girls would rotate our way. This might have been the only thing that Carlo liked more than the ponies, because it usually meant an overnight stay in the cabin with the ladies. Carlo loved the ladies and was the most frequent user of Big Tommy's brothels. Connie Bones said if they'd given out frequent-flyer points at the whorehouse, Carlo would have been a platinum member.

Carlo lived in Weirton, West Virginia, in the house that he had inherited from an aunt. The place was falling down around him, in part because the money he should have used to buy paint and have the lawn mowed was spent on losing horses. It goes without saying that he was in a great mood when I picked him up. The first words out of his mouth were, "I love it when they bring new talent to town."

"Really? I didn't know that about you." I laughed and slapped him on the chest with a backhand.

It was a three-and-a-half-hour drive to the hunting lodge. At his request, I stopped at a carry-out in Weirton and he picked up a twelve-pack of beer, which he drank on the way, flipping the empty cans out the window. The sun was shining and warm on our faces. He said, "It's a great day to be alive, isn't it, partner?"

"Yes, it certainly is, partner."

When we were driving up the mile-long gravel road to the lodge, Carlo said, "Give me the key. I'm going to piss myself if I don't get to the bathroom."

"We're alone in the middle of thousands of acres of forest," I said. "The whole world is your bathroom right now."

He snapped his fingers twice and said, "I'm not a fuckin' caveman." I dug into my pants pocket for the key. He unlocked the door, and I followed him in. I could have put one in the back of his head just after we walked inside, but I decided to let him empty his bladder first so I didn't have to deal with a corpse and a puddle of piss.

After hearing the toilet flush, Carlo asked me from behind the closed door, "When are the girls getting here?" I didn't answer. As he stepped out, still hitching up his pants, he was asking again. "Angelo, when are the girls . . ."

He stopped and his eyes widened when he found himself staring down the barrel of my 9-millimeter. "There are no girls, Carlo. Get your hands up."

He slowly lifted his hands to shoulder height, frowning; his pants fell down around his ankles. "What the hell's this?"

"You know what this is."

"No, I don't. I swear."

"The mark always knows why. Remember? That's what you always told me."

"But I don't."

"Sure, you do. You've been burning the candle at both ends—working with the Gemellis."

"What? That's crazy. I . . ."

"Shut up, Carlo. You set me up. It was you who told them I would be at the Federal Terrace that night. It was you that got my Jolie killed."

"No, Angelo, wait. Don't do it, for God's sake. You've got it wrong."

"How could you do that to me, Carlo? Huh? How could you betray me like that?"

"Look, I've been talking to the Gemellis, trying to work some deals for Big Tommy, but never about you. Never."

"You were the only one I told that I was taking Jolie to the Federal Terrace."

"I don't know who set you up, Angelo, but it wasn't me. I swear to God. Just let me go. I'll go away, far away, and no one will ever hear from me again, I swear to Christ. You can tell Big Tommy you clipped me. He'll never know."

"This isn't about Big Tommy anymore. This is personal." I pointed at his pants with the barrel of my pistol. "Pull your pants up. I want you to go out with some dignity."

He started to cry. "Come on, Angelo, we've been friends forever."

"You set me up to get killed and you got my wife and baby killed, and you call us friends?"

He started crying harder, pleading for his life. He was pissing me off. How many times had I heard Carlo Dello Russo say that a mark should take it like a man? And there he was, my boyhood idol, the Iron Mauler, my mentor, blubbering and begging, his pants down around his ankles. "Is this how you want to go out, Carlo, crying like a little girl in your boxer shorts?"

He extended his right hand, tears running down his cheeks. "Please, Angelo, I beg . . ."

I put one right in his heart. A clean shot. He dropped on his back and was dead before he hit the floor. I kicked him in the ribs and said, "Roast in hell, you piece of shit."

* * *

My phone had rung at six o'clock that morning. It was Big Tommy, and he wanted to meet me in his office at seven. This was unusual but not unheard of. I said, "Do you want me to call Carlo?"

"No. This is a solo mission. Don't be late."

I wasn't. I stood outside his closed office door until exactly seven, then I rapped twice. When I entered, Big Tommy was at his desk, but the chair was spun around and he was staring into the morning sun. The smoke from his cigarette was curling up around his head and dissipating into the open blinds. "Do you suppose that Christ really knew that Judas was the one who would betray him?" he asked. I didn't answer. "It's not a rhetorical question, Angelo. Do you think Christ knew it was Judas? The gospel of

John says that Jesus knew all along that Judas was his rat. What do you think?"

Chills raced up my spine, and I felt as though I was trying to swallow a dish towel. What had I done that he perceived to be an act of betrayal? He spun around in his chair. "And he didn't betray Christ for some moral or ethical reason. He betrayed him for thirty pieces of silver. It's always been about the money, hasn't it? Even back in the days of Christ. No matter what anyone tells you, it's always about the money. So, what do you think?" Big Tommy asked again. "Did he know for sure?"

"He was Jesus Christ, the son of God. Don't you think he would have known that he had a traitor in his ranks?"

"I don't know. Maybe he instinctively knew that Judas was a rat, but he didn't want to believe it. And if he knew, why didn't he just push him off a cliff?"

Because he was Jesus Christ, not a mob boss, I thought.

"This conversation is making me more than a little nervous, Tom. Why are you asking me this? Do you think I've been disloyal?"

He didn't answer. Big Tommy Fortunato, one of the toughest human beings I'd ever known, rolled his tongue over his teeth and looked to be fighting off tears. His right fist clenched and relaxed, clenched and relaxed. The cigarette he had wedged between his index and middle fingers took a bow with each contraction of muscle. He said nothing. I waited. Through the window, I could see a blackbird perched on the limb of a small elm. The sun reflected off its feathers, producing a prism of colors that cascaded down its back. It tilted its head toward the window, as though it, too, was questioning my loyalty. Big Tommy's left hand clutched the handle of his center drawer. An invisible force, it seemed, was preventing him from opening it, as though it was his personal Pandora's box, and sliding open the drawer would unleash a personal hell.

When finally he pulled open the drawer, it was slow and deliberate. He reached in with his right hand and picked out a piece of the familiar folded flash paper and slid it across his blotter. He looked at me, and it was a long moment before he released his fingers from the paper.

When I picked it up and unfolded the paper, a flush of heat consumed my face. The name on the paper was Carlo Dello Russo.

"Can you do this?" he asked.

It felt like I was trying to talk through a mouthful of steel wool. "Why?"

"Carlo . . ." His voice faded out. "Carlo has been playing double agent with the Gemellis. His disloyalty has been of the highest level, both to me . . . and to you."

I let the words settle for a moment. "Jolie?"

He nodded once. "Carlo is Judas in pinstripes. His betrayal pains me to my core." He tapped his cigarette on the edge of the ashtray, then looked up at me. "I'll ask you again, Angelo. Can you do this?"

"Yes, sir. My loyalty is to you and the family, first and always."

"You're a good man. Take him to the hunting lodge. Tell him there's a shipment of girls coming in. He'll go without question. I don't want the sun to ever shine on his body again."

I thought my face would combust. "Okay," I said. "Consider it done."

I handed him the flash paper. Big Tommy put it in the ashtray and touched it with the end of his cigarette. When it flashed, I turned to leave the room. As I took hold of the doorknob, I turned and looked at the head of the Fortunato family. Where Big Tommy was concerned, I was largely a man of blind obedience. I rarely questioned him. But I had to ask, "You're sure about this, right, boss?"

"If I wasn't sure, his name wouldn't have been on that piece of paper."

* * *

I took Carlo's 9-millimeter Beretta out of his shoulder holster and thought for a minute about going through his wallet, but figured that would be an exercise in futility. He never had any money. I went back out to the car and got the paint tarp I'd taken from Big Tommy's garage and rolled him up, securing both ends with a roll of duct tape. There was a wheelbarrow in the garage that I wrestled his body into. What an ignominious way to go out, wrapped in a dirty paint tarp with his pants down. I wedged a shovel between his body and the side of the wheelbarrow, then started pushing him into the woods, following one of the hunting paths that snaked into the hills away from the lodge.

It was eighty-one degrees. I struggled up hills and fought Carlo's weight coming back down, pushing it for more than a mile until I came to a creek bed that ran hard with the spring runoff, but was dry the rest of the year. It was after three PM when I started digging in the sandy bottom of the creek. I can't tell you how long I dug, but the sun was heading down over the hills when I stopped and my eyes were below ground level. I unceremoniously tipped the wheelbarrow forward and dropped Carlo Dello Russo to the bottom of the hole, then began throwing dirt and sand on top of him.

When I got back to the lodge, I put my mouth under the tap and drank for a long time. My hamstrings and toes were cramping up. I found some vegetable soup in the cupboard that I ate cold out of the can. Then I laid down on the couch and slept hard until midmorning. Every muscle in my body ached. When I awoke, I made myself a cup of coffee, gathered up the pistols, and headed back to Steubenville. I stopped at my apartment to shower and shave before driving to the compound to see Big Tommy.

He was in the office. When I walked in, he pointed at the door and I closed it behind me. Big Tommy walked to the bar in the corner of the room and grabbed two tumblers and a bottle of bourbon. He returned to his chair and poured three fingers in each glass. His hand seemed to quiver, like the nervous relief after a near-miss car accident. "It's done?" he asked.

"It's done."

He held his glass over the desk, and we toasted a man we had both loved.

He nodded. "Good." He reached into his desk, grabbed a wad of cash wrapped in a rubber band, and set it on the corner of the desk nearest me.

"I don't think I want paid for this one," I said. I sat down in the chair in front of his desk and massaged my temples. "Tom, I think you owe me an explanation . . ." I let my words trail off as I remembered who I was talking to. "Let me back up and try that again. I would appreciate it if you would tell me how you knew."

"How did I know that Carlo was colluding with the Gemellis? I've known for a while that we had a Judas in the ranks, and in my heart, I knew it was Carlo. But I didn't want to believe it. Not Carlo Dello Russo." He sipped his bourbon. "It was confirmed to me by John Scardino."

"The head of the Cleveland mob?"

"That's him. We're, let's say, cordial. Even though Cleveland is the big brother to Youngstown, and they're supporting them, he hates Donny Gemelli, Frankie's kid, who's now the family boss. Donny Gem also is the one who ordered the hit on you. According to Scardino, Donny's got diarrhea of the mouth; it's always running. He told Scardino that he had someone working on the inside at my compound. He wouldn't say who, but he said the guy was a bad gambler and was into the Gemellis for tens of thousands. Sound like anyone you knew?"

"I don't understand. How did he get upside down with the Gemellis?"

"Carlo was gambling in town and ran up thousands of dollars in bad debt. I noticed that our bars were short on their collections, and there was a consistent answer—Carlo Dello Russo. When he could no longer get credit at one bar, he'd move to the next, and the next. He was lucky that I was backing the play. I took care of it and told Carlo he had no more credit. If he wanted to gamble, he had to have the cash. Well, you know Carlo. When he didn't have any cash, he still needed his gambling fix, so he had to find a place where he could get credit. In an uncharacteristically bad move, he drove up to Youngstown and started laying down bets with the Gemellis. They knew who he was, and they allowed him to go way into debt. Which,

I've got to admit, was very clever on their part. Once he was upside down about twenty grand, they sent four of their goons into the bookie joint to have a little chat with our Carlo. They'd let him continue to gamble, but at a price. They wanted information on my operation. Carlo was the rat."

"What kind of information? Did he tell Donny Gemelli that I clipped his dad and uncle?"

"That would be my bet."

"And he told him I'd be at the Federal Terrace with Jolie?"

"Who else?"

"But he told you I was thinking of leaving the organization. Why would he care if he knew they were going to have me whacked?"

"What better cover than to pretend to be concerned about your welfare? Did you tell him you were using my room at the Federal Terrace that night?"

"Yeah."

Big Tommy smiled. "Angelo, if it quacks like a duck . . ." He let the words hang for a minute before asking, "You remember Orly Lanaro, don't you?"

"Yeah, the Gemelli capo in Monaca who we were supposed to rough up, but he drew on Carlo and . . ."

"Carlo's dead, Angelo. You don't have to protect him anymore. Lanaro never drew on Carlo. We both know that. I told you and Carlo to go to Monaca and settle up with whoever the Gemellis were sending in. Carlo told the Gemellis what was going down. This guy, Lanaro, was apparently trying to organize some kind of coup to overthrow Donny Gem. Donny found out and sent Lanaro to the bar that night, knowing you and Carlo would be there. It was all arranged. Carlo killed him, not because Lanaro drew on him, but because Donny Gemelli ordered the hit. You went to Monaca working for me; Carlo went working for Gemelli. He was a double agent."

"John Scardino told you all this?"

"Every word."

"And it came right from Donny Gemelli?"

"Every word."

"And I thought it was you or Ricky Bones that set me up." I drained my bourbon. "Okay, I agree that this looks bad, but what if someone else knew I was going to be at the Federal Terrace? Carlo's fingerprints aren't on anything. What if I killed him and it was a fluke?"

"There are no flukes when I operate. You should know that by now." He rubbed out the nub of a cigarette in the glass ashtray. "Do you remember a guy named Isaac Marsh?"

"Sure. Reverend M. He was the preacher who disappeared back in the . . ." I could feel the ridges on my forehead pushing down on my brow, recalling the details about the minister's disappearance. "He went to some kind of conference or convention and vanished. They found him floating in a river or lake. That's all I remember."

"Marsh was a giant pain in everyone's ass. He was a self-ordained minister and had a little storefront church on South Fourth Street. He got his church members to picket my brothels, and he forced the county to convene a commission to investigate illegal gambling. He told me he'd pull the pickets off the brothels and shut his mouth for fifty grand. If I refused, he was going to cause more problems, and the next time he came back, fifty thousand was going to look like chump change compared to what he'd demand."

"How come I never heard about this?"

"Don't take this personal, Angelo, but sometimes issues arise that need to be handled at a higher level than where you're standing. I was trying to figure out how to eliminate my problem, but I was afraid our traditional method would draw too much attention, and I didn't need Jesse Jackson and every social justice warrior in the country coming to town, because when that happens, the FBI and DOJ are never far behind. Walter Snodgrass was still the chief of police. I called him and told him I needed a meeting at the old brewery warehouse. Turns out, I wasn't the only one the good reverend was trying to squeeze. Snodgrass had a son who was a rookie cop, and Reverend M was threatening to release some compromising information about an improper relationship the married son was having with a police dispatcher. Apparently, they had been somewhat less than discreet."

"Not good."

"Not good at all. The chief and I had what you might call a mutual interest in seeing that Reverend M was no longer a problem, but he harbored the same concerns I had about drawing attention from the feds. Trust me on this, the Steubenville Police Department doesn't want the feds investigating them any more than I want them looking at my books. Fortunately, sometimes things work out. There was a little article in the newspaper about Reverend M attending a conference in Kansas City for black ministers. I made a call to an associate in Kansas City. A deal was made, and some things happened. A week later, Reverend M was found floating in the Missouri River. It was ruled an accidental drowning. It was a drowning, but it was definitely no accident. I told you all that to tell you that Chief Snodgrass and his son, Robert, owed me a favor for making their problem disappear."

"Robert? Bobby Snodgrass? The chief of police in Youngstown?"

"The very same."

"You waited all those years before calling in the marker?"

"I didn't need it until then. I told Bobby I had a problem, some suspicions, and I needed him to confirm them." Big Tommy opened his desk drawer and retrieved a DVD. He walked to the corner of the room, turned on the television and DVD player, and slid the silver disc into the machine. Static filled the screen for a moment before the image of an alley and a brick building with a windowless steel door appeared. After a minute, a familiar figure came down the alley, rapped twice on the door. Someone opened it, and Carlo Dello Russo disappeared inside. Before the door closed, Donny Gemelli stuck his head outside, looked up and down the alley, then shut the door. Twice more, similar footage replayed, with Carlo each time rapping on the door and disappearing into the building that housed the Gemelli-owned Eastern Ohio Refuse and Hauling.

"Snodgrass hid a camera in the alley," Big Tommy said. "In all honesty, he just confirmed my suspicions. I knew Carlo was the Judas."

I shook my head. "I still can't believe it. I saw it with my own eyes, but I still can't believe it. Carlo Dello Russo, a rat. He killed my Jolie and my baby, then went back to work with me. I'm sorry I couldn't kill the son of a bitch more than once."

"Once is enough. I'm just curious. How did it go?"

"He went like the coward that he was, crying and begging."

Big Tommy shook his head. "I figured as much."

"I've got to go clear my head, boss."

He nodded. "Understood." As I got up to leave, he pointed at the cash on his desk. "People don't work for me for free. Take it."

I put it in my pocket and left. I drove across the river to Undo's. Our regular waitress said, "Where's your friend?"

"I haven't seen him lately," I said.

I ordered the shrimp with linguine in a cream sauce and a bottle of chianti. The waitress asked, "Do you want an extra glass in case your friend shows up?"

"Sure. Two glasses would be great."

I never again uttered the name of Carlo Dello Russo in the presence of Big Tommy Fortunato.

CHAPTER

31

August 2019

As my visits to the compound became less frequent, it was difficult for me to keep track of the players. You needed a scorecard to chart the trash running in and out. After agreeing to train Little Tommy's latest candidate to take my place, I called Matteo's grandson, Alfie, to see what I could find out. He was nervous to be talking to me and declined my invitation to take him to dinner at Naples. "I don't think it would be in my best interests to be seen with you," he said.

"What's that supposed to mean? I'm a made guy."

"That doesn't hold a lot of sway with the current administration. As far as Little Tommy is concerned, you don't bring any value to the table. That's what he said in a meeting the other day. I'm sorry, Mr. Cipriani, but I've got to protect myself."

"Understood. But what can you tell me about this guy he wants me to train?"

"I don't know much about him. He's been hanging around with Tommaso for a while. All I know is that he grew up in Steubenville and has a reputation for being a rough character. He's a jerk to me, so I stay away from him. From what I can tell, he's pretty raw and undisciplined."

Raw and undisciplined. Great.

"Oh, I can tell you one more thing. His real name wasn't Gaetano. It's Louis. He started calling himself Gaetano to sound more Italian."

"Little Tommy thinks the old Italian ways are archaic and stupid. Why would that be important?"

"I don't know what to tell you, Mr. Cipriani. It's kind of crazy up here these days. I think I'm going back to college."

The cops had returned the Cutlass, and I drove it to the compound at nine that morning. Little Tommy and Gaetano were in the kitchen. Little Tommy was eating a bowl of some kind of kids' cereal that probably had a prize in the bottom of the box. Gaetano was pulling on a can of Pepsi. "Angelo," Little Tommy said, as though he was announcing a prizefighter entering the ring. He grabbed the kid's shoulder and said, "This is your pupil." They both laughed at that.

I don't know why it was supposed to be so funny, but I'm guessing it had something to do with the stegosaurus teaching a kid who believed he had nothing to learn. I was in no mood for any of it. "You ready?" I asked.

"Yeah, time to drop it into gear, Pops," Gaetano said.

"Let's go."

He reminded me of Anthony "Tony Gem" Gemelli. He was a good six-two and muscular. It was natural strength, not the kind you get from pumping barbells. Even though Little Tommy was desperate to find my replacement, I wanted this kid to go down in flames like Timmy Sweets and Bruno De Luca. It was like being the second-team quarterback and hoping the guy in front of you throws six interceptions or breaks an ankle so that you can get back in the game. That's what I wanted, back in the game. But I was worried about this kid. I had to admit, he cut an impressive figure. And then, he managed to piss me off before we even got out of the driveway. He slid into the passenger seat and said, "Jesus Christ, Pops, what did you do, buy this car from Fred Flintstone or something?"

I dropped the Cutlass into gear and pulled out of the driveway without comment. I'd never told a living soul that it was a gift from Big Tommy, and the insult went up my spine like a flare. When we pulled onto Sunset Boulevard, I asked, "What's your name, kid?"

"Di Vittorio, Gaetano Di Vittorio."

"Di Vittorio, huh? I heard you were from the Spaghetto."

"They don't call it the Spaghetto anymore, Pops. Now it's just the ghetto. But, yeah, I grew up down there."

"Your family's house was right next to ours. One of my buddies growing up was Reggie Di Vittorio."

"That was my grandfather. I grew up around the corner on Carnegie Avenue."

The same street as Carlo.

"Who was your father? Benny?"

He nodded. Benedetto Di Vittorio had gone to prison for what they used to call "general principles." That meant he had been a low-level criminal for so many years—a few burglaries, shoplifting, assaults—and was such a colossal pain in the ass to the judicial system that they finally gave him a maximum sentence on a minor theft charge just to get him out of their hair. His wife was pregnant with this kid—Gaetano or Louis, take your pick—when he had gone to prison. He reportedly joined the Aryan Nations in the joint and got stabbed to death during a riot at Lucasville—a "backdoor parole," as they called it.

This kid had grown up on the same streets of the Spaghetto as me. Maybe I could work with him. He could become my prodigy. It wasn't difficult. I mean, it wasn't like I was teaching him to become a concert violinist.

"Where did you go to school?"

"Big Red, but I quit after my freshman year. School's for chumps and losers."

"I see. So, what do you know about this business you're getting into?"

"Whacking people? How tough can it be? You do it, right?"

"See if you can keep the insults to yourself. When it's time to pull the trigger and take another man's life, we'll see how easy you think it is. And just so you know, whacking someone is the easy part. Doing it without getting caught is the challenge."

"If you say so, Pops."

"Have you ever killed another man?"

He smirked. "No, but I'm looking forward to the opportunity."

"We'll see." I turned off Route 22 at Hopedale. "There's a code we follow. Number one, if you can avoid it, never shoot anyone in the face."

Out of the corner of my eye I could see his head jerk back and one brow arch. "Why?"

"Respect for the family. You want them to be able to display the body in a casket at the funeral."

He started laughing. "Man, you've got some, like, King Arthur kind of rules about killing people. I say, fuck it. Smoke their ass and dash. What do I care if they get a nice funeral?"

"It's not about you, and it's not about the guy you clip. It's about the family."

"Whatever you say, Pops. What else have you got for me?"

"You don't get style points. When you have a job to do, just do it and get out. Don't make it dramatic or more difficult than it needs to be. Tommaso is not going to care that you did it with flair. All he's going to be concerned about is that you left a corpse on the floor."

"Okay, that's good."

"No fishing. That means you don't go through a mark's wallet or pockets for money or jewelry."

"Why not?"

"It's considered bad form."

"Do you know how much money some of these drug dealers carry? And they're always draped in gold and diamonds. I ain't followin' that rule, guaranteed. I'm taking their shit."

I didn't want to argue with him. I said, "Never kill anyone in front of their family."

"You mean like their kids?"

"Yeah, their family—wife and kids."

He blew out a puff of air. "We're living in different worlds, Pops. Tommaso says that you think things are like they were when his old man was in charge. That ain't the way it is anymore." He looked over at me and shrugged. "The guys we're dealing with, they aren't having Sunday afternoon picnics with the kids. These are bad motherfuckers."

We pulled onto the gravel and mud road that led to the abandoned strip mine where I had tried to train Gaetano's predecessors. I set up some cans and bottles. I had wanted to talk a little bit about gun safety. I know that isn't something you'd think a professional hitman would be concerned about, but you want to make sure you don't get careless and shoot yourself. I could already tell it would be a ridiculous waste of time with this kid.

He was good with his pistol. He may not have killed anyone, but it was obvious to me that he knew how to handle a gun. We had spent about thirty minutes at the strip mine when he said, "I'm bored with this, Pops. Let's get out of here."

We rode back in silence. I'd tried to make a connection with our Spaghetto background, but it didn't work. There wasn't anything else to say. Well, there was, actually, but he wasn't going to listen, so what the hell? In his mind, he already knew it all. Gaetano leaned back, his right arm resting on the door, blowing smoke from his cigarette out the window. He chewed at the fingernails on his left hand, and I noticed they'd all been gnawed down to the tender, pink skin. Beneath the bravado, there was an anxious psyche. I made a mental note of that.

When we returned to the compound, he got out of the car and walked away without a word. Little Tommy came out of the manse before I could get two steps from my car. "How'd it go?" he asked.

"He's about as likable as poison ivy, and he's got a nest of snakes in his head. He's full of himself and arrogant and disrespectful."

"Angelo, you're wearing me out. I don't care if he's full of himself and arrogant."

"And disrespectful."

"We can work on that."

"Tommaso, I've always had some beliefs about men. I believe you can gauge a man's strength by the size of his wrists. You can gauge his character by his choice of words. And you can gauge a man's ability to take a life by the look in his eyes. That kid has it. When the time comes, he'll drop the hammer. I have no doubt."

"All right. That's good. Very good."

"I'll tell you the same thing Carlo told me. It doesn't take a Marine sharpshooter to do this job. It just takes some balls and some smarts. I think he's got the balls, but the jury is still out on the smarts."

Little Tommy didn't even hear me. He was already imagining a world in which Gaetano was his right-hand man, and I did not exist.

* * *

My cell phone was ringing before I got to the bottom of Market Street hill. The call was blocked, and I knew it was Agent Ross on the other end. I took the call and said, "Hello, Ross."

"You didn't forget about me, did you, Angelo?"

"I'd like to forget about you, but you won't let me."

"Good to hear. When are you coming in?"

"I didn't say I would, for sure."

"Tomorrow, then."

"You don't hear so good."

"I hear fine. I just don't like to take no for an answer."

"I can't tomorrow; I'm busy."

"Thursday, then."

I took a breath. "Okay, Thursday."

"Nine o'clock?"

"Fine."

"Do you know where you're going?"

"Text me an address."

"It's a smart move you're making, Angelo."

"Ross, it's the dumbest thing I've ever done in my life. And believe me when I tell you, that covers some considerable territory."

CHAPTER 32

March–May 2013

When I walked into Big Tommy's office that morning, he was sitting at his desk with one fist stacked atop the other, his forehead resting on the knuckles of a thumb and index finger. He heard the door squeak on its hinges and looked up at me. His stare was empty, unfocused, and he frowned a bit, as though unable to place my face or name. His skin was pale and sweaty, and he looked like he had aged dramatically since I'd last seen him. In all the years I'd known Big Tommy Fortunato, I couldn't remember him having anything worse than a cold. I didn't ask him if he was okay. It was obvious that he wasn't. "Boss, what the hell is wrong?"

As I knew he would, he said, "I'm fine."

"You don't look fine."

"I'll be okay."

"'I'll be okay.' I wonder how many people have said that just before they keeled over from a heart attack. I think you need to go to the emergency room or at least go see a doctor."

I knew Big Tommy. I might as well have said, "Let's take a rocket ship to Mars."

"I'm fine, Angelo. It's just my stomach. It's all knotted up. Something I ate, probably."

"You're white as a sheet and short of breath. That's got nothing to do with your gut."

He was waving me off when Little Tommy walked into the room. I wasn't giving this up. "He needs to see a doctor."

"I asked him about it a little while ago. He says he's all right," Little Tommy said.

"He's not all right. I know what all right looks like, and this ain't it. He's a hardhead when it comes to doctors." I poked Little Tommy in the chest. "You've got to make him go."

In those days, I could still talk like that to Little Tommy. Even though he was the heir to the throne, I was still ahead of him in the pecking order. Technically, but not really. Little Tommy's last name was still Fortunato, so you do the math.

"It's a family matter, Uncle Ange. If he goes into the hospital today, what do you think will happen tomorrow when the Gemellis find out? You know how this business works. They'll swarm into our territory like locusts."

"It won't make a hell of a lot of difference if he's dead by tomorrow, will it?"

"You need to take care of your own business."

"The business of this family *is* my business. I was taking care of things here long before you were born, junior." I probably stepped over the line with that last remark, but I didn't care. This was a time to state my piece. "He needs a doctor."

"No doctors," Little Tommy said, his voice climbing.

"Mother of Christ, both of you, shut up," Big Tommy said. "Angelo, I'm okay, I promise. It's just a little stomach bug. What do those last, about twelve hours? I'll be fine."

We've all known guys who were married to their jobs. Nothing was as important to them as their work—not their wife, their girlfriend, their relationships with their kids, or friendships. For Big Tommy Fortunato, that was his life on steroids. Neither his blood family nor his health was as important to him as his operation and his allegiance to the omerta. He would have sooner died in that chair than risk the Gemellis learning that he was sick.

I left. There was no use arguing. It was my day to make rounds, and I had to go see a couple of bookies whose numbers were down. As I drove out Rosemont Street, I couldn't recall a single time that Big Tommy had seen a doctor in all the years that I had known him.

Big Tommy was strict about his diet and had set up a gym in the basement with weights, a treadmill, and a heavy bag that he pounded. He was a complete health nut, except for the paradoxical habit of chain-smoking every minute he was awake. He always had a cigarette in his hand. I'd seen him light one off the stub of another. The only time he wasn't smoking a cigarette was when he was smoking a cigar. I'd seen him at the Federal Terrace with a thick T-bone and a cigarette burning on the side of his plate.

I'd been worried about Big Tommy for a while. He was constantly clearing his throat, and his voice had started to sound like gravel crushing under truck tires. He would take horrific coughing fits where his face would turn purple, and I sometimes feared he was going to suffocate. On several occasions, I saw him lie down on the floor of his office, trying to cease the attack and catch his breath. But as soon as he was back in his chair, the first thing he would do was fire up a stick.

He was Big Tommy Fortunato, the lord of eastern Ohio rackets, and no one was going to tell him how to live . . . or die, I guess. After one of his more severe coughing fits, I said, "Tommy, you've got to give up the smokes. Those things are killing you."

"Something's got to kill me," he said.

"Yeah, but you don't have to go knocking on the door. Cut back to a pack and a half a day, for the love of God."

He never did.

The following Monday, Big Tommy said he felt better. He still looked a little peaked and drawn, but not in the pain that had roiled through him on Friday. Four days later, we were in a replay of Black Friday. The sweats, the stomach pain, nausea.

"Are you sure it's in your gut?" I asked. "Could it be in your back or lungs?"

"I don't know," he said. "I can't tell."

Little Tommy was there and visibly agitated with me. "Uncle Ange, you need to leave and let Dad rest."

A dark thought kept creeping in from the outer reaches of my consciousness. Maybe there was a reason why Little Tommy didn't want his father to see a doctor. Maybe he wanted to expedite his father's trip to the other side and leave him as the head of the family. Unchecked cancer didn't take long to ravage a body. I tried to block that thought, but couldn't. It made no sense. Big Tommy needed to be in a hospital, and the kid seemed to be doing everything he could to keep him suffering at home.

Big Tommy had several more rebounds and an equal number of setbacks, daylong bouts of pain and misery. However, the time between the attacks began to shorten. Big Tommy's complexion had gone permanently to gray, and his eyes fell deeper in their sockets and were rimmed with dark circles. He rarely left the house. I knew just how sick he was when he told me that cigarettes made him vomit. His illness became a source of continuing irritation between us. I insisted that he needed to go to the hospital and he insisted that I needed to go to hell.

Six weeks after the first illness, I was in the office with Big Tommy. He was stretched out on a couch, a mop bucket near his head—half-full with vomit. He'd lost so much weight, the tendons in his neck looked like straining bridge cables. I said, "Tom, for the love of God, please go to the hospital."

Before he could answer, Little Tommy yelled, "He's not going to the fuckin' hospital. Get that through that fat dago head of yours."

I got up and left.

It's a terrible thing to watch someone you love suffer and wither away, especially someone as vibrant and larger than life as Big Tommy Fortunato. When I lost my Jolie, the pain was the worst of my life. But that quick, it was over. She was not in pain, and though the road back from her death was long and hard, I could start to heal. You can't heal when you have to watch someone struggle to their finish line.

(Note: It is not lost on me that I was responsible for inflicting great pain on many other people by killing their loved ones.)

I'm sure there were people who felt differently about Big Tommy. The head of an organized crime family was dying a slow and agonizing death? Great. Good riddance. But I loved Big Tommy, warts and all. I'd been with him through the death of his father and the birth of his son, and all the sorrows and joys associated with each. I always knew that when Alphonse died, the family would still be in good hands. How many crime families have a boss with a bachelor's degree in business? He was a man of character and loyalty, and I would've taken a bullet for him.

We were on a roller coaster ride with Big Tommy for several months. We suspected it was lung cancer and it had probably metastasized in his stomach. The further along we got, the harder it became for him to breathe. He walked around the house dragging a little oxygen tank on a cart behind him, wheezing for air. It is one of the saddest things I've ever seen in my life, and I executed people for a living.

Finally, after much coercing by Rosebella and me, he agreed to see a doctor, but only if he was brought to the house and sworn to secrecy. I contacted an oncologist in Pittsburgh and put five thousand dollars cash in his hand in exchange for a visit and his silence. I picked him up and personally delivered him to the compound. He examined Big Tommy, then wrote out several prescriptions in my name in order to keep Tommy's name off any records. We huddled in the living room after the examination, and the doctor said, "I can't tell you exactly what's wrong; it's quite possibly cancer. The weight loss and pain are certainly indicators. However, I'd need to do some tests and take X-rays to know for sure. Whatever it is, it's moving quickly and, without treatment, I suspect that he doesn't have much time."

Rosebella's knees buckled, and Ricky Bones caught her. It just didn't seem possible.

I went to Big Tommy's bedside late on a Wednesday afternoon. The drapes were drawn, and the tang of testosterone and body odor were heavy in the room. A stubble of salt and pepper beard covered his jaw. He was weak, but aware, his breathing labored. I couldn't believe the toughest man I'd ever known was lying in bed, struggling just to take a breath. He said, "I need you to do me a favor, Angelo."

"Name it, boss. I'll do anything you need."

"When I'm gone, I need you to look out for Little Tommy. He's going to be the head of this family, but he's not ready."

No kidding. He's a train wreck with the maturity level of a nine-year-old.

"I'll look after him, Big Tom. I promise."

"He respects you."

No, he doesn't. He wishes I'd get hit by a train.

"I thank God for that. I really do. He's a good boy."

"I'm going to have Nickels run the business end of things. He knows the numbers and the organization better than anyone. But I need you to guide Tommy. He's smart, but impetuous. I need you to make sure he doesn't get himself in trouble."

He won't listen to a word I say.

"My right hand to Christ, Tom, I'll do everything I can."

"Make sure he sticks with our traditional revenue streams. Don't let him drag the family into the drug trade."

He'll be dealing drugs before your body is cold in the ground.

"Little Tommy, he knows what you and your father built here, and he holds it in high regard. You raised him right. But, heaven forbid, should someone try to wrongly influence him, I'll handle it."

He grabbed my hand and squeezed. "I'm counting on you, Angelo."

Of course, I had every intention of being loyal to my word. I also knew it would be easier to wrestle a pit of snakes than to get Little Tommy to listen to anything I had to say.

I went back to the compound to see Big Tommy on Saturday afternoon. I had waited too long to come back. He was out of his head, talking about a vacation in Florida and something about pineapples and horses. Rosebella sat on the bed next to her husband, her knees tucked beneath her. She stroked his stubbled cheek and smiled. She looked at me and sadly shook her head. His time was short. This was family time, and I needed to go away. When I stood to leave, Big Tommy looked at me. The light of recognition came back into his eyes for just an instant, and he said, "We had us some times, didn't we, Angelo?"

I said, "You bet we did, Big Tom. You bet we did." And that quickly, he was again lost, lingering somewhere between Steubenville, Florida and the hereafter. That was the last time I ever saw him. He died the following Tuesday morning. Little Tommy had his father's body cremated at Hilltop Funeral Home, the same crematory where the family had long enjoyed a special relationship. Cremation went against the rules of the Catholic Church and was personally upsetting to Rosebella. Even though she had the final word, she did not argue with her son, who said, "Warriors should be cremated."

The Steubenville *Herald-Star* ran a front-page obituary under the headline:

Crime Boss Tommaso Fortunato Dead at 66

The capos collectively had to stop Little Tommy from going to the newsroom with a baseball bat. Services were held at the Church of the Holy Cross the Saturday afternoon after his death. A reception was held at the compound afterwards. We toasted Big Tom and told stories and laughed. It was a sad day, but a good day.

When most of the people had left and Rosebella had retired to her room, Little Tommy called me to a corner of the living room and said, "I want to have a meeting with the capos in fifteen minutes."

"Whatever you want, Tommy, but are you sure you don't want to spend this time with your family?"

"We've got business that can't wait."

He was his father's son.

I walked outside and told Connie Bones of the meeting. "Now?" he asked. I shrugged. We rounded up the rest of the capos and went to the office. Finding Little Tommy at the desk his father had used for years signaled the official end of an era. That, and the three guys in ratty jeans and T-shirts who were slouched on the chairs and couch. I looked at one of them, but he quickly broke eye contact, and I swear to Christ I saw him roll his eyes.

When everyone was in the room, Little Tommy said, "I'll keep this short. Nickels, I know my dad talked to you about running the financial end of the operation. You'll keep the books, but I'm going to be in total charge of this family . . ."

"Tommy, I don't think . . ."

"I don't want to be rude, Nickels, but it doesn't matter what you think. My father wasn't of sound mind the last month of his life. I'm going to do what I think is best for this family."

Nickels's facial expression never changed, but I could feel a burn that consumed my neck and ears. How dare he insult Nickels, a man who had been loyal to the family for more than a half-century. I wanted to pull Little Tommy across the desk and throttle him.

"These are three of my new associates. They're going to be helping me. We're moving away from our traditional areas of business and more into the drug trade. I know my father resisted doing that, but he's not here anymore. Our business thrived in the Ohio Valley because the steel mills thrived. Simple as that. We had sixty thousand steel workers who were eager to spend money gambling and whoring. Things have changed. The states all have lotteries. No one plays our daily numbers anymore. Casinos are opening up everywhere. We have to change or die. We've always provided for our customers. Well, our customer base has changed. There may not be a demand for whores and gambling, but there's a definite demand for drugs, and that's the route we're taking. I've been working on a business plan for a couple of years. The supply chains are set up. In the coming weeks, I'll be letting each of you know your new roles. Any questions?"

Jimmy Beans said, "Your father always said . . ."

"Irrelevant," Little Tommy said. "My father's dead."

"Your *father* . . ." Jimmy Beans continued, refusing to be denied, ". . . always said the drug trade would draw too much attention from the cops."

"My father, God rest his soul, ignored the realities of our changing world. We're down to two brothels and they're both falling down. The gambling receipts are a fraction of what they were just five years ago. We cannot continue down this path. The money is in illegal drugs. There's a fortune to be made out there, but it's not the way we did things yesterday. I want you all to be part of the operation, but it's going to change, and it's going to change quickly. That's all I have for now."

As the capos began to leave the office, Little Tommy said, "Oh, one more thing. Muzzie, go downtown and tell that whore in the penthouse of the Fort Steuben Hotel that the free ride is over. She's got thirty days to get the hell out."

I remained behind, as did the three slugs.

"Something on your mind, Uncle Ange?" he asked.

"Can we have a few minutes alone?" I asked.

He nodded, and the trio got up and left. When they were gone, he said, "I'm not changing my mind, Uncle Ange."

"I'm not asking you to change anything. You're the boss now. You're the final word. Do I think it's wrong to go into the drug trade? Yes. But that's your decision. I've worked for your grandfather and father, and I didn't always agree with them, but their word was the law. With that said, your father always gave me the latitude to tell him when I thought he was going to walk off a cliff. Sometimes he took my advice, sometimes he kept walking. That was his call. Now, you're the head of the family. You're giving the orders, and I'll follow them. The oath of loyalty wasn't just to your father, it was to this family. All I ask is for is the same privilege of speaking my mind."

Little Tommy nodded and smiled. "Of course. You're always welcome to speak your mind, Uncle Ange."

"I also think it's time we dispense with 'Uncle Ange.' You're now the head of the family, and I'm one of your subordinates. You should start treating me as such."

"Agreed. But you'll never stop being my Uncle Ange."

CHAPTER

33

August 2014

MAYBE I WOULD never stop being his Uncle Ange, but the ostracism began almost immediately. Not just for me, but for all the old capos. Little Tommy kept one brothel open, and the sports betting was still pretty good money, but nothing close to what Little Tommy began raking in from the drug trade.

He kept Nickels around to take care of the books. Nickels said there were times when the money was coming in faster than he could count it. He tried to get Little Tommy to stash some of the cash in the offshore accounts that his dad had set up, but he refused. He kept stockpiling it in the downstairs vault. "If the feds ever raid this place, all that money is lost. You've got to move some of it offshore," Nickels said.

"Just count the money, Nickels," Little Tommy said.

We don't know what happened to Jimmy Beans. One day, he just wasn't around anymore. When we didn't hear from him for a couple of days, we went to his apartment to check on him. It looked like he had left for lunch and never come back. We didn't think anything nefarious had happened, because Jimmy was a low-level earner. We figured he headed to Florida and was living on the beach. At least that's what we hoped had happened to him.

Connie Bones died of the bad headcheese a few months after Big Tommy. He had never really recovered from the shooting at the Delmonico Steakhouse in Empire. One of the bullets tore up his gut pretty good and he'd had problems for years; he was always in pain. Poor guy.

Muzzie Lollini was pushing ninety by the time Big Tommy died. He told Little Tommy, "I'm too old for this shit; I ain't comin' around no more." And he didn't.

Carlo Dello Russo . . . Well, Carlo went away.

Then there were me and Jimmy D watching over the whorehouse and running the sports gambling. When you've outlived your usefulness at big corporations, they hand you a cheap wristwatch and send you out the door with your pension. Little Tommy wasn't offering a retirement plan or a handsome severance package. In organized crime, when you are no longer needed, you simply cease to exist. I had read that in Japanese companies, nobody ever gets fired. If you turn out to be a complete screw-up, they make you the vice president of paper clips or something like that, but you get to keep hanging around and it saves your dignity. To a much lesser extent, that is what Little Tommy did to us. We were like a couple of kids who had gotten on their parents' last nerve. They shoved us into the corner and said, *Play nice and don't make a mess.* Then, after a few years, Little Tommy shuttered the last brothel, and even our long-time customers were making sports wagers on their cell phones. Who needed us? That quick, Jimmy D and I became completely invisible. Jimmy D had a fatal stroke not long after he was put on the shelf.

I was hurting financially, but I never wanted to let anyone know. I'd put back a little money, about fifteen grand, and I started chipping away at that. I sold my gold jewelry, my watches, rings, and necklaces, and even the cufflinks that I had shown off to Austin Adams at the Federal Terrace. I moved out of the nice apartment in the Hollywood Addition and into the dump on Slack Street. With Social Security, I was able to stay afloat, if barely.

CHAPTER

34

Thursday, August 15, 2019

IT WAS A few minutes before nine when I walked into the lobby of the FBI's Pittsburgh field office. By the way I was greeted, you would've thought I was a crown prince, instead of a career mobster. Ross and another agent were waiting in the lobby. They were all smiles, and Ross extended a hand and acted like we were old high school pals. He introduced me to the other agent, a pasty looking guy named Stanton, who called me Mr. Cipriani, like I was some kind of celebrity. I guess that was some indication of how much they wanted my testimony.

It was all a game.

The FBI agents knew that if they could flip me, it would be a booster rocket for their careers, and bringing down the house of Fortunato would result in medals and certificates of commendation, and all of the gratuitous awards that law enforcement agencies like to shower upon their own people. Stanton scanned his ID badge and opened the door into the inner sanctum. My stomach churned like I was walking in for a root canal. Cops and dentists; I had long regarded them with the same amount of trepidation.

We walked into a conference room where a female stenographer was seated behind her little machine, ready to record every word. A lawyer from the Department of Justice, Weldon something or other, was seated at the head of the table in a starched white shirt, a pair of cheaters on the end of his nose, and a yellow legal pad before him. He made no eye contact. My guess was that he was the one who would decide if I got into the witness protection program. A third agent entered the room. His name was George Malcolm. He was the agent in charge of the Pittsburgh field office. When I was introduced, he nodded curtly, but made no effort to exchange a handshake or pleasantries. He thought I was the lowest form of life, a societal bottom feeder. That was fine. I preferred to deal with guys like Malcolm. You always knew where you stood.

"Can I get you something to drink?" Ross asked. "Coffee, soda, water?"

"Water," I said. I was already wired and didn't need any more sugar or caffeine.

Ross distributed draft copies of the contract that would place me in the United States Federal Witness Protection Program. There were numerous lines dictating my obligations to the federal government. In return, the government agreed to give me a new identity, a home, a car, and a stipend of sixty thousand dollars a year for two years.

I underlined the two-year agreement and said, "Unacceptable. Sixty grand is acceptable, but it has to be for life," I said. "I'm sixty-nine. With my skill set, there are a limited number of jobs available to me."

"That would require approval further up the chain," Ross said.

"Of course it would."

"Let's say we get this approved. Does that mean you're in?"

"Let me ask a couple of questions here. I guess these are directed to you, counselor." Weldon finally looked up from his legal pad and used a middle finger to push his cheaters to the bridge of his nose. "Just exactly how does this dance work?"

"What do you mean?" Weldon asked.

"It's a simple question. How does it work? You obviously aren't going to put me in the witness protection program and give me immunity until I prove to you that I have incriminating information that will put away Little Tommy Fortunato, correct?"

He nodded.

"Nodding ain't an answer."

"That's correct," he said.

"That makes sense from your end. But how do I protect myself? Let's say I tell you something that you find interesting, maybe even damning. What's to say you don't just forgo the witness protection program and indict Little Tommy and try to force me to be a witness?"

"That would never happen."

"Sure, because what could possibly go wrong when the federal government is in charge? What protection do I have against self-incrimination?"

"You'll just have to trust us."

I started laughing. "Seriously? That's your answer? Trust us. Give me a break. It sounds to me like I need to lawyer up if this is going to move forward."

"God dammit, Angelo," Ross said. "We're giving you a chance to start your life over without ever being charged with any of the murders you and Carlo committed."

"So, you're mad at me because I want to protect myself, is that it? I'm not sure any of you appreciate how difficult this is."

"How many more times are we going down this road? I don't understand why the decision is so difficult."

"Just so you know, Cipriani, I don't give a damn how difficult it is for you," Malcolm said. "This is your circus, not mine. You and your buddy Della Russo make Dillinger look like St. Peter. I know that; you know that; everyone in this room knows that. And now, you're on the verge of getting a get-out-of-jail-free card, and you want to whine about your precious loyalty oath? Spare me. If you're having doubts . . ." He pointed to the door. "Hit the road. I don't care one way or the other. Eventually, your boss is going down, with or without you. If you decide not to work with us, no problem. But rest assured, there'll come a day when we knock on your door, and it won't be to ask questions; it will be to put you in handcuffs. Once Fortunato goes down, all the little rats in his organization will be scurrying around, looking to cut deals. So, think hard about this, Cipriani. If you sign the agreement, there's no backing out. Your ass belongs to us. It's just that simple."

"I know how the game's played, Malcolm. You've made it abundantly clear that this is a path of no return. Basically, I can slit my throat however I like. I need some time to think on it."

Malcolm flipped through a notebook he had brought into the room. "Let me ask you this: The name Bruno De Luca, does that ring a bell?"

"He was around for a while. I knew who he was."

A thin grin pursed his lips. "I'm sure you did."

Now, I clearly understood. These guys were playing hardball. They weren't asking me any questions that they didn't already know the answers to.

"You see, Angelo, Nickels isn't the only one we've been talking to," Ross said. "For example, I'm sure you remember a kid named Timmy Sweets. Wasn't that a wonderfully failed science experiment? It took us a while to track him down, because he changed his name and was hiding, afraid that Little Tommy would find him expendable. He moved down south and became a barista. In case you don't know what a barista is, it's a guy who works in one of those foo-foo coffee shacks where you pay eight bucks for a latte. Probably a better profession for him than trying to kill drug dealers in Youngstown, wouldn't you say?"

"I wouldn't say one way or the other."

Stanton asked, "Why did Little Tommy move away from gambling and prostitution to concentrate on drugs?"

"Are you serious? Why do you even need to ask me that question? The amount of money in illegal drugs is crazy."

"Why didn't Big Tommy move the operation that way?"

There didn't seem to be a lot of reasons for holding anything back at this point. "Tommy thought it was bad for business because it would draw too much attention from your organization, and he also thought it was bad for society."

This caused Malcolm to look up from his notebook. "Big Tommy Fortunato was concerned about the direction of our society?"

"Absolutely. Big Tommy was a patriot. He loved this country."

"I'm sure he did. Where else could you spend your entire life in organized crime, set up offshore accounts so that you only pay taxes on about three percent of your net income, and never go to prison? God bless America, huh? So, he didn't want to move the organization toward the drug trade. Is that why Little Tommy killed him?"

I wasn't sure I'd heard things correctly. "Do you want to run that one by me again?"

"It's a softball question. The drug trade, is that why the kid offed the old man?"

I was trying to process that information and respond. It's difficult to do when every hair follicle on your body has caught on fire and a wave of ice has sprinted up your spine and paralyzed your cerebral cortex. Imagine the worst ice cream brain freeze of your life.

Ross smiled and looked genuinely surprised. "Angelo? Really?"

"What?" I finally said. "Little Tommy didn't kill his dad. Big Tommy died of cancer."

All three agents laughed at once.

"You don't really believe that, do you?" Ross asked. "This perfectly healthy guy suddenly gets sick, never sees a doctor, and dies at home. The family physician signs the death certificate, and his body is cremated before any kind of investigation can be launched. Little Tommy knew he couldn't leave a body in the ground and risk an autopsy or an investigation. Poison doesn't leach out of the bones or hair or nails. You can dig up bones from an archaeological site a thousand years old and find out if someone was poisoned because traces of the arsenic are still there. Little Tommy Fortunato's a vicious prick, but he's not stupid, and that's what you're dealing with."

I remembered a thought I had when Big Tommy had his second attack. *Maybe there was a reason why Little Tommy didn't want his father to see a doctor.*

Big Tommy would do virtually anything to please his son. It was an odd relationship. Instead of the boy striving to win the approval of his father, it was the father always trying to win the approval of the boy by showering him with gifts and money. But there weren't enough gifts on the planet to make the kid happy. The only time I ever saw Big Tommy stand up to him was on dealing drugs. I think it might've been the first time in his life that Little Tommy ever heard the word "no" come out of his father's mouth. That's what I was thinking as I tried to convince myself that Little Tommy couldn't possibly have murdered his father.

"No, that didn't happen. Little Tommy, he loved his father. It's impossible."

"Come on, Angelo, you've been in the game too long to be that naïve," Ross said. "Little Tommy killed his father. He poisoned him to death. It was all very Shakespearean. Little Tommy wanted to sit on the throne, but the old man had too many years left in him, and he wouldn't move the operation to illegal drugs."

"That's bullshit. You're just saying that to get me to flip."

"Let me ask you this: You've spent your entire adult life with the Fortunatos and their Italian-Catholic cadre. How many of them were cremated?"

I thought about this for a minute, then said, "One."

"That's right. One. Big Tommy. What a coincidence, huh?"

Malcolm got up to leave. "You boys take it from here." He looked at me, shook his head and said, "Jesus Christ."

"We think it was arsenic. It attacks your central nervous system. If you do it right, over a couple months, it looks like cancer or leukemia. If your victim doesn't have the common sense to go to a doctor, like Big Tommy, even better. You check out and no one suspects anything, particularly if you're a big smoker. He was poisoned, Angelo, and it wasn't the FBI who did it. It was an inside job. I can't believe you didn't know this. Think about it. Little Tommy slips a little arsenic into the old man's coffee. It's tasteless and odorless, but it starts eating away at his insides. It's like a rat in your gut, trying to gnaw its way out. I was no fan of Big Tommy, but that was a terrible way to go."

It began to seem more plausible than I cared to admit. I recalled the day Little Tommy unloaded on me. *He's not going to the fuckin' hospital. Get that through that fat dago head of yours.* I had been stricken by how fast Big Tommy had gone downhill. But I never once suspected that it was anything but cancer. He was a heavy smoker, he had trouble breathing, and he was forever hacking up lung custard. It all seemed like the logical sequence of events.

"How do you know all this?" I asked.

Ross and Stanton looked at each other. Ross held an open palm to the other agent and said, "Go ahead and tell him."

"Technology's a beautiful thing, Angelo," Stanton said. "We were able to access Little Tommy's Internet searches. The kid was researching poisons for months before his father mysteriously became sick. The symptoms Big Tommy exhibited were consistent with the poison that his son was researching. Now, the courts would call that circumstantial evidence, and since we don't have a body . . ." He winked at me. "But we know what really happened, don't we?"

"What about Bruno De Luca and Timmy Sweets? How did you know about them?"

"Remember when I called your unlisted number and you were shocked that I had it?" Ross said, grinning. "Let's just say that we have a lot of resources that are available to us, and we don't always play by the rules."

"You have no warrants. None of it will hold up in court."

"It doesn't have to. Once we get the information, we'll find another avenue to nail it down so that it's admissible in court. And like I said, you and Nickels aren't the only ones we're talking to. You should remember that while you're considering your options."

I stood to leave.

"I need an answer in seventy-two hours," Ross said. "And don't go back to the compound and do something stupid."

"Like strangling Little Tommy."

"Yes, exactly like strangling Little Tommy."

"Why, because if I strangle him, you won't get your trophy?"

I walked out of the conference room and headed toward the door. Malcolm was standing in the hall. As I grabbed the doorknob, he said, "Watch what you eat at the compound, Cipriani."

CHAPTER

35

Thursday, August 15, 2019

IT WAS LATE that night, and Carolyn and I were lying under the sheets, a cool breeze wafting in through the open bedroom window. Far down the hill, a police siren wailed. Someone or something rattled a trash can in the alley. On the Ohio River, a towboat shoving a train of barges was scanning the water with its spotlight, illuminating the banks on both sides of the water. I didn't like for Carolyn to sleep with the window up when I wasn't there and my 9-millimeter was not on the nightstand. She said I worried too much. That may be true, but I was also somewhat familiar with the criminal element in Steubenville, Ohio, and didn't want the woman I loved taking stupid chances with her life.

She was naked and lying on my shoulder; my left arm was wrapped tight around her back. I was raking my fingers through her hair and wishing that I never had to leave that spot.

After dinner, I told her about the possibility that I would enter the witness protection program. I told her that because I didn't want a life in which she wasn't a part. She asked, "What does that mean, exactly?"

"It means that the feds would give me a new identity and relocate me somewhere in exchange for my testimony in a federal racketeering and drug case against Little Tommy."

"Relocate you where?"

"I don't know. If I have a say in the matter, it'll be Florida or Arizona, somewhere warm."

"I'd miss you."

"There's a reason I'm telling you all this. I'd want you to go with me."

"Oh, thank God. I thought you were telling me goodbye." She had little tears in her eyes.

"No. If I decide to do it, I want you to go, too. Will you?"

"And give up my fabulous career as a waitress at the Starlighter Diner? Let me think about that for a minute. Okay, when do we leave?"

Man, I loved this girl.

As we were lying together in bed, she asked, "When will you know if you're going to enter the witness protection program?"

"I don't know. It's a moving target. They have to make me some guarantees before I commit, and I don't know if they're willing to do that. We'll see. If it happens, you know that wherever we go, we'll always be looking over our shoulders. I can't change who I was."

"I don't care who you were. All I care about is who you are going to be moving forward. Who are you right now?"

"Right now? I don't know the answer to that."

"Why?"

"It's hard to explain."

"Try me."

"I have this belief that loyalty should stand for something. I swore an oath. On his deathbed, I told Big Tommy that I would look out for his son."

"Even if his son turns out to be a total shit?"

"His son was a total shit when I made the promise."

"Did Big Tommy want his son to deal drugs?"

"Of course not."

"Do you think he would be happy about it?"

"Not even a little bit."

"Do you think Big Tommy would want you run out of the organization?"

"No."

"And yet, those things have happened and you still feel this sense of loyalty toward him."

"Yes."

"You're going to have to help me here. I'm not understanding this whole loyalty pledge when it's not reciprocal."

"You should be working for the FBI. They don't get it, either."

"Let me see if I have this right. You swore an oath of loyalty to the Fortunato family. The guy you loved, Big Tommy, may have been murdered by his son. So, even though you despise his son, you still must be faithful to your oath because it was to the family."

"Correct."

"You need to reassess your values, Angelo." She smiled, slapped me twice on the chest, and said, "You know, a psychologist would say that you are in a terribly dysfunctional relationship."

"Or that I'm a profoundly disturbed human being."

"I love you anyway."

"Part of the problem is, I'm still not completely convinced that Little Tommy poisoned his father. I think there's a strong chance that the FBI made that up to piss me off and make me flip on him. It's a perfect scenario for them. They can make the allegation, it sounds plausible, but they don't have to prove it because the body was cremated and Little Tommy scattered the ashes. They might have just tossed it out there to give me something to stew about."

"But you said that Little Tommy was researching poison on the Internet."

"No, I said the FBI agents want me to *believe* he was researching poison. Again, how do I know if that's true or not? The cops lie all the time, and it's not like I can walk up to Little Tommy and say, 'Hey, boss, did you murder the old man?'"

"What do you believe in your heart?"

"I don't know. I believe it's possible. I believe Little Tommy is a vicious prick, but I don't believe he would kill his own father."

"You don't believe it or you don't want to believe it?"

"A little of the former and a lot of the latter."

"And you really believe the FBI would make that up to get you to turn on him?"

"Without question."

"You operate in an interesting world, Angelo Cipriani." She drummed her fingers on my chest for a moment before asking, "And we couldn't just get in the car and drive away from all of this because . . . ?"

"Because I've got nothing to offer you. I've got no money, I've got no place for us to live, I've got no transferable skills. Should I go on?"

"Not right now," she said. "Just rest."

She drifted off to sleep. I couldn't. I stared at the ceiling for hours and listened to the sounds of the valley below.

CHAPTER

36

Monday, August 19, 2019—Little Tommy Fortunato's 30th Birthday

Carolyn Melvin had given me a new purpose in life. For the first time since Jolie was murdered, I had a reason to live beyond my loyalty to the Fortunato family. This relationship was more important to me than my oath. Lunch at the Starlighter was no longer the highlight of my day. Two PM became the hour I most anticipated; it was the time when Carolyn hung up her apron and walked out of the diner. The rest of the day, she was mine. I didn't know what my future held, but the only certainty was that I wanted her in it.

Then, at eleven-fifteen, just as I was toweling off from my shower, my cell phone rang. It was the compound number. Little Tommy was on the horn.

"I need you to take care of someone for me, Angelo," he said.

What can I say about this? You may look down upon my profession, but it was what I did, and I was immediately excited to think I might be back in the fold. I wanted to feel needed, like I mattered somewhere in the world . . . or, in this case, the underworld. I also knew in my heart that this could nix any deal I might have with the

FBI. I justified this by convincing myself that Little Tommy hadn't poisoned his father and the feds were lying. At least, that's what I wanted to believe.

"Whatever you need, boss," I said. "When?"

"Tonight."

Again, no time to prepare. "What time?"

"Come by at seven."

"I'll be there."

The kid would get a burr to take someone out, and he wanted it done yesterday. I'd tried to tell him that these things take time, that you needed to be careful, but like I said, he didn't want to hear any of that. "Just get it done," he'd say. Someday, Gaetano would be the perfect hitman for Little Tommy. He was impetuous and careless, and not concerned about stealth or cunning. I guess that's how you look at things when you're in the drug business and spraying down the homes of rivals in drive-by shootings. It wasn't much different from what the Gemellis had done Delmonico's Steakhouse. Actually, it wasn't different at all.

The thing Little Tommy didn't understand was this: It just wasn't as easy to clip someone as it used to be. I'm not making excuses; it's a fact. Nowadays, there are cameras on the freeways, inside of buildings, outside of buildings—everywhere. You're always on camera. And, if you're carrying a cell phone, the cops can track you by the pings off cell towers. It's crazy. That's how they nailed Joey Labitto for the Carsoni hit in Philadelphia a couple of years ago. I'm telling you, it's tough these days. They're either watching you on camera or tracking your every move. It's not like the old days when you could walk down an alley, through a back door and boom, the job was done. Thirty minutes later, Carlo and I would be at Undo's opening a bottle of chianti.

I pulled a black suit out of the closet and took a brush to my shoes. Dress like you have some respect for yourself and your job. Then, I took my 9-millimeter apart and cleaned and oiled it, and jacked one into the chamber. It would be in my waistband that night. I called Carolyn at the diner and told her that I had to run out on a job and didn't know if I would be over to see her that night. There was a cold silence on the phone. "What kind of a job?" she asked.

"Consulting."

"Angelo!"

"I don't know yet. I'm going to meet with Little Tommy later tonight."

"After what we just talked about?"

"It's work, Carolyn. I need work."

"I don't like this."

"It'll be fine. I promise. I'll call you later."

When I pulled up into the compound in my Cutlass, Rosebella was in the garden—a handful of freshly picked daisies in one hand. "Hi, Rosebella," I said. "Picking yourself a fresh bouquet of daisies, I see."

She stared blankly for a moment, struggling to caption the image in her mind's eye. It wouldn't come. Alzheimer's was eating away at the last vestiges of one of the best women I'd ever known. "Yes, picking daisies," she finally said. "Have you seen my Tommaso?"

It was breaking my heart. She asked that question to everyone she saw and was lost in a time and place where no one else could visit.

"I haven't, Rosebella, but if I see him, I'll tell him you're looking for him."

"That would be nice," she said.

As I watched her wander further into the flower bed, I realized I was simply a nameless character passing through the last chapter of her life. It was yet another sign that my best days with the family were behind me.

The scary future the old guard had been afraid of was sitting on the veranda—three guys in their twenties, wearing Hawaiian shirts, garish floral things of red, yellow, and orange that hid the snub-nose .38s they had tucked in the waistbands of their blue jeans. I'm not sure any of them would actually pull the trigger, but they liked making a show. They were talking in hushed tones, most likely about me. They sniggered, and I overheard one of them say, "The human fossil has arrived." I should have gone back to the car and grabbed the piece of cast iron pipe I kept under the seat and laced him across the temple, showing him what the fossil was still capable of.

Their blue jeans, by the way, had holes in them when they were bought. Explain that one to me, please. Why in God's name would you buy pants that have holes in them? It's another thing I don't understand about this younger bunch. That, and all the tattoos. They were wearing penny loafers and no socks. They looked like they were on vacation in Key West instead of working at the Fortunato compound. Before I could get to the shade of the overhang, the mouthy, tubby one, the guy called Gummy Bear, got up and walked inside. Gummy Bear. Yeah, there's a gangster's name for you. Why didn't they just call him Snickerdoodle, for Christ's sake? Gaetano and the Tipplehorn kid, who headed up the drug distribution operation, continued to sit; they acknowledged my presence with the slightest of nods. Tipplehorn had a glassy look in his eyes. He was high on something. This was a calamitous amateur show.

Little Tommy walked out the back door and made a slight move of the head, indicating that he wanted me to follow him away from the crowd. We walked past his mother, who showed not the first sign that she recognized her only son, and stopped at the edge of the paver bricks.

"You're taking Gaetano with you tonight," he said. "It's his test run."

And that quick, the elation I had been feeling melted away. I was again the teacher with the belligerent and unteachable pupil. I could feel the heat building under the collar of my dress shirt, but there was no sense in arguing. He wasn't going to change his mind. I leaned toward Little Tommy and whispered, "You know, his real name is actually Louis."

"Please, don't start, Uncle Ange."

"Who's the mark?" I asked.

"Gaetano has all the information." He put a hand on my shoulder and squeezed once. "I want him to get involved. I need to know if he's got the stomach for this."

I nodded. "I'll take care of it."

Gaetano knew he would be going with me and was already cutting across the yard toward the driveway. "Hey, Pops, ready to rock 'n' roll?"

When he called me "Pops," it scalded me to my marrow.

"I'll drive," he said. "I'm afraid that bucket of bolts of yours will never make it."

I followed him down the driveway and grabbed the handle on a garish yellow car. As I opened the door, I watched Little Tommy help his mother in from the garden. It was a tender moment that I didn't think the boy was capable of. *Uncle Ange*, I thought. He had called me *Uncle Ange* for the first time in years. I watched until they disappeared under the shade of the veranda.

"Hey, Pops, you coming?"

I slid into the passenger seat. "What kind of car is this, other than one every cop in the world would remember seeing?" I asked.

He laughed. "You're funny, Pops. It's a Camaro. Sweet ride, huh? They call it the bumblebee."

"Yeah, sweet. Look, Gaetano, this car is a mark for every cop between here and Altoona." He squealed the tires as he pulled onto Sunset Boulevard. I glared at him and he eased off the gas. "You have to be discreet in this business. We're not like the gangbangers. They roll into town with those Jap cars all jacked up with the big wheels and the music blaring. They want everyone to see them. That's not the way we operate. We work in the shadows. We get in, we get the job done, and we get out. If we do it right, nobody even knows we were there. Sometimes the poor son of a bitch we are going to see doesn't even know. Get yourself a boring car, brown, gray, something that mixes in with every other car on the street. That way, if the cops ask somebody what they saw, they don't remember the car. You drive this thing, they say, 'Yeah, I remember a car. It looked like a big bumblebee with loud mufflers.'" This made Gaetano smile. "I'm serious, boy."

"That's what you don't understand about the business, Pops. You guys drove around in black, boring cars because you didn't want to get noticed. I drive into the 'hood in this, and it's like a magnet for teenage boys. It's a recruiting tool. They all want to own a ride like this one. They see me in this car with a lot of bling, a lot of gold, and that's how I get them to sell drugs for me. I tell them, work with me and you could be driving a sweet ride like this and buying all the gold you want. It's like dangling a present in front of a kid at Christmas. They can't wait."

"See, you're not listening to a word I'm saying. You're not selling dope or recruiting at the moment. You're on an operation."

He laughed. "You worry too much, Pops."

I leaned my seat back and inspected the dashboard. It looked like it belonged on a fighter jet.

"Do you know where we're going?" I asked.

"It's over on the other side of Midland, Pennsylvania, north of the river."

"That doesn't tell me anything. Everything in Midland is north of the river."

"I've been there once. I'll look it up when I get a little closer."

"Have you got a map?"

"A map? Who uses maps? I got a GPS on my phone."

"See, that's exactly what I'm talking about. You've got to start listening to me. You shouldn't use a cell phone on the job. If the FBI wants to track you, all they've got to do is get your cell phone number. You can't leave an electronic record for them. No phones or credit cards. If you need gas, or something to eat, you pay cash, so no one knows you were there."

"I swear, Pops, I've never seen anyone who worries like you."

"You'd be wise to worry a little bit. It'll keep you alive. I'm supposed to be training you, but you don't listen. You got your own ideas, and they're going to get you killed. You're careless, and in this business you can't be careless."

It started spitting rain. I slouched and looked out the window as raindrops beaded on the glass and raced past. I might as well have been talking to the wind. This kid, he was born careless. He would never make it to my age.

Gaetano drove through East Liverpool and turned north on Route 30 toward Calcutta. "If we're going to Midland, why didn't you just take sixty-eight across?"

He looked at his phone and tapped some buttons with his thumb. "It's not right in Midland. The GPS says this is the shortest route."

"You kids couldn't find your way to the crapper without looking at your GBS."

"GPS, Pops."

"Whatever."

The rain had stopped as we crossed Little Beaver Creek north of Calcutta and turned east on Fredericktown Road, crossing over the Ohio-Pennsylvania line in the middle of nowhere, driving through heavy woods on two-lane asphalt. "Jesus Christ, who are we after, Sasquatch?" I asked.

"It's not much further," he said.

"Okay, here's your final prep. Tommaso, he wants to make sure you're ready for this job. Do you think you can pull the trigger tonight?"

He smiled and nodded. "Oh, yeah. I'm ready. I was born ready, Pops."

"Taking a man's life is no small thing, you know?"

"I want to do this. I'm ready."

"What are you carrying?"

"A Luger."

"A Luger? What are you, a member of Hitler's SS?" I retrieved the revolver that I had tucked into my inside jacket pocket and held it out on my palm.

"What's that?" he asked.

"I want you to know something, Gaetano. You and me, we're not that different. We're not connected by blood, but we're brothers of the Spaghetto. We share a common experience. There was one other person who shared that experience. I believe he's here with us tonight. If you're going to be a pro, you need a pro's piece. For your first job, I want you to use this. Pull this off, and it yours. It belonged to a great man—Carlo Dello Russo."

Gaetano looked at me, then the pistol, then back at me. "Really? You're giving me Carlo Dello Russo's gun?"

"Carlo never called it a gun. It was his 'piece.' I think it would do him proud if you took this guy out with his piece." He reached for the .38, and I pulled it back. "Before I hand it over to you, I expect you to treat it with respect. You treat your weapon and your job with respect, and you don't get careless."

I held the .38 back out, and Gaetano snatched it out of my hand. "Thanks, Pops." Gaetano examined the pistol as he drove, rolling it around in his hand. "I appreciate it. I'll make ol' Carlo proud, for sure." He drove with his knee while releasing the cylinder, checking to see each chamber loaded.

"It's ready to go—hollow points," I said. "Remember, your first option is to put one in the back of his head. He can't fight back if he doesn't see you coming. Put it right behind the ear if you can. If not, fill his chest with lead—heart and lungs. Don't shoot him in the face."

"Yeah, yeah, yeah, the whole disrespect thing. Seems to me that shooting them in the face sends a message. It tells them you mean business."

"Sometime tonight, maybe for just two or three seconds, try to listen to one thing I tell you." I took a breath and rubbed my eyes with my fingertips. "So, what's the story?"

"Same deal as usual. Some gangbangers from Youngstown are poaching on our turf again. Little Tommy's warned them. Tonight, they'll learn that Little Tommy's serious as a prison fight. This guy we're meeting thinks I want to score a couple bricks of heroin."

"Okay, remember, don't get careless and don't get cute. This ain't the movies. Don't be talkin' to him and makin' him beg for mercy. You're not playing for style points. Do the job and let's get out."

"I've got it. You'll be with me, right?"

"And what, hold your hand?"

"No, just be my backup."

I chuckled. These guys Little Tommy sends out with me, they want to be all John Wayne until it's time to pull the trigger. "What happened to all that bravado? Five minutes ago, you couldn't wait to clip this guy."

"Come on, Pops, it's my first time. I'm a virgin."

I waved at the air. "Fine, Johnny Bravo."

We cut down Route 168, crossing over Island Run toward Ohioville. We snaked along country roads until I saw a sign that we were entering the state of Pennsylvania game lands. He pulled onto a dirt and gravel road and said, "I think the meeting point is up here."

"You *think* it's up here?" I asked, my voice climbing. "We're coming out here to clip someone and you're not even sure where you're meeting him?"

He swallowed. "This is right," he said. "I remember now. For sure."

He drove a quarter-mile into the woods and heavy underbrush. The fading light was blocked by the canopy of maples and oaks. Foxtail and low branches scraped the sides and top of the car. He drove into a vale of ivy-covered slopes and pulled onto the soft loam lining the road. I said, "Your bumblebee is going to get all muddy."

"Let's get out," Gaetano said. "I don't want to be sitting in the car when he shows up."

"What if he brings company?" I asked.

"Then I'll double up on the message."

We exited the car. He turned off the engine but left the headlights on.

"Wait by the car," I said. "Lean against the hood; look relaxed. You want him to let down his guard." I pointed to a thicket of trees. "I'll back you up from over there in the brush, out of sight."

I'd only taken a few steps when I heard the click of the .38's hammer locking into place. Gaetano said, "That's far enough, Pops."

I turned to find him standing in the glow of the headlights, his arm extended, the pistol I had just handed him pointing at my forehead. "Me?" I asked.

"You've been a bad boy, Pops. You've been talking to the FBI."

"No, no, no. They've just been talking to me. They want me to flip, but I haven't told them anything."

"Right, we know you went to their headquarters in Pittsburgh for a meeting, but you want me to believe you didn't tell them anything. You know who doesn't believe that that shit either? Tommaso. And you know why, because he's still got an agent at the bureau on the payroll. He told Tommaso that you were going to sell him out for a little house in the country."

"That's not true. Look, can't we talk about this?"

"Nothing to talk about, Pops. You've got a big mouth and you've outlived your usefulness." He rolled his wrist, and the chrome plating on the revolver glinted in the beam of headlight. "Ironic, ain't it, Pops? First, you trained your executioner, and now you're going to cash out on the wrong end of Carlo Dello Russo's gun. I'm sorry, I mean, his *piece*." He chuckled, but just for an instant before his upper lip curled and his eyes turned to slits. "By the way, after you're out of the way, I'm going to go pay a visit to your buddy Nicolosi and suffocate him with a pillow. Then all the old fucks will be extinct. I'm glad to be getting rid of your tired ass and your whining and your bullshit about the old-fashioned ways. Say good night, Pops." He squeezed the trigger, and the hammer fell. *Snap.* The echo was crisp in the night air. He squeezed again. *Snap.* Still, nothing.

Gaetano looked down at the revolver and frowned. "What the . . ." It took only a moment for him to realize what had occurred, but by then I had pulled my 9-millimeter out of my waistband and had a bead on Gaetano, or as I now preferred to call him, Louis.

"Checkmate, Louis. Keep your hands up where I can see them." I took two steps closer. "You actually thought I would give a punk like you Carlo Dello Russo's weapon? I would never let you touch his piece. How many times did I tell you that you were careless and it was going to get you killed? The answer is, too many, and now it has."

There was a moment in time, an instant, or whatever passes faster than an instant, between my last word and the report of my 9-millimeter echoing off the slopes of the vale, when the fear melted from Gaetano's face. His mouth puckered to the size of a cherry, his head titled slightly, and his eyes took on a look of confusion, or perhaps bewilderment, as though he could not comprehend the living form before him, that the creature about to end his life was not Angelo Cipriani, but a beast from a different time and place. A dinosaur, perhaps.

The first bullet hit him in the chest, yanking him off his feet like a hapless marionette and dropping him on his back. He was dead before he hit the ground, but I emptied the magazine into his heart. Why the overkill, so to speak? Just because I could. I rolled him over with my foot and pulled his wallet from his pants pocket. There were three twenty-dollar bills inside, and I took them. Sorry, Carlo, but I needed the cash. I fished through his pants pockets and found the ignition fob to the Camaro. As I was about to walk away, his cell phone started to chime, and I could see it glow inside his pants pocket. I pulled it out. On the white screen were the initials TF—Tommaso Fortunato.

I touched the green button on the screen and said, "Good evening, Tommaso."

He stammered for a minute. "Uncle Ange, hey, uh, can I speak to Gaetano?"

"I'm sorry, Tommaso, but he can't talk right now."

"Is he busy?"

"No, he ain't busy at all; he just can't talk."

There was a long pause on the other end. "Oh, okay, tell him to call me when he can."

"Yeah, I don't think that's going to happen anytime soon."

"Why's that?"

"He wasn't as ready for this job as you thought. Remember, I told you he was careless."

"What happened?"

"You sleep tight tonight, Tommaso. Don't wait up for your buddy. Oh, and by the way, happy birthday."

He was still talking when I hit the red button.

I picked up the revolver and slid behind the wheel of the bumblebee. And just that quickly, the dark horse had moved into the lead.

* * *

For the first time in years, I felt like I was in charge, and that I mattered again.

Little Tommy and Gaetano thought I was beyond my prime, and maybe I was, but I was smart enough to walk away from another attempt on my life. You see, when you've been in the business as long as me, you know when something is going down. You feel it in your bones. That's why I filed down the firing pin on the revolver and made up the story about it being Carlo's pistol. You don't live to be sixty-nine in this business being careless.

As I crossed over Little Beaver Creek, I rolled down the passenger window and tossed the revolver and Gaetano's cell phone into the water. It was a beautiful night to still be alive. And, I had to admit, the bumblebee was a pretty sweet ride. As I drove, I decided that I was done with the loyalty thing. It was time to change teams, and I planned to take Special Agent Lawrence G. Ross up on his offer. What the hell, the damp Ohio winters were starting to wear on me, anyway. Having a little place in the sun might be nice.

Before I committed, maybe I'd go back to the compound and shoot Little Tommy in the face.

I'd have to think on that for a while.

In the meantime, I'd use Gaetano's money to treat myself at Undo's. I'd get the corner booth, order the bucatini with clam sauce, a chianti, and maybe a cannoli.

CHAPTER

37

Tuesday, August 20, 2019

EVEN THOUGH I had pledged my loyalty to the Fortunatos, I had long had a backup plan, just in case things took a hard left with the family or the Gemellis overran the fort and I had to blow town in a hurry. That's why I drove to Indiana once every six years to renew the driver's license of Pete Cola, the ball bearing rep from Indianapolis. Eventually, I opened up a bank account and got a couple of credit cards in his name. I kept a couple hundred bucks in the bank and used the credit cards sparingly, just enough to keep them active. It's the kind of thing you think about when you work for the mob.

At three AM, I parked a block away from my apartment, then walked along the shadows and slipped through the back door of the building. I went up the stairs with my shoes in one hand, my 9-millimeter in the other. The hall was empty, and the tiny piece of tape I had put in the corner of the door was undisturbed. On the negative side, my socks were soaked in dog piss from the carpet, and I had to wash my feet in the sink. I hated those dogs.

I packed the few belongings I wanted to take. There are some advantages to living a Spartan lifestyle. I never carried around a bunch of memories, like photo albums or treasures of my youth. The reason, I guess, is that I didn't have either. The only mementos I had were my father's watch—and it was on my wrist—and the pool trophy I had won at Bixby's when I was seventeen. My move was quick—a couple suitcases of clothes and toiletries, and another, smaller suitcase of guns and ammunition. There was a framed photo of Jolie and me on our wedding day on my dresser. I put it in the suitcase; then, I took it out and set it back on the dresser and stared at it for a long moment. It had to stay. It was a painful memory of the life that was sliding past me at a terrible speed.

When the suitcases were packed, I opened the small safe I had hidden behind the detergent in the cabinet below the sink. I pulled out the 9-millimeter Beretta that I had taken out of Carlos's shoulder holster that day in the mountains of Pennsylvania, and an envelope in which I had tucked Pete Cola's driver's license, Social Security card, checkbook, and credit cards. I stopped at the door and looked around the sad apartment. The clock that Big Tommy had given to me continued to tick off seconds from the mantel, each stroke echoing through the apartment. You know what I thought? Good riddance. I cracked the door and peeked into the hall. It was empty. Five minutes later, I was back in the Camaro and headed south.

I got off of Route 7 at the Georges Run exit and doubled back to Deandale and Paddy's Diner, a twenty-four-hour greasy spoon popular with truck drivers and guys trying to sober up before heading home. I went to a booth and ordered coffee, bacon, and fried eggs over medium. It probably wasn't what my doctor would want to see me eating, but after the night I'd had, what were a couple of extra points on my cholesterol level?

I had two more cups of coffee. It was a little before six AM when I left the diner. I stopped for gas in Mingo Junction, then drove back to Steubenville and crossed over the Ohio River on the Veterans Memorial Bridge and into Weirton. I parked in the lot of the Pinecrest Rehabilitation Center and set the alarm clock on my phone—it's crazy the things these cell phones can do—for 7:45 and crashed. Sleeping in a bright yellow car was probably not the smartest move when the reigning crime boss of the Ohio River Valley had already made at least one attempt on my life, but I couldn't help it; I was fading fast.

The shift change was at eight; I walked into Nickels's room before the day-shift nurse had made her first rounds and popped him full of pills. He was in bed, unshaven, wearing that stupid hospital gown. "Where are your clothes?" I asked.

"I ain't got anything but this gown."

I opened the three drawers of his dresser. There was nothing in there except a copy of the New Testament, his wallet, and a black pocket knife, the same one I'd watched him use to clean his fingernails for years. I shoved the wallet and knife into my pants pocket. His artificial leg was propped in the corner of the room—a titanium stick with a cup to go over his stump and a tennis shoe over the foot. "Can you wear that thing?"

"I can wear it. Walking's a challenge. I look like Muzzie Lollini on a Saturday night bender."

I went back to the lobby and grabbed a wheelchair from the little corral by the front door. As I was helping him out of his bed and into the wheelchair, I looked down on his nightstand and, I swear to Christ, there was a half-eaten prune Danish on a paper napkin. "Where'd that prune Danish come from?" I asked.

"The same place it always comes from. Alphonse brought it to me earlier this morning."

A nurse's aide walked in with a fresh pitcher of water. "Where'd that Danish come from?" I asked.

She swapped out the pitchers and shrugged. "I just got here."

"Has he eaten breakfast yet?"

"It's not for another fifteen minutes."

Nickels winked at me. "Alphonse said to give you his regards."

My chest constricted with the pricks of a thousand icicles. When the aide had left, I grabbed the artificial limb and said, "Stuff this up under your gown. We're going to get some fresh air."

"Where?"

"Just follow my lead."

I pushed him down the hall and into the lobby. The woman at the front desk looked up and said, "Where are you two going?"

"Just outside for a minute," I said. "He wants a little sunshine on that pasty puss of his."

"Don't be long. He's due for his meds."

"Just a couple laps around the parking lot."

The automatic doors slid open, and I rolled Nickels onto the asphalt. "How many times a day do they give you those pills?"

"Who fucking counts?" he said, lifting the back of his left hand to his eyes. "Jesus Christ, I forgot what the sun looks like."

"That's what happens when they treat you like human veal."

I rolled him up to the Camaro. He said, "Is this your ride?"

"I borrowed it. The guy who owns it didn't need it today."

"Nice. Is this the 455-horse, small-block V-8?"

I had forgotten that Nickels was a car guy, but how was it that someone who thought a long-dead mobster had brought him a prune Danish could remember the horsepower options of a Chevy Camaro?

"I don't know, Nickels. It's got an engine, and it runs."

"Where the hell are we going? That nurse said I needed my meds."

"You don't need any more of their meds. They do nothing but keep you loopy. Just get your fat ass in the car."

I opened the passenger side door and helped him off the wheelchair and into the seat, his bare rear hanging out of the gown. It was a tight squeeze, and he banged his head hard on the edge of the roof. "I'm going to need meds if you keep beating me up."

I slammed the door and ran around the car. The wheelchair rolled to the edge of the parking lot and tipped over the curb and into the grass. As I was backing out of the parking space, the nurse from the front desk was coming out the front door, waving for me to stop. I hit the gas and laid rubber on the asphalt.

Nickels was off balance with only one leg. He fell against my shoulder, then rolled back and hit the door. "Slow the hell down, Mario," Nickels said.

"Put your seat belt on," I said.

"Seat belts are for pussies."

"Then try not to do the Humpty Dumpty routine when I'm driving."

"You're an asshole."

"Yeah, so I've been told."

He strapped on the seat belt as his face crinkled. "Good God, can you cut the heat in this thing?"

"I turned it up for you. You're the one who's always cold."

"Who's always cold? I've never been cold in my life."

I was beyond the point of arguing. I dialed back the heat and turned on Colliers Way to get on Route 22 back to Steubenville. As we reached the bottom of the hill and Veterans Memorial Bridge appeared before us, Nickels looked around and frowned. "Where the hell are we?"

"Weirton."

"West Virginia?"

"Yeah. It hasn't left the state. Where did you think you were?"

"I thought I was in a room at the Steubenville Country Club."

"What?"

"Yeah, I thought I was at the country club. There were always golfers walking past my window."

"Jesus H. Christ, Nickels. What kind of drugs were they giving you?"

He shook his head and said, "The good stuff, apparently. So, why did you bust me out?"

"Because Little Tommy wants to kill you."

"Kill me? Why?"

"For the same reason he tried to have me killed last night. He's got a snitch inside the FBI, and he knows they've been trying to flip us."

"How come you're not dead?"

"Because I was smarter than the guy he sent to kill me."

"He must have been a complete retard if you're smarter than him." He grinned.

"You're hilarious. I'm over here juggling hand grenades and you're cracking jokes."

"Do you think I could get a cup of coffee that doesn't taste like warm dishwater?"

"Sure. You want something to eat?"

"No, just coffee, couple of creams. I'm not hungry. I had half a prune Danish."

He was screwing with me. I pulled out my cell phone and called Carolyn. She picked up after one ring. Without pleasantries, she said, "Do you know how to answer your cell phone?"

She had called several times during the night and that morning. I had ignored the calls while I was scrambling for my life and trying to bust Nickels out of hell. "I can explain everything later. Can you meet me out front of the diner in five minutes with two coffees—one black, one with two creams."

When I turned onto Slack Street, Carolyn was already standing outside, a foam cup in each hand.

"Whoa, who's the tomato?" Nickels asked.

"Before you say anything insulting, that's my girl."

"Cipriani, my man, you have completely outkicked your coverage." He actually licked his fingers and ran them back over his hair, as if that could improve things in four seconds. "How do I look?"

"Nursing-home fabulous."

Carolyn leaned down and looked into the interior of the bumblebee and said, "This is an improvement." She handed Nickels both cups. There was no softness to her face. "What's going on, Angelo? And why is there a one-legged man in pajamas in your car?"

"It's a hospital gown," Nickels said.

"This is my friend Nickels. We had to leave his former residence in a bit of a hurry, and that's all he had to wear."

She wouldn't be distracted. "I asked, what's going on?"

"You're still game to get out of here, right? If I can get us a place in Florida or Arizona, you'll still go with me?"

She took a deep breath and said, "Angelo, say the word, and I'll put the for-sale sign in my front yard this afternoon."

It bears repeating. What a top-drawer babe.

"When you get off work, pack two suitcases. I've got a job to do, and if I'm still alive when it's done, we're getting out of here."

"Why, exactly, might you be dead?"

"Because right now I've got a first-class ticket on the Hindenburg and there's a lightning storm coming."

"What's that mean?"

"It means, please don't ask questions that you know I can't answer."

"You mean you won't answer."

"Correct."

"I hate you so much right now."

"No, you don't."

"You'll be back tonight?"

"Yes. Maybe. Probably not, but maybe."

"You're making me very angry, Angelo." She looked down at Nickels. "Get him some clothes to wear." She spun on a heel and disappeared back into the diner.

"She's a spunky little thing," Nickels said. "I like her."

I peeled the plastic lid off my cup of coffee and pulled away from the curb. I drove over the Market Street bridge and back into West Virginia. It was another ten minutes before I pulled up to a familiar spot in Oak Grove Cemetery. "I'll be back in a minute," I said. I walked over to Jolie's modest tombstone. Her parents had erected it using her maiden name, Jolie Frankfurth. I eased myself down on the grass by the stone. "Jolie, I'm afraid this is the last time I'm going to be able to come see you. You know that I have loved you since the first time I laid eyes on you. That was a long time ago, love. It hardly seems possible that so much time has passed. For the first time since then, I found someone who I really care about. Her name's Carolyn, and I love her. I don't know if I should have said that in front of you, but I want to be honest. I need this woman in my life, and I hope you understand."

A cardinal landed on the cement wing of an angel a couple of rows away from me. I think in life we sometimes look for signs or signals that we believe those who have gone before us are sending. I'd like to believe that. I would like to think that Jolie sent that cardinal from the heavens. I don't know what the corridor between this world and the next looks like, and I don't know if souls have free passage back and forth to see what we are doing. When I think of how I have lived my life, I would hope that isn't true so that the souls of those I sent to the next world are not creeping back into my life. I guess that's a little hypocritical, hoping that Jolie could somehow send me a message, but not Tony or Frankie Gemelli. They would certainly be very different messages.

I got onto one knee and pushed myself up. "I've got to leave now, my love. You take care. I'll be seeing you someday. If things go badly later, it might be very soon."

When I climbed back into the bumblebee, I was blinking away tears. Nickels looked at me with furrows across his brow. "Who is that?" he asked.

"Jolie."

He looked at the tombstone, then back at me. "Your wife? The one who . . ."

"Yeah, the one they murdered."

He seemed to ponder the morning's events. "Was that your final goodbye?"

"That was it."

"Where the hell are we going, Angelo?"

I dropped the bee into gear. "I've got some unfinished business to attend to, and he's going to wish to God he had killed me when he had the chance. After that, it's a roll of the bones. First things first, I need to get some cash and buy you something to wear."

"I've got cash."

I looked at Nickels. "There are no pockets in that gown. That only leaves one place you could be hiding it, and I guarantee I don't need it that bad."

"I'm tellin' ya, I've got some cash squirreled away."

"How much?"

"One-point-six million."

I pulled the Camaro off the side of the road. "How much?"

"You heard me."

"Dollars?"

"No, bunny rabbits. Of course, dollars."

"Where did you get that kind of money?"

"Where do you think? I stole it from Little Tommy. I was doing the books for three years and had access to the vault."

"He wasn't watching the books?"

"He was a hawk about watching the books, but he wouldn't let me move anything offshore, like Big Tommy. He wanted to put everything in the vault in the basement. Mother of Christ, there's so much money in there you can't turn around—floor to ceiling, nothing but cash. I was very careful with the books and reviewed things with him three or four times a week. The books were right, but when he was gone one day, I went to the vault and walked out of the house with one-point-six million in my duffle bag. The only way he would ever know it's gone is if he counts what's in the vault and compares it to the books. That ain't going to happen. There's so much money in there, he'd think it was just a rounding error. He'll never know it's missing."

"So, where did you hide it?"

"I had a false bottom put in an old steamer trunk that my grandfather brought over from Italy."

"Where's the trunk?"

He shrugged. "Beats me. I think my niece put it in storage or something."

"Or something? It's holding one-point-six million dollars and you don't know where it is?"

"Jesus Christ, Angelo, cut me some slack. I didn't know where I was until an hour ago."

"Do you know how to get in touch with your niece?"

"Sure. She's a good kid. She stops in to see me a couple times a week. She'll freak out if she shows up and I'm not there. You want that I should call her and get into the storage unit?"

"No. I don't need one-point-six million. I was talking like a hundred bucks."

"Oh, why didn't you say so? Look in my wallet."

I had forgotten that I had stuffed his wallet and pocket knife into my pants pocket. I arched my back to get my rear off the seat and dug the wallet out of my hip pocket. It contained eighty-six dollars. "They didn't steal this while you were loopy?"

"Apparently not."

"Let's go get you some clothes."

We went shopping at the Salvation Army Thrift Store in Steubenville—the same store where Mom bought Steve Casey's old shirt, which led to me getting suspended the first day of the fifth grade. I'm not sure words can accurately paint the picture of the ridiculousness of the scene. I looked like I hadn't slept all night, which was largely true, and had a stubble of heavy beard and wrinkled clothes. Nickels put on the artificial leg and was limping along beside me, his right foot bare, the titanium rod and tennis shoe extending from the stump of his left leg beneath a pale blue hospital gown. He was using his right hand to clutch my left biceps for balance and his left arm was wrapped around his back, a wad of gown bunched up in his fist as he tried to keep from showing the world his sagging ass. Yes, we were quite the dapper pair.

I put him in a dressing room and started passing in clothes—a package of boxers and three pairs of black socks. It's not easy finding pants in a thrift shop for a guy who is a thirty length and a fifty-two waist. The Humpty Dumpty analogy of that morning might have been a little more accurate than either of us cared to admit. I also bought a couple of shirts, a belt, and a pair of black dress shoes.

With a pair of matching shoes, he was a little steadier on his feet. He stepped outside the dressing room and looked in the mirror. "Not bad, I guess," he said. "But you know, I'm used to something a little more stylish than Salvation Army attire."

"A guy who was wearing a bedsheet is going to talk to me about fashion?"

"You're an asshole."

"Yeah, you keep reminding me."

As we walked to the parking lot, Nickels lightly held onto my arm. He seemed to be gaining strength and confidence. The gray pallor of his face had been replaced with a little pink in his cheeks. His blood was pumping, and the fog and cobwebs were blowing out of his head. He complained about a headache, and I assumed that was the result of withdrawal as his body reacted to coming off the meds.

I wasn't sure if Little Tommy was on the hunt for us, but if he was, the bumblebee was an easy target to spot. I pulled out of Steubenville and headed south on Route 7. I got off at the Georges Run exit and drove west to New Alexandria, then back down over the hill through Riddles Run to Brilliant, making sure that we hadn't been followed. I parked at the O.K. Carry-Out and bought us both microwave burgers and sodas. When we were finished eating, I called Agent Ross, setting my phone on the center console and pushing the speaker button.

"Ross, it's Angelo."

"Thank God. Are you okay?" he asked.

"I'm fine. Why would you ask that?"

"We received some intel that Little Tommy was going to have you executed."

"Who are you talking to?"

"Never mind who I'm talking to. What happened?"

"The boy tried to put his old Uncle Ange on ice, but obviously, he came up a little short. That's not important at the moment. Let me tell you something that is important. You've got a giant leak in your office. Little Tommy knows that we've been talking. He also knew you'd been talking to Nickels. The only place he would have learned that was from your office."

"Can't be."

"Trust me, Ross. You've got a rat posing as an FBI agent who's on Little Tommy's payroll. And I'll tell you another thing, if your intel from inside the compound is coming from Alfie Fortunato, and that's my bet, you better get that kid the hell out of there, because his life ain't going to be worth a shit. Now, I'm ready to make this deal happen. However, it's got to include Joey Nicolosi."

"Nicolosi? Why? He's practically brain dead."

"Fuck you, G-man," Nickels yelled. "Brain dead would still make me smarter than a half dozen FBI agents."

"Nickels said to say good morning. And, as you might have deduced from that outburst, he's not as brain dead as you thought. In fact, he was the one doing the books for Little Tommy, and he has a very clear memory. I'd say he's critical to your case."

"You know I can't make these decisions on my own. I've got to run them up the chain of command."

"Come on, Ross, don't blow me a bunch of smoke. You've been telling me all along that you're working on a tight deadline, and now you're dragging your feet? Nickels and I will give you the information you want, but we both need protection."

"I'll call the U.S. attorney as soon as we get off the phone."

"Carolyn Melvin is coming with me. It's a package deal."

"Sure, fine. Are you on your way?"

"Not yet. I've got some unfinished business to attend to."

"What's that mean?"

"Just what I said. I need to take care of some things before I go underground."

There was a moment of silence on the phone before Ross said, "Oh, no. No, no, no. You get your ass back up here to this office."

"Why, so your little office rat can let Little Tommy know where I am? No, thanks."

"You're going to do something stupid and ruin this entire operation. I don't want Little Tommy dead; I want him in prison for the rest of his life."

"I know, you want your trophy. You have a good day, Agent Ross. Get Nickels into the program and we're all sunshine and kittens. I'll be in touch."

He was still yelling into the phone when I hung up.

"That went well," Nickels said.

"Do you think you could drive a car?"

"Do you think you could be any more insulting? I'm not an invalid."

"You were this morning," I yelled, "And you've got one fuckin' leg."

He yelled louder, "I've got my right leg. I can drive. Why?"

"Because I've got a plan."

"Uh-huh. Well, plan to feed me something better than microwave cheeseburgers, and I'm all in."

"Let's go get the—oh, shit. I left the Cutlass at the compound last night."

"Do you think you could sneak in and get it?"

"No chance. Besides that, as soon as we left last night, Little Tommy probably had it taken to the scrap yard and crushed into a brick. Damn, I liked that car."

"Isn't that the one Big Tommy bought for you?"

"Yeah. How'd you know that?"

"You kiddin'? Everybody knew."

I hit Carolyn's number again. She answered on the first ring. "So, you're still alive up to this point."

"I need to borrow your car."

"For reasons that you can't, or won't, tell me."

"Correct."

"Am I going to prison if you get caught using it in the commission of a felony?"

"No, I'll tell them I stole it and eventually they'll give it back to you."

"Fine. It's parked outside. I'll put the keys under the floor mat."

"Carlo would be proud of you."

"What?"

"Nothing. Thanks."

I pulled out of the O.K. Carry-Out parking lot and took the entrance ramp for Route 7 north, back toward Steubenville. The plan I was concocting was still swirling in my head, and I was wondering if Nickels had the mental acuity to pull off his role when, a mile south of Steubenville, he adjusted my interior rearview mirror, nodded, and said, "Yeah, I'll tell him."

"Tell me what? Who are you talking to?"

"Big Tommy."

"Big Tommy? Where's he?"

"He's not here anymore. He was in the back seat. You didn't smell his cigarette?"

"No, I didn't smell anything. What did he want?"

"He just said that you should do what you have to do. It's not the same organization that you grew up in."

"I already knew that."

"Well, don't shoot the messenger. I'm just telling you what he said."

"Anything else?"

"Nope. That was it."

"Nickels, how am I supposed to believe you're lucid enough to drive a car and help me with my plan when you're still talking to ghosts?"

He just smiled.

I didn't think Big Tommy was riding in the back seat of the Camaro. But then, I still couldn't figure out how the prune Danish got on his nightstand.

CHAPTER

38

Tuesday, August 20, 2019

NICKELS DROVE CAROLYN's car and followed me to Youngstown. In the midst of the chaos swirling around my life at that moment, I've got to admit it was hilarious watching a one-legged fat man squeeze behind the wheel of her Kia Forte. We parked the Camaro in a shopping mall parking lot, and I went inside and bought a burner phone for Nickels with Pete Cola's credit card. We cruised around in the Kia until we found a motel without security cameras everywhere. The Carousel Inn was a rent-by-the-hour dive in Niles, a city just northwest of Youngstown. I paid for the room with the bogus credit card. After we got settled, we went back for the Camaro. I parked it in front of our motel room door, moved my luggage to the Kia, then wiped down everything Nickels and I had touched in the bumblebee.

Nickels was hungry, so I drove the Kia to Renato's Pizza and picked up a pie for him, a cavatelli with meatballs and garlic knots for myself, and a couple of Cokes. The pizza apparently agreed with him because he attacked it like a hungry bear. I'd never seen anyone devour a large pizza by himself, but Nickels did it. As he crammed the last piece in his mouth, and talking around enough dough, pepperoni and double cheese to choke a horse, he said, "Oh my God, this is delicious."

"You're eating it so fast I'm surprised you can taste it," I said. "You act like you haven't eaten in a year."

"I'll tell you one thing, we never had food like this at the country club."

My head jerked around, and he started laughing. "Relax, Angelo. It's a joke."

"You're a funny guy, Nickels. Seriously, are you sure you're up for this?"

"How difficult can it be?"

"For the old Nickels, a piece of cake. But this Nickels, who still thinks he's conversing with Alphonse and Big Tommy . . . I'm not so sure."

"You seem pretty certain that these conversations are all part of my imagination. You should have a little faith, brother."

I had no idea who I was dealing with here. Off the drugs, he seemed to be in charge of his faculties, other than talking to dead people, which I will admit is a major drawback to declaring complete sanity. Still, I didn't have any other options, other than to just walk away, and I couldn't do that. I couldn't live the rest of my days knowing that the man who ordered the killing of Jolie and my baby was still breathing.

At 3:30 PM, I drove the Kia to the east side of Youngstown and parked across the street from the offices of Eastern Ohio Refuse and Hauling. I stopped a black kid of about twelve on a bicycle and said, "Hey, pal, you want to make a quick twenty bucks?"

"Maybe," he said.

"Good answer, kid. Never accept a deal without knowing the particulars." I handed him a twenty-dollar bill and an envelope. Printed on the envelope was *Donny Gemelli—Personal*. "As soon as you see my car disappear around the corner, I want you to take this envelope into that building, set it on the first desk you see, and walk out. That's all. Leave before anyone can ask you who gave you the envelope."

"That's all?"

"That's it."

He shrugged and said, "Okay."

I drove around the corner and watched out the rear window as the kid disappeared behind the building's steel front door. He didn't even bother to close it behind him. A few seconds later, he ran out the door, hopped on his bike and pedaled away like he'd dropped off a letter bomb.

In a way, he had.

Inside the envelope, on a piece of plain typing paper, I had printed, *Do I have your attention?* and the number to the burner phone I had bought for Nickels. Wrapped inside the paper was a business card for Pete Cola, ball bearing distribution rep. It was identical to the card I knew they had found in Tony Gemelli's pocket the night I put three bullets in his skull.

I stopped at Renatos's to get Nickels another pie. About that time, the burner phone rang in room fourteen at the Carousel Inn.

"Talk to me," Nickels said.

There was a moment of silence.

"Is this Pete Cola?" Gemelli asked.

"No."

"Did you send me this card?"

"You called the right number, didn't ya?"

"Who are you?"

"That's irrelevant."

There was another moment of silence.

"Where are you?"

"Instead of playing twenty questions, how about we cut to the chase, Gemelli? I know you want Pete Cola. You've wanted to find him for years because he killed your uncle. What you might have suspected, but didn't know for sure, was that he also smoked your old man in that Florida hotel room. He didn't work for no ball bearing distributor, either. He was a button man for the Fortunatos, and his real name ain't Pete Cola, which you've probably figured out. You want him, and I know where he is. All it's going to cost you is twenty large, ten up front and ten after you have his head on a stake."

Nickels could hear the hot exhaust coming from Donny Gemelli's flared nostrils. "If this is some kind of a joke, I'll cut your throat."

"I happen to know from good sources that you have absolutely no sense of humor, Gemelli, so I wouldn't attempt to bore you with humor. Ten thousand up front, ten when I deliver."

"How do I know you won't skip after I give you the first ten?"

"I don't move very quickly these days. You'll see that when you get here."

"Where's 'here'?"

"There's a hot pillow joint on Robbins Avenue in Niles—the Carousel Inn. Room fourteen. The door's unlocked."

My phone rang a few seconds later. "He's breathin' steam and on his way," Nickels said.

I pulled into the parking lot of a white trash plaza—Tattoos by Lou, Juanita's Nail Salon, Abe's Discount Smokes, Ace Pawn Shop, and a payday loan operation with a walk-up window—across the street from the Carousel Inn. I slipped the Kia between a beater Chevy with the rearview mirror held in place with duct tape and a Dodge pickup truck with a black garbage bag pinched into the passenger side door to cover the window opening. From this vantage point, I could keep an eye on room fourteen. Thirty minutes later, Gemelli and two of his goons stepped out of a black sedan. One of the goons had a pistol wrapped in his left hand; he tapped on the door before pushing it open. The second goon entered. A few minutes later, one of the goons opened the door wide and Donny Gemelli disappeared inside.

After entering the room, Gemelli reached into his pants pocket and pulled out the business card, holding it between his index and middle finger. He looked at the one-legged man sitting at the foot of the bed, his pant leg extending down from the stump. "Is this your handiwork?"

"You got my down payment?"

The key to working with a guy like Gemelli is to show no fear. You have to make him believe you're bargaining from a position of power. Granted, there was always a chance he could have his goons use your face for batting practice, but being aggressive was still the best approach.

"What's your name?" Donny asked.

"Nicolosi. Joseph Nicolosi. Pleased to meet your acquaintance."

"This is a pretty ballsy move, Nicolosi."

Nickels shrugged. "You want Pete Cola or don't ya?"

"What's to say I don't just start cutting off body parts until you tell me what I want to know?"

"You can try that if you like, but I can take a lot of pain, and I'm an old man with not much longer to live, so I won't be losing out on that much. And since I don't like you or your family to begin with, it'll give me great pleasure going to my grave knowing that you'll never find the man who killed your father and uncle."

Gemelli nodded, just twice, then pulled a thick envelope out of an inside jacket pocket and dropped it in Nickels's lap. He slid open the flap and found two neatly wrapped bundles of hundred-dollar bills. He smiled and tucked the envelope under his left hip. "Where's the other ten grand?"

"When I have Pete Cola, you'll get your money."

"Show it to me." Gemelli swallowed hard, and scarlet flares ran up his neck. He reached into the other jacket pocket and pulled out a second envelope, waved it at Nickels, then returned it to his pocket. Nickels said, "See, that wasn't so difficult, was it? The guy you're looking for, Pete Cola, is Carlo Dello Russo."

"Bullshit," Donny said.

"I thought that one might scald you a bit. All that time you thought Carlo was working as an inside agent for you, he wasn't. He and Big Tommy Fortunato were playing you for a chump. Muzzie Lollini took the ID of a guy the Chicago mob killed and created Carlo's fake identity—Pete Cola. He killed your father in Florida using one of Big Tommy's prostitutes as bait. He went to dinner at the Vine Cliff, and your uncle thought Pete was going to make him a billion dollars selling frozen lasagna—your grandmother's recipe. He laughed about that for years. Big Tommy wanted to infiltrate your organization because he was afraid of the Gemellis. He knew you had the backing of the Cleveland mob, and he figured it was just a matter of time until you took control of the Ohio Valley. So he had Carlo go to your bookies and intentionally make bad bets so he could run up a debt that you figured he couldn't pay. That way, you'd blackmail him with his gambling debt. You thought you had him by the balls, but he was feeding Big Tommy information all the time, and all you were getting was bogus intel."

"It wasn't bogus," Donny said between clenched teeth. "Carlo was the one who told me a guy named Cipriani killed my dad and uncle."

Nickels started laughing. "That was the best one ever. Big Tommy hated Angelo Cipriani. *Hated him!* In fact, all of the capos, myself included, hated him. He was this part Italian, part Ukrainian or Russian, or some shit like that, who thought he should be a full capo. And Big Tommy was pretty sure he was skimming on his collections. He let Cipriani and his wife use his private dining room at the Federal Terrace for an anniversary dinner, so Carlo could tell you exactly where to find them. It was a complete setup. Big Tommy was going to get rid of his problem child while you thought Carlo had given you the crown gem—the guy who murdered your uncle and old man. The only problem was, your boys screwed up. They killed his wife and left Cipriani shot to pieces. It was so pathetic that Big Tommy started feeling sorry for the putz and let him back into the fold. It's like beating a dog until he pisses himself, and then you feel bad about it. Cipriani became this pathetic character that we all felt sorry for, but even then, no one liked him."

Gemelli didn't say anything. He was perplexed, believing that Nickels's story was just wild enough to be true. He was embarrassed that he had been played for a fool.

"So now you're probably wondering why Carlo disappeared all of a sudden. A couple of things happened. Carlo had a thing for Cipriani's wife. He was crushed when she got killed. See, he was hoping that you'd off Cipriani, then he could move in on the old lady. After she got killed, he lost his nerve. I think all those years of being undercover and infiltrating your organization started to get to him. He got the shakes and started having that nightmare shit the combat soldiers have, that post-traumatic stress thing. When people are under stress, the crazy rises to the top. That's what happened with Carlo. He couldn't pull the trigger on his marks. It was sad, because in his day, no one was a better button man than Carlo Dello Russo, but it caused him to lose his edge. He was living in Florida until a couple of months ago. He's had some health problems, a stroke or something, and his niece moved him back in the area."

"Why are you ratting him out?"

"Because he screwed me. When I was working the books and Dello Russo was heading up the gambling in Jefferson County, we skimmed one-point-six million dollars from Big Tommy. We were supposed to sit on it for a couple of years, then split it. But he took it all to Florida with him, the motherfucker. What was I going to do, complain to Big Tommy that Carlo had made off with the money we'd stolen from him? I got nothing. I've got one good leg and a hard-on for that son of a bitch. I'd like to see him go out the way he deserves."

"If you know where he is and a beef to square with him, why don't you take care of it yourself?"

"For one, as you can clearly see, I'm not as nimble on my feet—or foot—as I used to be. Having one good leg makes escaping a bit of a challenge. But more importantly, I can't pay myself twenty grand for the privilege."

This seemed to satisfy Gemelli. "Where is he?"

"The Pinecrest Rehabilitation Center in Weirton, West Virginia. It's up on the hill. He's a couple of doors down from the nurses station, room four or five, something like that."

"How do you get there?"

"Jesus Christ, Gemelli, how helpless are you? I just gave you the location of the guy who killed your uncle and father. Figure it the fuck out."

Gemelli turned back to his goons. "You got it." They nodded in unison. "I want him back here alive. He doesn't have to be in good shape, but I want him alive. Understood?"

"Understood," said the shorter of the two.

"I'm going to wait here with Mr. Chatterbox." He turned to Nickels. "You'd better hope they come back with him, or I'm going to cut off your other leg, just for starters."

After the goons left, Nickels wouldn't shut up. He asked Gemelli for a job. "I'm good with numbers, you know?"

"Yeah, so good that you skimmed a million-six from your old boss. Sure, you're just the kind of guy I'd want to hire."

Nickels was relentless, question after question, until Gemelli said, "Please, just shut the fuck up."

"I'm hungry. I'm going to order a pizza."

"Good. Put something in your mouth so you'll quit talking."

"You want anything?"

"Just silence."

Nickels dialed my number. "Renato's Pizza," I said.

"Yeah, I'd like one of your large pizzas, pepperoni and extra cheese . . . No, nothing to drink . . . No, no salad, just the goddamn pizza . . . Room fourteen at the Carousel Inn. You sure you don't want anything?"

Gemelli waved him off.

"Twenty to thirty minutes," I said.

"Step on the gas, would you, pal? I'm starving here."

I hung up.

"You ever had Renato's Pizza?" Nickels asked.

"I've lived in Youngstown all my life," Gemelli said. "Yeah, I've had Renato's Pizza."

"It's stellar pizza. Not as good as Original DiCarlo's, but pretty good."

Gemelli shook his head and rolled his eyes. "You Steubenville guys and that thing you've got for DiCarlo's. I don't get it. It's the most overrated pizza in the world."

If I wasn't already going to kill him, he deserved to die for that last comment. Original DiCarlo's is the greatest pizza on the planet.

"By the way, I don't have any money, so you're going to have to pay for it," Nickels said.

"I just handed you ten grand."

"I'm not giving a pizza delivery guy a hundred-dollar bill, for Christ's sake."

"Fine. Anything to shut you up."

Twenty minutes later, I pulled my ball cap low on my brow and started the Kia; my 9-millimeter with the silencer was lying on a piece of wax paper on top of the pizza. I pulled up next to the Camaro, slid my hand under the pizza box and headed for the door.

(Note: No, I don't know why they didn't ask Nickels how it was that a guy with no money had a forty-thousand-dollar car parked outside his room. Maybe they hadn't made the connection.)

I knocked twice on the door and said, "Renato's."

Donny Gemelli opened the last door of his life and motioned me inside. As I entered, I pushed the door closed with the heel of my shoe. "Fifteen fifty," I said.

Gemelli said, "Lift up your shirt and turn around."

I frowned. "Why?"

"Just do what I said."

"He's got bad nerves," Nickels said.

I pulled up my shirt and turned in a circle.

Satisfied that I wasn't carrying, Gemelli began digging for his wallet.

"Let me have a look at that pie," Nickels said.

I opened the lid, pulled out the 9-millimeter with the suppressor, and dropped the box on the bed.

Gemelli froze at the sight of the pistol. A look of anger without any sense of fear consumed his face. He had yet to make the connection between the one-legged man on the bed and the pizza delivery guy. "You're robbing me? You have no idea in the world who you're screwin' with," he said.

"You know what's funny, Donny? Those were the exact words of your father right before I scrambled his brains."

He frowned. "Pete Cola?"

"Sometimes. But for your purposes, I'm Angelo Cipriani. Jolie Cipriani's husband."

His eyes widened long enough to put the puzzle pieces together, then I put my money shot right in the middle of his forehead. It opened up a hole in the back of his skull the size of a baseball and blood and bits of brain and bone sprayed across the wall and the cheap woodland print that hung over the bed. The impact blew him backwards into the nightstand. He rolled to the floor, his eyes and mouth open, blood streaming from both holes in his head, his nose and mouth.

Nickels never moved from his spot at the foot of the bed. He looked at the pizza and said, "Angelo, I specifically asked for extra cheese."

"Sorry, Nickels. I had other things on my mind."

He slapped the cardboard lid shut. "I can't eat this without extra cheese."

I pulled Gemelli into the bathroom so we could open the door without putting him on public display. "Grab that envelope in his inside jacket pocket," Nickels said.

I peeked in the envelope. There was another ten thousand dollars in hundred-dollar bills. "He actually was going to pay you the twenty grand for the information?"

"No, he wasn't. Even if they'd found Carlo at the nursing home, he would have killed me and taken back the envelope. There's no honor among thieves anymore."

"How about we get out of here?"

I went back to the car and got the artificial leg out of the trunk and helped Nickels strap it on. He was a little wobbly at first but shunned my offer to help him to the car. "I think I've got the hang of it," he said. "I can make it to the car. You grab the pizza."

"I thought you said you couldn't eat it."

"I can't, but I think it would be ever so lovely if it wasn't here when the cops show up so they can't go back to Renato's and check the video footage to find out who bought a large pepperoni pizza without extra cheese."

A shudder went through my entire body. It was a near-fatal error. "You're pretty smart for a crazy guy," I said.

"Spread the word, brother."

As we cleared Youngstown, following the same route as the Irish bartender who gave me a three-hundred-and-sixty-dollar ride to East Liverpool years earlier, Nickels folded his hands over his ample belly and said, "I gotta admit, Angelo, I really got a kick out of that tonight. That was beautiful, the way his eyes opened up when he realized who you were. Stuff like that makes life worth living."

"Think about what you just said."

"I know what I said. You did society a favor by getting rid of that scum. What about Little Tommy? I think you've got a score to settle there, too."

"I'll flip and turn it over to the FBI. All I can do is kill him; they can make the rest of his life a living hell."

Nickels waved at the air. "We ought to kill him. The FBI will just screw it up. They always do." He stared out the window into the darkness for a few minutes. "You know, if the FBI does its job and Little Tommy goes away for a long time, it would open up opportunities for us in the valley. We could get the sports gambling book up and running, get the loan-sharking game going again, jazz up the brothels. You and me, we could be running the show, just like the old days."

"I think we need to leave the old days where they are, Nickels. This should be our farewell tour. I'm getting too old for this, and you've got one-point-six-million reasons to leave the past in the past."

"That's a good point."

I smiled. As the lights of Steubenville lit up the Ohio River in front of us, I hit a speed-dial number on my phone. "Are you ready to go?"

"Thank God. You're alive."

"Very much so. Meet me in the alley with your suitcases in ten minutes. Don't turn on any lights."

Nickels again started spitting on his fingers and running them back through his hair. "Any chance Miss Carolyn has a thing for guys with one leg?"

"Her dance card is full right now, Nickels."

"Too bad. See if she has a sister."

Like the champ that she is, Carolyn was standing in the shadows of her garage, a suitcase in each hand. I threw them into the trunk with mine as she climbed into the back seat. We were moving again in seconds. "Where's the sporty car?" she asked.

"It didn't have the trunk space we needed," I said. I drove down the hill toward Route 7. Mostly to Nickels, I asked, "Are you hungry?"

"I could eat." He pulled twenty thousand dollars in hundred-dollar bills out of his jacket pocket. "And . . ." He rolled his thumb over the edge of the stack so that it snapped like a deck of cards. "I had a good night at the track, so it's my treat."

"What did you guys do, rob a bank?" Carolyn asked.

"Don't ask questions that you know I can't answer," I said.

"Can't or won't?" she said, sitting back in the seat.

"Where are we going?" I asked Nickels.

"Is this our last night in the Ohio Valley?"

"Probably forever."

"In that case, let's go over to Undo's. I'd like one last plate of their ravioli."

It was starting to rain as we passed the Starlighter Diner and turned from Slack Street onto Route 7. In the soft yellow glow cast by a full moon, I could see the sagging outline of the Spaghetto and the darkness of the hulking Wheeling-Pittsburgh Steel plant, its furnaces long cold. I remembered that morning decades earlier when I walked through the Spaghetto's dark streets in polished shoes toward my first day of work for Alphonse Fortunato. I also remembered the afternoon when Alphonse gave me a ride home and how everyone in the Spaghetto looked at me like I was some kind of big deal. Images of Frankie and Tony Gemelli flashed before me, as did Carlo, Alphonse, and Big Tommy.

I didn't know what the future held, but I knew it would look nothing like my past. I checked the interior rearview mirror. Carolyn was looking out the window as rivulets of rain streaked past. Sitting next to her was Big Tommy Fortunato, his thick hands resting on splayed knees, a cigarette glowing orange between an index and middle finger. We made eye contact in the mirror, but there was no emotion on his face, nothing to show displeasure or approval. There was, however, a barely perceptible nod, a slight dip of the chin, before he brought the cigarette to his lips and broke eye contact. He blew smoke into the front seat, and this time I swear I could smell burning tobacco. I slowed for the light at Washington Street, and when I again looked in the rearview, he was gone.

Nickels looked at me and grinned.

C H A P T E R

39

Wednesday, August 21, 2019

AFTER FINISHING DINNER at Undo's, we drove to Pittsburgh and got rooms at a hotel in Robinson Township. I called Ross at seven o'clock the next morning. He acted like a long-lost child had called him out of the blue. I'm sure he'd gone to bed thinking the next time he saw me was when they fished my body out of a strip-mine pond. He and agent Stanton picked us up at the hotel. Stanton drove Carolyn's car, and Ross drove the three of us to the FBI field office in the unimpressive building between Carson Street and the Monongahela River.

When I'd completed my paperwork, agents were still questioning Nickels and processing Carolyn. I was in a conference room watching a morning news show when Ross came in. "Hungry?" he asked. "Those two are going to be tied up for a while. Let's get some breakfast."

"Sounds good," I said.

We took the elevator to the ground floor and walked across Carson Street to a diner. "I've got to tell you, Ross, before I visited your office the last time, I always had a mental image of the FBI offices being a little more palatial."

"We're the FBI, Angelo, not U.S. Steel. We try to keep a low profile."

"Smart," I said. "Keep a low profile, just like the mob."

"Exactly the same, but without the corruption."

"Yeah, I'm not sure I'd go that far."

Ross fought off a grin as he opened the door to the diner. We sat in a booth and ordered coffee and omelets. "I was serious when I told you that you've got a rat in your office," I said. "Someone has a pipeline to Little Tommy."

He nodded. "I'm working on it."

"Work on it all you want. Just make sure no one else in your office knows where we're going, because I don't want one of Little Tommy's emissaries showing up at my door."

"You don't need to worry about that, Angelo."

"Well, I'm worried plenty. Little Tommy was obviously funneling information to that Steubenville detective. If he had any more information, I could end up going down on state charges."

"Oh, that wasn't Little Tommy. It was me."

"Excuse me?"

"Yeah, I did that. I was trying to squeeze you into the witness protection program. I'm really surprised you didn't pick up on that."

"What the hell, Ross. I could have gotten indicted."

"Give me a break, Angelo. I wasn't feeding them enough information to get you indicted. I was just trying to make you squirm a little. It was for your own good. I was trying to save you from yourself."

"Oh, hell yes, you FBI agents are such compassionate souls. Did you tell them to impound my car?"

"A hundred percent."

"I asked you if you were the one feeding information to the Steubenville cops, and you said no."

"Yeah, I lied."

I wanted to punch him. "Where did you get that information?"

"Did you really think that you and Carlo were working in a complete vacuum? We've had files on the two of you for years."

"If that's true, how come you never came after us?"

"Just because we had a dossier on you doesn't mean we had enough information to indict. Or maybe we just thought you were providing a public service by eliminating your competition."

The waitress set our omelets on the table and warmed up our coffees. "I've got a question for you, Ross."

"Fire away."

"You have the Gemellis in Youngstown. They've got a drug pipeline coming out of Cleveland that looks like a four-lane highway. What's left of the Santoro family in Pittsburgh is now largely a cocaine and heroin operation, and Santino the Crab in Erie is pushing hard stuff all the way down to Youngstown. They're all deeper into the drug trade than the Fortunatos. Why do you have such a hard-on for Little Tommy?"

"Because Little Tommy is the only Fortunato left."

"Yeah. So what? He's still small potatoes compared to the other families."

"It's personal."

"Everything's personal. What's that mean?"

Ross picked the paper napkin off his lap and wiped his mouth. "You're right, Angelo, everything is personal, isn't it?" He rolled his coffee cup between his palms and stared out the window for a long moment, thinking, wondering if he should reveal the next chapter of the book. "The Fortunatos killed my uncle."

My brows converged onto the bridge of my nose. "Your uncle?"

He nodded. "That day we met at the old brick factory, I was telling you how my father's family turned on him because he went into law enforcement. You said, 'He didn't patrol the streets of the Steubenville Spaghetto, did he?' I brushed it off."

"I remember."

"Well, he never patrolled the streets of the Spaghetto, but that's where he grew up."

I shook my head. "Who?"

"My dad's name back then was Gilberto Dello Russo. That uncle I told you about, the one I wanted to go visit . . ."

Waves of prickly ice rolled up my spine. "Carlo Dello Russo."

He nodded. "Uncle Carlo, the Iron Mauler."

"I'm having a hard time making the ends meet on this one."

"We were quite a bit different, that's for sure. We reconnected as adults. I reached out to him. I knew who he was and what he did, but he was still my uncle and as far as I knew, my only relative."

"Carlo kept a low profile. How'd you find him?"

"You keep forgetting that I'm an FBI agent. I have a few resources at my disposal."

"I guess that slipped my mind."

"I was glad he was in my life, as odd as that sounds. We'd meet for dinner once in a while and talk. We kept our professional lives out of the conversation, mostly. He asked about my job and how I was doing, but he never tried to pry information out of me. We just talked about life and the family. When I was a kid, he'd been my idol. Before the divorce, we'd go down to visit my dad's family, and I didn't want to be around anyone but Carlo. I'd go out back with him while he was hitting the bags. It was cool to have an uncle who was a champion boxer. We were tight. Then, after the divorce, Mom and I went to live with her parents. I used to ask my mother about Uncle Carlo and pestered her to take me for a visit. She'd placate me and tell me that we'd go visit him someday, but someday never came."

I stared across the table for a long minute, remembering the image of a young boy following Carlo to the heavy bag that hung from the oak tree. "You were the little guy who used to shadow box with him when he worked out in the backyard. Once in a while, he'd put the gloves on you and let you hit the bag."

Ross nodded. "Yeah, that was me. How'd you know that?"

"I saw you. We lived right around the corner. I could see his yard from my back porch. I used to watch Carlo work out. I remember seeing you out there with him."

"Small world, huh? All these years later and we're sitting across the table from each other, about as opposite as two people could be."

"But your last name is Ross."

"After Carlo quit boxing, he went to work for the Fortunatos. That devastated my old man. He thought Carlo was going to be a world champion and make us all proud. Instead, he became a button man for Iceman Al. The old man decided that he no longer wanted to be a Dello Russo from Steubenville. He was working at the police department in McKees Rocks and thought if other cops found out he was Carlo Dello Russo's brother, they would always look at him with suspicion. But in reality, I think he changed it out of spite. Either way, Gilberto Dello Russo became Gilbert Ross, very American."

I couldn't believe what I was hearing. "That association didn't bother you? The FBI are the pretty boys of law enforcement."

"It wouldn't have made the honchos in Washington happy, if that's what you mean."

"And you never once asked him about his profession?"

"One time, I asked him if he'd ever considered getting out of the life. He said, 'And do what? I know how to box and how to take orders from the Fortunatos. That's the extent of my talent.'" Ross's voice trailed off and he smiled. "He said it was no fun walking around wondering if someone was going to put a bullet in his ear, but the days when he could have gotten out of the game were behind him. His exact words were, 'That train has left the station. I'm not fit for anything beyond the life I'm leading.' Then, one day, he quit answering his phone. I drove down to his place in Weirton, and it was locked up tight. The neighbors said they hadn't seen him in weeks. It didn't take an FBI agent to figure out what had happened. After a while, I got word that Big Tommy had taken him off the board. Over the years, I've heard a lot of rumors about who was responsible, but nothing solid. It seems that there were only two people who knew what really happened—Big Tommy and the man who pulled the trigger. Big Tommy isn't talking anymore, and I imagine the hitman is smart enough to keep his mouth shut." I slid my omelet to the side of the table. Our eyes locked for a long moment. "What's the matter, Angelo, lose your appetite? I thought you were hungry."

"It's been a crazy couple of days," I said. "My stomach's a little upset."

A faint smile pursed the lips of Special Agent Lawrence G. Ross. "I like you, Angelo, and because of that, I'm never again going to ask you what happened to my uncle. One, I'm not sure I really want to know, and two, I don't want you to have to lie."

EPILOGUE

EVERY ONCE IN a while, a plan comes together exactly the way you sketch it out on paper. It's a beautiful thing.

When the goons returned to the Carousel Inn after finding an empty room at the nursing home in Weirton, they made the night manager open the door to room fourteen, where Donny Gemelli's corpse was stretched out on the tile floor of the bathroom. According to a story in the Youngstown *Vindicator,* the goons bolted after the manager freaked out and called the police. One detective was quoted as calling Gemelli's death "suspicious." It made me choke on my coffee. *What was your first clue, officer? The bullet hole in the middle of his forehead?*

The story noted Gemelli's ties to organized crime and said police were searching for two individuals for questioning—Pete Cola, an Indianapolis, Indiana, man who had rented the room at the Carousel Inn, and Louis "Gaetano" Di Vittorio, who was a known associate of the Fortunato crime family of Steubenville. Di Vittorio's car was found abandoned at the motel.

Fortunately for us, God kept one in his back pocket to drop at the perfect time.

Two weeks later, authorities announced the end of their investigation into Gemelli's death after hikers found the rotting corpse of Di Vittorio in a Pennsylvania game reserve, about forty miles from

Youngstown. Authorities surmised that Di Vittorio had killed Donny Gemelli as part of long-standing bad blood between the Fortunato and Gemelli families. Di Vittorio was subsequently executed by members of the Gemelli family. Police noted that Di Vittorio had been shot twelve times in the chest, indicating it was a revenge killing. They further surmised that De Vittorio was using the alias of Pete Cola, and his Camaro had been abandoned at the motel because he most likely left in the trunk of a Gemelli associate's car. And since there were no security cameras at the Carousel Inn to prove otherwise, case closed.

It was an easy out for the cops. While it was wildly erroneous speculation on their part, what did they care? It was slimy Donny Gemelli, and there wasn't a cop in the Mahoning Valley losing sleep over that one.

Nickels and I signed agreements to enter the United States Federal Witness Protection Program. We were put up in rooms in a downtown high-rise hotel, where we were grilled for two solid days by FBI agents and lawyers from the Department of Justice. They were salivating over the information we provided. They arranged for us to live in a duplex near Gulf Shores, Alabama, while they pursued their charges against Little Tommy. There would be other days of interviews, and the FBI posted agents outside the building around the clock. It was overkill. Little Tommy could never find us. And in all candor, I don't think he was looking.

Here's the beautiful aspect of this entire arrangement. Remember when I told you there was no loyalty in the new regime—Gummy Bear and the Tipplehorn kid and that bunch? What is it the kids say these days? *True that!* When the FBI raided the compound and seized the millions of dollars Little Tommy had stored in the vault, the rats scattered, just as Agent Malcolm had predicted. Ross said Little Tommy's closest lieutenants were pounding on the FBI's door the next day, trying to cut deals in exchange for their testimony.

The feds did what the feds always do. They hammered him with charges, more than a hundred. Little Tommy pleaded guilty to two or three and took a deal that could let him out of prison in forty years. Meanwhile, Nickels and I never had to testify and got to keep our deals with the government with income for life.

What a great country.

Did I want to kill Little Tommy? Absolutely. But I couldn't make myself do it. Why? A couple of reasons. For one, he was still Big Tommy's son. That fact alone kept him alive. I also understood his reasoning for wanting me dead. He knew I was talking to the FBI and was a rat, and the mob kills rats. That's why I killed Carlo. I took great offense that Little Tommy wanted to kill his Uncle Ange, but I understood his reasoning. Besides, knowing that he would go to prison and wouldn't breathe free air for at least four decades was more satisfying to me than seeing him dead. He knew that I was taking long walks in the sunshine with sand squishing between my toes, so let him stew on that for a while.

Trooper Andrew Donaldson of the Pennsylvania State Police was parked in the median of I-79 near the Heidelberg exit when a southbound Mercedes sedan blew past him and registered a hundred and thirteen miles per hour on his radar. Donaldson hit his lights and pulled onto the interstate. Almost immediately, the Mercedes moved to the right lane and onto the gravel berm. Donaldson pulled in behind the Mercedes, but before he could call in the license plate number, he heard a bang and saw a spray of red fill the interior of the Mercedes. Its driver, FBI Agent Charles Sheridan Walker, slumped sideways onto the passenger seat, dead.

That morning, Agent Malcolm had called Walker into his office and taken his badge and Bureau-issued handgun, and told him that he was immediately suspended with pay pending the outcome of an investigation into allegations that he had shared sensitive FBI investigative information with the Fortunato crime family. Malcolm said, "Just so you know, Chuck, this investigation is just a formality. When we arrested Little Tommy Fortunato, we confiscated his computer and cell phone. The evidence is overwhelming. We've got text messages, emails, and the bank records for your fictious corporation where they wired your payoffs. We had that account frozen, by the way. It surprises me less that you were corrupt than how stupid you were to leave such an electronic trail of evidence. You might want to think about getting your affairs in order because once you're indicted, you'll never see anything but the inside of a prison wall."

Walker knew what happened to cops in prison and decided to take the easy way out.

Rosebella died shortly after her son went to prison. Alzheimer's is a terrible disease, but I was glad she was afflicted and wasn't cognizant enough to realize her only son had been sent away. The Federal Terrace closed down, and the Fort Steuben Hotel was converted to apartments. Ross and Stanton received numerous commendations for shutting down the Fortunato crime family. Neither of them bothered to send me a thank-you note. Jerks.

Carolyn sold her house, and the FBI had everything she wanted shipped to us. There wasn't much. Nickels had the contents of the storage unit shipped, too. He told Ross, "Tell those sonsabitches to be careful with that steamer trunk. My grandfather brought that over from Italy."

It arrived with one-point-six million beneath the false bottom.

He gave me a half-million dollars in hundreds and fifties. I said, "Nickels, you stole it fair and square. You keep it."

"I don't need it all," he said. "Besides, if you hadn't snagged me out of the nursing home, Little Tommy would have punched my ticket and some junk dealer would have bought the steamer trunk for three dollars at an auction."

Carolyn and I are living in Florida. I'm not supposed to tell you where, but it rhymes with maples. We have a nice cottage and a miniature schnauzer named Eleanor. Nickels said Florida was too hot and muggy. He convinced his niece to move to North Carolina, somewhere near the Outer Banks, and he built her a house. He said his niece put him on a strict diet and he's lost a hundred pounds. Every time we talk, he asks if Carolyn is going to set him up with her sister, which she doesn't have. To the best of my knowledge, Alphonse and Big Tommy are leaving him alone these days.

My alias is Waldo Eugene Parker. That's two steps north of embarrassing. More so, in fact, than the nun suggesting I take the stock boy gig at the M&K Market. I still go by Angelo. Carolyn loves Florida. She said she was too young to retire and took a job as a receptionist in a dental office. She likes the work and doesn't come home smelling like a deep fryer.

I'll make a confession. Walking on the beach was fine, for about a week, then I started getting bored with sunshine and salt water. In Steubenville, I knew my place in the world. I had a reputation, good or bad. Here, I was just another schmuck walking the beach. All I needed was a metal detector, a stupid hat, and a coat of zinc oxide painted on my nose to complete the picture. I had no desire to return to my previous life, but in Florida I was wholly without purpose, prematurely put out to pasture.

A little more than a year after I landed in the Skin Cancer State, I was coming back from the post office when I saw a dark blue sedan parked outside of my cottage, and a man I had hoped never to see again was leaning against the fender. My gut cinched up, and I crossed the street and ducked back behind a liquor store. It never ends, I thought.

I crept closer. The dude was dressed in a familiar bad suit and plastic neck tie. Warning sirens were going off in my head, and I should have turned around and started walking to Fort Myers. Even when you're in the Federal Witness Protection Program, you can't always run from your past. As I neared, he said, "I'll tell you something, Angelo, I could get used to this sunshine."

"It's overrated," I said.

I was in cargo shorts, flip-flops, and a T-shirt. "Looks like it agrees with you."

"What the hell are you doing here, Ross? When I signed that agreement with the feds you said that I wouldn't be getting any unwelcome visitors."

"Can't a guy come visit an old friend?"

"We're friends now, huh? That's interesting. I always viewed myself as something of a commodity for you."

There were constants that Iceman Al taught me early in the game, and one of those was that an FBI agent, or any cop, doesn't just show up unannounced to make a social call. They show up unannounced when they want something, and FBI agents always want something. It doesn't take a career criminal to figure that out.

"Can we go inside and talk?" he said.

"I'm in an eight-ball league at four o'clock, so you'll have to make it quick."

"Eight-ball? Wow, sounds like you've got a full schedule."

That went up my spine. As we entered the house, I turned and said, "And just whose fault might that be?" I poured us each a glass of lemonade. "Want to go out on the patio?"

"It's probably better if we talk inside."

"Sounds serious."

"It is, and you're going to hate it." We walked into the living room. As soon as we sat down, he said, "The Pittsburgh field office has been asked to assist in a project, and I need your help."

"How about instead of doing the waltz, you do the boogie-woogie and get to the point?"

"I need you to go undercover and infiltrate an organized crime family."

I blinked, waiting for the punchline. None came. "My hearing ain't so good anymore, Ross. It sounded like you just said you wanted me to go undercover and infiltrate an organized crime family. Let's try it again. Why are you really here?"

"The FBI needs help infiltrating the DeStafano crime family in Detroit. Much like the Fortunatos, the DeStafanos are looking for alternative revenue streams, and they've turned to flesh-peddling."

"It's the mob, for Christ's sake. They've peddled flesh for as long as there's been organized crime."

"True, but generally not thirteen- and fourteen-year-olds."

I winced. "That's terrible, but why would you want me?"

"We need someone who understands the inner workings of the mob. No one knows that better than you. Detroit is still run by the old guard, and that's your groove swing. You speak the language. We resurrect Angelo Cipriani, figure a way for you to get involved from a distance, and eventually let you ingratiate yourself with the DeStafanos so we can bust this up."

"Oh, is that all? Insert my seventy-year-old ass into one of the most brutal crime families in the country and expose their child sex ring. What could possibly go wrong? You've lost your marbles, Ross. Get out of here."

"It's not that easy, Angelo." Ross reached into his jacket pocket and pulled out a document. My throat tightened when I recognized it as a copy of my witness protection agreement. He handed it to me and said, "I've taken the liberty of highlighting the pertinent line in our arrangement."

The undersigned agrees to assist federal authorities on any future audits, investigations, or prosecutions as dictated by, but not limited to, the Federal Bureau of Investigation. Degrees of assistance may include work on federal investigations that include, but are not limited to, civil rights violations, cybercrime, white collar crime, public corruption, and organized crime.

The slightest of smiles pursed Ross's lips. "It's the last one, Angelo. The organized crime part."

"I should have told you to go to hell that day in the Starlighter."

"Actually, I think you did tell me to go to hell. I don't know why you're upset with me. It was included with the, uh . . ."

"Fine print. I think the phrase you're looking for is fine print."

"Yes, the fine print."

"You are a son of a bitch."

"That may be true, but you signed the document."

"Because I didn't think you'd come knocking on my door trying to drag me into some looney plan to infiltrate the DeStafano family."

"Thirteen- and fourteen-year olds, Angelo. Kids from Mexico and Guatemala, South Carolina and Massachusetts. They're scared and trapped. We've got to bust this up."

"And I'm your first choice?"

"You're my only choice. That's why I'm here. Let me ask you this: How old is that granddaughter of yours?"

Carolyn's son had three children—two boys and a girl, Bridget. I had only visited with them a couple of times, but I had grown fond of Bridget. She was a good kid, an A student and a field hockey player. She called me Grampy Angelo. I liked that.

"Ross, if you're asking me that question, I'll bet you already know the answer."

"I do. She's fourteen, the same age as some of the kids who are getting trafficked."

"What if I say no?"

"The first thing that would happen is the checks would stop coming. And if you're in violation of a contract that you signed with the federal government, I imagine they would not look kindly on that. It would be a messy ordeal, Angelo."

"How would it work? I can't just knock on Georgie DeStafano's door and ask for a job trafficking kids."

"We have a plan and a backstory for you."

"You think the underworld doesn't know that I'm a rat?"

"First of all, you need to get over yourself. You weren't that important to the Fortunato family after Big Tommy died. Remember, you were sitting in that apartment, watching game shows. Besides, people have short memories. As far as anyone outside of Steubenville knows, Angelo Cipriani scattered when the house of Fortunato caught fire. You took cover for a while, then re-emerged in Pittsburgh with your own operation, and you need young girls to keep your clients happy."

"How long of a commitment are we talking?"

"How fast could you infiltrate the family?"

"Faster than you would think, Ross."

"That's the spirit, Angelo."

We sat in silence for a long moment. I smiled and nodded. "You know, Ross, to quote Michael Corleone, 'Just when I thought I was out . . .'"

"I know. We pull you back in. But Corleone was with the mob; we're the good guys."

"Yeah, that's what you keep saying, but I think the jury is still out on that one."

* * *

I have another confession. I was not all that upset by Ross's visit or the forced assignment. It gave me a renewed sense of purpose. Clearly, I was going to be on the other side of the ball. But would I really? I thought of Woodrow Golightly and how the mob used to handle pedophiles. In my mind, that hadn't changed. If the DeStafanos were peddling young girls, they had no honor, and they needed to go down.

That night, I sat down with Carolyn to explain the situation. She listened intently, then asked, "And you're contractually obligated to do this?"

"I am."

"And if you're successful, you'll help these young girls?"

"That's correct."

"Angelo . . ." She paused a moment, biting her upper lip. "You don't play golf, you don't play tennis, you don't play shuffleboard. I've never seen you more miserable than when you're sitting on the beach. You've got to have a reason to get out of bed in the morning, and maybe this is it. You have a chance to do something really good. I love you to pieces, but get the hell out of the house. Go do this, and please try very hard not to get yourself killed."

What a top-drawer babe.

AFTERWORD

THE CHARACTER OF Carolyn Melvin is a tribute to the real Carolyn Melvin. For years, Carolyn was a driving force in the Columbus, Ohio, chapter of Sisters in Crime. She was an attorney by trade, but her passion was the written word. She loved mysteries, writers, and her sisters in the club. In early 2022, Carolyn was diagnosed with brain cancer. In her last days, I told her that I would name a character after her in a future book, and I would make her beautiful, smart, and funny, just like her namesake. Carolyn died on June 5, 2022. We all miss you, sweetheart.

In 2022, I was named the Honorary Chairman of Education and Libraries for the General Federation of Women's Clubs. I'm not sure how that happened, but it was quite an honor, and I guess I partially qualified for having a unisex name. I spoke at the GFWC International Convention in Louisville, Kentucky, in 2023. To help raise money for the Ohio Educational Foundation's Whisper Grant Fund, I raffled off a character for a future book, and the winner was Jolie Frankfurth. I'm sorry that Jolie's fictional counterpart didn't make it to the end of the book, but that's what can happen when you marry into the mob.

ACKNOWLEDGMENTS

I OWE A DEBT of gratitude to my beloved Ohio Valley, where I spent my youth and formative years. In those days, when the steel mills were booming and spewing grit along the river, the Youngstown mob controlled the vice in Steubenville—the gambling, the Water Street brothels, and the loansharking. It's difficult these days for people to wrap their brains around how commonplace this was. So commonplace, in fact, that very few people considered it problematic. Simply, it was just the way things operated.

As a boy, I would go with my Grandmother Yocum into Lane's Lounge in Mingo Junction, where she played the daily number. I was too young to understand what she was doing, but my recollection was that the only things being sold in the lounge were chewing gum, newspapers, and cigars. Louie Lane had a very nice house, so I assumed the profit margin on chewing gum must have been enormous. Of course, he was a bookie and making all his money on the vig.

In this novel, I have set up competing mob families in Steubenville and Youngstown. This is literary license on my part. Down the river a bit, in Wheeling, West Virginia, the vice was controlled locally, but Youngstown controlled Steubenville, which in those days was the steel capital of the Ohio Valley and home to many first-generation Americans.

This novel was inspired by my short story *The Last Hit*, which first appeared in the July 2019 issue of *Strand Magazine* and was later selected for the 2020 edition of *The Best American Mystery Stories*, published by Otto Penzler and edited by C. J. Box. My thanks to Andrew Gulli and Lamia Gulli at *Strand*, and Otto and C. J. for providing a launching pad for *The Last Hitman*.

This is my first lap around the track with Crooked Lane Books and editor Tom Wickersham. I hope it's the first of many. They've been great to work with. The suggested edits of my first draft by Tom and publisher Mark Martz made this a better book, and I'm appreciative of their input.

As she has been for years, my warrior agent Colleen Mohyde was firmly in my corner for this book, sponging my face between rounds and at times walking me in off the ledge. In publishing, it does take a village, and Colleen is the mayor. I couldn't be more appreciative of her efforts.

It seems that I answer to a variety of mayors, and that includes the one I live with, my beautiful wife, Melissa. The number of hours needed to write a book can be staggering, but Melissa has never been anything but supportive. In fact, there are times when she'll raise one eyebrow and say, "Shouldn't you be writing?" While this usually occurs when I'm doing something she finds particularly annoying, the answer is almost always yes.

As I was making the final edits on this novel, the woman who had been in my life the longest, my mother, Carroll Yocum, left us on April 11, 2025. She had a good run of eighty-nine years. I was hoping that she would stick around to see this one hit the shelves, but she was tired and wanted to see Dad and the two children she had buried. Mom was always my first editor and never missed an opportunity to tell people, "You know, my son's a novelist." I'll miss her dearly.

And finally, thanks to all my readers, particularly those from the Ohio Valley, who find familiarity and comfort in the words that describe the world we once knew.